THE MAHLER MAYHEM

A Megan Crespi Mystery Series Novel

Also by Alessandra Comini from Sunstone Press

Schiele in Prison
Egon Schiele's Portraits
Gustav Klimt
Egon Schiele
Egon Schiele: Nudes
The Fantastic Art of Vienna
The Changing Image of Beethoven
In Passionate Pursuit: A Memoir

The Megan Crespi Mystery Series

Killing for Klimt
The Schiele Slaughters
The Kokoschka Capers
The Munch Murders
The Kollwitz Calamities
The Kandinsky Conundrum

THE MAHLER MAYHEM

A Megan Crespi Mystery Series Novel

ALESSANDRA COMINI

SUNSTONE PRESS
SANTA FE

This book is a work of fiction. Names, places, characters, and incidents are either the product of the author's imagination or used fictionally. Any resemblance to actual events or persons, living or dead, is entirely coincidental.

Sunstone books may be purchased for educational, business, or sales promotional use. For information please write: Special Markets Department, Sunstone Press, P.O. Box 2321, Santa Fe, New Mexico 87504-2321.
Book and cover design › R. Ahl
Printed on acid-free paper
∞

Library of Congress Cataloging-in-Publication Data

Names: Comini, Alessandra, author.
Title: The Mahler mayhem : a Megan Crespi mystery series novel / by
  Alessandra Comini.
Description: Santa Fe, New Mexico : Sunstone Press, [2018]
Identifiers: LCCN 2018045525 (print) | LCCN 2018048085 (ebook) | ISBN
  9781611395679 () | ISBN 9781632932471 (softcover : alk. paper)
Subjects: LCSH: Murder--Investigation--Fiction. | GSAFD: Mystery fiction.
Classification: LCC PS3603.O477 (ebook) | LCC PS3603.O477 M34 2018
(print) |
  DDC 813/.6--dc23
LC record available at https://lccn.loc.gov/2018045525

WWW.SUNSTONEPRESS.COM
SUNSTONE PRESS / POST OFFICE BOX 2321 / SANTA FE, NM 87504-2321 /USA
(505) 988-4418 / ORDERS ONLY (800) 243-5644 / FAX (505) 988-1025

TO Ehrengard Syverson von Gemmingen, cherished former student, co-roamer around Europe, professional cellist, and mother of two adorable musician boys.

AND to the memory of Henry-Louis de la Grange (1924–2017), Mahler scholar extraordinaire and dear friend.

Auguste Rodin, *Gustav Mahler,* bronze, 1909,
Schwind Foyer,
Vienna State Opera

LIST OF MAJOR CHARACTERS

Megan Crespi: retired professor of art history and enthusiastic musicologist, she is an expert on early twentieth-century European culture and is now active in solving crimes in the art world.

Egga Streicher: renowned German cellist, founder of the quartet *Streicher Vier*, and former student of Megan Crespi.

Mary Neff: senior vocal coach at the Vienna State Opera.

Erich Decker: Chief of Police in Vienna and friend of Megan Crespi.

Max Brandes: demanding guest conductor from Cologne at the Vienna State Opera Orchestra.

Gabor Alexander: regular conductor of the Vienna State Opera Orchestra.

Jared Bogenstein: elderly principal cellist of the Vienna State Opera Orchestra and a borderline alcoholic.

Basileus Schmidt: fifty-eight-year-old director of Vienna's National Library.

Sabina Schmidt: wife of Basileus Schmidt and an amateur pianist.

Adele Schmidt: daughter of Sabina and Basileus Schmidt, in her late twenties, and works as head of the women's repertory tailoring department at the Vienna State Opera.

Stefan Schmidt: son of Sabina and Basileus Schmidt, in his late twenties, second principal cellist in the Vienna State Opera Orchestra.

Ottokar Weininger: contrabass trombonist for the Vienna State Opera Orchestra; always sits in the orchestra pit whether or not there is a part for his instrument.

Cristina Paloma: harpist for the Vienna State Opera Orchestra.

Rudi Wittkower: longtime portier at the Kärntner Strasse stage door of the Vienna State Opera.

Harry Howell: American documentary film maker, flutist and pianist, partner of Haim Elisaf.

Haim Elisaf: a Romaniote Jew from Ioannina, Greece, documentary film maker and cellist; partner of Harry Howell.

Callas: daughter of Harry Howell and Haim Elisaf and fraternal twin of their son Bell.

Bell: son of Harry Howell and Haim Elisaf and fraternal twin of their daughter Callas.

Tonik Nektar: ardent Mahler fan from Iglau.

Rita Rausch: cultural contributor to the *Wiener Morgenblatt* and television reporter for ORF.

Gerald Chaplin: brilliant American self-taught conductor, specializes in Mahler's Second Symphony.

Henri-Claude de La Granger: renowned French authority on Gustav Mahler.

Homer Bläser: first French hornist of the Vienna State Opera Orchestra.

1

"I can't explain it, I just know there is something wrong about it. Terribly, terribly wrong."

It was intermission at the Vienna State Opera and Act One of Beethoven's *Fidelio* had just concluded with Don Pizarro's dreadful decision to murder his detested opponent and prisoner, Florestan.

The excited Sunday evening crowd in the opulently decorated Schwind Foyer was becoming noisy, and young but already renowned German cellist Egga Streicher was forced to ask her former art history professor Dr. Megan Crespi to repeat what she had uttered with a look of such alarm on her face. They were standing at one end of the long foyer in front of the white marble fireplace that displayed Rodin's bust on its mantelpiece.

"It's just not right, Egga. Something is out of kilter," Crespi said, never taking her eyes off the bronze bust of Gustav Mahler, who had reigned as controversial conductor of the Vienna Opera during the city's ten golden years of 1897 to 1907. A Jew in the anti-Semitic waltz capital of the world, he had been hounded out of Vienna by the press only to begin a dazzling new career in America as conductor of the New York Metropolitan Opera and later the New York Philharmonic Orchestra. His career in the New World lasted from 1908 until his untimely death at the age of fifty in 1911.

Megan Crespi had often emphasized the composer's love-hate affair with Vienna when teaching students about him, even though she was not a trained musicologist but an art historian. Nevertheless, she managed to insert the cultural content of specific artistic forms into every one of her class lectures and seminars at Columbia University and later at Southern Methodist University in Dallas. She touched upon music, ballet, architecture, literature, medicine, science, and politics whenever pertinent. And now, although she was retired, she spent much of her time in Europe as she was repeatedly called upon to investigate art crimes.

But this time she was in her favorite European city not as a detective but in her role as distinguished scholar. She had been invited to give a lecture on a Mahler contemporary, the Expressionist artist Egon Schiele, at the Albertina Museum where so many of his extraordinary graphic works were housed. A second lecture by her on Schiele's time in a Neulengbach prison had been set for one afternoon at that town where the basement block of six prison cells was now a heavily visited Schiele museum. She was also scheduled for a book signing at the Leopold Museum, possessor of the world's largest collection of Schiele paintings. And she had been invited by the University of Vienna to give a lecture, "The Two Gustavs," about the painter Gustav Klimt and the composer/conductor Gustav Mahler.

While in Vienna Megan had linked up with a treasured former student now living in Berlin who was concertizing in the city with a string quartet she had founded, the *Streicher Vier*. Married to an American physician and the mother of two talented young boys, both of whom played string instruments, Egga had happily agreed to remain in Austria another week to "do Vienna" with Megan. It would be like the old days before she was married when they traveled in Finland, England, East Germany, and Russia together following Megan's art history pursuits. In the meantime, they had carved out a free evening to attend the Vienna opera together. And as luck would have it, famed maestro Max Brandes was guest conducting *Fidelio*, that musical drama which Mahler had colored with his daring encouragement of stark staging and novel lowering of the auditorium lights during the performance.

Egga, whose amber eyes matched her dark ginger hair, stared at Auguste Rodin's famous bust of Mahler, created when the conductor was visiting Paris briefly in 1909. Fruitlessly, she attempted to perceive what her teacher was reacting to so adamantly.

"I'm afraid I don't see what you mean," she confessed finally. "It looks just like Mahler to me."

"Oh, yes, it looks exactly like him but it's a *muted* Mahler we're looking at. His high forehead, flowing hair, fine features, and their proportions are all correct but they are less distinct than they should be. Not as pronounced, not quite as large as they would be in the original bronze casting. I've known and loved the Rodin bust here at the Opera House since I was a student in Vienna."

The cellist looked fondly at her teacher—a lively, perpetual brunette who allowed that she was "eightyish." She knew all about Megan's aborted study of art history at Vienna University, in order to help refugees fleeing the Hungarian Revolution. Megan owned an Opel station wagon and drove to the Austrian/Hungarian border several times a day, transporting displaced Hungarians to shelters in Vienna. It was an event that had changed her life, Megan always claimed.

"I tell you, Egga, we are not looking at the original bronze here. We are looking at a surmoulage—a cast of a cast. The original cast is not here. Not here where it has always been.

"*This, Egga, is a very clever substitution!*"

2

℘art of the Vienna State Opera's multi-layered history since its completion in 1869 was the fact that neither of its two architects lived to see their finished magnum opus. Eduard van der Null committed suicide, so devastated was he by Kaiser Franz Josef's observation to an adjutant that the neo-Renaissance building under construction appeared too low in the ground. His broken-hearted colleague August Sicard von Sicardsburg died some weeks later of tuberculosis. Sadly aware of the havoc his remark had created, the emperor made it his policy thereafter always to utter the same sentence at public events: "It was very beautiful, I liked it very much."

As she trotted up the stairs from one of the building's soundproof basement rehearsal rooms, sixty-six-year-old vocal coach and pianist Mary Neff was thinking about the circumstances occasioning the emperor's unfortunate remark. He had chosen the Opera House site on Vienna's expanding Ringstrasse himself and no one realized at the time that filling in the trenches around the demolished old walls of the inner city had raised the encircling boulevard about three feet higher than anticipated, thus creating the sunken effect observed by Franz Josef.

One of the contemporary satirical verses ridiculing the two architects had been set to music for a new opera and Mary Neff had just come from helping one of its soloists master the Viennese dialect enunciation.

Der Sicardsburg und van der Nüll,
Die haben beide keinen Styl!
Griechisch, gotisch, Renaissance,
Das ist denen alles ans!

The Sicardsburg and the van der Nüll,
They both have no style!
Greek, gothic, Renaissance,

It's all the same to them!

The singer was Bulgarian and had only just arrived in Vienna. Neff was American but had lived and worked in Vienna for thirty-one years. Her brown hair was beginning to show a topping of distinguished gray, set off by a pair of penetrating, merry blue eyes. Fluency in many languages, as well as her renowned ability to draw the best out of singers as she partnered them on the piano, had come to the attention of the Vienna State Opera. As *Solo Korrepetitorin*, she had been a valued staff member there for the past twelve years. Despite her busy schedule, she had brought out seven recital CDs featuring her accompanying baritone Jeremey Bony as well as other individual singers from the opera. Neff's repertoire comprised unfamiliar songs by German, French, Italian, and Russian composers. Her latest CD—a grouping of Beethoven's Scottish, Irish, and Welsh song arrangements—included a cellist as well and had been a signature success.

Right now, Neff's attention was on whether she would get upstairs in time to join the back standers for *Fidelio's* second act. As a staff member she was allowed entry to the *Stehparterre* behind the orchestra seats where she could stand during the performance. She need not have worried. Intermission was still in progress and the sound of spirited conversation floated above the crowd. Making her way to the front of the building and the Schwind Foyer, she automatically looked over to the white marble fireplace on the far side of the room with Rodin's celebrated Mahler bust on its mantel. This time she was unable to see it because two women were standing in front of it. The large gold framed mirror behind the bust showed they were in animated conversation and much too close to the artwork. In fact one of them looked as if she was about to kiss Mahler's mouth! No, she was trying to *smell* the bust. Actually sniffing up and down the bronze! What was going on? Would she be licking it next? Mary Neff crossed the room and got within earshot of the two peculiar Mahler admirers.

"I'll tell you what else is wrong, Egga," the older woman was saying in English. "The nostrils of this bust are actual holes. Miniature tunnels. They go all the way up and back as far as I can see. There should not be full nasal cavities." She was crouching now, craning for a better view up the bronze nostrils.

Just then the overhead lights began to blink, signaling it was time to return to the auditorium for Act Two.

"We'd better go back." Egga looked urgently at Megan, eager to stop her excruciating examination of the Mahler effigy that was beginning to attract attention. And she hated the idea of entering the auditorium late.

"Give me a few more seconds." Megan quickly placed her right ear up against Mahler's right cheek. Blocking out attendant noise with her left hand, she listened the length of an unabashed quarter-minute. For Egga, worried a guard might intervene, it seemed more like half an hour. Finally Megan drew away in resignation, turned, and began following her relieved friend back to their orchestra seats.

Mary Neff could no longer contain her curiosity as she fell in behind them.

"Might I ask what you found so interesting about our Rodin's Mahler bust that you were actually touching it with your ear?" Mary was surprised to hear herself saying "our," but as a member of the Opera House staff she found herself feeling a certain proprietary protectiveness toward the bust.

"Oh, dear, I know it looked odd," Megan answered, turning around and smiling with as much charm as she could muster at the woman who had obviously observed and been mystified by her examination. Perhaps even offended.

"It's only that I've admired and seen that wonderful bust here for many, many decades, and yet this evening it didn't look the same for some reason."

Egga paused to look back at the woman who had justifiably quizzed her friend. She gave a start of recognition and astonishment.

"Say, aren't you Mary Neff?" she asked.

It was Neff's turn to be surprised.

"I am. Do I know you?"

"You might know my CD recordings. I certainly know yours. Especially your most recent one, the Beethoven songs with..."

"Ah, *that* one! It just received the 'Best Lieder Recording' of the year from the *Voix des Arts,*" Neff said proudly.

"I know, I know," Egga smiled. "Congratulations."

"And you said I might know some of *your* CDs?"

"It's possible. My most recent one features a group of French Romantic songs by Gounod, Fauré, and Lili Boulanger arranged for voice, piano, and cello obbligato."

"Say no more. You must be the *cellist* on that recording because I know both the soprano and the pianist."

"That's me," laughed Egga. Megan, relieved to have had the spotlight turned off her impulsive Rodin investigation, decided on the spot to ask their interesting new acquaintance if she would like to meet for drinks after the opera. The invitation from a fellow American was jovially accepted and the trio hurriedly broke up, Megan and Egga striding down the aisle to their seats, and Mary slipping into a standing spot one of her usher pals had saved for her.

After they had taken their seats Megan, as she had done before the beginning of the first act, surreptitiously opened the sling bag satchel on her lap, placed her Tascam DR-05 digital recorder so that the two minuscule mics faced the stage.

"I sure hope the orchestra mishap at the beginning of Act One doesn't happen again with the start of Act Two," Egga giggled to Megan.

"Oh, don't be silly. You can't have *two* mishaps in one orchestra on the same evening," shushed Megan. Egga was referring to the sudden sound of an instrument falling to the floor of the orchestra pit during the opera's opening scene when Marzelline, responding to a knocking on the door, sings "*Das war ein willkommener Klang*—That was a welcome sound." Megan pressed the enter button of her Tascam.

Act Two, with its recreation of Alfred Roller's partly abstract 1904 stage design for Mahler, began a few seconds later. Megan noticed with approval that there were fifteen women in the orchestra. The curtains opened to show Florestan—sung this evening by Italian tenor Aldo Finzi-Contiti—alone in his dismal dungeon cell. After singing of his trust in God he has a vision of his wife Leonora coming to his aid. Torn out of him suddenly came the famous lament: "*Gott! Welch Dunkel hie*r! *O grauenvolle Stille!*—God! What darkness here! O horrible silence!" Just as the despairing tenor sang the word "silence," a booming explosion was heard. The great auditorium ceiling chandelier went dark. So also did the stage and orchestra pit. Cries of surprise and fright filled the auditorium and its four balconies. People began jumping up from their seats. Within seconds the darkness on stage and in the pit and auditorium was illuminated by hundreds of cell phones flashing ineffectively in all directions. Seconds turned into minutes.

"*Please everyone, remain in your seats,*" a man's voice commanded authoritatively over the house loudspeaker system. The voice continued as the din suddenly died down.

"This is Chief of Police Erich Decker. There has been an explosion outside the auditorium in the Schwind Foyer. We do not yet know whether this is due to an in-house systems failure or to other causes. We ask that no one in the auditorium leave their seats. All orchestra members, singers, and stage hands are to remain where you are as well. For safety precautions, all building exits have been temporarily locked."

The sound of anxious murmuring filled the air. Megan and Egga looked at each other incredulously.

"See? I *told* you there was something suspicious about the Mahler bust," Megan said. "Just think. The hollow interior would have been a perfect place to insert a grenade or something explosive like that and then set it off remotely. I bet that's exactly what happened."

"*Aber!*" Egga exclaimed. "We don't know how the explosion took place yet. It may well have been a systems failure as the police officer mentioned. But even if it was an intended explosion, placing the explosive inside the Mahler bust seems like a long shot to me. More likely, such a device might be hidden behind one of the radiators, or inside one of the two fireplaces. And one would really have to know the layout of the building. An inside job, perhaps?"

"Very possibly. I'm thinking this may have been a bungled attempt. If the release of a dangerous chemical is involved, for instance, it must have been intended for all of us—everyone in the house."

"Then why set it off in a small foyer rather than right in the auditorium or orchestra pit or even on stage?" Egga asked.

"We'll have to wait for the police to explain. But if I'm right, the triggering 'grenade' was concealed in Mahler's bust."

"Hold on a minute. I'm getting confused. Do you no longer think that someone removed the Mahler effigy because they coveted it and substituted the surmoulage so the robbery wouldn't be noticed? Or are you now saying that someone stole the original Rodin bust in order to substitute a cast taken from the original bronze head and that it contained an explosive mechanism?" Megan paused before she answered.

"Why not both?"

"Scary!"

"Well, we can't know at the moment, can we? But it's unlikely that someone *not* connected with the substitution of busts would somehow, all of a sudden, think 'hmm, what a good place that bust over there on the marble fireplace mantel would be to hide a bomb.' How would they know there was *room* in the bust for such a thing? And anyway, they could hardly have done it on the spot. Certainly anyone attempting to do such a thing had to avoid the likelihood of being caught in the act, no matter what time of day or night. Okay, well, perhaps two in the morning is when they could get away with doing it— switching busts, keeping the original, and substituting the loaded surmoulage."

"This is beginning to boggle my mind," said Egga, in her singsong accent, proud of knowing the English expression.

"I agree," Megan answered, too intent at the moment to notice her former student's command of vernacular English. They sat in silence for a while. Then Megan burst out.

"Egga, I think I know why this has happened!"

3

ℱifty-eight-year-old director of Vienna's renowned Austrian National Library, Basileus Schmidt, had grown up in the midst of the first Arab-Israeli war. Orphaned at the age of three by a bombing attack that killed his parents and siblings, he was adopted by the family of his best friend in kindergarten, Ahmed Suleiman, and grew up in the troubled Gaza Strip. Upon migrating, with the blessing of his adoptive parents, to the Austrian metropolis at the age of eighteen, he had immediately changed his name. To be an Arab, a Muslim in Europe was not the most advantageous thing. He converted his surname, Suleiman, into the innocuous sounding Schmidt, and transformed his given name from Basel into Basileus. He especially liked the latter as the meaning of the name in Greek was king. He liked to joke with his Austrian wife Sabina that she had only married him because of his "royal" first name.

They had met within a few months of Basileus's arrival in Vienna—she a Catholic and he a Muslim—although neither of them practiced their faith. They had two children, the older, a daughter Adele and the younger, a son Stefan. Adele had always doted on her brother and both of them, although only in their late-twenties, had found fine, respected professions that brought them into contact almost every day. A talented seamstress, Adele worked at the Vienna State Opera as head tailor in the *Damen Repertoireschneiderei*—Women's

Repertory Tailoring—where any alterations or repairs needed before or during a performance of one of the season's repertoire operas were taken care of. If on evening watch, tailors provided their own sewing machines. Adele's was a portable white vintage Singer and she kept it in a rolling tote that was twenty inches high, fifteen inches wide, and fifteen inches deep, absolutely perfect for accommodating a beautiful machine like hers. With a head for mechanics, computer savvy, and quite strong physically, Adele enjoyed maintaining the powerful appliance herself. This placed her in great demand for "emergency" repairs needed by her colleagues. Sewing machines always seemed to break down when a non-repertoire opera was being performed and unique costumes needed quick alteration. When she was not on duty, Adele's hours were pretty much her own.

As for Stefan, he had demonstrated an early love of music and was especially drawn to the cello. He began lessons at the age of seven and was admitted into the Vienna Conservatory by the time he was fifteen. He landed a position with the Vienna State Opera at the age of twenty-two and soon advanced to the position of first chair second cello. Sister and brother were extremely close and Basileus was understandably proud of both of them.

And now here he was at the peak of a long and distinguished career as director of what had originally been the imperial and royal library of the Austrian emperors. A man of unusual height and vigor, but recently greatly disabled by ankylosing spondylitis—AS—Basileus was the guardian of over 7.4 million items stored at the library's Josefplatz building in the heart of Vienna.

He was a zealous guardian. For in his many years of personally and privately examining many of the thousands of untouched file boxes of documents, he had come across one box, the contents of which, were he to reveal them, would startle the world of music and compel recent biographies to be amended.

At present he would do nothing. The box resided in a safe next to his treasured Mahler bust at his small home office in the attic—a site his AS allowed him to visit only painfully now. Not even the family knew about the contents of his safe. At the right moment he planned to reveal the momentous findings to his adored Stefan, who, as a musician, would understand the significance of his discovery. But not now. Basileus knew that Stefan was about to initiate an orchestral "chess move" he had worked out that required concentration and exquisite timing.

Concentration and exquisite timing.

4

$\mathcal{M}$ore than half an hour had passed. Lights were restored in the auditorium, orchestra pit, and on stage, but it was obvious that Act Two of *Fidelio* was not going to be performed that evening. The buzz of anxious, angry conversation had become louder by the minute. However, an immediate hush fell when Chief of Police Erich Decker's voice crackled over the loudspeaker again.

"Ladies and gentlemen. We are sorry for the delay. The specific cause of the explosion you heard has not yet been conclusively determined but we are now making sure that no poisonous gasses of any type have been released. It is imperative that everyone continue to remain here in the auditorium where all doors are closed and you are safe from any possible exposure until the situation has been completely resolved. This should only take about half an hour."

There was a pause. Then Decker spoke again.

"I regret to inform you that when we do receive the all-clear signal and before you leave the building, a body pat-down will have to be carried out on everyone. We will begin with audience members first, then members of the orchestra and staff."

Gasps filled the air. Shouts of protest and indignation were heard.

"Please, please! Ladies and gentlemen, we are as eager as you to facilitate evacuation of the building. Therefore, since a body search will be involved, we ask that women take the far-left exit by the stage and men take the far-right exit by the stage. Our experienced search teams will be as respectful and as quick as possible. I shall ask that we begin with the top balcony and work down."

Loud curses rose from the audience as people began rising to their feet and gazing around in consternation. A few people who had paid top price for their orchestra seats volubly expressed their resentment that they would now be the last to leave the building.

Megan and Egga stood up as well and began stretching.

"So tell me, Megan, now that we know *what* has happened—an explosion, and possible release of a chemical of some sort just as you predicted—*why* has it happened? You told me that you thought you knew why. But you have not said a word for the last fifteen minutes. You've just been buried in the program brochure and in your iPhone."

"I've been checking on things."

"*What* things?"

"The full season schedule for this year's *Fidelio* performances here along with their casts and conductors."

"What a weird thing to have been doing. How could that possibly have anything to do with what's happened tonight?"

"Remember, I told you I thought I knew *why* this explosion has happened?"

"Yes, yes. So?"

"Well, it was just a hunch, but after making a list just now of who was singing and who was conducting for every performance this season, I did a crosscheck and here's what I came up with. This evening is the only time we've had both a Jewish tenor and a Jewish conductor. And in addition, the set designer who recreated Alfred Roller's sets for Mahler is Scotter Cantrell, a recent convert to Judaism, I read recently."

"Okay. So?"

"I'm thinking that if the Mahler bust was indeed used for the explosion, *then this whole thing could be the work of a fanatical anti-Semite.*"

5

Although there was no scoring for his instrument in the trombone family in the original score of Beethoven's only opera, Ottokar Weininger, contrabass trombonist from Mannheim at the Vienna State Opera, never missed a performance. Pit manager Kerstin Jesse and other members of the orchestra were used to having the quiet, self-effacing opera fanatic in their midst. Even when operas not requiring his instrument were being performed, the quiet, slightly stoop-shouldered man still religiously took his seat in the orchestra pit, black instrument case always at his side like a large, faithful hound.

This evening was no different. Weininger sat quietly with his case behind the brass section of four French horns, two trumpets, and the two trombones specified in Beethoven's orchestration. When Act Two of *Fidelio* began, however, Weininger had not returned to the orchestra pit. No one gave it a thought.

6

The protracted evacuation of the Opera House had begun at last. Spotting their new acquaintance Mary Neff far behind them but edging down their aisle, Megan and Egga waved at her vigorously and waited for her to catch up to their row of seats.

"I still can't believe something like this has happened," Mary murmured indignantly after she joined them. "Not here in Vienna, not at this beautiful Opera House." She looked at Egga and Megan beseechingly.

"Well, Megan has a theory about why it happened," Egga said, lowering her voice discreetly.

"Why? What do you think?" Mary looked at Megan demandingly.

As they moved with excruciating slowness down the aisle toward the far-left exit by the stage, Megan gave her a summary of the cross-index of the information she had put together, citing the interrupted performance's tenor, conductor, and recreation by Scotter Cantrell of Alfred Roller's original *Fidelio* staging for Mahler.

"Does that suggest anything to you?" Megan finished, without revealing her own conclusion.

"Only that all three men are well-known."

"Yes, that, and something else they have in common?" Mary's eyes rolled up in thought for a few moments, then met her questioner's eyes.

"I can't identify anything," she said.

"I'll give you a clue," teased Megan. "What ethnic background or religion might all three men have in common?"

Mary's forehead wrinkled in concentration, then she shook her head.

"I'm afraid I'm just dense. Do tell me what you mean." Mary looked inquiringly from Megan to Egga and back to Megan. Egga spoke up.

"What Megan has deduced from studying the casts and conductors of all *Fidelio* performances for this season is that this evening's event, and only this evening's event, brings together a Jewish tenor, a Jewish conductor, and a recently converted Jewish set designer."

"And?" Mary frowned for a second, then brightened up with comprehension.

"I see. So you are saying that some hate mongering madman had it in for all three men because they're Jewish?" Megan and Egga nodded in sad affirmation.

"Then what about the original set designer, Alfred Roller?"

"Don't think Roller was Jewish," said Megan. "Although I've never really thought about it."

"I'm asking because I visited the big Jewish cemetery La Tablada in Buenos Aires when I was vocal coaching there and I saw several gravestones with the name 'Roller.' I remember because the name Roller sounded Scottish to me and I wondered why there were Scotts in an Ashkenaz cemetery?"

"Roller sounds French to me," contributed Egga musingly.

"Either way, we have at least three Jewish connections to tonight's sabotaged performance," said Megan.

"Hey, here's something to consider," Egga said, her voice rising with excitement. "If we're looking for Jewish connections, how about members of the chorus and members of the orchestra? They might all be in danger."

"We should study the program and find out," Mary said, warming to Megan's theory. They had almost made it to the exit and could see the female police officers deftly conducting body searches on the women in front of them.

"Well, this shouldn't take too long," Megan said in relief, looking back at her friends and smiling assuredly.

She was correct and ten minutes later the three women had exited onto the Operngasse side of the building.

"Are you still up to having a drink, ladies?" Mary asked, realizing the hour was far later than any of them had thought attending a performance of *Fidelio* would be.

"Absolutely!" exclaimed Egga, eager to talk to a fellow musician and one with whose work she was acquainted. Megan vigorously nodded agreement.

"I say, then, shall we remove to the Café Mozart?" Egga asked in a mock British accent. She knew the café was Megan's favorite one in the Opera House vicinity and it was just across from the renowned Albertina Museum where she had conducted so much fruitful research studying Schiele's graphic art.

"Perfect. Let's just hope everybody else hasn't had the same idea," Megan laughed, wheeling in the direction of the café.

Five brisk minutes later they were seated outdoors in front of the historic meeting place and had ordered drinks from a jovial waiter who recognized Mary Neff. She was a regular patron and always tried to sit at the indoor table where Graham Greene wrote *The Third Man*. Tonight however the interior was already filled with café-goers taking shelter from the still blistering heat.

"Oh, god, this hot spell is truly overwhelming," Egga said, glad that her instrument was safe in her air-conditioned hotel room.

"You should still live in Texas. You'd be used to it," joked Megan.

Their view of the Albertina façade this evening was obscured by a swarm of randomly parked squad cars that had responded to the explosion in the Opera House. Seated so near them, it was difficult to stray very far in conversation from the grim reason why the police had descended upon the neighborhood. Talk of music seemed forced when all three were still reeling from the baffling and frightening event they had just experienced.

"*Megan Crespi*! What on earth are you doing in Vienna?" A man's voice sounded on their left and they turned to see a lanky man with curly black hair in his fifties smiling at them.

"Erich!" Megan half stood in her excitement. "Off from the scene of the crime so soon?"

The two had become friends after she had been instrumental in helping him solve a murder connected with a stolen Schiele painting a few years earlier.

"*Ach*, so you know about what happened at the opera this evening."

"Know? We were there! All three of us." Megan gestured toward her companions and introduced them: "Meet Mary Neff from America, chief vocal coach at the Opera House here, and Egga Streicher, renowned cellist from Berlin." Megan turned back to the smiling man.

"And this is Chief of Police Erich Decker. Erich, can you join us for a minute, or are you on the way somewhere?"

"I shouldn't, our investigation is still in progress—we're just about to interrogate the staff and orchestra members—but a short break would be welcome right about now." Decker sat down next to Egga and smiled at her.

"What brings you to Vienna?"

"My love for the city and the fact that I am on a concert tour of Austria with my string quartet."

"Hmm, you don't sound like a Berlinerin."

"I'm not, I'm Swabian, but my sons are Berliner boys. Right now, they're at home in Berlin with my husband."

"She's married to a wonderful American physician," Megan added. "And their children are not only bilingual, they are also musicians. The older one plays cello like his mother, and the younger one plays violin."

"And how is it that you know Megan?" Erich asked. Egga looked at Megan and smiled broadly.

"She was my favorite professor when I attended Southern Methodist University in Dallas, Texas. She brought music into her art history classes. And we've been friends ever since. Before I met my husband David and had children, we used to link up at some of Megan's European lecture sites—London, Berlin, Leipzig, Helsinki, even Saint Petersburg. Oh gosh, was *that* an adventure! Remember, Megan?"

"I certainly do. After the lecture I wandered over to an upright piano in the reception room and began playing *Show Boat's* 'Can't Help Lovin' Dat Man,' and the Russians came flocking over, humming the melody. They knew it! Very touching. A sort of East-West moment."

"You play piano then?" asked Mary, intrigued by the sprightly fellow-American, an art historian who appeared to be comfortable in the world of music.

"Oh, well, only by ear," Megan replied. "Folk guitar too, but again, only by ear."

"Her main instrument is flute, and for that she does read music," Egga added.

"True, but only the treble clef, Egga," Megan laughed modestly, but she was actually rather proud of being able to read music for at least one instrument and one she enjoyed.

"We've played the Bach B minor flute sonata together a number of times and each time it's been a happy experience. And it's a real challenge for me to supply the keyboard part on cello," Egga smiled. Erich looked at Mary.

"And as vocal coach for our opera singers, I take it your main instrument is piano and that your ability to read music is top notch."

"Yes, piano is my instrument and yes, I can sight read pretty much anything you put in front of me. I don't play by ear, however," she added.

"Hey, are we all purposefully *avoiding* talking about what just happened tonight at the Opera House?" Megan interrupted, certain that the explosion was not due to any "in-house" malfunction and impatient to know what Erich's investigation had turned up so far. And whether he had any suspicions as to who might have set off the blast. Most of all, she was eager to find out whether her instincts were correct that Mahler's surmoulage bust had been the hiding place for the explosive agent. This would certainly strengthen her theory that the motive for destroying the bust was part of a well-planned anti-Semitic stunt meant to capture newspaper headlines and TV coverage.

All eyes now turned to Erich Decker.

"Avoiding? No, not exactly. I can tell you one thing. What I just released to the media before coming back here to my squad car for something."

"What is that?" Megan could hardly conceal her curiosity.

"The explosion you heard was purposefully set off by some unknown person and yet it was not intended to inflict great damage."

His listeners looked puzzled. Erich continued, rather pleased to have such an attentive audience. He spoke slowly and gestured extensively with his hands.

"I'm sure you can all picture the Schwind Foyer with its wall and ceiling paintings and its busts of famous composers lining the long walls. And the entrance on the right, if you're coming up the grand staircase, that features two marble portrait busts set against the wall on either side of the tall gold-framed mirror above the large fireplace."

Decker paused, an inquiring expression on his face, and Mary quickly identified the busts as being of Karl Ditters von Dittersdorf on the left and Giacomo Meyerbeer on the right. The officer continued, sounding like a teacher quizzing his students.

"And you will recall that the famous bust in bronze of Gustav Mahler by Auguste Rodin has the place of honor, placed alone on the white marble mantelpiece of that same fireplace?" Megan looked as though she wanted to tell Erich to hurry up at this point but she remained quiet.

"Yes, yes," Mary and Egga said in one voice.

"Well, thankfully, nobody was hurt, but those three busts are no more. Mahler, Dittersdorf, and Meyerbeer. The explosion came from that particular wall of the foyer and, although the marble fireplace was more blackened than damaged, the three effigies were totally smashed when they fell. There were dozens of marble fragments, some of them from the black marble pedestal that supported the Mahler bust. Also, there were various bits of melted metal from the Mahler head scattered across the hall's floor. It seems absolutely certain that the bronze head, which of course would have been hollow inside, was the site of the explosive agent. And that's why it was blown into smithereens when it was set off. Actually, a rather clever place to hide a small, volatile IED."

"See? I *knew* it had to be the Mahler surmoulage!" Megan exclaimed.

"What is a 'surmoulage?'" Erich asked, surprised by Megan's sudden excitement.

"It's usually a fraudulent taking a bronze cast of another bronze cast, literally an 'on mold'—and not from the original master model. As the metal cools it shrinks somewhat and so the features become a bit less pronounced. That's what was bothering me about the Mahler head Egga and I were looking at during the intermission. Rodin would never allow his bronzes to be reproduced by surmoulage during his lifetime. His marbles could be copied, yes, but not his bronzes."

"So could that mean the original Mahler bust by Rodin is not lost?" Erich was confused.

"Correct. The original bronze bust was removed from the Schwind Foyer at some point and the surmoulage cleverly substituted. So whoever did this understood the enormous value of the original and went to great means to preserve it."

"But why would that person not just steal the original bust and be done with it? Why go to the trouble and danger of replacing it with a copy, or as you call it, a surmoulage?"

"Because I am certain this person was not only a Mahler fanatic of some sort, but he, or she, was also a hate-monger, in this case of Jews, and wanted to make a dramatic statement by blowing up the effigy of a famous Jew."

"That is quite a theory. What makes you think this with such certitude, Megan?" Erich asked, intrigued and fixing his large brown eyes upon her.

"Tell him about your cyber research while we were stranded in the Opera House," Egga urged.

Megan explained her data search and the intriguing results suggesting that the attack might have been initiated by a rabid anti-Semite. Someone aware of the fact that three of the participants in and only in that evening's particular performance were Jewish. Megan's friends nodded in agreement. Mary spoke up.

"And there is one more element now if it was the work of a Jew hater. The bust of Meyerbeer may have been planned collateral damage," said Mary. Egga looked at Mary blankly for a moment, then nodded comprehension.

"I don't get your gist," said Erich.

"Ah, well you see Giacomo Meyerbeer was born Jacob Liebman Beer," explained Mary. "And he was faithful to his religion throughout his life despite experiencing growing prejudice against him as a Jewish composer. Nevertheless, his operas were immensely popular."

"Yes," added Megan, "and a jealous Richard Wagner became his most outspoken critic, even after obsequiously borrowing money from him during his early years."

She expanded to her rapt audience on something that had always intrigued her: Wagner's pseudonymous publication in 1850 of an essay he wrote titled "Jewishness in Music." Mendelssohn had died recently and, with both that Jewish composer and Meyerbeer in mind, Wagner was emboldened to characterize "Jewish music" as not being able to escape the "jumbled blabber" singsong of Jewish speech. The Jew, according to him, would never be able to speak European languages fittingly. And this prevented Jewish composers—the outsiders—from writing what he called 'true music.'"

"But that's terrible!" Egga exclaimed. Mary and Erich nodded in vigorous agreement.

"Ha! That's the least of it," Megan continued. "Twenty years later, capitalizing on the growing anti-Semitism in Germany, he published the essay again, this time with his own name and with a frenetic new section as long as the first part."

"But I don't understand," said Egga. Wagner's favorite conductor was Jewish, Herman Levi."

"Right. Wagner had a number of Jewish friends, especially in his later years, but they were all *of use to him*, remember that."

Curious to know what else Decker had released to the press, Mary changed the subject.

"And so did you tell the news media all the details you have just told us, *Herr Polizeioffizier*?"

"No. I purposefully did not identify the exact site where the IED was hidden. And if Megan is correct *it is possible that the swapped original Mahler bust is still in the Opera House.*"

7

The French horn had not been Homer Bläser's first instrument. He came from a family of double reed players and was happy to carry on the tradition, choosing the oboe over the bassoon. He loved its melancholy sound.

But when he was in his early thirties he developed an excruciating pain in the middle finger of his right hand which would lock when playing. Unlocking it was almost unbearable. It was a condition his doctor called Dupuytren's contracture, more commonly known as "trigger finger." Apparently, it was common among people like industrial workers and musicians whose jobs involve repetitive finger movements, just as trigger thumb was the new ailment assailing cellphone owners who used their thumbs to type.

Taking up the French horn was the ideal solution for Homer. The instrument called for the index, middle, and ring fingers of the left hand to do the key work while the right hand was used to cup the flared bell of the instrument. Homer never regretted his choice. He sometimes actually told people that he was glad he had trigger finger; it had introduced him to a whole new repertoire and he joked that sitting in the back row of the orchestra instead of the middle row gave him more leg room.

The fact that Homer's lungs and lips were already well attuned to channeling breath jumpstarted his mastery of the double horn when he switched instruments. He did have to get used to the fact that the F/B flat instrument was built a quarter-tone sharp, giving the right hand the job of correcting the pitch, but it also allowed greater range. And the notes he played felt physically closer together and it was easy to crack or miss a note. He knew that there was always some spoilsport in the audience—usually a newspaper critic—who just waited for the first French horn gaffe and who greeted it knowingly without understanding that the horn's normal tessitura is higher in its overtone series than other instruments in the brass family.

But Homer had mastered all that and had, with diligence, worked up to first horn at the Vienna Opera Orchestra to the pride of his musical family. His horn of choice was the Kruspe wrap horn with its several tubing bends, dark tone, and large, open bell. Homer did not keep his horn in the heavy molded horn-bell design of most French horn cases, but in a large modular case made of a lightweight wood covered by durable double-zip black nylon, outside strapped pockets, and padded straps. The straps enabled him to either to carry his instrument by hand or wear it on his back—his usual choice, as he customarily brought with him a black nylon gear kit every bit as large as his horn case. For the opera this evening he had shown up with both items.

8

"But why do you think the original Rodin bust might still be in the Opera House?" Egga was asking police chief Erich Decker as they sat at the Café Mozart.

"Couldn't the substitution have been made days or even weeks earlier?" she continued.

"No, that's not likely. The perpetrator would not want to take any chance of his IED going off in the bust ahead of time."

"That makes a lot of sense," Megan agreed. "Speaking of time, I was thinking that the surmoulage substitute could have been acquired at any time previous to the crime, weeks, months, perhaps even years before this happened. So perhaps tonight's event was long in the planning."

"Well, if *I* were committing the crime," Egga said, "I guess my cello case could be a good place to hide the substitute bust. Just hide out in the women's restroom until the house was empty, then sneak up to the Schwind Foyer in the middle of the night and switch out the two busts, hoping no fireman was about."

"That's a bit simplistic," Mary said, shaking her head in amusement." And what about your cello. Where would that be in the meanwhile?"

"Where? I could park it in one of the women's restroom booths and the whole scenario could probably take place in less than twenty minutes."

"I don't mean to rain on your crime, but all booths in all restrooms are checked every night," Erich smiled.

"And how would you get your cello *and* the bronze bust home?" Megan jumped into the fray.

"You couldn't leave right away because the Opera House, any Opera House, is locked up tight during the night. Right, Erich?"

"Yes. Only a very few persons have the keys; in this case the main person would be the head fireman overnighting there."

"Firemen sleep at the Opera House?" Egga was surprised.

"Indeed they do. It's been a long tradition with the Vienna Opera," answered Erich.

"And if you left when things opened up in the morning," added Mary, "the portier at either of the two stage doors would see you leave and he would notice and remember that you had a presumably full cello case as well as an uncased cello with you—adding up to two cellos. He wouldn't forget that unusual sight."

"There's another important thing you'd have to be sure of, if you were the criminal, Egga," Megan said, picking up the argument with zest. "You would have to have the *correct* surmoulage with you. One that was made from Rodin's more naturalistic Model B casting, which was the one preferred by the family, and not from the more expressionist Model A. Mahler's widow Alma gave the Vienna State Opera a copy of Model B in nineteen-thirty-one on the twentieth anniversary of Gustav's death. It was destroyed by the Nazis when they got to Vienna, of course. Just the way they destroyed the statues of Mendelssohn in Leipzig and Düsseldorf. But after the war, in nineteen-forty-eight, Alma gave a second casting of Rodin's Model B to the Opera House. And that's what your police are searching for now, right, Erich?"

Before Erich could answer, a policeman ran up to their table and addressed him. There was urgency in his voice.

"Good that I found you, *Chef*!"

"What's up, Viktor?"

"Just a moment! I must tell the units where you are." Viktor quickly sent a text, then handed a small object to his commander.

"*This* was just found in the Schwind Foyer at the opposite end to where the damage is. Behind the bronze bust of Richard Strauss."

"His daughter-in-law Alice was Jewish," Megan whispered to Mary, who nodded knowingly.

Erich took what appeared to be a metal index card box wrapped in singed tinfoil and opened it. There, wrapped in a single sheet of aluminum foil, was a single index card. A terse message was handprinted on it in capital letters. Erich read it out loud for all to hear:

TAKE THIS AS A WARNING!
NO MORE JEWS IN OUR OPERA HOUSE!
NO MORE JEWS DEFILING OUR CULTURE!

"I'm afraid this confirms your suspicion, Megan," said Erich grimly. "*Somewhere in Vienna we have a Jew-hating madman in our midst.*"

9

"But why hasn't Stefan *called* us?" Sabina Schmidt asked her husband Basileus for the fifth time. They had been glued to television ever since the State Opera's live broadcast of *Fidelio* was interrupted by a news bulletin reporting the unthinkable. Someone had purposefully set off an explosion in the Opera House. Their daughter Adele had called from her apartment almost immediately after the breaking news flash. Thank goodness she hadn't been on duty tonight she told them. And not to worry, she was sure Stefan was safe. She was coming right over.

That was a little before nine o'clock. Adele had arrived soon after and now it was nearly eleven. Why hadn't Stefan called to let them know he was all right, Sabina kept asking her husband and daughter. This was one of his regular performance evenings. He assuredly was at his usual place in the orchestra pit. Perhaps the explosion had happened there!

"Mutti, everything will be all right. Don't worry. Really, I just know things are okay."

Hardly hearing her daughter's reassuring words, Sabina continued to gaze imploringly at the telephone cradled on the couch between them, willing it to ring. Nothing.

Basileus had no words of comfort for his wife. He was even more perturbed than she but hid it well. He knew that Stefan had become increasingly miserable in his job at the Opera House even though he had a position envied by the other cellists there. He was, after all, second first chair—co-principal cello. Something to be proud of in a section of ten cellos. And yet Stefan was unhappy. And rightly so. The principal cellist, Jared Bogenstein, had held his chair for well over twenty years. This despite the fact that he was a closet alcoholic who increasingly could no longer control his drinking. Unnerved that the talented young man next to him who played so assuredly might one day replace him, Bogenstein had taken to arriving early and practicing his part in the orchestra pit which, with an empty house, magnified his sound and boosted his self-confidence. Then, plopping his bow down on the rack of his music stand and leaving his cello on its side by his chair, he would stretch out on a couch in the musicians lounge. There he would empty the small thermos of whiskey stored in the outside pocket of his instrument case cover and take a snooze until the sound of other players arriving woke him up. Stefan had complained to the resident conductor, but his criticisms were of no avail. Maestro Gabor Alexander had been at the Vienna State Opera for as many years as his first principal cellist, in fact a bit longer, and he was not going to signal incompetence just because a player was in his or her late sixties and drank a little.

Stefan had spoken bitterly to his father about the unfairness of not relieving an increasingly incompetent Bogenstein from his post. And just that afternoon Stefan had told Basileus that he had a plan. One that would require concentration.

"Concentration and exquisite timing," he had said.

10

*W*hile the quartet at the Café Mozart was pondering the index card warning brought to Erich by one of his officers, another policeman ran up. He was breathless.

"What is it, Peter?" Erich demanded, standing up.

"We've just found something important. *A disposable cellphone at the back of the orchestra pit.*"

"Ah ha, excellent! That's it! Now we know." Erich immediately reached for his own cellphone, tapped it twice, connected, and gave an urgent command to the officer he had left in charge at the Opera House.

"Listen to me, Paul. *No one is to leave the building. No staff or orchestra members are to leave the Opera House.* We've already lost the audience but continue to detain everyone who's on the premises. I believe the cellphone you just found has to be the one used to ignite its mate hidden inside what is most likely to have been a substitute portrait bust of Gustav Mahler in the Schwind Foyer. It's highly possible the original bust is still hidden somewhere on the premises. So have your men examine the large instrument cases. And I want every centimeter of the building searched. The auditorium, the balconies, loges, foyers, stage, backstage, closets, toilets, corridors, and all basement areas searched. I'll be right there to start interrogating the orchestra members. So continue keeping them in place. What?"

Erich listened for a moment, then answered, "Yes, the conductor too." Megan and Mary suppressed giggles.

"Well," Erich continued, hanging up and looking at them, "now we know for sure exactly how the explosion occurred. It was triggered by a cellphone, a disposable cellphone. And the bad part is that disposable cellphones can't be traced."

"Wow!" Megan exclaimed. "That would mean whoever used one of those to set off the synchronized one inside the Mahler bust had to be within physical hearing distance of the Opera House, wouldn't it? To set it off exactly at the word *Stille?*"

"Most probably. But it could also have been someone anywhere in the house where there's a monitoring screen," Erich answered. "And, I think you know that nowadays our Vienna Opera live-streams many of its performances. Forty-five of them. And this evening's performance was one. That was the first thing we checked. So theoretically the blast could even have been triggered by someone following the performance on television in Berlin or New York, say."

The women gasped.

"Then anyone, *anywhere in the world*, could have triggered the bomb?" Megan burst out.

"Taking into account the time change, yes, that is correct," said Erich. He turned to go, then looked at Megan.

"I know it's getting late, Megan, and it's going to get later, but could you come with me? I think your observation of the people we are going to have to interview could be helpful." He was referring to a situation that had arisen during their Schiele investigation in which her correct reading of a lying suspect's body language—constant blinking, eyes roving to the left, sitting perfectly still and drawing hands and feet inward, and distancing—had enforced his persistence in exposing the woman's guilt.

Megan was thrilled by the request and readily agreed to accompany Erich back to the Opera House. But then she paused and looked at their new friend.

"Erich, perhaps you should ask Mary here to be in on this as well, since as head vocal coach she is certainly well-versed in the Opera House personnel."

"Might you come with us?" Erich asked, turning to the quiet, intelligent looking woman.

"I'd be happy to. It is not impossible that I could have some insights that might be helpful."

Megan turned to Egga, who was watching them all with amusement. She shrank back holding her palms up in front of her.

"No! Don't ask me too," she laughed. "I have a concert right here in Vienna tomorrow evening and need to get my rest."

"Of course, of course," Megan soothed as she stood up. "Here are some euros; would you mind taking care of the check?"

"Leave everything to me. Not to worry."

Heading back up the Operngasse, Megan and Mary tried to keep up with the three policemen striding ahead of them. So much for staying out of mystery cases, Megan was telling herself. Despite her age, she felt invigorated, intrigued, and definitely up to the task. Only irritated that her gait was so slow.

She heard an inner voice intoning the love duet toward the end of *Fidelio*, "*O namenlose Freude!*"—"O unnamed joy!"

11

¶It was not because fifty-three-year-old Ottokar Weininger had no desire to return to the orchestra pit that evening. But he needed the money. Aside from Wagner's *Ring of the Nibelung*, Verdi's last two operas, *Otello* and *Falstaff*, and Puccini's *Turandot*, there was so little operatic music calling for a contrabass trombone that his annual salary was correspondingly low. The young man in a short-sleeve blue-striped shirt who had approached him when he exited the Opera House stage door on the Kärntner Strasse side after a performance of *Fidelio* three evenings earlier, had made an intriguing if curious proposal to him. Would he be interested in trading his ancient contrabass trombone for a brand-new German-style Kühl with slide extender, bell garland, and long water key? It would come with a modern carrying case that, although it weighed a bit more, had plenty of space for all the ancillary items any bone player would want to have, like cleansing oil, cleaner snake for the slide, wrench to adjust the hand brace, and space for two different mutes. And to make up for any possible inconvenience, a payment of one thousand euros would accompany the swap, since his old instrument had a reasonably nice mellow tone and there might be a short adjustment period with the new one.

Ottokar was overwhelmed with delight and did not have to think even one instant before saying yes. Now at last he could self-publish and advertise the important book he had written at the age of twenty-three and which had been rejected by dozens upon dozens of ignorant publishers through the decades that followed. Titled *Personality and Gender*, it was an appalling display of self-hatred. Despite the fact that he was Jewish, his treatise excoriated the archetypal Jew and womanhood in general. Both Jews and women were amoral and passive. It was they who were to be blamed for the decay of modern civilization. Ottokar had maintained a blog to circulate these truths until the amount of hate mail he received scared him into discontinuing it.

By curious happenstance, such demented ideas had been expressed decades earlier in a 1903 book that had seen the light of day entitled *Sex and Character*. And by an even unlikelier coincidence, the Viennese author's name was Otto Weininger. Ottokar knew nothing of the strange man or that, a few months after publication of his book, he chose to commit a dramatic suicide by pistol in the same house where Beethoven had died.

Ottokar only knew that one thousand euros along with a new instrument was a fabulous offer he could not turn down. In saying yes, he also accepted the one proviso mandated by the stranger. The instrument exchange would take place just outside the Kärntner Strasse stage door exactly five minutes before the beginning of the next performance of *Fidelio* three evenings hence. His old instrument would be appropriated at that time and the new one would be handed over. At intermission he was to leave his new trombone in its locked case next to the chair behind the brass section where he always sat when not playing. Then, as soon as Act One was over, he was to return to the stage door where he would be given the promised one thousand euros and the key to his new instrument case.

The peculiar request did not in the least diminish Ottokar Weininger's ecstasy at the heaven-sent bargain. Now at last humanity would have his desperately needed masterpiece explaining why the world was falling apart. Beware of woman; beware of Jews!

12

"No, I'm definitely not releasing that to the press," Erich Decker said in answer to Megan's question as they hurried through a corridor in the back of the Opera House toward the auditorium.

"Public knowledge of the hate note could inspire copy-cat actions and then we'd really have our hands full," he added.

"Or the same person might be encouraged and strike again," Mary added. "Perhaps even here in the House, say during another performance, or at midnight."

"I don't understand," said Megan, looking at Erich and Mary. "Aren't there any guards walking around and checking the premises at night?"

"Minimal, I should think," Mary spoke up before Erich could answer. "It's been the custom ever since the Opera House was built to have members of the fire brigade sleep here overnight. There's such a fear of fire here at any hour of day or night. And yes, during the day, there are a number of guards on duty. I know most of them."

As they entered the Opera House Erich looked back at the two officers who had walked back from the café with them.

"Viktor, Peter, you've heard what we've been saying. I want you to interrogate last night's in-house fire crew. When exactly they relieved each other. Then interrogate every usher and member of the stage crew on the job this evening. Any tailors on duty. Also, what time everyone concerned clocked in today and what their specific location was this evening at the time of the explosion. We'll deal with the musicians."

"Yes sir, we're on it," Viktor answered for them both as they peeled off from the group. Erich nodded and addressed the two women.

"Right now of course because the disposable cellphone was found at the back of the orchestra pit, it's the orchestra players themselves who are under the greatest suspicion. But it's also possible that the phone was discarded there by someone *after* the explosion. Perhaps to cast suspicion on one of the orchestra players."

The trio entered a narrow walkway that separated the orchestra pit from the front row seats of the orchestra floor. Walking briskly to the center they looked down over the guardrail at the conductor's podium in the pit. The pit was only about three feet below them and the fact that audiences had a good view of most of the orchestra players was one of the plusses of the Vienna State Opera auditorium. Megan had especially enjoyed watching the brass and percussion players from that position after checking out the flute section.

"Hey, where's your baton, Max?" The police chief jokingly called down to the young man seated on the conductor's stool below him. Although all lights were on, the police officer was beaming a flashlight at a small object.

"Good you're back, *Chef*," the man called Max answered, jumping up and flashing an object at them.

"*Here's the disposable cellphone we found*. It's a, just a minute, I'm looking at a very small label here. It's a something—can't read that first word—Mobile Micro Ten."

"That would be a Posh Mobile Micro Ten—a very small android."

"Oh, boy, is it ever. Not even as long as the palm of my hand."

"Excellent! Now where exactly was it discovered?"

"Near where that harp is over there."

"Can you be more specific?"

"Beyond the harp music stand and chair facing it. It was jammed down inside a break in the baseboard. That's why we missed it in the first sweep."

"All right. Great work." Erich turned to his two companions.

"Okay. This is terrific. Now we know how the explosion was triggered. Sometime very late last night or very early this morning the perpetrator switched Mahler busts—the original for the explosive-loaded surmoulage. That's all he'd have to do. Then, in possession of the linking disposable cellphone we just found, he could pick the precise time he wanted it to go off. Ruling out for now any outside instigator, somebody here this evening did it. And very likely someone in the orchestra pit."

Erich paused, a wan smile on his face.

"The pit location of the find acquits the audience at least."

"Thank goodness for that," said Megan. "It would be impossible to reassemble this evening's audience!"

"At least we have the ushers, orchestra members, singers, and stage hands right here," Erich continued. "The dressing rooms and restrooms have been cleared, the stage manager—the *Inspizient*—and all stage hands are confined to their lounge, the singers and ushers to the canteen, and the orchestra players with their instruments, plus His Highness conductor, are all in the musicians lounge waiting to be interviewed."

"Let him wait a little," Mary suggested impishly. She had not been particularly impressed by his tempi in the first act.

"Now," Erich said to his companions, as they sat down, "when we question the performers we are looking for a number of things. There is the possibility that more than one individual was involved—the person who made the bust switch, and the person who triggered the explosion. If the switch occurred within the last twenty-four hours, then the original bust could still be on the premises. God knows what could be hidden inside a large case minus its instrument. And of course we'll be examining the largest instruments themselves as well."

"How do you recommend we begin?" he asked his companions. Megan was the first to answer.

"I think we ought to start with the percussion section. The players stand along the back of the pit and are closest to where the cellphone was found."

Mary nodded. "Let's call the player of the kettledrums to the pit first. Those two giant copper bowls are hollow, after all. Could presumably contain something. Even something like a bronze bust!" She was pointing to the back center of the pit.

Erich made the call and a few minutes later a slim man in his thirties with black sideburns and long hair in a bun appeared. He was constantly intertwining his fingers and looked anxiously up at them. Erich began the questioning.

"I see from the program here that you are Hans Trommel. How long have you been employed by the Opera, Herr Trommel?"

"Five and a half years, sir."

"Where were you when the explosion in the Schwind Foyer occurred?"

"Um, right here, at my drums."

Megan posed the next question. "May I ask you to tilt your drums, one at a time, back and forth so we can hear if there is any object inside. Any rattling noise."

"Huh? It'd be impossible to push anything under the calfskin heads on top of my drums, sir. They're stretched really tight." The man looked puzzled.

"I agree, but please oblige us. Just tilt them all the way back and forth."

Trommel obeyed vigorously. The kettledrums were silent. Satisfied, Erich changed the subject.

"Just before the explosion did you see or *hear* anything unusual anywhere around you. In any of the orchestra sections—the strings, or woodwinds, or brass?"

The young man was obviously thinking hard, raising his eyes to the right. Then he looked perplexed. "Do you mean at the beginning of Act One?"

"Why do you mention Act One when we're asking you about Act Two?" Mary asked, leaning forward.

"Well, because that's when he fell over. Crashed to the floor with his instrument."

"Who? What instrument?" Mary followed up quickly.

"Um, his cello. The principal chair's cello. The near audience could hear the commotion and our guest conductor was furious, hissing at Jared Bogenstein, telling him to leave the pit immediately."

"And did he?" asked Megan.

"For sure. He scooped up his instrument and made his way past the cello section which, with our orchestra disposition, is right in front of the conductor. He kinda' staggered and went to the pit door on our right. He was sobbing. I felt real sorry for him."

Megan voiced a quiet "Hm." So that was the noise she and Egga had heard when Marzelline sang about the "welcome sound." Mary may not have heard it back in the *Stehparterre*. Megan described what they had heard to them.

"Interesting. Don't see how that could have anything to do with the explosion in Act Two though." Erich had one last question for the instrumentalist.

"Think hard now, Herr Trommel. "Did you hear anything unusual *after* the explosion?"

"No sir. Everybody was yelling and screaming. We were all getting the hell out of there! Running from the pit down the stairs on either side to the lockers and the lounge, even the restrooms."

Erich turned to his two companions. "All right, I don't think we need our kettledrum player any longer, do you?" They agreed.

The musician was dismissed with thanks and Erich called to have the other timpanist sent in, the bass drum player. While they waited for him—it turned out to be a her—Mary began holding forth on Beethoven's important use of the bass drum. It was he, she said, who first thought of tuning it on the tonic and dominant, with the stunning effects achieved in the *Scherzo* of the Ninth Symphony. Her listeners were fascinated and almost did not notice that the bass drummer had entered the pit.

A tall, very young woman, Theresa Canales, told them a story that matched Trommel's. They were both standing behind their instruments during the beginning of Act Two and neither one saw or heard anything unusual before the explosion. She confirmed it happened just as the word "*Stille*" was sung by Florestan. Erich dismissed the cooperative woman with thanks and turned to his friends.

"You know, Erich," Mary said, "I'd like to take a look at the orchestral score from which the maestro was conducting. It would be useful, I think, to know which players were actually playing their instruments when the trigger word '*Stille*' was sung, and which players were not, meaning which had hands free to access a putative hidden cellphone. As in the case of the two timpanists we just interviewed."

"Fine idea. I'll have the score, which I see is still on the podium—at least that's what I think it is—I'll have it brought up to us. In the meantime, I have a feeling that we are going to hear the same story from all the players."

"Most probably," said Megan. "But still, after we determine how long they've been with the orchestra, let's continue asking exactly when each one heard the explosion—make sure their stories match—and exactly where they were at that moment and whether they heard or saw something out of the ordinary," she urged.

"And, of course, Megan, you'll be watching their body language," urged Erich.

"Who should we call in now?" He deferred to Mary.

"I think we should start with those first violin players whose seat assignments here at the Opera place them in the very back of the left-hand section," she answered. "Aside from the timpanists, they would be the ones closest to the spot where the disposable cellphone was found."

"There is one thing I find a bit peculiar concerning the orchestra pit," Megan said.

"Oh, what's that?" Erich asked.

"Well, why is there a *harp* in the pit? The instrumentation for *Fidelio* doesn't include a harp."

They looked in admiration at the large gold concert grand pedal harp standing forlornly in the far end of the pit on audience left and fronted by empty black music stands and chairs.

"It's not totally odd for a harpist to leave her or his harp in the pit if it's going to be played several nights in a row," Mary said softly, as though to herself. "Although they usually cover it with a soft fabric dust cover if so."

"Do you still have the program booklet?" she asked Megan.

"Yes. Here, just a second. It's deep down in my bag." Pushing her Tascam recorder to one side Megan triumphantly pulled out the thick program booklet from her cross-body satchel purse and handed it to Mary. Due to the unusual heatwave in Vienna these past few days she had regretted wearing it. But now it was coming in handy.

"Ah, here we go. Let's just see what we've got." Mary turned to the page listing the performances and their dates for that year's season.

"Last night's opera was Richard Strauss's *Elektra*," she informed them.

"Wow! There are *two* harps in that opera!" exclaimed Megan, her eyes widening.

"Let's see if anyone remembers noticing a harpist here tonight," Erich said. He pressed the number on his cellphone for his man supervising the musicians lounge and told him to find out. Perhaps there was even a harpist in the lounge along with the other players.

"I'll call you back as soon as I determine this, sir. There *is* a harp case outside in the corridor, along with the large double bass cases and the timpani flight cases, I noticed that. But we haven't finished searching all the big cases yet."

"Interesting. Keep searching." Erich hung up and Megan turned to Mary.

"Let me have the program back for a second, Mary. I want to check something else." She studied the page where the brochure had been opened. She found what she wanted.

"Look here! For the next two evenings there are no operas with harps in them. They're performing Mozart's *The Magic Flute* tomorrow, and the next evening it's *Fidelio* again."

"Well!" exclaimed Mary. "Maybe we're getting somewhere. Why didn't the stage hands remove *both* harps after the show last night? After *Elektra*? Did one of the harpists tell them not to remove her harp? But why would a harpist leave her instrument in the pit if she would not be playing for a stretch of days?"

13

Thirty-eight-year-old Cristina Paloma was furious. When the police discovered she was a musician, she had been required to leave the wings from where she had been watching the opera with her stage-hand buddy Oliver. She was told to go directly to the musicians lounge along with the other instrumentalists. She was not allowed to approach her precious Salzedo harp, marooned now in the orchestra pit. Nor was she allowed access to her own harp case. It stood with the double bass cases along the wall of the semi-circular basement hall just outside the locker rooms where the smaller cases were stored.

Her fellow orchestra members were in the same boat. With the exception of the timpanists, they had been ordered to take their instruments with them to the musicians lounge. As they waited, crowded uncomfortably in the lounge, their instruments and their instrument cases outside were being examined one by one, and things were going excruciatingly slowly. The Italian harpist cursed heartily under her breath and looked woefully at her friend Matías, a Jewish Argentinian viola player whose father had been Astor Piazolla's pianist. Then she blew up.

"*Dannazione,* Matías! I must to drive to Graz this evening after the performance. I to give master class there tomorrow morning at nine. Now if we ever let out of here, I must to drive through the night just to get there in time!"

"Stay calm and carry on," he grinned at her, showing his beautiful white teeth and imitating Winston Churchill's accent as best he could. "There's nothing we can do about it."

"Maybe I pretend having epileptic attack," Cristina said, clutching at her long dark hair and dramatically rolling her brown eyes upward.

"And be wheeled out on a cart without your harp? Doesn't sound like the Cristina I know."

"*Hai ragione.* You are right. But I like to see them open harp case without key." She patted her purse. "They not even have give me time to tell them case locked."

"Well, let's hope they don't just blast it open when they discover that."

Matías had meant his remark as a joke but Cristina took it seriously and jumped up, her face pale.

"*Dio mio*, I must to give them key before they force it open!"

She ran out of the lounge and into the arms of a policeman.

"Hold on there, *Fräulein*. No one is allowed to leave the lounge until we finish searching all the instrument cases and you've been interviewed by the police."

"That's why I come out. I need give you the key to my harp case. See? Here it is. My case is locked. Take it, just take it, *per favore*. I not want you force it open."

"All right, all right, *gnädige Harfenfrau*, I'll take it over there. You, however, must return to the lounge."

Cristina turned back inside and closed the door with a bang. Matías looked at her questioningly. She shrugged and rolled her eyes upward in exasperation.

Never mind that *esplosione*! She absolutely had to reach her harp languishing in the orchestra pit.

14

"So you're saying Beethoven scored his opera for four French horns, two trombones, and two trumpets? That gives us eight more suspects to interrogate," Erich Decker sighed, looking at Megan and Mary.

"We probably don't have to question them if their cases are found to be empty," Megan soothed him.

"*Ach ja*, let's see how that's coming along." Erich raised his cellphone and called one of his officers backstage. He listened intently to what turned out to be a lengthy answer. When it was concluded he turned to the women with a tired expression on his face.

"Okay, This is what we have so far. Even though they're too small to hold a bronze bust, a search was made of the two trumpet cases. Nothing, of course. Same with the two trombone cases, still hardly large enough to hold something the size of a bust. And again, nothing. But searching the four French horn cases turned up something that might be interesting. They were all empty except for the small items I'm told are needed for the upkeep of the instrument. But the officer said that while three of the empty French horn cases have flared bells, bells that could not possibly hold a life-size bust, the fourth French horn case isn't flared. It's rectangular in shape, larger, longer, deeper and quite a bit wider—could possibly hold a bust. But the case was empty. The interesting thing is that my men also found a very large black nylon kit bag right next to the rectangular case, in fact they both had identical name tags on them."

"Yes?" The women asked in unison.

"Well, they looked inside and found something odd. Something that might possibly have a bearing on our search."

"*Yes?*"

"A second French horn." Both women looked disappointed.

"Tell you what I'm going to do," Erich said.

"We didn't interview all the brass players who play smaller instruments, but I'm going to have that French horn player with the two cases sent to us right now."

A few minutes later a man in his mid-forties walked into the pit from audience right. A French horn was cradled in his left hand and a smile of inquiry was on his face. He identified himself as Homer Bläser and yes, he was the owner of the rectangular French horn case and also of the kit bag containing a second horn.

"Why do you have a second horn?" Erich asked peremptorily.

"Well, the horn you're talking about, the one you found in my kit bag, is my regular Kruspe horn. But this evening I was trying out my brand-new Vienna horn with its *Pumpenvalve* engagement. Our conductor this evening is notorious for demanding a more mellow, more liquid legato from his horns, and, as first horn, this was an incentive for me to invest in one of these old-fashioned instruments." Bläser held up the horn.

"You can see it's slightly smaller than our modern French horns, and instead of rotary valves it has double-cylinder valves so there's less resistance for the player. The *Pumpenvalve* lets the air flow straight unless the valves are actuated, so there is less resistance . . ."

"All right, all right, thank you," Erich interrupted. "And where were you when the explosion happened?"

"Sitting in my chair in the brass section. I am principal hornist."

"Let me sum up then," Erich said. "You're saying that you own two French horns and that your old one is the instrument we found in your kit bag next to your empty case and this one, your new one, is the instrument you used this evening, correct?"

"Yes, sir, correct. Of course my 'new' one is not really new, as the Vienna horn has been around since the middle of the nineteenth century, but . . ."

"Thank you for your help," Erich interrupted again. "You and your instruments are free to go." Looking somewhat disappointed the garrulous French hornist left the pit.

"God save me from valves!" Erich mouthed to his two comrades.

15

Riveted by TV news reports of the explosion at the Opera House, Basileus, his wife, and daughter almost jumped off the couch when their landline phone finally rang. Sabina grabbed the receiver, yelling yes into it and heard a familiar voice.

"Hey! Mutti, it's me!"

"Stefan! *Liebling*! Where are you? Why haven't you called us? I've been sick with worry you'd been hurt or even killed in the terrible Opera House explosion. We've been glued to TV!"

"Hold on, Mutti. I'm perfectly all right. All of us orchestra players were cordoned off right after the explosion by the police and our cellphones were taken from us. They just now gave them back. I called you the second I got mine. Wanted to let you know I'm okay."

"Oh, thank god! Here, your father wants to talk to you, hold on."

Basileus grabbed the phone.

"Son," he said urgently," please tell me the explosion didn't have anything to do with your plan."

"Ha! No, Papa. The strategy went like clockwork. A few minutes after Act One began, just as I calculated. I'll tell you all about it when I get there."

16

An hour and a half into the interviews of instrumentalists being conducted by the police, Kerstin Jesse had very nearly tripped over the almost invisible black rectangular box on the floor behind the brass section. As pit manager, she had been methodically clearing the site of any forgotten paraphernalia after it became obvious that Act Two of *Fidelio* would not be recommenced that evening. And then the police arrived and began frisking people and opening instrument cases one by one. In the excitement Kerstin totally forgot she had half kicked, half pushed with her foot the heavy box into the narrow storage space at the back of the pit that doubled as a bench for the timpanists. Its wooden flap had swung down reluctantly over the irksome object and Kerstin had moved on to more urgent things.

And so it was sheer luck that, in a last inspection of the orchestra pit, while Officer Decker was finishing up his interviews, she spotted the partly open flap of the storage bin. She raised it and pulled out the rectangular black box she had pushed inside. Then she turned around and looked up at Decker. He had just concluded questioning one of the soloists and appeared to be free.

"*Chef,*" she called, attracting his attention. "I have found something that might be of interest." She picked up the case by its large handle and carried it to the side of the conductor's podium, raising it up a bit so the officer could see.

"Certainly looks like an instrument case," he said. "But for what instrument? It's really large. And we've already questioned all the relevant timpani, strings, woodwind, and double reed players." He was thinking in particular of the amusing contrabassoonist he had questioned after interviewing the two bassoon players in the orchestra scored for *Fidelio*. He had made the mistake of asking what the difference was between a contrabassoon and a bassoon and the man's response was quite adamant and threatened to be lengthy.

"It's a different beastie altogether," he had proclaimed proudly. "For starters my double reed is much larger than a regular bassoon's. And my instrument is twice as heavy; comes in at a little over six-and- a-half kilograms. And consider this long maple bore—if you stretched out its four looped curves you'd have an instrument that was almost five-hundred-and-fifty centimeters long. Think of that!"

Decker had adroitly cut him off while Mary was whispering to Megan her calculations from kilograms into pounds as a little over fourteen, and from centimeters into feet as being about eighteen—no wonder the four compact curves of the bore!

But now Kerstin Jesse was holding up the large instrument case she had found in the pit awaiting Decker's instructions.

"Good. Open it up. Is it heavy?"

"You bet it's heavy!" Kerstin was only too happy to put the oversize case down. She easily flipped open two latches along the front side of the rectangular box but when she got to the lock itself, its latch would not lift.

"It's locked," she called out.

"Hold on. I'm sending someone in." Decker summoned help on his cellphone, specifying what was needed. It only took a minute or so before two policemen appeared in the pit, one of them with a crowbar, the other with a set of small keys. After trying various keys, the officer with the crowbar went to work. It took longer than anyone would have expected but finally the case was pried open and its lid flew back. What it contained was immediately evident.

Six red bricks held in place by bubble wrap.

Had Ottokar Weininger been there he could have told them what was supposed to be in that case. A brand-new German-style Kühl contrabass trombone.

17

The investigative trio, as Megan dubbed them in her mind, had finished interviewing the back row, first section string players, Erich tried to answer Mary's puzzled inquiry as to how an explosive device and a cellphone could have been hidden in the Mahler bust which was, after all, life-size and not all that capacious.

"It's easier than you might think," he answered. "All you really had to place in the hollow bust is a small amount of gun powder wrapped in paper, a headphone jack plugged into a small cellphone like the mini Posh Ten we found, and the wires from the headphone. The wires would have an igniter attached which would go to the gun powder." Erich did not notice his listeners' eyes were glazing over.

"Then you configure the bust phone so that only the matching cellphone's call could set off the device; no other call from any other number could be picked up. Then when the configured phone gets a call or text from the other phone, the headphone wire receives the small electric signal which immediately sets off the igniter which in turn ignites the gun powder. And boom! That's what happened with the Mahler bust."

Erich's listeners looked grateful but a trifle uncomprehending and it was with relief that they heard Erich's own cellphone ring after his last sentence.

"Good. Send her to the pit." Erich turned to the women.

"The harpist has been found."

18

The longtime portier on the Kärntner Strasse side of the Opera House stage doors, Rudi Wittkower, took his job seriously. Should he tell the police about the slightly strange thing he had witnessed earlier that evening? He had been told to stay at his post while the police investigated the mysterious explosion of earlier that evening. And now, almost two hours after the explosion, stage hands and orchestra members were at last coming out through his door, if only just one or two at a time. A bassoon player Rudi had known for years stopped to tell him that they, their instruments, and their instrument cases had been searched and in addition, they had been privately interrogated, one by one.

"I stood in the pit next to the conductor's podium and had to look up at the fancy uniformed officer who was quizzing me. He was sitting in the front row and there were these two women with him, and they were also asking questions."

"What were you asked?"

"Oh, just what you'd expect more or less. What was my name and how long had I been with the Opera. And exactly where I was when the explosion happened. They already seemed to know what instrument I play. You know we had to take them directly from the pit to our lounge. And they actually inspected our instruments—turned them upside down. Can you imagine? Then, after they'd examined my case over in the locker room, I was reunited with it, packed up my bassoon, and here I am finally getting out of this place."

"Do they have any idea how the explosion happened?"

"Don't know about that, but word is that it wasn't an accident. Some idiot with a grudge, I guess. Maybe a former Opera employee. We're lucky it was confined to the Schwind Foyer. Police don't seem to have a suspect yet. Well, I gotta get going now, Rudi, see you tomorrow."

This scene was repeated a number of times as the house was slowly cleared of stage hands and performers. Rudi watched in amazement as one elderly man he didn't place stormed through his door swearing and headed for a white limousine that had pulled up to the curb.

"That angry man was our guest conductor this evening," one of his favorite flute players whispered to him as she exited behind the raging figure. "He had an absolute fit when he was searched. But we were all searched. I guess he thought an exception should have been made for him." The flutist giggled and left.

Rudi again wondered if he should notify someone in charge about the unusual scene he had witnessed outside his entry just about five minutes before the performance began. Although he was not suspicious at the time—the scene had only seemed hurried and hectic to him—now in the light of things, perhaps what he witnessed was worth passing on to the authorities. Of course he could not leave his post so he called the police headquarters on Minoritenplatz and after stating the reason for his call, was switched to the proper department officer. Rudi identified himself and said that what he had seen earlier in the evening might be useful to the investigation going on right then in the Opera House.

"What exactly did you see, Herr Wittkower?"

"Now mind you, musicians do occasionally arrive at the last minute."

"Yes?"

"Yes, in hindsight however, it was most unusual."

"What?"

"Yes, the more I think about it, the odder it seems."

"Could you just describe what happened that you think could be of interest, Herr Wittkower?"

"Well, the Opera orchestra has a contrabass trombone player who comes to every performance with his instrument in its case, whether or not it's required in the orchestra on certain nights. Lots of certain nights. You see, there's not much need for contrabass trombones in the standard opera orchestra."

"You are saying this person comes to every performance evening regardless of whether or not he has a part to play in the orchestra. And he brings his instrument case with him as well. Have I got that right?"

"Yes. That's right."

"Hm. And?"

"Well, this evening, with only about six or seven minutes to spare before start time, he's standing outside with his trombone case, like he's waiting for someone. He doesn't enter the building. Just waits."

"And?"

"So, somebody, a tall, young man, wearing a blue striped shirt, no jacket, mind you, on a hot evening like this, so, he walks right up to him. He's carrying a second case similar to the one the trombonist is holding, only it's larger."

"Yes?"

"Appreciably larger, I would say."

"And?"

"And they swap cases then and there and the young man leaves and the trombone player dashes past me to get to the pit before the performance starts. You see, he's got the new case under his arm. Then just after intermission begins he appears without his new case and stands outside like he's looking for somebody. Maybe the young man he'd met before. He just stands there, right by my door, and then he begins walking back and forth. He seemed quite agitated."

"And his name, Herr Wittkower, his name?"

"Oh, did I forget that?"

"You have so far not supplied it." The police officer's patience was being stretched to the breaking point.

"I guess I thought I'd mentioned his name at the beginning of our conversation. I certainly meant to."

"How about mentioning it *now*?"

"Oh, yes, well, of course, sure. His name's Ottokar Weininger. Unusual first name, huh? Ottokar. But very nice man, mind you. Loves the opera. Attends every performance. Even brings his instrument case with him."

"All right. Fine. Thank you for calling the police. I'll have this checked out."

Rudi Wittkower was surprised to hear the nice officer hang up abruptly, but he must be a very busy man after all. Yes, very busy.

19

"All right. Let's hear what our harpist has to say," Erich said as he watched a youngish brunette with long hair swept up in a bun stride briskly to the podium. Before he could question her, the woman began speaking. Her lilting pronunciation sounded Italian. Her high voice was borderline hysteria.

"Officer! I am Cristina Paloma, first harpist here, and before that, first harpist with Berlin Philharmonic. I have been unjustly detained by your men. I must get to Graz with my harp this evening and what is going on here is unforgivably inconvenient. Why are you doing this to me?"

Erich was so taken aback by the woman's defensive manner that he was silent for a moment. Megan jumped in, affecting a conciliatory tone.

"Ms. Paloma, it is not with any pleasure that you have been detained by the police. You have not been singled out. As you know, from having been in the musicians lounge this past hour, every musician in this evening's orchestra is being questioned in regard to the explosion here at the Opera House. And this is our question to you: why are *you* here at the opera this evening, since there is no harp part in Beethoven's opera?"

"Why am I here? Because she is here!"

"Who is 'she'"?

"My harp! She is here."

"Yes, we can see that," Megan persisted, "but why is your harp here when it is not needed for performance? It is common practice that stage hands remove unnecessary instruments before each evening's opera. Your fellow harpist's instrument, for instance, has not been left in the pit after last night's performance of *Elektra*. And there is no harp part for the next two performances. Why was her harp removed and yours not?"

Suddenly Cristina Paloma began to sob, covering her face with her hands. Her cries were piercing.

"Pull yourself together," Mary commanded, impatient at Paloma's prima donna act.

"You people not understand. Only Oliver understand. I cannot take harp home with me now. I am thrown out of my apartment because I need always to practice. I am in hotel for short time looking for new, understanding apartment place. They not allow instrument in hotel room and I cannot keep harp in hot car, not in this dreadful heat *ondata*. Nice Oliver say I can leave *la mia arpa* in pit."

"The pit?" Mary asked, her blue eyes honing in on the harpist. "But stage hands always remove instruments not being used in the next evening's opera."

"Yes, but Oliver say I can keep her in pit because he know how other harpist try to sabotage me."

"What?"

"Is true. You ask Oliver. She already put hot pack against my harp case thinking her inside."

Erich turned to his companions.

"Do you think this is true? Is there such jealously, such hatred among the orchestra members?" Mary laughed.

"Don't get me started. Just suffice to say yes, there is. In every orchestra, symphonic or opera."

"You call Oliver! He confirm me!" Cristina began shrieking.

"Yes, we will indeed call him. And now." Erich's patience was beginning to run out. He communicated with the stage hands' lounge officer and within minutes a pleasant-looking, robust man barely in his twenties, if even that, stood before them. He looked with concern at Cristina who was still sobbing dramatically.

"You tell, you tell I not lie!" she implored him before Erich could even begin questioning the man.

"What is your name and how long have you been here at the Opera?"

"My name is Oliver Kräftig and I've been at the Vienna State Opera eight months," he answered proudly.

"And what is your relation to Cristina Paloma?"

"She's my best friend among the orchestra players. I roll her harp back and forth from the pit and she's always so cheerful and thanks me. And she is giving me Italian lessons. But right now, we're leaving her harp in the pit because the other harpist tried to do something sneaky to it when she thought it was in its case backstage. And Cristina has taught me how to clip her electronic tuning fork to the harp back so I could keep it in tune on days she's not here. It has to be done every day, you know."

"Yes, yes, Oliver is very fast learner and I am good *maestra*," Cristina added, beginning to regain her calm.

"Well, the stories match at least," Erich turned to Megan and Mary.

"One last question." Megan was not completely satisfied.

"Why didn't you place a dust cover over the harp while it was in the pit not being used? That's what is usually done."

"I not believe in that rubbish!" Cristina's high-pitched voice cut in before Oliver could answer. "My strings must *breathe!*"

Megan leaned over to Mary and giggled. "I think we have *gut* a very high-strung harpist with us here."

"Yes, all forty-seven gut strings of her," Mary whispered back, referring to the total number of strings a concert grand pedal harp has.

"I guess we're going to have to accept her story," Erich said to them. "But before I excuse her let's just check with the officers who examined the instrument cases. Maybe they found something of interest in her harp case." He made the call, listened, and said: "I'll ask the experts here, but I wouldn't think that's suspicious. Call you back if it turns out to be important." He hung up and faced his friends.

"The officer who searched Fraulein Drama's case says he came across something odd. He found almost fifty slim packets. At first glance he thought they might contain some form of crack cocaine, but they turned out to hold gut strings. For the harp, obviously. But here's the thing. A few of the strings were what he called 'color coded,' some in red, others in dark blue. So he became suspicious again."

Erich wondered why the women began smiling.

"No, no, Erich," Mary laughed. "Those are the C strings in red and the F strings in dark blue." Erich began laughing as well. Then he turned to the two people standing in the pit.

"All right, Oliver Kräftig and Cristina Paloma. You may go now."

"And Oliver is to roll my harp to me immediately? So he can load my car and I go to Graz and acclimatize in time?"

"Yes, yes, so you can drive to Graz and acclimatize in time." Erich was almost smiling.

They left the pit at once and headed for the storage room where the harpist's light two-wheel trolley was. The three interrogators simultaneously breathed a sigh of relief. But all of a sudden Megan gave a gasp.

"This may sound crazy, *but has anyone checked out the inside of that harp?*"

20

The third-floor adjoining apartments 22 and 23 at Liechtensteinstrasse 68/70 in Vienna's ninth district, Alsergrund, had formerly been home to composers Arnold Schönberg and Alexander von Zemlinsky. Not far away was Sigmund Freud's residence at Berggasse 19 where the founder of psychoanalysis lived and worked for forty-seven years until forced to flee Nazi-occupied Austria in 1938. Eastward and directly across from Alsergrund, but separated by the Danube Canal, Vienna's second district, Leopoldstadt, known as "the Jewish district," had become the quarters for a large number of Jewish immigrants and refugees. Alsergrund grew into the home for middle class and professional Jews and housed a high percentage of Jewish businessmen, lawyers, and physicians.

The elderly couple who now resided at historic Liechtensteinstrasse 68/70 were well aware of its two famous former inhabitants. They had in fact engaged in several shrewd machinations to snag the two eight-room apartments which they had immediately made over into one continuous space. A space now crammed with extraordinary examples of eighteenth-and-nineteenth-century musical instruments of all sorts and sizes. A spate of statues and ornately framed paintings accompanied the richly diversified display which continued in all the rooms.

Harry Howell, a banker's son from Muncie, Indiana, and Haim Elisaf, a Romaniote Jew from Ioannina, Greece, had been a couple for forty-nine years and counting. They had met while playing on summer tour with America's National Youth Orchestra; Harry was a flutist but also quite adept at the piano, Haim was a devoted cellist. His parents, owners of an expanding Greek wine export business, had immigrated to New York a few months before his birth and he and his siblings had grown up taking luxury for granted. Harry, as well, had come from a family of comfortable means and as an only child he had received a fine education at Columbia University and had been exposed to many countries on travels with his parents. The two men couldn't have been more different in appearance. Although pretty much the same height, Harry was slim, had fair skin, blue eyes, and blond hair whereas Haim was a good twenty pounds heavier, with olive skin, luxurious black hair and penetrating brown eyes set in an ovoid face.

Both Harry and Haim were interested in making documentary films on noted performers and composers and both had enrolled in Columbia's famed School of the Arts film program. That was where they met. Their joint project on the cellist Mstislav Rostropovich, undertaken as part of their Master of Fine Arts degree, had received top accolades, not only from Columbia but a coveted BAFTA award as well as a showing at the Austria International Film Festival. Neither man had been to Austria before and both fell instantly in love with Vienna. They decided then and there to form *Dokumentarfilm International* company with headquarters in the Austrian capital. Sixteen successful years and eleven acclaimed documentaries later, when it became known that the Liechtensteinstrasse apartments once belonging to Zemlinsky and Schönberg were going to become available, they successfully pulled every string, both legal and illegal, to obtain the historic apartments.

Then, employing discreet workmen and paying them for their silence, they had the walls separating the two apartments ripped out to create one continuous grand room—their "studio." It ran all the way from the building's west side windows to those on the east side. This gave them the necessary space in which to recreate the famous atelier of Austria's extravagant nineteenth-century history painter after whom an entire age had been named, Hans von Makart. The flamboyant Makart age of décor and glamour had preceded the graceful Art nouveau age of Gustav Klimt. Built by Makart at his own expense in 1872 and located on Vienna's Gusshausstrasse, the studio was copiously furnished with furniture, carpets, antiques of all kinds and ancient weapons. No less a notable than Empress Elisabeth herself was a visitor. Although the studio was demolished in 1916, its layout and lavish furnishings had been carefully recorded by several of Makart's painter colleagues, notably Rudolf von Alt. It was his depictions of Makart's studio that Harry and Haim painstakingly followed when creating their lookalike.

Since it was not possible to have Makart's full staircase, as their aggrandized apartment was only one story high, the enthusiastic filmmakers built a partial set of broad stairs that opened in the back onto a large landing encased with a dark wooden balustrade. The enormous rectangular room itself was decorated with heavy crimson velvet draperies hanging from carved wooden cornices, a plethora of Persian rugs, a capacious Italian carved wood cassone with its lid permanently open, a nineteenth-century French chaise, and four Savonarola carved wood side-chairs. The center of the room was dominated by a magnificent Hamburg Steinway concert grand.

When the two Hs, as they were referred to by close friends, had been twenty-five years into their marriage and were approaching their fifties, they had made an important and life changing decision. They wanted a child. A child with both their genes. After much research they made arrangements to visit California and a noted Los Angeles clinic that specialized in surrogate birthing. They met with the future mother, liked her exceedingly, and reached agreement on all sides. A small, private room was located at the rear of the clinic and that very afternoon the two men delivered their sperm samples without having to utilize any of the various forms of pornography made available by the clinic. Around eight weeks later, back in Vienna, they received good but surprising news: a fetal Doppler exam had revealed not one heart beating but two! The heart rate in both babies was a healthy 140 beats per minute. A grainy printout of their first sonogram was emailed to them. The future fathers decided they did not want to know the sex of their twins. They wished to be surprised.

This wonderful news had obliged the two Hs to make some modification of the floor plan of the two contiguous apartments they had acquired. Unlike the Schönberg apartment, the one formerly belonging to Zemlinsky had a very spacious servant's quarter which they divided into two equal-sized chambers so that later their two children could have their own bedrooms. In the beginning, of course, they would be sleeping with their dads. This had been an easy decision. Far more difficult was the choice of names. For weeks they batted around different notable names in the field of music. Finally, for Harry, they settled on Bell in recognition of Indiana's famous violinist Joshua Bell, and for Haim, they chose Callas in honor of the renowned New-York-born Greek opera singer Maria Callas. It did not matter to them whether the twins were both boys or both girls, or one of each sex; their given names would be apt and illustrious. They had shared the names with the surrogate mother and she had been delighted with the choices. For the hundredth time she asked if they didn't want to know what sexes the twins were, and for the hundredth time they had declined. They truly did not care, so taken were they that such a miracle had occurred.

The miracle became flesh and blood when, seven months later the twins were born. One was a girl, one was a boy. How appropriate their given names then, Callas and Bell! And what joy the twins had brought Harry and Haim over the next twenty-five years. In an odd game of genetics as they grew, Callas looked more like Harry with blonde hair and blue eyes whereas Bell resembled Haim, with an oval face and brown eyes and hair.

Early on the children had both demonstrated such musical talent that their fathers hired private tutors to teach them piano and later other instruments—violin for Callas and trombone for Bell—he had fallen in love with the instrument the first time he was taken to an orchestra concert. And how they loved to attend the symphony and the opera. The family had season tickets for both. Their home was filled with Hausmusik and even now, when the twins were in their mid-twenties and living in their own apartments, the family still gathered three times a week to make music around the concert grand. Bell's pleasant day job was as a guard at Vienna's Upper Belvedere Museum while Callas was curator of the Jewish Museum of the City of Vienna on the nearby Dorotheergasse. Both of them loved their jobs and got along well with their colleagues.

There was one other family member who was equally happy listening to any of the household instruments being played. He was a ten-year-old golden retriever named Houdini, so named because of his escapologist talents. Standing on his hind legs he could exit or enter any room with a closed door in the household and did so often. He was intelligent, curious, and loving. And he was especially devoted to Haim who loved him dearly.

Nestled against the far end of the Steinway stood a new Casio digital piano, as the children found its electric keyboard touch to be so ever so much more subtle and infinitely variable than an "old-fashioned" acoustic piano. The setting for these pianos was truly magnificent. To one side, three free-standing four-foot high Ionic capitals supported two pairs of Middle Eastern champlevé-lidded urns. On the verdurous tapestried walls, instead of paintings, hung a magnificent display of antique musical instruments, sometimes three-deep. They were divided by categories: string, woodwind, and brass. Below the violins and violas in a glass case stood Haim's recently acquired Stradivari cello, insured by him for forty million euros. His regular cello, a French Mircourt from 1810, stood guard in the open case next to it and alongside in a specially constructed heavy glass case stood his nineteenth-century Villaume bow.

Harry's gold Haynes flute, his wooden Haynes flute with open holes, and his platinum Powell flute resided, ever ready, in their black cases on the concert grand. Next to them, also in closed cases, was his collection of low flutes: two altos—one of them made of wood—one bass, and one contrabass. They all received regular workouts by Harry even though it meant having to clean and polish the silver ones after each session. In addition, on the rectangular studio's short walls hung Harry's collection of American open-hole Indian flutes.

To the other side of the concert grand were three more free-standing Ionic capitals. But no urns rested on them. Instead life-size bronze busts of Felix Mendelssohn and Arnold Schönberg graced the two outer ones. The middle capital awaited an appropriate bust.

Standing in their Makart Age atelier, darkened now by the late evening sky, Harry saw Haim's eyes rest briefly on the middle capital, bare of a load. Then Haim looked back at what they had been talking about—the brass instruments on the wall behind the busts.

"Perhaps, some day," Harry murmured, resting his hand lightly on his partner's shoulder.

21

"Get someone back down into the pit! Now!" Erich Decker shouted into his cellphone. Almost simultaneously two policemen appeared at either entry to the pit and stood looking up at their chief inquiringly.

"Go to that harp, pick it up, and turn it upside down," he commanded.

Mary and Megan glanced at each other in concern. Regardless of things, that was no way to treat a harp. Good thing Cristina Paloma was out of sight.

"Gently," Mary couldn't help calling out just as Erich's officers began to pick up the harp. The two men carefully began turning the enormous wooden instrument upside down. They had barely tilted it a few inches when two objects fell on the floor. One was immediately recognizable as an electronic tuning fork. The men shook the harp cautiously in case anything else dropped to the floor but there was nothing further. After the harp was eased back into place one of the officers picked up the articles that had fallen to the floor and held one of them up for his chief to see. It was black and relatively small, the length of a man's hand, but with what looked like a trigger toward one end, it appeared to be a pistol.

"What the hell is that? A revolver?" Erich exclaimed.

"Don't know what it is, sir. It's not a pistol. It seems to be made of rubber and this part here, what seems like a trigger, is hollow. It fell from one of the cavities in the back of the harp."

"Oh," Megan grinned, "not to worry. That's simply a rubber tuning key for the harp. Cristina must have hung it and her electronic one on two of the sound holes." Mary joined her as they laughed in relief. It had been a tense few moments.

22

Basileus, Sabina, and their daughter Adele jumped up from their seats when they heard the sound of Stefan's key opening the front door.

"At last!" sighed his mother running down the hall to hug him. He stood his cello case on the floor, turned, and gave her a long embrace, looking beyond her at his father and sister. Father and son exchanged a knowing look.

"I couldn't call you. The police sequestered our cellphones while we were being kept for questioning."

"You have to tell us all about what happened," Sabina commanded as they walked to the living room. "Are you hungry? Thirsty?"

"I'm fine Mutti, just fine. Only irritated that they kept us so long. Everyone had to go immediately to the musicians lounge with our instruments. They wouldn't even let us put them in our cases. The police actually examined my cello! God, I don't think even the piccolo was exempted from scrutiny. Then we had to wait until our cases passed inspection. And in the meanwhile we were called, one by one, to the pit for questioning by, get this, the chief of police himself! Two women were with him and seemed to be involved somehow. Their occasional questions were very authoritative."

"Were they also police officers?" asked Sabina, who had been hanging on her son's every word.

"I don't think so. I recognized one of them—she's head vocal coach at the opera. The other woman was older, I could tell her hair was dyed. She spoke

German with a sort of Italian accent, although I don't think she was Italian. They spoke English to each other, so maybe both were American or British."

"Have the police discovered who set off the bomb, or whatever it was?" Basileus asked.

"It they did, they're not telling us. What they did say is that several images of musicians in the Schwind Foyer were destroyed by the blast, including that famous head of Mahler done by Rodin. Such a pity about that."

A look of keen interest registered on Basileus's face. His son continued his excited debriefing.

"And it was hilarious about our conductor. You know it wasn't Gabor, our usual conductor, but a pompous, very demanding guest conductor from Cologne by the name of Max Brandes. He hated being cooped up with us lowly instrumentalists in the musicians lounge and he let everyone know it. It was just too funny to watch him simmer."

"Hmm. Gabor Alexander, Max Brandes. Aren't they both Jewish?" Basileus asked.

"Just as Jewish as my dear bête noir is," Stefan said, looking meaningfully at his father. They traded complicit glances.

"But something happened in the pit while we were playing this evening, something that's going to change things," Stefan continued

"Something happened in the pit?" asked his mother.

"Right. We'd just finished the overture and the first act was underway— you know, when Marzelline is trying to avoid Jacquino's insistent declarations of love and then there's a knocking on the door that makes her sing an aside about it's being a 'welcome sound.'"

"Yes, yes. We were watching it on television. And?"

"Well, at the very moment those two words were sung, my stand partner, that old alcoholic Jared Bogenstein, suddenly keeled over onto his instrument and crashed to the ground on top of it. I bet the noise could be heard in the balconies."

"How awful!" Sabina said.

"No, Mutti, how wonderful. The conductor was furious, hissed at him to get the hell out of the pit and I'd bet it's pretty unlikely he'll keep his job."

"Oh my god! What a lucky outcome that would be for you!" Adele was gleeful to the point of high drama: she ran over to her brother and hugged him, then began jumping up and down in joy and chanting "Out of the pit!" over and over, running around the living room.

"Son, let's get some wine and glasses and celebrate," said Basileus, rising from his seat and heading for the kitchen. Stefan followed immediately.

"*How'd you do it*?" his father whispered urgently when they were alone.

"Well, I've told you how that old bastard comes really early on performance nights and practices in the pit, then leaves his cello by his stand while he goes off to our lounge for a shot of whiskey and then dozes there on the couch till people start arriving. It's a regular routine. We all laugh at him as he snores away."

"Yes. And you told me the operation would take 'precision and exquisite timing.'"

"Oh boy, you bet it did. So early this evening I took advantage of his cello left there on its side by our stand and sneaked into the pit right after Bogenstein finished practicing and left for the lounge. I ran over to the silly strip of thick carpet he sticks his cello endpin into, pierced and looped the back corner of the carpet nearest me with a thin wire the color of the pit floor. After that I ran the wire underneath his chair and brought it around the back two feet of my chair, then down again to just back of where I place my right foot when playing. There I made a large loop on the floor under my chair so that when I stuck the ball of my foot into it and pushed forward really hard, his carpet strip would suddenly jerk back and send his cello flying. It was easy to retrieve the wire unobserved when we broke for intermission."

"What an incredibly simple maneuver!"

"Yeah, well, I practiced it a lot at home with two of our pit chairs I'd absconded with years ago and a carpet sample and it worked every time. So I was pretty sure about its reliability."

"And the 'exquisite timing' was the moment of Marzelline's two words, 'welcome sound.' Correct?"

"Correct, Papa. The irony is delicious, don't you think?"

"It's beautiful, my boy, beautiful. Surely the man will be retired now. Congratulations."

Basileus reached for an open wine bottle while Stefan quickly put four glasses on a tray.

"Not a word of this to your mother. Not even to your sister."

"Oh, I was going to tell her after we left here. She can keep a secret."

"Perhaps so. And I know how close you two are. But this should remain just between you and me. I want you to promise."

"If it means that much to you, Papa, of course I promise not to tell Adele."

Father and son returned to the living room and within minutes the family was clinking glasses to the fortuitous fall of Jared Bogenstein. And in thankfulness that Stefan had not been hurt in the explosion at the Opera House.

23

After the last interview was concluded that evening Erich decided to release to the late-night media the fact that Gustav Mahler's bust in the Schwind Foyer had been destroyed by the explosion in the Opera House but that it was possible a switch involving the original and an excellent copy had taken place. Perhaps the more people who knew about this, the more the search for it would expand. He hoped so.

"Well, ladies, I can't imagine we have any surprises left now," he said, turning to them after hanging up his cellphone. Every pertinent musician had now been questioned by them and Erich's officers had interviewed all the singers and staff on duty with no results. The search of the Opera House and personnel had revealed nothing that could not be explained and the disposable cellphone find was the only bit of evidence relating to the explosion.

"I'm telling you, those six bricks and that rubber tuning fork 'pistol' were the last straw." He grinned an uncustomary grin.

"My friends, shall we call it a night?" he asked.

"Absolutely," Megan said at the same time that Mary nodded a vigorous yes. Suddenly they all felt tired. The idea of sleep was most attractive.

Exiting the opera at the Kärntner Strasse they exchanged email addresses and phone numbers, said goodnight, and walked off in three directions—Erich to his car parked by the Café Mozart, Mary to the D tram station in front of the Opera House, and Megan to the small Römischer Kaiser Hotel in the nearby Annagasse off the Kärntner Strasse—her favorite place to stay in all of Vienna.

24

The loud unlatching of the front door to the grandiose apartment on the third floor of Liechtensteinstrasse was heard by both parents as well as Houdini, who eagerly dashed to the door. Which one of their children could that be? They left their bedroom and looked toward the vestibule where their son Bell had just relocked the door. Wearing a short sleeve, blue striped shirt that seemed to match his upbeat mood, he walked briskly toward his parents and came to a stop. A triumphant grin lit up his face. Resting on the floor at his side was a long rectangular black case. He looked joyfully at his parents.

"*Happy upcoming fiftieth anniversary to you both!*"

"Oh, how exciting! What on earth could be in that? But our anniversary isn't until Friday." Harry's protest was mild. He was tickled by the idea of an impetuous, early anniversary gift. And Haim was equally enchanted.

"Right, Dads, but I wanted to give it to you tonight, since I'll be working at the museum all late afternoon and evening Friday. Come on, let's go to the salon and see what I got for you!"

Eagerly followed by his parents, Bell carried the instrument case into the grand studio room. He laid it on the Steinway piano bench and opened it up for his amazed onlookers. It couldn't be! They were staring at an eighteen-eighty Jérome Thibouville-Lamy contrabass slide trombone. Ah, the simplicity of it, the classic lines, the aristocratic nickel-silver color. What an addition to the family collection of antique brass instruments. What a find!

From the moment a very young Bell had spotted it in the orchestra pit during a four-evening performance of Richard Wagner's Ring cycle, he had been in love with the instrument and its thunderous low tone. On the last evening of the Wagner cycle his two dads had allowed him to wait at the stage door to get the autograph of the contrabass trombonist, one Ottokar Weininger. The man had seemed stunned that anyone should want his autograph but he had willingly obliged. Now, seven years later, the same contrabass trombonist had no idea that he had once given his autograph to the young man in a blue striped shirt who had approached him with a proposal so attractive that he had agreed to switch instruments—his old trombone that was practically an antique, for a famous modern brand, Kühl. What musician could have turned that down, or the one thousand euros that came with it? The offer had been irresistible. And Bell was of course unaware of what an unknown author of an unpublished treatise on the inferiority of women and Jews intended to do with the money.

"Where would you like me to hang it?" Bell asked his parents, holding up the mighty instrument and turning it slowly from side to side for them to admire.

"I think there, right there below the gold valve trombone," Harry said, walking to the spot he had in mind.

"We might have to raise that one a bit in order to accommodate the larger Thibouville-Lamy," said Haim, bringing over a tape measure.

"Right," Bell agreed. "But let me give this beauty a little workout first." He began to play prolonged Wagnerian phrases on the contrabass. After all, trombone was his number one instrument. The two dads stopped to admire its tone.

Then while the two men repositioned a smaller valve trombone, Bell tried out the dramatic bars written for the instrument by Puccini for his opera *Turandot*. The commanding tones masked the sound of the front door being opened. No one, not even Houdini noticed Callas enter the studio until she yelled out her brother's name.

"Bell! What are you *playing*? Oh my god, that's a contrabass!" She went up to him and gave him an affectionate hug. Then she ran her hand lightly along the length of the beautiful slide instrument.

"Where on earth did you find that? It looks like a real rarity."

"Just luck. Right pawnshop at the right time. I knew it was the perfect gift for our fathers' fiftieth anniversary. And for the collection. Couldn't wait until Friday when I have to work at the museum late."

"Looks like you're making a really splendid place for it with the other brasses," Callas said, watching her dads make room for the new arrival. Harry turned to her, his face suddenly serious.

"Just remember, while we live, the entire collection stays with us, on our walls. After we're gone, everything is divided equally among you."

"There's no room for treasures like these in your apartments and you realize that," Haim added. "It's our great desire, as you children know, that you will take over our Makart studio and continue the tradition of preserving and acquiring some of the world's most precious instruments."

"Oh, dear ones, of course we're going to do that," Callas answered for them both. Bell nodded his vigorous affirmation. The family fell silent for a few minutes. Then Callas thought of something cheerful to tell them that would dispel the sudden gloom that had descended upon them.

"Hey, everyone. Great news about my exhibition." She was talking about the new show at the Jewish Museum she had curated. It was called "*Genosse. Jude*—Comrade.Jew" and attendance had been record-breaking.

"The show is going to be extended for another three months!"

"Oh, that is great, Sis!" The two parents smiled with pleasure and pride. They and Bell had attended the opening night of the exhibition with its fascinating pictorial and documentary look at Jewish activists in the founding years of Communism. Personalities such as Rosa Luxemburg, Viktor Adler, and Leo Trotsky were featured along with an illustrated chronology of Karl Marx's life, writing and influence. The exhibition also revealed, with meticulous documentation, the high probability that there was something Vladimir Lenin had not known about himself: that he had Jewish blood in his veins. His mother was the daughter of a German-Swedish mother and a Russian Jewish physician father who had converted to Christianity. New documents pointed to the fact that their mother's half-Jewish ancestry was only discovered by Lenin's sister Anna after his death. The veracity of this part of the exhibition had been hotly debated in the newspapers and on television.

After this bit of good news concerning the prolongation of Callas's show, attention turned again to the contrabass trombone.

Once the new acquisition had been secured and admired, the family settled down in the quartet of Savonarola chairs near the piano and began discussing the strange explosion that took place at the Opera House earlier in the evening.

"We've been watching the news and they said that it took place in the Schwind Foyer," Harry said, looking at his children.

"Yes. That's why I came over to tell you, just in case you hadn't heard about it," Callas said.

"And now they've narrowed it down even further," Haim took up the story. "They think that the bust of Mahler was the hiding place for the explosive device and that, since the bust is so valuable, being by Rodin and everything, it may well have been replaced before the explosion with a lookalike bust, you know, a surmoulage. In that case, if it's true, the original Mahler bust still exists."

"It could be on the black market even now and . . . *available,*" Harry theorized.

Simultaneously their heads turned to the free-standing Ionic half-capitals with the busts of Mendelssohn and Schönberg gracing the outer two. Their attention focused on the middle capital that as yet supported no load. Here was the perfect place for their most cherished Jewish musical idol, Gustav Mahler.

25

The head tailor of the women's repertory costumes division at the Vienna State Opera, Adele Schmidt, had not been on duty the evening of the explosion in the Schwind Foyer. But she had been the night before. In fact, after the performance of *Elektra* that evening, she had returned unobserved to the small in-house costume room one floor below the auditorium where, undetected, she spent the night in one of the room's deep, costume-filled closets. Except for some twenty-five minutes before four in the morning.

Adele knew that the in-house fireman on inspection duty made his rounds every two hours and it was thirty-five minutes after his three o'clock inspection when she initiated her plan. Avoiding any possible noise the wheels might make when in contact with flooring, she had hugged her portable Singer tote close to her chest. With its contents, along with three items in the large outside zipper case, it weighed forty-three pounds.

Her first destination was up the stairs into the orchestra pit. Entering from audience left, she had walked straight to the wall behind the harp and jammed a disposable cellphone into a fracture in the wall's baseboard. Wriggling it hard, she was able to push the phone down exactly to the point she wanted. Not totally out of sight, but not readily discernable.

Adele's next destination had been the Schwind Foyer. Selecting the shortest route up through the auditorium, it took her fewer than three minutes to reach it.

Soundlessly, she placed the roller tote on the floor next to the bust of Gustav Mahler on the fireplace mantel. Opening it wide, she took out a pair of latex gloves and slipped them on. From the outside pocket of the case she removed a small pair of manual hydraulic pliers and locked them around one of the two nuts bolting the bust's horizontal V-shaped bronze mount to the white marble mantel of the fireplace. Fifteen seconds later the nut was loosened. Another twenty seconds and the other nut was loosened. Adele pivoted them off with her fingers, placed them on the fireplace mantel, and slowly raised the Mahler bust up from its anchoring screws. Silently she placed it on the floor, positioning it so that it leaned against the fireplace wall. Turning to the roller case, Adele removed some bubble wrap then gently lifted up an identical bronze bust of Mahler. It was alike in every respect. True, the details were a shade less pronounced but only the practiced eye would notice the difference. And only if the original bust were next to it.

Suddenly Adele froze. Had she heard something? She remained riveted to the spot listening. Moments passed. No, it was nothing. She continued with her work, raising the cellphone-loaded surmoulage up to the marble mantelpiece and bringing its V-shaped support base slowly down exactly onto the two support screws. She replaced the nuts on top and used the locking pliers to tighten them. Then she pulled a small kit out of the roller case and opened it up. It contained five bottles of nail polish in varying shades of black and russet brown. She picked the closest match and applied it to the nuts, screws, and mount, then stood back to examine her work. It was perfect. Perfect positioning, perfect color match. The whole operation had taken nineteen minutes.

Moving quickly now, after glancing at her watch, she lowered the original bust gingerly into her empty tote and returned the pliers and nail polish bottles to its outside pocket.

There was one more thing she had to do on the scene. She removed the third item stored in the tote pocket. It was an old-fashioned metal index card file box wrapped in tinfoil. Sprinting lightly across the long room to the marble mantelpiece opposite the Mahler one, she slipped it behind its bronze bust of Richard Strauss. She ran back to the tote and once again holding it tightly to her chest, she slipped back down to the costume room. Another minute and she was lying in the closet listening to her racing heart and waiting for the beats to return to normal. She remained there until eight that morning, grabbing only short stretches of sleep. Then rolling her loaded tote bag behind her, she casually exited the Opera House on the Operngasse side, the portier there scarcely taking note of her.

This evening her outrageously mistreated brother would be avenged, and she controlled the exact moment when.

She had spent the next hours at home catching up on sleep. After preparing and relishing a full meal, she turned on her television to catch the Opera's live broadcast of *Fidelio*. She watched it with intense concentration. At the beginning of the second act, at Marzelline's phrase containing the word "*Klang*," Adele triggered the disposable cellphone in her hand.

Her brother had been avenged.

26

An emergency meeting of the Vienna-based International Gustav Mahler Society had been called for the morning following the explosion in the Schwind Foyer that had seemingly destroyed Rodin's famous bust of the composer. If it were true then the treasure was lost forever. If, as the latest police bulletin issued to the media theorized, there had been a switch with a surmoulage, then there was hope that the Rodin could be located.

The large room in the six-story orange building at Wiedner Gürtel 6/2 was crowded with Mahlerites, famous and unknown, musicologist and musician, rich and poor. One thing united them: outrage at the use of a bust of Mahler to cause mayhem at the Vienna State Opera. Whether or not it was the original. It was the desecration of the persona of Mahler, of his reputation, that was so mortifying. And, as a number of agitated members pointed out, the identical sort of disgrace had occurred at the same Opera House where malicious intrigues and an increasingly vocal hatred of Jews overshadowed the great composer's final years as conductor there.

"We must issue an immediate statement for the press and television," urged the society's president Ben Geistert for the fifth time. Dissention had broken out each time over whether or not the question of anti-Semitism should be brought into the statement.

"Is this an affront to Mahler the Musician or is this an affront to Mahler the Jew?" asked one of the older members of the organization, summarizing the arguments that had taken place.

"*Both! It's both*! And we have to spin it that way to the public," a tall, boney, middle-aged man with receding hairline shouted. Of Czech descent, his name was Tonik Nektar and he was well known to the society as a somewhat nutty lecturer on Mahler's Bohemian beginnings, having been born in the same Bohemian town of Iglau where Gustav had spent his childhood. Nektar, who was also Jewish, had taken to heart as the theme of his lectures what Mahler had once claimed— that he was "thrice homeless: as a native of Bohemia in Austria, as an Austrian among Germans, and as a Jew throughout the world. Everywhere an intruder, never welcomed." Without exception society members who had heard Nektar lecture came away with the impression that he spoke more about himself than about Mahler.

"It's both, I tell you, it's both!" he proclaimed.

Elderly Berta Zuckerkandl, the society's revered matriarch, leaned forward, looked over at Tonik Nektar, and made one loud disapproving click. An interesting, well-traveled, and wealthy woman, she was the granddaughter and namesake of Vienna's most famous salon giver in the first four decades of the previous century. The notables who attended her salon had included musicians Johann Strauss Jr. and Gustav Mahler, artists Auguste Rodin, Gustav Klimt, and Oskar Kokoschka, the theater director Max Reinhardt, and the authors Hugo von Hofmannsthal, Arthur Schnitzler, and Stefan Zweig.

The latter-day Zuckerkandl was a no-nonsense person who dealt with facts not suppositions. When Nektar began repeating his claim that the opera explosion was a double hate crime she rose magisterially and faced him.

"We shall deal with a judeophobic hate crime if proved pertinent."

"*Pertinent*? If you don't think being a Jew matters then why did a Munich critic write while Mahler was alive that he 'doesn't compose, he *Jewdles*'"? The room was silent. Most of the members had heard Nektar's quotation before and it was only painful to hear it milked again. Frau Zuckerkandl ignored Nektar's outburst and continued her plea for common sense and caution.

"At this moment it is imperative that we declare our common concern over the purposeful destruction of an image of one of our city's, our *nation's*, greatest cultural figures."

"I am going to take a vote on the wording you have just framed for us, Frau Zuckerkandl," said Ben Geistert quickly, cutting off further discussion. "All those who vote yes, please raise your hands."

The vote passed overwhelmingly. The few dissenters gathered in the entry hallway where a woman from the press stood and mumbled their disapproval. The loudest voice was that of Nektar, who was heard to say something to the effect that the bomber could just as easily have chosen to blow up the bust of Richard Strauss if he was not an anti-Semite.

This quixotic remark caught the attention of the reporter and she followed Nektar out of the building and onto the Wiedner Gürtel. There, in front of the International Gustav Mahler Society building, she accosted the angry man.

"Herr Nektar, my name is Rita Rausch, cultural contributor to the *Wiener Morgenblatt* and television reporter for ORF. I am extremely interested in your views on last night's dreadful incidents at the Opera House. Might you speak to me on the subject?" Tonik Nektar's eyes gleamed with pleasure.

"Yes, certainly. I would be only too happy to speak to you on the subject." Then his eyes narrowed and he looked at the intense woman facing him with curiosity.

"You mentioned last night's *incidents*, plural. I only know of the explosion that destroyed the bust of Gustav Mahler. What makes that plural?"

"Oh, you don't know about the incident that occurred during Act One of *Fidelio*?"

"God, no! What?"

"The collapse of principal cellist Jared Bogenstein. He and his cello fell right onto the pit floor. Made a huge crash. The conductor threw him out."

"How do you know that?"

"I was sitting in the second balcony. I saw it happen."

"Bogenstein? That's a Jewish name, isn't it?"

"I suppose so, sir."

"That clinches it. You can tell your newspaper and your television channel that there is a Jew-hating terrorist on the loose right here in Vienna."

27

Sabina Schmidt had waited until Basileus was out of the apartment before calling her daughter at work in the Opera House the next morning. She needed to discuss something with Adele in confidence.

"Hi, Mutti, what's up?" Adele had answered immediately.

"Nothing to be worried about, dear, but I wanted to speak to you without the family around."

"That sounds serious!"

"It's just that your father is in more pain than he lets on. He hasn't told you that, in addition to his AS condition which is debilitating enough, he is going to have to go to the hospital for several days."

"What? Why?" The surprise news agitated Adele greatly. She was extremely fond of her father.

"Because at his yearly physical exam this past week a long-term skeletal imbalance was discovered and recently it's created some very painful tendon tears that need to be repaired surgically. But because of the AS factor it is going to be an intricate operation lasting several hours."

"Oh, that's terrible. Papa didn't let on that he's in pain."

"That's just like your father, dear. He doesn't want to be a burden or worry his family. The doctors say that after the tendon repair he'd have to be on crutches for a number of weeks."

"Do you think he'll still be able to work?"

"Of course, dear. Nothing could tear him away from the National Library, you know that." Sabina permitted herself a short laugh.

"Is there anything I can do to help?"

"No, nothing, except to give him the joy he always gets from you. But I wanted you to be aware of one thing, Adele. Because the operation is not deemed 'necessary,' the costs of the very expensive surgery will not be covered because of the recent reform of our health care system."

"Could Papa go without the surgery then?"

"Not really. At least not for very long. He's in terrible, terrible pain, can only get around the house for the most part. He uses a rolling walker to get to and from work now, but doesn't want you children to know. He's humiliated by not being able really to fend for himself."

"Well, in that case he should definitely have the surgery, even if the costs are not covered."

"That's the problem, *Liebchen*. We don't have enough money to cover the horrendous costs."

"Can I help? Can't Stefan and I help with the costs?"

"No no. Your father would never hear of it. You know how proud he is. He plans to work until mandatory retirement, you know that. But I don't want him to be in increasing pain these seven years before that. Thank god the National Library is just across the street!"

"Papa is too proud. This is a time when the family should face things together."

"Please, please don't let him know that you have any idea of this. I just wanted you to understand why we aren't taking vacation this year and why your father may seem grumpy sometimes. He's just hiding his pain. I'll be telling your brother about the situation as well."

"I won't let Papa know if you promise that you'll allow me to give you as much money as I can to help out with the operation."

"We'll talk about that another day, my angel. I have thought of calling his father in Palestine, but he would then be so worried, and sooner or later Basileus would find out that I'd contacted his father. For now, I just wanted you to know the situation at home."

"All right, Mutti, and thank you for telling me."

After hanging up, Adele sat at her sewing machine in a daze. She had never even noticed that Papa was in pain. Or that her parents were short on funds.

She had a way to help. But how to go about it in the face of all the publicity given to what the media was calling "the Mahler Bomber"?

28

Seventeen-year-old Karl Lueger was still only a child when his great granduncle of the same name was, in his grandmother's bitter words, "dumped by the city of Vienna." The handsome, popular mayor who remained a bachelor—with a hidden mistress—in order to garner the goodwill of women and their voting husbands, had benefitted enormously by raising the "Jewish Question" during and after his five elections as mayor of the city for thirteen consecutive years from 1897 to 1910. As with other political populists in Europe, anti-Semitic rhetoric was a key to success with the working classes who resented the recent competition afforded by increases in immigrant Jewish tradesmen. He voted to restrict the immigration of Romanian and Russian Jews to an over-crowded Vienna and created the pun "Jewdapest" in reference to Budapest's large Jewish population. Lueger, who in private life had many upper-class Jewish friends, gave the famous reply when asked why, "*Ich entscheide, wer Jude ist.*—I decide who is a Jew." A starving young artist living in Vienna at this time was an early admirer of the mayor. His name was Adolf Hitler.

After Lueger's early death from diabetes, the city of Vienna honored its popular mayor by naming that part of the Ringstrasse in front of the University after him and for the rest of the twentieth-century and beginning of the next, it was known as the Karl-Lueger-Ring. Only in 2012 was the name changed, under international pressure, to Universitätsring. Other tributes to the former mayor, including a square, a bridge, a cemetery chapel, and two statues, now had "contextualizing" texts added to their identifying plaques.

This was what young Karl had grown up hearing about from his indignant grandmother who never forgave their native city for dishonoring her uncle. All because of "justice for Jews."

And so it was that when media coverage of the "Mahler Bomber" damage exploded that morning, the latter-day Karl sat mesmerized in front of the family television set. The mayor's namesake was tall and thin, with long sideburns and thick black hair swishing around his face. Tattoos decorated his arms and the back of his neck. When the contents of the threat note were revealed by the media, Karl suddenly felt he had found his purpose. He would find a way to help so that "no more Jews be allowed to defile our culture." He would begin at the University, where he was a first-year student.

29

𝔐egan was surprised to be the first one up after the stressful evening at the Opera House the night before. Then she realized that Egga's cello case was not in the corner to which it had been assigned in the large double room they had reserved at the Römischer Kaiser. Egga had already been in the room a week while performing with her quartet and, typically, had charmed the hotel staff into letting them practice in the hotel basement. So that must be where she was now. Egga would probably not be back until mid-afternoon for some quiet time before tonight's concert.

Good. Time to get her morning exercises in before dressing and going down for breakfast, Megan thought. At her age she preferred to exercise in private as the sets she put herself through were rather demanding and left her quite breathless. She had a name for her strenuous arm and leg routine which was done lying down with face up, then face down. Then she lifted weights, did cord exercise stretches, and trotted, in that order. She called it "FSAB," which stood for flexibility, strength, aerobic, and balance. When home she used four-pound weights; when traveling she used water bottles. At home the routine took her forty minutes; on the road as she called it, she did a shortened version lasting only twenty-five minutes. Nevertheless, as she was now in her mid-eighties, the shorter routine seemed just as taxing as the long one. But "it's what keeps me going" Megan would say to herself, looking at her "robust" stomach in the mirror critically but forgivingly. After all, some of that weight gain was due to the medications she must now take to keep a bipolar disorder under control. Her first episode of extreme depression had occurred just a few years after she retired and friends who were used to her cheerful, bouncy spirit told her it was just because she "missed teaching." But Megan knew, *felt* it was something quite different and the experienced psychiatrist she consulted confirmed her thoughts that it could be the result of a chemical imbalance in the brain. After much trial and error, her caring physician was ultimately able to prescribe the right combination of drugs to keep her permanently on an even keel. Now she was no longer plagued by the idea that her mind might be degenerating, and she was able to talk about her disorder without embarrassment. In fact she hoped that she might be helpful to others afflicted by bipolarity. She had actually counseled two former students by email concerning the subject. The result of this medical encounter—so different from the "touch" of breast cancer she, with immediate surgery had easily overcome—was to make Megan far more empathic concerning the illnesses of others.

Breakfast downstairs at the Römischer Kaiser was always a treat: fruit, yogurt, sprinkled cinnamon, cereal, and hot coffee with cream. And usually Megan got her favorite corner table from which she had a good view of the Annagasse and of everyone in the room. It was a never-ending parade of various types of tourists and business travelers and she had fun trying to identify their nationalities before they sat down and began talking. She also enjoyed reading their body language which appeared to range from excitement and apathy in some of the few children to gusto and impatience in the adults.

But right now, she was looking at her fellow hotel guests with unseeing eyes as thoughts and questions about the meaning of the events of last night tumbled unsorted through her head. She started to reach for one of the nearby early morning newspapers but changed her mind. She should be up and out, taking advantage of having a free day. What to do first?

Her book signing at the Leopold Museum wasn't until Wednesday and this was only Monday. The Albertina Museum lecture was the following day, and her lecture for the University she once attended was the day after that, Friday. For that event she had tweaked her image-rich PowerPoint presentation for the umpteenth time. So, although she would be attending Egga's final Vienna concert this evening, she had the entire day free. First she would take a look on her iPhone at her little Maltese Button back in Dallas via her Wireless IP Camera. Then she would visit an old friend just a few steps down the Annagasse. And oh, yes, it would be nice to invite her new friend Mary Neff to attend tonight's concert. Megan picked up her iPhone and dialed Neff's number. An answering machine announced that Neff was at the Opera House and to please leave a message. Megan did so, giving the time and location of the concert—seven o'clock at the Brahmssaal of the Musikverein—an acoustically perfect room for a string quartet.

Leaving that message suddenly gelled what Megan wanted to do most. Two things. Walk over to the nearby Secession Museum with its Klimt *Beethoven Frieze* and then, in blissful solitude, visit the first floor of the Upper Belvedere Palace Museum where Klimt's celebrated *The Kiss* reigned. But that was not Megan's reason for visiting the vast baroque palace museum. No, she wanted to determine for herself whether or not the Rodin Mahler bust she remembered being on display there in the same room as Klimt's work was the same as the one at the Opera House. Model B, it was called, smooth and realistic with precise delineation of the features, in contrast to what became known as Model A, more expressionistic, swiftly articulated with a rougher touch, probably a later conception and the one preferred by Rodin.

Model B and the Vienna State Opera House had an unusual history. For the twentieth anniversary of Mahler's death in 1931, his widow Alma Mahler gave her Model B to the Opera where it was exhibited until the Nazis destroyed it. After World War II, Alma Mahler again gave the city of Vienna a Model B cast as replacement for the Opera's lost bust.

Megan was eager to confirm that the Belvedere cast was what she remembered, Model B. She wasn't absolutely sure now because the previous year she had been in Paris for a week staying, as she always did, with her cherished friend Henri-Claude de La Granger, the world-renowned Mahler expert. They had visited the Rodin Museum together as neither of them had been there for many years and it was there that Megan got her fill of the sculptor's Mahler busts.

The museum possessed seven preparatory studies: three terra-cottas of

Model A and four plaster casts of Model B. In a mystifying addition, one of Rodin's assistants had created a marble version of Model B soon after Mahler's death with the name "Mozart" on it. Megan and Henri-Claude had asked the museum staff why such a misnomer and the answer had been out of respect for Mahler's legendary last words, "Mozart! Mozart!" They liked the reason but felt it would be misleading for the general public. But their protests were in vain.

"Well, at least the Mahler bust Model B we have at my *Médiathèque Musicale Mahler* has the name Mahler on it," Henri-Claude had consoled Megan as well as himself.

After leaving a note for Egga as to the places where she would be during the day, Megan emerged onto the Annagasse and turned to the right, walking past a few storefronts down to the shop that had been her home base for so long in Vienna, the Antiquariat Christian M. Nebehay. It had belonged to her dear friend Christian Nebehay. Although he and his wonderful wife Renée had both long since passed away, the business was now run by Christian's genial former assistant, Dr. Hanskarl Klug. The shop was empty when she entered and she had to call out his name before anyone came to the front room where a few graphic works were displayed on the walls.

"Megan! What a lovely surprise!" It was Hanskarl himself and the last time Megan had seen him was when she was investigating a murder involving the artist Gustav Klimt. Hanskarl looked older and grayer now and some of his former energy seemed to have evaporated. Megan soon learned why.

"It is good that you have visited me this month because next month I close down the business."

"*What*? Closing down the shop? Why it's a Viennese institution!" Megan was correct. The Antiquariat had been on the Vienna scene for almost a century as the place to go to for rare books and prints.

"I am only too painfully aware of that," Hanskarl said. "And it is certainly not because I want to. It is because the age of the Internet and cyber sales have taken over the world."

"Golly, I never realized that could apply to a business of rare books and art like yours, where people like to touch and see in person. But of course that does make sense." Megan felt rather foolish for not having thought about the consequences of the cyber age for a business like the Nebehay shop.

"It's sad but true. I have almost no visitors in the flesh anymore. Sometimes entire days go by when the shop is empty." His eyes wandered over to the prints on the wall. "I've sold more graphic work via email than I have to visitors to the shop."

"I still can't get my head around this, Hanskarl. Vienna will never be the same."

After a few more minutes they said goodbye and exchanged long, hard hugs.

Megan was quite downcast as she reversed her direction and walked up to the pedestrian Kärntner Strasse, center of downtown Vienna. So many memories were conjured up concerning the happy hours spent with the Nebehays, hours that included playing flute and piano duets with ever merry Renée. Megan had recently stopped bringing her flute with her on European travels. There just wasn't enough time for it and it was something one had to keep up—you couldn't just blow into the embouchure after a lapse of months and expect a beautiful tone to issue forth. In fact, she had almost given up playing any instruments at all—her guitar from folk music days stood unused in a corner of her Dallas music room. The only instrument she still regularly played was the old Steinway grand she had inherited from her parents. When she had time, she enjoyed playing the old Italian, French, and Spanish songs her violin-and-mandolin playing father had loved, and she missed their duets.

Oh, well, enough reminiscing. Megan knew how she wanted to spend her free day. Klimt at the Secession and Mahler at the Belvedere. What more could one ask for?

30

Chief of Police Erich Decker was at work early that Monday morning. He was simultaneously furious and encouraged. Someone had just leaked to the morning papers the fact that an anti-Jewish harangue had been found printed on a note in the Schwind Foyer after the explosion and that it was a "warning." Which one of his many officers on the scene would have done that?

But there was also cause for encouragement. Overnight an interesting report had come in from an officer at the Minoritenplatz office. The opera house portier, Rudi Wittkower, had telephoned to report something he thought might relate to the explosion in the Schwind Foyer. As portier for the Kärntner Strasse stage door, he had been on duty both before and after the blast incident and he had seen something that might be called unusual. One of the orchestra's players, its contrabass trombonist Ottokar Weininger, almost missed getting to the pit for last night's performance because he was waiting for someone outside the stage door. At the last minute, a young man in a blue striped shirt appeared with a large instrument case and the two men switched cases. Then, right at the start of intermission, Ottokar Weininger exited the opera house, and here was the unusual thing, according to Wittkower. He wasn't carrying any instrument case with him. The musician did not leave immediately, however. He seemed to be waiting for someone. Possibly the man he had exchanged instruments with so recently?

"Find that orchestra player and bring him in for questioning immediately," Erich had urgently instructed two of his officers. Here was a real lead. An orchestra musician, not scheduled to play that evening, who nevertheless arrives with his instrument case just a few minutes before the opera begins and who at intermission leaves immediately without taking his instrument case with him? And right before the beginning of the second act when the explosion occurred? This could explain the disposable cellphone found in the orchestra pit. Herr Ottokar Weininger had a lot to explain.

While he waited for the man to be brought in, Erich tracked down the pit manager's phone number and gave her a call.

"Hallo, here is Kerstin Jesse," she answered after three rings. She sounded in a hurry.

"This is Officer Erich Decker. We met last night."

"Oh, yes, of course I remember. *Have you caught the Mahler Bomber*?"

Erich was taken aback. That was the exact wording of the headline in this morning's paper: "Mahler Bomber Sought in Opera House Explosion."

"No, but we're actively working on it. I need to ask you about the large instrument case you found last night stowed away in the back-storage area of the orchestra pit."

"Oh, yes, of course. The one that was locked and took two policemen and a crowbar to open. And then there was nothing except six bricks!"

"Well, in the surprise we neglected to ascertain which musical instrument would require such a big case."

"Oh, sorry. I thought that was self-evident. It's for a contrabass trombone. Probably a new, modern one."

"How would you determine that?"

"By its size. Many of the newer trombones of all sizes now have large roomy cases in which essentials, including several mutes, can be stored."

"And how many contrabass trombonists play in the Opera orchestra?"

"Goodness! Only one," Kerstin had to laugh. "Except for Wagner, there haven't been too many parts for that monster instrument until the early twentieth century."

"What is the name of the orchestra's contrabass trombonist?" Erich wanted to see if the portier's identification matched Kerstin Jesse's.

"Ottokar Weininger. He's been with us for quite a few years now. Loves opera. He's never missed a performance, whether or not there's a part for his instrument."

"And there is no part for contrabass trombone in last night's opera *Fidelio* is there?"

"Definitely not. But you see Ottokar doesn't care. He's a true opera fanatic. And he always brings his instrument with him, just out of habit, I guess. Or because that way he is admitted at the stage door without having to pay for a ticket. The portier isn't going to know the instrumentation of each opera. He probably thinks *every* opera requires a contrabass trombone, if he's ever even thought about it. Yes, come to think of it, that's probably why Ottokar always brings his trombone with him—free admission!"

"Is the case still there?"

"Yep. We intend to use it to play a practical joke on Ottokar the way he played one on us. We've thought of filling it with flower pots!"

"Don't even *think* of doing something like that! We'll need to take prints off that case. I'll send an officer over there immediately to pick it up."

"Oh, dear. Sorry! We'll have it ready. And we'll handle it with gloves from now on."

"One last question. Do you know anything about the man's financial situation? Do you think he might be in need of money? Is he a womanizer, for example? Or could he have had to sell his trombone since there wasn't one in the case when we opened it."

"Sorry, Sir, I really don't know anything about his personal life. He's a very quiet man and really keeps to himself. I've never seen Ottokar with a woman and I don't think he has any close friends in the orchestra. He's just sort of amusedly tolerated, if you see what I mean."

"And the name. Ottokar Weininger. I presume it's Jewish?"

"I've never thought about it, Officer. Here we tend to judge musical ability, not racial happenstance."

Erich Decker realized he had gone too far in Kerstin's eyes. But he was actually collecting the names of Jewish members of the Opera orchestra because he feared their lives might possibly be in danger. After all, in addition to the threatening note his officers had found, there was that curiously timed disaster last evening with the principal cellist, Jared Bogenstein.

31

Satisfied at last with her detailed photography of Klimt's gold-and-silver-studded *Beethoven Frieze* at the Secession, and without looking at the contemporary show on the ground floor, Megan entered the gift shop. There she bought two new books on Klimt and a few souvenir 3D lenticular postcards of the frieze as presents for friends back home. Unfolding her miniscule tote sack that was decorated with musical staves, she stored them carefully away, and walked back to the opera house. Once again throwing caution to the wind, she did not take the underground crossing, but stood at the great horse-shoe shaped Ringstrasse watching for the moment she could cross between oncoming streetcars. That done, she walked to the front of the opera house where the D tram took her down the Prinz-Eugen-Strasse along the Belvedere's complex wall to the entrance of the Upper Belvedere in just under eight minutes.

To her right was a separate small structure where one bought entrance tickets and ingenuous souvenirs, and after doing both—"gifts" was her excuse for acquiring the latter—she returned to the side of the palace and sat down on a hedge-shaded bench that had a good view of the great garden that sloped down to the Lower Belvedere.

She automatically looked to her left, remembering that the elderly composer Anton Bruckner—Mahler's great Austrian contemporary—had spent the last year of his life, 1896, in the nearby gate-keeper's humble lodge. It had been offered to him by Emperor Franz Joseph himself. Even on his final morning Bruckner had tried in vain to complete his ninth symphony—something not lost on a superstitious Mahler who was only too aware of the fact that Beethoven died after writing his colossal ninth symphony. Mahler was terrified of writing anything that could be called a ninth symphony. After he had completed his eighth symphony, in the hopes of cheating death, he "disguised" his next one as a song cycle, *Das Lied von der Erde—The Song of the Earth—*a symphony for tenor and contralto or baritone and orchestra." The great irony was that as soon as he completed the work Mahler immediately began writing a tenth symphony but never finished it as he died several months later. So like Beethoven, he too died after writing his ninth symphony.

These gloomy thoughts tumbled through Megan's head as she watched giggling tourists line up to take selfies in front of the huge pair of winged female sphinxes sitting on their haunches and calmly observing the never-ending stream of curious tourists. Megan remembered the time when she was twenty-one that she herself had posed for a mischievous photograph one evening, "riding" on top of one of them after coming across the mysterious mute monsters. Oh, how she loved Vienna!

All right, enough of nostalgic reminiscing; time to do the investigating you came here for, Megan chastised herself. She stood up, walked past her sphinx friends to the museum's grand entrance foyer with its four baroque marble Atlas figures supporting the ceiling, entered, and presented her ticket. She was surprised to note that there seemed to be no check-in for coats or packages. And only two museum personnel within sight. But for now the far more pressing question was to climb or not to climb. She stared at the great white marble staircase leading to the first floor and the twenty-plus Klimts. Surely she should climb up. She'd just been sitting—on the tram, on the bench. Come on, now! But the counterargument was that she had done her exercise routine that morning and she didn't want to be breathless upon arriving at her goal.

Megan decided in favor of the small gray elevator seductively nearby. A minute later she was walking toward the object of her intense interest, the Mahler bust. The large windows of the room were on her left, the bust on her right. It faced inward, looking at the artworks on the wall in front of it. Mahler's eyes were commanding, the pupils and direction of gaze had been specifically indicated. She thought of what Mahler once said of himself: "If I were not obliged to wear glasses, I would conduct with my eyes." Elongated small dabs of clay turned bronze in the lost-wax casting process were noticeable on the base of the throat. This was definitely Model B, the more naturalistic one.

A young guard with an oval face and brown eyes and hair had been watching with amusement Megan's intense study of the Mahler bust and followed her movements after she finally turned from the bust and stepped forward to look at and photograph the famous paintings in the room. There was no point in taking shots of Klimt's *The Kiss*, as there was always a crowd of eager onlookers in front of it. Megan turned to the room's other works and delighted in taking close-up details of some of the images she had used as illustrations in her books.

Then she came upon the only work in the room she did not already know. And it was the only work in the room by a female artist. The almost five-foot high, three-foot wide oil painting showed a gathering of some six willowy nude boys in the background all looking at a pubescent nude girl who dominated the foreground and faced the viewer. *Adolescentia* was the title and the work was dated 1903. The artist was someone Megan had never heard of, Elena Luksch-Makowska, born in St. Petersburg in 1878, worked and exhibited in Vienna at the turn of the century, and died in 1967. Megan was fascinated and just as she raised her iPhone to photograph the work the young guard who had been observing her stepped in front of the painting with his hand held up, saying quietly, so not to attract other museum visitors' attention, that photographing the work was not allowed.

"But I've been photographing all the other paintings in this room," Megan murmured in surprise, genuinely puzzled.

"Yes, the other artists have been dead long enough so there is no problem, but this artist only died in nineteen-sixty-seven, so photography is not permitted yet of her work."

Megan was struck by the gentle and affable manner of the young guard and after chatting—she mentioned her work and books on Klimt and Schiele to justify why she was photographing in such detail—they parted on friendly terms. Before moving on to the Schiele room, she returned to the Mahler bust and photographed the large bronze cast next to it: Leipzig sculptor Max Klinger's heroic 1902 image of Beethoven. It was this work and Gustav Klimt's accompanying allegorical frieze that had spurred her to write some three decades earlier what turned out to be the first reception-history of the composer, *The Changing Image of Beethoven: A Study in Myth-Making*. And now, after all that time, the book was going to be translated and published in German by the Viennese publisher Hollitzer. How could she *not* photograph dear Ludwig one more time?

Abruptly Megan realized she felt tired and walked to a beautiful gold-and-white-legged table with matching chair she had noted in the small elegant room beyond—the "Klimt Selfie" room. People were lining up to be photographed in front of the replica of the great golden icon and Megan sat down and watched the proceedings with amusement. After about fifteen minutes there was a break and the room was suddenly empty and quiet. Admiring the baroque ceiling paintings and gold and white architectural décor, she was surprised when the pleasant guard she had spoken with earlier suddenly appeared in front of her. A big smile was on his face.

"Professor Crespi, I saw you leave the Klimt room and come in here. Would you like me to take your photo in front of the Klimt *Kiss* reproduction with your cellphone?" he asked.

Starting to decline his offer, Megan thought the better of it and jumped up, saying a hearty yes. Leaving her fold-out tote bag filled with Belvedere souvenirs at the side of the table—something that would have been impossible to do in most major museums around the world—she struck several dramatic poses in front of the kissing couple.

"What's your name?" Megan asked laughingly as the grinning guard came up to hand her iPhone back to her.

"I have double surnames but people just call me Bell,"

"Well, Bell, you have to be the most genial guard I have ever met. Thank you for everything and I hope to be back when it's permissible to photograph the *Adolescentia*." Megan picked up her tote sack and started to continue on to the adjoining room that contained canvasses by Schiele.

But before she could get there something happened that caused both her and Bell to stop dead in their tracks.

It was an overwhelming, nauseous stench and it was coming from the Mahler bust room.

32

Ottokar Weininger had woken up in a daze. Not only was he out one thousand euros, he was without a contrabass trombone. How could he have been so foolish as to trust a stranger? And yet the locked case he was given at the stage entrance last night seemed legitimate enough. Certainly it was heavy enough to contain his big brass instrument. And his instructions had been to leave it in the pit at intermission and return to the stage door where his benefactor would give him the key to the case as well as one thousand euros. He must work up his courage to return to the opera house and attempt to locate the instrument he had left, fulfilling his part of the ill-fated bargain, in the orchestra pit at the beginning of intermission.

But in the meantime, something had come up that totally deflected his attention. Grabbing a newspaper at his local café that morning he had read about the "Mahler Bomber" and his demands. He now knew that after he had left the opera house an explosion had occurred in the Schwind Foyer during Act Two of *Fidelio*. And that a note had been found there cursing Jews and demanding their removal from the opera house. Then Ottokar turned to the editorial and he could feel his pulse racing as he read it.

"The hatred issuing from the bomber's note is reflective of historic anti-Jew sentiments in our city from the likes of Otto Weininger and Adolf Hitler."

Who was this "historic" namesake, this Weininger? This man who had feelings similar to his own? This man who, like him, was Jewish yet anti-Semitic? Who was he? Having come to Vienna from Mannheim, Ottokar had not grown up in the cultural environment of the "waltz center of the world." He must find out more about the man who apparently held views similar to his own. Even his given name was close to his. Ottokar returned to his modest attic room in the Leopoldstadt district and spent the next two hours on his laptop. What he found was so riveting he temporarily forgot the crisis with his missing instrument.

The Internet coverage was as vast as the man's life was brief: four months after the June 1903 publication of his bizarre book, *Sex and Character*, he rented a room at the famous Schwarzspanierstrasse 15, the very building in which Beethoven had died. Weininger wrote a letter to his father and another to his brother, then shot himself in the chest. Mortally wounded, he died the next morning, on October 4, 1903. He was twenty-three years old.

What had he written and why had he committed suicide?

Ottokar looked up contemporaneous reviews of the man's book and was even more intrigued. One in particular from the now defunct *Wiener Allgemeine Zeitung* held his attention: "But it is the book itself, even more than its author's individuality, which is abnormal. It is nothing less than an attempt to construct a system of sexual characterology on the broadest scientific basis, with all the resources of the most modern philosophy." And the *Allgemeine Wiener Medizinische Zeitung* called it "an extraordinary book . . . that will henceforth be in the hands of every doctor who has occasion to study the antithetical character of the two sexes."

Totally fascinated, Ottokar located a PDF of Weininger's *Sex and*

Character and quickly recognized the author's self-directed hatred as a Jew and a homosexual as his own. Similar, too was his rejection of Jewishness by becoming Protestant, just as he, Ottokar, had done. The unfolding chapters offered biological, psychological, cultural, and philosophical justification of male superiority. Weininger judged the characteristics of the Jew, "who believes in nothing," as worse than those of "the passive, unproductive, unconscious, amoral Woman whose life is consumed by the sexual act," but who "at least believes in the active, productive, conscious, and moral Man." Weininger characterized Man's primary objective as striving to become a genius, and "forgoing sexuality for an abstract love of God, which is to be found in himself."

Ottokar was electrified. Here was an important cultural figure, a famous author who thought as he did! Energized, he now felt strong enough to confront the problem of his lost instrument.

By noon he stood on the south side of the Ringstrasse facing the imposing neo-Renaissance façade of the Vienna State Opera opposite him. Should he cross over to the stage door and make conversation with the day portier, perhaps learning something about what had happened last evening? Or should he just nod, hold up his ID card, pass him by, insert the card into the red chip reader on the wall, and see for himself whether his new instrument case was somewhere in the house. Perhaps it had been placed in one of the large instrument storage bins. Or maybe still in place in the orchestra pit?

Not recognizing the portier on duty, he did the latter and almost immediately ran into the pit manager.

"*Ach*, Ottokar, there you are! We've had to hold your instrument case for the police. But tell me, were you playing a practical joke on us, filling it with bricks?"

"*Bricks*?"

"Come on now, man. Why do you pretend to be surprised?"

"But I am surprised. How can you know this? The case was locked."

"*Ja*, it certainly was. Took two policemen and a crowbar to open it. And out fell six red bricks. I can tell you the police were as surprised as we were. But why did you do it? Have you *always* done it when there's no orchestral part for you?"

"Believe me, Kerstin, I did not put bricks or anything else into that case. It contained a brand new Kühl I had traded my old instrument for just before *Fidelio* began."

"Well, all I know is that the police are looking for you. They quizzed me about you. Even wanted to know if you're Jewish."

"What business is that of theirs?" Ottokar was mortified.

"That's more or less what I said. Told the policeman our orchestra players are judged by talent, not by ethnicity or religion."

Without saying another word to Kerstin, Ottokar turned on his heels and left the building.

"I'll show them who is Jewish," he thought angrily to himself. His thoughts turned to Gustav Mahler, the target of last night's bomber.

Now there was a Jew, if ever there was one, even if he did convert to Catholicism in order to help his career. His tortured music is one long assault of interminable whining racket or whimpering stasis. Why was it so static and then suddenly so violent, so tragic and then so sentimental? Why did it include cliché trivial tunes like *Frère Jacques* and farcically assign it to a solo string bass? Yes, here was the eternal, harping Jew. The Mahler Bomber was right to make such a bold statement.

And Ottokar knew where another bust of Mahler in the city was. Purposefully now, he turned away from the opera house and entered a small stationery store where he bought a bottle of black ink. He then walked to the nearby popular toy store for children, *Das Spielzeug* on the Kärntner Ring. Minutes later he emerged with three items and caught the D tram heading south.

33

ℳary Neff had listened to Megan's recorded message on her cellphone with interest. Yes, she was free this evening and would love to attend Egga Streicher's quartet concert. The list of music Megan said her friend would be playing included someone whose name immediately piqued Mary's interest: Erwin Schulhoff. She had heard of him only in regard to some Dada-type songs he had composed in the nineteen-twenties for baritone. The songs were amplified by four winds and percussion. Few people knew his work nowadays. Since Mary's first vocal coaching appointment was not until eleven that morning, she decided to educate herself a bit more concerning the composer.

Opening her laptop she went to Spotify, and chose Schulhoff's String

Sextet for two violins, two violas, and two cellos. As she listened, she read a URL reference mentioning that no less a musician than Paul Hindemith played the second viola part and his brother Rudolf, second cello. What a treat that performance must have been to hear in person with its twisted tonality and textures. The sextet ended with pulsing music that was close to the way a beating heart gradually slows down and then reluctantly ceases. Hmm. What was that line by T. S. Eliot? "This is the way the world ends. Not with a bang but a whimper." The sextet was a frightening and frightened, brooding work. What had Schulhoff been so afraid of in the 1920s?

Mary looked up the composer's biography. His dates certainly covered rich and definitive periods in world history. And ah ha! He was a child prodigy. That alone could complicate things later on. Wikipedia told her he was born in Prague to a German-Jewish family, encouraged by fellow Czech Antonín Dvořák, and studied with Claude Debussy for a brief time in France. When World War I broke out in 1914, he was conscripted as an Austro-Hungarian citizen into the army. Apparently what he went through during four years of military service served to radicalize him, culturally and politically. After the end of the war in 1918, he associated with New Objectivity artists like Max Beckman, George Grosz, Otto Dix, and the apocalyptically-minded Ludwig Meidner. There came a short Dada period and the discovery of jazz. Schulhoff then fell under the spell of Joseph Stalin, actually composing a choral setting of passages from the *Communist Manifesto*.

Mary was shocked by the final two sentences in the biography: "In 1941, Schulhoff was deported to the Wülzburg concentration camp near Weißenburg, Bavaria. He died there on 18 August 1942 from tuberculosis."

What a rich but jagged, fractured life!

So what did Schulhoff's first string quartet have in store for her? The one that would be played this evening by Egga's quartet? Unable to curb her curiosity, Mary "Spotified," as she called it, the piece and listened to it closely. The first movement was full of energy; the second began and ended as a pseudo waltz: the third recapitulated the buzzing vitality of the first with lots of pizzicato and high harmonics. But it was the fourth and final movement that revealed Schulhoff to Mary. It was a reflective, melancholy, and slow termination of energy as an eternal F/D alternation faded into nothingness. An omen?

It was with the greatest of impatience that Mary looked forward to hearing this evening the unusual composer to whom history had dealt such a horrible Finale.

34

The morning paper had one other item of interest pertaining to the Mahler Bomber. Inside on page three above the bend a black-rimmed rectangle framed the following message:

ATTENTION MAHLER FRIENDS!
A REWARD OF FIFTY THOUSAND EUROS IS OFFERED FOR DELIVERY OF THE MISSING
RODIN BUST OF MAHLER REMOVED FROM THE
OPERA HOUSE IN LAST EVENING'S EXPLOSION.
Contact: missingmahler@hotmail.at
NO QUESTIONS ASKED.

Eighteen responses had already come in by noon and Harry Howell had determined that they were all untrustworthy, concocted by people hoping to pass off one of the several surmoulages available in a few music stores around town. In fact, he learned by calling the store, that Vienna's time-honored Doblinger on Dorotheergasse in the center of town, had already sold its two surmoulages, and they were by no means inexpensive. Some customers had even bought cheap miniature models of Mahler made of fiberglass painted in white to look like marble.

Such was the intelligence level of those who hoped to pass off their wares.

But a nineteenth response had just come in that seemed worthy of follow-up. The email return address was obviously fabricated by someone with computer savvy and was likely to be closed down within hours. It too ended with "hotmail" and read: mahlerorbust@hotmail.at.?

The message stated: "As one who also mourns the loss of Rodin's Model B bust of Austria's greatest composer, I am in a position to verify that it has been safely removed from the Vienna State Opera to a location far from the intrigues of quarreling collectors and blundering officials. The bust is undamaged, in excellent condition, and is ready for acquisition by the right person."

Harry read the email out loud five times. He hesitated, his fingers poised over the computer keys. No, don't be foolish. Don't be blinded by desire. But if the email is legitimate, is truthful? Harry typed out a short answer.

"Send color photos of all sides; indicate dimensions and weight."

Within ten minutes a second email arrived from the person at *mahlerorbust*. There was no message but the data Henri had asked for came in just as requested: six color photographs showing not only all sides but also the top and the bottom of the bust. It looked convincingly real. But Harry decided he was fooling himself. That his eagerness to acquire the stolen Mahler bust was so intense that he was easily duped. He magnified the images on his screen and took his own magnifying glass to them. The bust certainly looked genuine. All the details were correct and matched Model B of Rodin's casting. The weight given was certainly within the range of accuracy, nineteen kilograms—close to forty-three pounds. The speed with which the information and images had been supplied was a convincing factor as well.

Harry decided to respond.

"Be at the American Bar on the Kärntner Durchgang at fourteen hours today. I will be waiting inside and wearing a bow tie."

Harry sent the email and then chastised himself. Had his wish to surprise Haim with such a marvelous fiftieth anniversary gift clouded his judgement? Was he setting himself up? Perhaps even courting blackmail? But his curiosity had gotten the better of him and he was ready to deal with any consequences.

He deactivated the email address he had set up earlier that morning and checked his watch. An hour and forty-five minutes to go.

35

Standing behind the Japanese tour group crowded reverently in front of Klimt's *The Kiss* at the Upper Belvedere, Ottokar Weininger inconspicuously surveyed the room holding the Mahler bust. His gaze took in the other paintings on the Klimt wall and fixed on a troubling picture of a totally naked young girl in front, with naked young boys eyeing her in the background. A look at the label revealed the vulgar painting was by a *woman*. Typical lack of taste. And it was pompously titled *Adolescentia*. As if this tasteless picture had anything to do with the adolescence *he* had endured, striving to negate his embarrassing attraction toward the same sex. It was then he had committed to a virginal life unblemished by sexual activity. And how he hated coming upon this vulgar painting that reminded him of his own difficult puberty.

He looked around, scrutinizing the people in the room. Most of the tourists were still densely grouped in front of *The Kiss*; a few were gazing at pictures in the room by other artists. No one was in front of the *Adolescentia*. Nor was anyone looking at the Mahler bust. Not a single guard was in sight. The moment was ripe. Quickly Ottokar pulled out two prank items from his breast pocket: one was a squirt pen filled with black ink, the other was a glass ampoule filled with a pungent malodorous liquid. He stepped into the middle of the room. The Mahler bust was a mere three feet away. All eyes were on the artworks. In two swift, simultaneous motions Ottokar squirted the offending painting with his right hand and with his left hand hurled the stink bomb at the Mahler bust with all his might. The glass container broke upon striking its bronze target and a horrible stink immediately pervaded the room. People began covering their noses and faces, screaming and running from the room. Some scuttled into the Klimt selfie area where Megan and the guard stood momentarily transfixed by the unbearable odor. Ottokar was one of those scuttlers and as he ran past Megan he tripped and almost fell to the floor. Megan glanced at him. She had seen him before. But where?

Within minutes the rooms were filled with guards. All persons were asked to remain where they were. And downstairs the doors were closed and manned by museum personnel. The exodus to the outdoors proceeded very slowly, as one by one the visitors were questioned. No one had seen anything or noticed something unusual. The nice guard Bell hustled Megan outdoors ahead of the others and it was a blessing to be out in the open again. Megan headed for the bench she had requisitioned earlier and sat down, thankfully and methodically breathing in the fresh air. She discreetly smelled her blouse. The awful odor was clinging to it. As soon as she calmed down she had better head back to the hotel and change. For now, however, she would just sit and recover.

Where had she seen the man who tripped in front of her before?

36

T he fellow obviously believes he is the incarnation of Mahler, Rita Rausch was thinking as she listened to what could only be described as the ramblings of a lunatic."

They were sitting inside the busy Café Belvedere at Wiedner Gürtel 6, where the International Gustav Mahler Society's headquarters were located. Ignoring the iced tea set in front of him, Tonik Nektar, his long face perspiring, had been holding forth on how unjust the public of 1900 was to Mahler. Now he was fervently talking about the busts of famous Vienna State Opera conductors in the Schwind Foyer.

"I meant it when I said why not bomb the effigy of Richard Strauss there? He was conductor of the Opera from nineteen-nineteen until nineteen-twenty-four when he resigned. And you know his own works didn't go over all that well with the postwar opera-going public. They found them old-fashioned, and rightly so, I say. Certainly they don't come close to the genius of Mahler."

"I'm afraid I'm not following you," Rita said, totally at a loss in her attempt to understand what the man was aiming at.

"Don't you see? With all the cash Strauss raked in with his opera *Salome,* he built a fancy villa at Garmisch-Partenkirchen where they all lived, his crazy wife, their son and his Jewish wife and his two Jewish grandsons. So why not destroy *his* effigy at the Opera if they are going to destroy Mahler's?"

"I truly don't understand," said Rita helplessly.

"I mean a *real* terrorist would have taken care to destroy both busts."

Rita fought to suppress a hysterical laugh. Tonik took her silence to mean agreement.

"And I have figured out why the terrorist chose last night specifically for his message to the world." Tonik's voice lowered conspiratorially.

"Why is that?" Perhaps Rita would at last hear something worth writing about for her newspaper.

"Just think about it for a minute. Last night we had a Jewish conductor, Max Brandes, and a Jewish tenor, Aldo Finzi-Contiti. And *Mahler* had commissioned specific sets for that opera and had conducted it with success in both Vienna and New York.

"So?" asked Rita.

"So I am saying that three Jews were enough to encourage anti-Semitic hatred and that the program last night was just the right bait."

"I would say that if your theory is correct," said Rita, "the Mahler bomber must have been a pretty sophisticated and desperate one to draw that sort of triangle."

"'Triangle'! Yes! That's it! Thank you. Triangle."

Rita considered the useless interview concluded and drained her glass of beer in a gesture of wrap-up. But then Nektar uttered something that riveted her to the spot.

"And you know what? I wouldn't be surprised if there isn't another explosion at another public event or place today."

37

"At the Upper Belvedere, you say?" Erich Decker was in the central police office on the phone talking to one of his officers who was on the scene.

"And you say no one was hurt, correct?"

"That's right, no injuries as far as we can ascertain. It all happened so quickly and visitors dispersed so rapidly that the museum personnel were unable to check everyone leaving. So we weren't able to interview everyone."

"What about the ones you did interview. Did they see anything?"

"Nobody seems to have seen anything unusual. All the witnesses were in agreement about one thing: the simultaneous sound of glass breaking on something hard and the hiss of something squirting."

"Oh, yes? What sort of damage did that do?"

"Limited. Only one painting was hit. A streak of black ink dripped down from the top of the canvas and pretty much obliterated the main image of a girl."

"Give me the name of the artist, in case that has anything to do with last night's explosion and today's vandalism."

"Okay. It's a long one. Never heard of the name myself. Here you go: Elena Luksch-Makowska."

"Hm. I never heard of her either. Any more info on her?"

"Well the label next to the work says she painted the picture in 1903 and titled it *Adolescentia*."

"Adolescence? Okay. Find the museum's conservator and see if you can glean any more information about why her work might have been the only painting which was the object of defacement. It's pretty obvious from the attack on the Mahler bust that this was a hate crime inspired by last evening's event at the opera house. Maybe the painter was also Jewish? Or perhaps she was hit because she was a woman. And be sure to ask the conservator if there is any damage to the Mahler bust."

"Yes sir. I'll call you again when I have more info."

Erich Decker hung up and sat thinking at his desk. Several items to consider. One was a suspicious ad run in the morning paper offering 50,000 euros "for delivery of the missing Rodin bust of Mahler removed from the opera house in last evening's explosion." Whoever this person was, he must have inside information as to what actually happened at the Opera. Or was it just wistful thinking? He picked up the phone and asked one of his detectives to run down the person who had placed the ad. He read off the contact email address given and urged his man to follow up whatever leads he might uncover.

And then there was the grim fact of two racist attacks in two days. Erich decided he had better look for any public events this week that might somehow have a Jewish connection—either the author of a play, or composer of an operetta or opera, or even the opening of an art show. He had to protect such venues in the city at any cost! What deranged individual or individuals were out there and what did they hope to gain? The last line of that hate note was clear enough: "No more Jews defiling our culture!"

That possessive "our" indicated a Viennese perpetrator, a hate-filled maniac living somewhere in the city. Well, by god, he was going to flush him out!

38

At ten minutes to two o'clock that afternoon Harry Howell was sitting in the very back of upstart architect Adolf Loos's famed 1908 American Bar on the Kärntner Passage. Once a notorious shake of the fist at Art nouveau décor, the bar was now a hallowed tourist stop at night. But at this time of day, the narrow, dark, mirror-paneled rectangular room, no larger than a hotel suite, was almost empty. This was what Harry had counted on, positioning himself opposite the long bar on the green leather banquette so that he faced the entry door. He was immediately discernable to anyone entering the establishment and looking for a man wearing a bow tie. Harry glanced up at the bar's signature painting just behind him to his left: Oskar Kokoschka's haunting portrait of the feuilleton writer Peter Altenberg, society sniping delight of turn-of-the-twentieth-century newspaper readers. This was only a replica, of course, but it added the right historic atmosphere to the room which, thanks to ubiquitous mirror panels covering both long walls, seemed much larger, multiplying the intervening mahogany frames into seemingly freestanding columns. With wood, brass, glass, onyx, tile floor, multiply-recessed ceiling panels, and back-lit tortoise lamps, Loos had created an intimate haven much appreciated not only in his day but also by modern visitors.

Harry looked at his watch. It was one minute to two. He took a quick sip of the lemon berry prosecco sangria he had ordered and focused on the door. Two minutes later a Muslim woman wearing a full black body garment—a burqa—and outrageously huge sunglasses, entered. A large sling bag was on one shoulder and Harry caught a glimpse of blue jeans underneath her flowing garb.

Damn it! Now there will be a witness to my transaction, Harry cursed to himself.

But the woman was heading straight toward him. Six steps and she was standing at his table.

"Are you Herr '*missingmahler*?'" she asked quietly.

"Are you Frau '*mahlerorbust*"'? he answered. She nodded.

"Please, sit." Harry moved closer to the Altenberg portrait and the woman sat down next to him. Without saying a word, she pulled a folder from her sling bag, put it on the diminutive white table in front of them, and opened it. The photographs Harry had seen online were inside.

"Where is the cargo now?" he asked.

"Where is the payment?" she answered.

"I can hand over the full payment at the same time I can verify the authenticity of the cargo."

"I can hand over the cargo the moment I receive the payment," the woman countered.

"You will understand I was not prepared for any immediate financial transaction," Harry scoffed.

"When you provide the payment, and it should be in denominations one hundred euros, you will see the cargo. It is absolutely authentic, as these photos show."

"You do realize that I have to examine the cargo in person before any payment."

"We can do both simultaneously," the woman answered with authority.

"What are you suggesting?"

"We meet Thursday evening at a place that is both very private and very public."

"And where might that simultaneous place be?" Harry was beginning to lose patience.

"You don't know? Think of the film *The Third Man*. You are familiar with it, aren't you?"

"Of course I'm familiar with it," Harry snapped.

"Then the answer should be obvious."

"How so?" Harry was almost yelling.

"Think of the highest place in the film that is both public but private."

"I give up. Why don't you just tell me?"

"The *Riesenrad* at the Prater amusement park. That giant Ferris wheel's highest point is sixty-four meters or two hundred-twelve feet tall."

"What? You expect me to finalize a transaction of such value on top of a Ferris wheel in front of strangers in an amusement park?"

"I do. I need to feel safe doing business with you."

"And you're suggesting we meet in such a public place and conduct *business*? That's insane!"

"Again, you are not following through. Think of the highest spot on the *Riesenrad*."

"You mean when one of the cabins is at the very top?"

"I mean exactly that."

"And I'm supposed to give you an enormous money payment and examine the Mahler bust in front of eight or ten other people? You are mad!"

Harry made motions to stand up. But the woman continued to speak.

"Obviously you are not acquainted with the recent makeover of the *Riesenrad* multi-windowed carriages into modern closed cabins with four large windows on either side."

"No, I am not. But so what?"

"A few of these new cabins are offered for rent at all hours of the day and night. It's popular, for example, to hold children's birthday parties in them. I can have one of the updated cabins at our disposal in three days at six o'clock. You will be able to examine the bust in privacy as long as you like, bring any equipment you might wish to use to verify the bust's authenticity. But you must also bring the full payment of fifty-thousand euros with you in cash."

Harry did now recall he had seen a short news clip on TV a few years ago detailing the makeover of the *Riesenrad* and that some of the modernized cabins were available to reserve for private parties. Conducting business in one of those cabins would indeed be "simultaneously private and public," just as the mystery woman had said.

"Okay, okay. You swear you will be bringing the bust with you?"

"Yes, I do. You will see that I have a rolling tote bag with me. It will contain the cargo."

"All right. I will be standing next to the *Riesenrad* entrance at six o'clock on Thursday with the full payment. But you goddamn well better be there, and with the *genuine* bust."

Without another word the mysterious woman who had never taken her sunglasses off in that dark locale got up and left. Harry realized he had no idea of what she actually looked like.

39

𝔐egan was still sitting on the bench near the Belvedere sphynxes. She was trying to solve a sphynx riddle herself. What was the motive for the stink bomb attack on the Mahler bust and, in mystifying conjunction, the black ink spraying of the painting *Adolescentia* she had heard about as she and the young guard left the building. Why would *both* items be the object of vandalism? Desecration of the Mahler bust made sense, considering last night's hateful event at the opera house. But why vandalization of the relatively unknown painting by an equally unfamiliar artist, Elena Luksch-Makowska? What could the two objects have in common that would attract the attention of a madman? She reflected upon other artists represented in the Klimt/Rodin room. Famous artists like the Norwegian Edvard Munch, the Dutchman Vincent van Gogh, and the Swiss painter Ferdinand Hodler. *They* had not been attacked. What was it about Elena Luksch-Makowska or her work? Oh, duh! Of course! Luksch-Makowska was the only *female* painter in the room. That must be why she attracted the vandal's hateful attention. So, if she were correct, the police would have on their hands a hater not just of Jews but also of women! Perhaps she should call Erich Decker and tell him her thoughts. Might be helpful.

She dialed the number he had given her and reached him immediately.

"Megan! I was just thinking about calling *you*. We have another Mahler hate crime on our hands. The Rodin bust in the Upper Belvedere was..."

"...hit with a stink bomb," Megan finished Erich's sentence.

"How did you know?"

"I was *there*! In the very next room. The terrible smell reached me as the guard and I heard the sound of breaking glass."

"*Ach*, Megan, *Liebchen*, leave it to you to be at the scene of a crime while in Vienna."

"Yup. It is a bit amazing, isn't it? But do you know about the other vandalism that occurred in the same room?"

"Yes. Black ink was sprayed on a painting done by..." Erich glanced down at his notes, "...an artist named Elena Luksch-Makowska. Dates from nineteen-and-three."

"Right. I'd not heard of her before. But now I've looked her up on my iPhone. She was Russian. Her husband, Richard Luksch, I do know about: he was a sculptor and exhibited with the Secession. His specialty was soft-paste porcelain figures, very willowy and very Art nouveau."

"I thought the name Luksch sounded somewhat familiar, but I just couldn't place it," Erich said.

"So the reason for the attack on her work could be simply because she was a woman—the only woman artist in a room filled with paintings by men? I didn't read online that either Elena or her husband were Jewish."

"I didn't either. Just looked them up as a matter of fact."

"Which could mean that not only do we have a despiser of Jews on our hands but also a woman hater."

"Or the criminal just didn't like that particular painting?" Erich gave a weak laugh. "I only hope this is the end of the rampage. There are no more original busts of Mahler in the city as far as I know. I checked that out."

"Hold on a second, Erich," Megan said. Bell, the guard she had befriended, and a policeman were walking briskly toward her.

"Hi, Bell. Have you caught the person who created all this havoc?" Bell did not answer the question. Instead the policeman addressed her.

"*Gnädige Frau*, we are going to have to look through your bag." He pointed to the foldout tote next to her on the bench.

"You're kidding!" Megan looked at Bell who looked embarrassed.

"No, *gnädige Frau*, I am quite serious."

Perplexed, Megan handed over the tote bag and the officer delved through it.

"What's this?" He drew out three squirt pens and held one up to her accusingly.

"That's a Klimt prank squirt pen. It shoots out gold that dissolves in a few seconds. I bought several at the Belvedere souvenir store before I entered the museum."

The policeman looked questioningly at Bell.

"Yes sir," he confirmed. "They're on sale at our museum shop and they're harmless."

"And I'm harmless too," Megan added. She turned and spoke into her iPhone.

"Erich? Have you heard all this? Would you please speak to your officer on my behalf?" After hearing his answer, she handed her phone to the still suspicious young officer. He listened intently for a minute and his body snapped to attention as though Vienna's chief of police were there in front of him.

"Yes, sir. Sorry, sir. Immediately, sir." He handed the phone, tote bag, and three squirt pens back to Megan.

"Thank you for your help, *gnädige Frau*, you are not to be detained any longer." Saluting them both he turned and walked quickly back in the direction of the museum.

"I guess we're no longer suspects," Bell murmured merrily to his new professor friend.

"I guess not!" Megan spoke into her phone.

"Erich? Are you still there? Yes. Good. Exactly what I was going to suggest. See you just as soon as I can get there." She hung up and smiled at Bell.

"Wow! You know the chief of police?"

"I do. And he's a very nice man. I was able to help him a little with a case having to do with the artist Egon Schiele a few years ago. Your chief of police is a very good amateur art historian."

"My dads are art historians too!"

"Perhaps we'll meet someday," Megan smiled in farewell, assiduously not responding to the interesting plural she had just heard. The priority now was to catch the D tram back to the center of town and meet Erich. He was as eager to discuss new developments with her as she was with him.

40

ℰgga found Megan's note when she returned to their hotel room after a long practice session with her quartet. The note specified where Megan was going to be during the day and suggested they have an early dinner at the Wienerwald restaurant on the Annagasse. That was fine with her. She loved the refurbished haunt of olden days.

She was the only quartet member who was staying in the center of town; the other three were sharing an atmospheric attic suite at the Tibet Guesthouse on the Schottenfeldgasse in the city's Josefstadt district. Following the street into the city center brought them right to the Kunsthistorisches Museum just off the Ring. Since all three musicians appreciated art history, they had already visited the palatial museum twice. But right now, back at their guesthouse, they were doing what Egga was doing in her hotel room, catching up with friends and relatives on Facetime.

After chatting on her cellphone with her husband and two boys while resting on her bed, Egga walked to the room's long desk and went over her notes for what she was going to say at the concert that evening. She liked to preface each quartet they would be playing with a brief introduction, and audiences always seemed to appreciate the information and insights she imparted with such enthusiasm. This evening's program would be chronological, beginning with Franz Joseph Haydn's string quartet Opus 77, Number 1 in G major, written when he was an old man but surprisingly sprightly. Its opening Allegro moderato was cheerful, the following Adagio, stately and thoughtful, and the last two movements, Menuetto and Finale, both presto and satisfying to play, with plenty for her cello to do. On Egga's cue, the first violinist would play the opening measures of each movement for the audience. This sort of brief motivic preparation seemed to be really liked by audiences.

Egga had something special to add, however, in the case of Haydn although she was not going to mention it until the next two quartets had been played, as the information might spook the audience.

The second number would be Mozart's String Quartet, Number 15, in D minor, Köchel Number 421 with four movements: Allegro moderato, Andante, Menuetto and Trio, Allegretto. The minuet in triple time was delightfully lively and Egga wanted to be sure to prepare the audience for its vivaciousness.

Proceeding chronologically, the third number played would be the familiar music from Beethoven's middle period, Opus 59, No 2 in E minor, the sublime second of his famous "Razumovsky" cycle of three quartets. After this beautiful selection was concluded, then would come the moment Egga would switch from the lofty to the *cryptic* and tell the audience about what had happened to the corpses of both Haydn and Beethoven soon after their deaths.

In the interests of verifying the presence of a "musical genius bump," said by phrenologists—so-called skull readers—to protrude above the eye, Haydn's head was severed and stolen for examination a few days after his burial. The skull eventually passed into the hands of Vienna's famed professor of anatomical pathology, Karl von Rokitansky, and from there to the Vienna Society of the Friends of Music. Haydn's head was not rejoined with his body until 145 years after his death.

As for Beethoven, who died in 1827, the theft of several large pieces of his skull was discovered in 1888 when he and Franz Schubert, who had died one year after Beethoven, were moved to Vienna's famous Central Cemetery. It was thought that Beethoven's physician friend Gerhard von Breuning was the culprit in this case, as both Beethoven's and Schubert's bodies had been temporarily above ground in 1863 in order to be reburied in more secure coffins as a protection against grave robbers. It was then that von Breuning, left alone with the body for nine hours, apparently broke off souvenir fragments of the composer's skull, fragments now at the American Beethoven Center in San Jose, California, where several strands of Beethoven's hair have been demonstrated by DNA testing to be a match.

Egga would summarize the gruesome events as speedily as possible. She knew from past experience, that after such information, the audience would be more than happy to give its full attention to the final piece of the evening, the First String Quartet by the twentieth-century Czech composer Erwin Schulhoff. Egga would go over the facts quickly in order to point out to the audience the elements that made up the cheerful string quartet they were about to hear: neoclassical structures mixed with dance rhythms from around the world and dominated by a jazzy edginess. In the past, performances of Schulhoff's vital music, after the triple dose of Haydn, Mozart, and Beethoven, had assured a successful concert and Egga was hoping it would be so in critical Vienna as well. Goodness knows the *Streicher Vier* had certainly practiced hard enough today!

41

Karl Lueger realized he did not have to wait until the wee hours of the night to post multiple copies of the document he had prepared and printed that afternoon. When he strolled down from his parents' large apartment on the Felderstrasse and over to the University's nearby original building around four o'clock to check things out in the lunchroom he found it completely empty. Ah! Good that he had brought his handbills with him. Quickly he affixed one to the center of the crowded notice board, then taped others on the top of each of the tables in the room. The whole procedure took under seven minutes. Dare he distribute others?

He walked over to the Great Reading Room. A few people were seated at several tables, bent over books and laptops. He pretended to be reading the various announcements on the poster board at the entrance. Most were about apartments for rent. Karl looked around and surveyed the room. All heads were down. No one was seated near him. Quickly he pinned up one of his bulletins and left the room. What a nice bit of luck!

He was proud of the eye-catching jagged layout he had conceived for his little posters. In thick black font on white they read:

ATTENTION STUDENTS!
ARE YOU SITTING NEXT TO A JEW?
DID YOU KNOW FREUD STUDIED THE
SEXUAL ORGANS OF EELS HERE?
JEWS CONTINUE TO SLIME OUR CULTURE.
DO SOMETHING ABOUT IT!

Thrilled at having used up his broadsheets, Karl left the old Renaissance-style building by way of the newly rearranged aula for which, over a century ago, Gustav Klimt's allegorical "university panels" had been commissioned, then harshly rejected as "pornography" by the professors. He walked over to the nearby Rathaus Park and sat down on a bench facing the Ernst Mach memorial white marble bust.

What else could he accomplish today?

42

Megan was the first to arrive at the historic Café Museum on the corner of the Friedrichstrasse and the Operngasse, just a stone's throw from the Secession where she had been that morning. She took the first booth on the left of the entry door and ordered a cappuccino. This was the café where, at the beginning of the last century, writers and artists regularly gathered to read the daily papers, talk, and trade ideas. The list of notables was long. Among authors: Peter Altenberg, the feuilletonist, Karl Kraus, cantankerous editor of an even more cantankerous magazine, *Die Fackel*, the poet Georg Trakl, who, aghast at the body count in the first year of World War I, committed suicide with an overdose of cocaine, and Franz Werfel, author of *The Song of Bernadette*. Composers as different as Franz Lehar and Alban Berg were regular habitués and among artists there numbered Gustav Klimt, Oskar Kokoschka, and Egon Schiele.

Quite a café. Megan looked around appreciatively. A moment later the tall figure of Erich Decker entered and she called out to him.

"Up here by the *door*?" he asked in surprise.

"Why not. It's a least favorite place to sit so we won't have neighbors who might overhear us."

"Ah, a shady character you are to the end, aren't you, Megan!" He sat down opposite her, with a view of both rooms in the L-shaped café and signaled a waiter. He too ordered a cappuccino and drank a sip with relish.

"Now, let's pool our information and see what we have," he said, rubbing his hands.

"Well, you know now that I was in the very next room, the Klimt selfie room, when the stink bomb exploded and one painting was vandalized."

"You were very close to the action then."

"Close, but not close enough to see the person who did these things."

"Do you think that person tried to flee by returning to the entry room to the galleries, or that he ran through the Klimt selfie room and past you?"

"Oh, I have no idea. People were running every which way. I think a few people were able to dash out of the building before the museum personnel closed the doors. But one of the tourists who ran past me in the direction of the Schiele room...well, I think I have seen him before. He half tripped in front of me and when I saw the top of his head—it had a perfectly circular bald spot—I thought I'd seen him before. He looked familiar to me somehow."

"He looked familiar to you. And how long have you been in Vienna this time?"

"I arrived early morning yesterday."

"All right, let's trace your movements and try to find out where you might have seen him. Where did you go yesterday, starting from after you checked into your hotel?"

Megan was a little embarrassed.

"I'll have to admit that I spent almost the entire morning catching up on sleep. Didn't even go downstairs for breakfast."

"And when you finally got up and about?"

"I walked over to the Zumbusch Beethoven monument to take some closeup photos for my Vienna publisher. He's bringing out my book on the composer in German so I wanted some fresh shots taken from different angles."

"And no one attracted your attention while you were there?"

"Can't think anyone did. But then I was focusing—literally—on the Beethoven statue."

"Where did you go when you finished there?"

"I walked back along the Ring toward the Karlskirche and stopped at the Brahms monument in the park next to it. Took more photos, even a selfie. Didn't see anyone close up; just passing tourists."

"After that?" Erich prompted.

"Then I spent the rest of the afternoon in the Wien Museum just behind it. You know, Erich, in my day it was called the Historisches Museum der Stadt Wien. I'm really sorry they changed the name. There's a vast Otto Wagner exhibition on right now, have you seen it?"

"He's my favorite architect of old Vienna, but I haven't had time to see the show yet."

"Oh, do please try to see it. Um, after I saw the exhibit, and again, I didn't see anyone who stands out in my memory, I walked back to the Römischer Kaiser to meet my former student for dinner. You met her last night at the Café Mozart. Egga Streicher, the cellist."

"Oh, yes. A lovely person. And she is concertizing this evening, yes?"

"Correct. Well, after we had dinner down the street at Salieri's—didn't notice anyone I'd remember there—we went to *Fidelio*."

"All right. What about at the opera house then? Certainly lots of people there. Where were you sitting?"

"We had orchestra seats, about half way down. So we had a good view of the stage and of some of the orchestra players. Mainly the string basses and percussion and brass."

"And then you were there when we interviewed them. Anyone already familiar to you at that time?"

"No, I would have said so right then and there. But this man, the one who tripped in front of me at the Belvedere, just stays in my mind. Now, what do you have for me?"

"We have a promising suspect. Someone from the orchestra. Someone who didn't return for the second act."

"Well, that certainly sounds suspicious!"

"It is, and he was reported to us very late last night; I've been following up on it today."

"So who is it?"

"The contrabass trombonist. A man by the name of Ottokar Weininger."

"Any relation to Otto Weininger?" Megan laughed.

"Who's that?"

"Shame on you, Erich. You live right here in Vienna and don't know who Otto Weininger was?"

"Enlighten me."

"He was a wacky young man who wrote an even wackier book about sex back in nineteen-o-three, then a few months later committed a dramatic suicide in the very house where Beethoven died. He became quite a cult figure. For instance, as a Jew he exerted quite an influence on the thinking of Sigmund Freud, Franz Kafka, and even James Joyce, with his "Leopold Bloom" character in *Ulysses*. And as a homosexual Jew, Weininger's writings impacted Ludwig Wittgenstein who was also Jewish and gay."

"Hold on, hold on, Megan! You're going too fast for me. Who the heck is Ludwig Wittgenstein?"

"The philosopher? That would take me an hour to tell more, but I bet you do know about the *family* Wittgenstein. They were among the wealthiest families in Europe at the turn of the last century. The father, Karl, was a steel industrialist. He owned a palais, practically next door to the Karlskirche, and held musical soirees to which Gustav Mahler was a frequent guest."

"After last night's explosion I've heard of Gustav Mahler at least," Erich smiled helplessly at Megan. His hobbies were archaeology and art history, not music.

"Well, three of Karl's sons committed suicide, and two achieved fame. Ludwig, as a philosopher, ending up at Cambridge, and Paul, who lost his right arm in World War One, as a concert pianist playing concertos and fantasias for the left hand specifically written for him by the likes of Richard Strauss, Maurice Ravel, Sergei Prokofiev, Erich Korngold, and Paul Hindemith, to name the best known."

"I'm sorry to say that other than Strauss and Ravel, none of those other names are known to me." Erich was uncomfortably feeling out of his element and in her enthusiasm, Megan had only now noticed.

"Here's something I am sure you know, Erich. You are familiar with the Bulgarian Embassy and its cultural department's modernist building on the Kundmangasse?"

"Oh! Yes, yes. The Haus Wittgenstein! It's very bare, no ornaments, not even window frames, just three floors of white cubes. Yes. And?"

"All right. Back in the twenties Ludwig Wittgenstein was asked by his sister Margaret, who was having the house built, to assist, and he applied his minimalist philosophy to the details, like door handles and window catches."

"Ha! I never associated the name with anything else. Thanks for the lesson, *Frau Professor Doktor!*"

"I truly didn't mean to give one. Let's return to your contrabass trombone player whose name ignited my lecture. Ottokar Wittgenstein."

"Since the family was so musical, maybe he is, in fact, related to *the* Wittgensteins."

"Do you have a photo of the man?"

"I now have publicity photos of every member of the orchestra," Erich said with gusto, pulling an iPad out of his slim briefcase. He raised the lid and within seconds produced a photograph which he enlarged to fill the screen. It showed the orchestra's brass section standing with their instruments lowered at their sides or held across their bodies and smiling for a group shot. Wittgenstein was standing in the back row next to the tuba player.

Megan spotted the huge instrument before she saw the owner. She concentrated on the man's face as hard as possible. And she checked out the faces of the other male brass players. There was only one female in the group and she stood with the French horn players. Megan wished as hard as she could that Wittgenstein's features were familiar. But they were not.

"I wish I could say this is the man I saw when he tripped in front of me, but no bells are ringing. If only I could see the top of his head in this photo. But you can't see that in this photo."

"But when you were in your orchestra seat, with a good view of the musicians in the pit, could you see the top of his head from there, perhaps?"

"No. I do remember that a man who wasn't playing an instrument was seated in the pit behind the active trombonists during Act One. I remember briefly wondering about that, but nothing more. I'm so sorry."

"There's nothing to be sorry for. We will find him. We have his home address. And we now have his instrument case. In fact he was here late this morning briefly. The pit manager told us he came by to pick it up and seemed genuinely surprised when she accused him of trying to play a joke on his fellow musicians by filling it with bricks."

"Oh, wow. How can any of us forget that noisy surprise when those red bricks crashed to the floor!"

"Right. We have lifted several sets of prints off the case now. We can confidently presume that one set belongs to Weininger. The others to the pit manager and two of my officers as they tried to open the locked case. We're also getting the prints of all the orchestra members but that's taking time and is mainly just for the record. Another thing that's taking time, if it's not a false lead altogether, is tracing the person who put that ad in the paper offering to buy the 'missing Rodin bust of Mahler removed from the opera house.'"

"Someone actually *advertised* for it?"

"Well, the ad was paid for in cash and in person and no one can provide a description. There was an email address listed in the ad but by the time we got to it, with everything else going on, it had been removed from the Internet without a trace. Extremely discouraging. What I've done now is to instruct all personnel citywide to be on the alert for any communication referencing the words 'Rodin, Mahler, or, of course, bust.'"

"Do you think the attacks of last night and today are connected?"

"It would seem so. But we are also entertaining the thought that the second attack might be a copy-cat."

"Oh boy, that's all you need!"

"Exactly. With that in mind I've drawn up a list of what performances are scheduled for tonight and for the week ahead. Performances and other events, say like art exhibitions, that might feature Jewish persons or themes."

"Of course. That makes so much sense." Megan looked at Erich.

"So what have you come up with for tonight?"

"*Ach.* You'd be surprised how many events could be classified as candidates for anti-Semitic attacks. For example this evening at the Burgtheater they are presenting Lessing's play *Nathan der Weise.*"

Megan smiled. She had studied Gotthold Ephraim Lessing's famous morality play *Nathan the Wise* at Barnard College and had seen it twice at the Burgtheater on the Ring. The play, written in 1783, was set in Jerusalem during a brief lull in the Third Crusade. Saladin, the Muslim, asks the wise Jewish merchant Nathan, which of the three religions, Islam, Judaism, or Christianity, is the one true religion. Nathan answers with his famous "ring parable." Using one original and two perfect copies of his greatly treasured opal ring, a father bequeaths each of his three sons with an identical ring, signifying that rather than choosing a single faith, religious tolerance of all three faiths is the solution.

"It's sort of an update of the call for tolerance in Shylock's great speech in *The Merchant of Venice*."

Erich nodded in recognition. Megan quoted the first two famous Shakespearean sentences.

"Hath not a Jew eyes? Hath not a Jew hands, organs, dimensions?"

"Terrific," Eric said. "But getting back to Lessing's 'tolerance' play."

"Yes, that piece of drama could certainly be a target for our fanatic," agreed Megan.

"And then there's the opera house itself. They're doing *The Magic Flute* tonight but *Fidelio* will be given there again tomorrow evening. No guest conductor, however. The regular conductor Gabor Alexander will be in the pit."

"So again we'd have the same combination we did last night," Megan said.

"What do you mean?"

"At least three Jews are associated with the opera performance: this season's set designer Scotter Cantrell, the Italian tenor Aldo Finzi-Contiti, and now the resident conductor, Gabor Alexander."

"I thought Alexander was a Scottish name," Erich said, puzzled.

"It is indeed, but it has also long been adopted as a Jewish surname."

"How do you know so much about Jewish things, Megan?"

"I suppose because I've never gotten over the concentration camp holocaust of World War Two, and I admire the talent and work of so many Jewish writers, artists, and composers. Plus my first two lovers in and after college were Jewish. And my father never knew who *his* father was, so maybe I've got some Jewish blood in me. I would like that."

"*Himmel!* That's some explanation, Megan. All right. Getting back to what's on tomorrow night at the opera house then, I've already assigned a number of guards to be on hand as early as six o'clock. I'll also have extra guards on duty this evening as it's possible that Jewish members of the orchestra might be the objects of attack." Megan nodded and Erich looked at the list he had drawn up.

"Tomorrow evening's event at the Musikverein with the Vienna Philharmonic is just asking for Jew-haters. They're performing . . . "

". . . Mahler's Second Symphony. Yes, Egga and I have tickets for it!"

"All the more reason for my posting men in and around the concert house!"

"Good. And of course you're keeping an eye on the Jewish Museums."

"You bet we are. Both sites." Erich looked at his list again.

"Now here's a target just asking to be hit: at the Volksoper three evenings from now they'll be performing Jacques Offenbach."

"Yes? Which operetta? He composed nearly a hundred."

"Oh. I just know it's *The Tales of Hofmann*."

"Ah. That was his one and only opera. He wrote it at the end of his life and it was left partially unfinished. The barcarole is so gorgeous, I'm sure you know it." Megan hummed it for Erich and he nodded in happy recognition. She decided to tell him a bit more about the prolific composer.

"Offenbach was the son of a synagogue cantor in Cologne but by the time he was fourteen the Paris Conservatoire accepted him as a student. He became a virtuoso cellist and a conductor, but his great love was composing light opera—operettas—most of them rather bawdy."

"Interesting, Megan, but back to business, we are definitely posting police at the Volksoper. Now that's all I could find for the week for high society type performances, but here's what I noticed is playing at the Flex all week: the indie-electro group *BustMyEars* from Tel Aviv. They could be in danger."

"What is 'indie'"?

"Huh? Oh, it's short for 'independent.' You know, independent of established recording labels; you know, self-produced." Erich looked at Megan in amusement. She might know a lot about classical music but she certainly seemed lacking in the contemporary pop arena.

"And what's 'the Flex'"?

"Come on now. You don't know what the Flex is? It's a club that's been around since the nineteen-eighties: live music for the nightlife scene. You really ought to expand your horizons, dear Megan, and visit the place. It's at Augartenbrücke number one, *but* you won't see it when you get there. It's inside a huge, unused tunnel under the Danube, and you can *hear* the Flex long before you see it. Plus, they serve bottles of sparkling water for free to the perspiring dancing public. You ought to experience it, Megan. Broaden your horizons."

"Or shrink them, if it's located inside a tunnel. Anyhow, you're so right about posting people there if a group from Israel is performing. And you say all week?"

"Yes, all week."

"Well then, maybe I can fit it in," Megan fibbed sweetly. In her multifaceted career she had participated in the folk music scene when in her twenties in San Francisco, but acoustic guitar, not electric, was as far as she was prepared to go.

Erich's cellphone rang, bringing Megan out of her reverie.

"Just now?" Erich asked. His face looked grim. He listened a few more seconds then hung up. His face was livid.

"Megan, the statue of Sigmund Freud at MedUni has just been spray painted."

43

Stefan Schwartz was stunned. He could not believe what had just happened. At afternoon rehearsal the day after the Mahler Bomber, conductor Gabor Alexander *had asked him to lend his cello to Jared Bogenstein*! This in front of the entire pit orchestra. That old husk of a cello player had dared come to rehearsal and take his chair as principal cellist. The man just sat there. Without a cello. And now here was Gabor Alexander, the orchestra's resident conductor, commanding that he, the second principal, hand over his precious instrument to an alcoholic!

Obviously there were two choices. To give in to the conductor's very public request or to refuse. Stefan could feel a vein in his forehead twitch. Silence. Everyone in the orchestra was looking at him. What should he do? What could he do?

Ashamed, and furious with himself, he opted for the second choice, lifted his cello and gently handed it over to Bogenstein. A murmur filled the pit. Was it approval or disapproval?

Stefan would never know. Just as Bogenstein reached out for the instrument a massive heart attack took his life.

44

¶It was five o'clock. Rita Rausch was among the first reporters to arrive at the campus of Vienna's Medical University on Spitalgasse 23. Separate from the old University on the Ringstrasse, the new "MedUni" was an unequal U-shaped conglomerate of seven structures grouped around a large outdoor area. Not knowing where the newly installed Freud sculpture was, Rita, like her fellow reporters, began searching the campus grounds. Dotted here and there were homages to famous physicians of the past such as Ignaz Semmelweis, the Hungarian doctor who realized in 1847 that the occurrence of puerperal fever in mothers giving birth could be dramatically reduced by the simple implementation of hand washing in maternity wards. Many physicians had gone straight from autopsies to the maternity ward with only a wiping of the hands. Semmelweis's idea was considered extreme and ridiculed. He was dismissed from the university hospital and after years of trying to convince his colleagues of the importance of cleanliness, he was committed to a mental asylum where he died without seeing his common-sense appeal answered. His plea for antiseptic procedures was only recognized after Louis Pasteur demonstrated the germ theory of disease in the early 1860s. Only then did Semmelweis's antiseptic hand washing policy become universal in hospitals.

Rita, very familiar with the "savior of mothers" Semmelweis story, was happy to see the acknowledgement tablet installed on a large white half column. But where was the new bronze Freud statue? She knew that it had originally been cast in Vienna in 1936 and that Freud's great grandson was there for the 2018 unveiling and that he had said on the public occasion: "Welcome back to Vienna, great grandfather." And she had read the memorable homage paid to Freud at that time: "Mozart and Freud are the most famous Austrians in the world and Berggasse 19, Freud's address in Vienna, the most famous address in the world." What a good lead this would be for the article she intended to write.

Rita walked around the corner of one of the nearer white buildings where the Rectorate office was located and came upon three policemen and several university officials. They were standing around Oscar Nemon's larger-than-life-bronze statue of the founder of psychoanalysis. He was sitting in the characteristic pose she had seen in photographs: legs slightly apart, torso leaning forward receptively, and elbows out with hands at waist level. The head was amazingly true to life, the eyes were in shadow, the nose prominent, and the forehead balding.

Only now the statue was streaked from head to foot with red spray paint.

Outrageous! What sort of deranged individual could have done this? And why was it only discovered late this afternoon? Considering how many people were on campus at all times of the day and night, how come nobody had noticed? The answer, she reasoned with herself, was that the defacement must have happened within the last thirty minutes or so. Most classes were over. Maybe a schoolyard prank? But this was a school of medicine, not a grammar school.

One of the policemen looked at Rita and smiled in recognition. He waved her over to him.

"Hey, Rita! Here's something for your newspaper. Look at this." He held out a legal-size sheet of paper so she could see the message printed on it:

ATTENTION STUDENTS!
ARE SOME OF YOUR FELLOW STUDENTS JEWS?
DID YOU KNOW SIGMUND FREUD ESPOUSED HIS CRAZY SEXUAL THEORIES AT THE VIENNA MEDICAL SCHOOL?
JEWS CONTINUE TO INFECT OUR CULTURE.
DO SOMETHING ABOUT IT!
I HAVE!
I AM THE MAHLER BOMBER!

"That is really sicko," Rita declared, raising her cellphone to take a shot of the offensive note.

"You're damn right it is," said the officer.

"Where was the note? Stuck to the statue's lap or something?"

"Oh, no. It wasn't over here at all. It was around to the back there. See that big group of people and police?

"I do now, what are they doing? Why are they over there and not here?"

"Because that's where the victim was found. About twenty minutes ago someone—a man—phoned in a report that a woman was lying just behind the Rectorate unconscious and with blood oozing from her forehead. So all attention was focused on her before we fanned out looking for the perpetrator and found what someone had done to the Freud statue."

"Was the woman able to describe her attacker?"

"Yes. She said he was young and skinny, with long black hair tied in a knot. And he had pronounced sideburns, she recalled."

"So knocking out the poor woman was the diversion, called in by the perpetrator himself, that allowed for the few moments it took to spray the Freud statue?"

"Sure looks that way. And this hate note claiming to be the Mahler Bomber was under the poor woman's head. Rita took a few more photographs. What an outburst of spite, of ethnic hatred!

That wacky Tonik Nektar was not so daft after all when he proclaimed to her this morning that he would not be surprised if there weren't another anti-Semitic attack today. There had been. Three. At the University, at the Belvedere, and now here at MedUni. Who the hell was the Mahler Bomber?

45

Erich and Megan had quickly parted company at the Café Museum when word of the Freud statue's defacement came in—he to the scene of the crime and she to the Wienerwald defacement where Egga was by now probably cooling her heels. They had agreed on five o'clock.

The popular restaurant on the Annagasse was already quite full but Megan spotted Egga sitting at their favorite table in the corner to the far right of the entrance.

"Sorry to be a bit late, dearie. Police events intervened."

"Not to worry. I already ordered for both of us. Wienerschnitzel with extra lemon, right?" Megan laughed her approval.

"How has your day been?" Egga asked.

"To say the least, it's been a very full day."

Megan brought her friend up to date as they attacked their schnitzels which were brought to them almost immediately. Egga could only shake her head in wonderment at Megan's story and she was worried that Megan could have been in actual danger at the Belvedere.

They skipped dessert and made a quick visit to their hotel room to pick up Egga's cello before walking over to the Kärntner Ring and down to the three-story Musikverein building that stood proudly within sight of the Karlskirche.

"Just picture Brahms walking from his apartment on the other side of the Karlskirche, then passing directly in front of the church to the Musikverein where he conducted the *Singverein* for so long. It's really appropriate that the room your quartet is going to play in is called the Brahms Room."

"And do you know, Megan, who the first person was to play in the newly created little auditorium back in eighteen-seventy? Before it was called the Brahms-Saal?"

"Well, I presume it was Brahms, wasn't it?"

"Ha ha! Now the student can teach the teacher," Egga declared with glee. She enlightened her former professor.

"Of course Brahms played there many times but he made sure that the very first musician to perform there was his dearest friend Clara Schumann. And as usual, she wowed the audience."

"Oh, I love that!"

"Did you know she was the first pianist who performed publicly from memory rather than with the music in front of her?"

"Yes, I did know that, Megan, and I know she was a composer as well and that she wrote chamber music, and songs, and solo piano pieces, and even a piano concerto."

"I didn't know about the piano concerto!" Megan loved learning new things.

"Yes. I actually heard it performed once in Berlin. I remember thinking it sounded a bit like Liszt, and you know she grew to detest him, along with Wagner. But she was only fourteen when she composed that concerto, so one has to go easy on her there."

"Tell me, Egga, do you think she and Brahms were ever sexually intimate after her husband's death?"

Megan was referring to the tragedy of Clara's troubled composer husband Robert Schumann, who, after attempting suicide, had been confined to an asylum for the final two years of his life. He died in 1854 and, despite being the mother of eight children, Clara managed to give hundreds of piano concerts for the rest of her long life, occasionally with Brahms, more frequently with their common friend, the violin virtuoso Joseph Joachim.

"If they were sexually intimate, you ask? I most certainly do *not* think so!" Egga was surprised by her own adamancy. "Clara was fourteen years older than he, and she and Robert both welcomed him into their Düsseldorf home as the young genius he was. That's not to say that Brahms didn't love Clara deeply and devotedly. But I really don't believe there was ever anything sexual between them. Do you, Megan?"

"No. I don't either. Too many children on the scene for one thing. No, they were loving friends and mutual supports, but most likely never lovers."

"You know they died within a year of each other; she, as the result of a debilitating stroke, at the great old age in those days of seventy-six in eighteen-ninety-six. He, just one year later."

"I'd forgotten the exact dates," answered Megan, "but I do know that in his grief at his impending loss of her—she lived two more months after her stroke—he composed the *Vier ernste Gesänge—Four Serious Songs*. Now, turn-about is fair play: I bet *you* didn't know that Brahms dedicated those songs not to Clara but to the Leipzig artist Max Klinger."

"You mean the sculptor Max Klinger who did the *Beethoven Enthroned* statue that was shown at the Secession along with Klimt's Beethoven Frieze? But Brahms died in eighteen-ninety-seven. He couldn't have known about that statue."

"Correct. But Klinger wasn't only a sculptor, he was a graphic artist of amazing, fantastic imagery. Imagery which would later be admired by the Dadaists. And he dedicated a fantasy series of engravings to Brahms in admiration for his music. That began a friendship by correspondence and is what sparked Brahms's dedication of the *Four Serious Songs* to Klinger."

As they walked Megan glanced at Egga, who by now must be in her late forties, valiantly lugging her cello case with its precious contents and decided to distract her by reading to her exactly what Brahms had written to Klinger upon receiving the bound volume gift of engravings. She searched for the letter on her iPhone, brought it up and, balancing herself lest she stumble by putting her left hand lightly on Egga's shoulder, read out loud from the phone's screen to her as they walked down the Bösendorferstraße:

I can see the music...without my knowing it, your drawings transport me; as I contemplate them, it seems the music continues to resonate in the infinite and thus expresses all I meant, more clearly than music alone could and at the same time with the same amount of mystery and anticipation. Sometimes I envy you the power of being so clear with your pen. Sometimes I feel happy that I am not. But finally I must think that any art is the same and expresses itself through the same language.

They had almost reached the imposing three-story, red and white Musikverein building. It was the work of the Danish architect Theophil Hansen, who designed the interiors of the two original concert auditoriums in beautiful Greek revival style: the "golden" larger, two-story concert hall with its magnificent organ—first played upon by Anton Bruckner in 1937—and the smaller, more intimate one where Egga would be performing. The acoustics of both halls were the envy of the music world both then and now. Egga and her quartet members were appropriately thrilled to be playing there.

The smaller chamber music auditorium, known as the Brahms Room since 1937, could seat up to 600 and still maintain the intimate character of chamber music. Four other performing rooms had been added to the basement in modern times and they were known in descending capacity size as the glass, metal, stone, and wood rooms. Ordinarily, Egga's quartet would have been scheduled for one of these smaller chambers, but with the release of the *Streicher Vier's* second CD, which had received resplendent reviews, the Brahms-Saal had been offered to the group.

A bit breathless, but still with plenty of time, Megan and Egga entered a side door of the building and made their way to the Brahms-Saal.

It promised to be a beautiful concert, with music "resonating in the infinite" as Brahms would have said.

46

The moment that rehearsal was over Stefan tried to find his sister. She should be in the women's repertory tailoring department in the back of the building, but she was nowhere to be seen. Her fellow workers said she had been in and out all day.

He tried phoning her and she picked up immediately.

"Adele! I need to talk to you. Where are you?"

"Oh, hi, Stefan. At the moment I'm on the Dorotheergasse walking back to the Opera. I've been at Doblinger's."

"At Doblinger's? Are you buying a musical instrument?"

"Ha! No. I was consulting with one of the clerks there. Tell you about it when we see each other. Are you still at the Opera?"

"Yeah. Let's get together. I have something amazing to tell you but I want to do it in person."

"And I have something to tell you, or rather, confess to you."

"You want me to come to the sewing room?"

"No. Let's meet somewhere else. I'm free until this evening's performance. How about Café Mozart?"

"Perfect. Outside or indoors?"

"Too hot to sit outside. Let's go inside, somewhere in the back if possible."

"Okay, Sis, see you there."

Ten minutes later brother and sister were seated in a corner table at the back of the famous café. They had both ordered refreshingly cold Berliner Weisse beer with raspberry syrup.

"Do you want to go first, or shall I?" Adele asked.

"I totally need to go first. Can hardly contain what I have to tell you and our parents," Stefan answered.

"*Himmel*! What?"

"Guess who dropped dead today at rehearsal?"

"The conductor?"

"Think again. Someone whose absence from the orchestra I, in particular, won't be missing."

"Oh my god! Not Jared Bogenstein?"

"Jared Bogenstein. Dropped dead of a heart attack. And just as he was about to play guess whose cello?"

"No idea."

"Mine! Can you believe this? Gabor Alexander had just asked me to lend *my* cello to idiot Bogenstein, who was sitting in his chair next to me, looking completely out of it and without an instrument. You know his cello got smashed when he crashed into it last night during *Fidelio*."

"No, I didn't know! But wait a second. You mean your conductor wanted you to let Bogenstein play *your* cello?"

"Right. I was tempted to stand up, take my cello, and leave the pit. But I thought better of it. And just as I started to hand it over, that's when Bogenstein keeled over dead."

"So will you be principal cellist now?" Adele smiled with excitement for her brother.

"That's still to be determined, damn it. Can you imagine that Alexander said he would hold auditions to replace Bogenstein? *Auditions*? And here I've worked myself up to second principal. Hell, I've earned the spot!"

"That's just not fair to you. Why on earth would Alexander even hesitate?" Adele was furious. All she had gone through, and for nothing?

"Why? Just think about it. Alexander is Jewish, Bogenstein is, *was* Jewish. Jews stick with Jews. And two of our section cellists are Jewish. It's only too obvious Alexander wants to give them a chance at principal chair. I am fucked!"

"Really, Stefan, you've got to be more positive. I'm sure things are going to turn out all right. You've got the talent and you've got the seniority." She looked at her brother adoringly—the child genius of the family.

"Maybe, maybe, but I can't help simmering. It's like some invisible hand has been dangling the position of principal cellist before me for years as bait. God knows I've worked my ass off to be worthy."

Adele massaged her brother's shoulder understandingly. She was so proud of him. And he had been so miserably, so unjustly treated. Her grand plan to help him in his career by sowing anti-Semitism with that note she left behind the Strauss bust in the Schwind Foyer had seemed to be working. In fact at Doblinger's she had heard of several incidents today ignited by Jew haters. Hate flyers around the University, a significant action at the Belvedere Museum, the location of Vienna's only other original cast of Mahler's bust, and then something on the campus of MedUni having to do with the defacing of that new horrible statue of a smug Sigmund Freud. She had a right to be proud. Singlehandedly, she had rekindled the enduring anti-Semitism that lay simmering in twenty-first century Vienna, just as it had in the past centuries. Let it lead where it may. All she wanted was justice for her genius brother.

"So what was it you wanted to tell me, Sis?" he asked.

To cheer her brother and show him her loyal support, Adele decided to share with him what she had done to forward his career. She recounted, step by step, her activities at the opera house in the middle of the night two evenings ago—planting a suspicious cellphone in the orchestra pit and substituting the opera house's original Rodin bust of Mahler with their father's treasured surmoulage into which she had packed the explosives and rigged cellphone. Yeah, she had learned how to do it online. Your Sis is a real techie! Then watching the live performance of *Fidelio* on television in her apartment that evening, and how she had waited for the keyword "*Klang*" in the second act, upon which she immediately detonated the Mahler surmoulage with her disposable cellphone.

"You did that for *me*, Adele?" Stefan was deeply touched. He was also amazed at his sister's bravery and ingenuity. He was moved to confess to her his own tampering in the orchestra pit. How he had, with precision and exquisite timing, pulled the wire that yanked Bogenstein's carpet strip out from underneath his cello endpin and sent man and instrument hurtling to the floor.

"Brilliant! You absolutely did the right thing, Stefan. I hope you don't feel any guilt. You know, like maybe that's what brought on the heart attack."

"Naw. He was an alcoholic and he'd lost control. He should have been retired years ago."

"You're right."

"So what were you doing at Doblinger's when I called you?"

"Ah, well, you know I gotta replace the surmoulage I secretly borrowed from Papa. He rarely goes up to his office now that his AS has made him so infirm, but still I have to sneak in a replacement before he finds out his treasure is missing. At Doblinger's. I was consulting with one of the salespersons to find out where they get their Rodin Mahler bust surmoulages of the Rodin Mahler bust from, and he was telling me about a bronze casting outfit in Tulln called *Kluger Guss* that owns a nineteen-twenty-six cast of what's called Model B. It has the 'fonderie Alexis Rudier' mark on the back of the neck. So it's from that legitimate cast that the Tulln foundry makes its surmoulages for Doblinger's. Perfectly legit."

"Good thinking! We sure don't want Papa to find out his precious Mahler bust is missing."

"Right, well, so I've called the firm and they've agreed, after much pleading on my part, to do a rush job. At an extra charge, of course. It'll be ready on Wednesday. It's gonna cost a fortune, but it's worth it."

"But how are you going to pay for it? I don't have much in my savings account but can I help?"

"It's totally okay. I have that covered. And on Thursday I'm selling the original Rodin bust I replaced with Papa's surmoulage with, to an anonymous buyer with big pockets. That money is going to Papa to pay for an operation he needs."

"*What*? Papa needs an operation? I know he's been quite fragile lately, but an operation?"

"Yeah, Mutti didn't want me to worry you about it and that's why she hasn't told you. But now Mahler's bust is coming to the rescue."

"What an awesome sister I have!"

"Desperate times call for desperate means, don't they say?"

"But won't you have to pay the fondeur *before* you sell the original bust?"

"*No problem if another plan I have works out.*"

47

Well, that was exhilarating! Young Karl Lueger had not stayed to watch the aftermath of his spraying of Sigi's statue. He knew the woman he punched in the face had gotten a good look at him before he knocked her to the ground. Best to get out of there. His new blue BMW motorcycle, hidden behind some sort of memorial to an Ignaz Semmelweis, was fast and silent.

This second adrenaline rush in one day was addictive. It was only six o'clock in the evening. Still plenty of time to do a little more mischief. Attract others to his cause. His thoughts turned back to the Mahler Bomber, as the newspapers and TV had called him. What about Gustav Mahler's gravesite? Where the hell was it anyhow? Karl looked it up on his cellphone. Ah ha! The cemetery in Grinzing. Out northeast in the Vienna Woods. And this month the cemetery was open nights until seven. Perfect. Karl revved up his bike and sped out to the Grinzinger Friedhof.

He still had one can of red spray paint.

48

From her front row seat in the Brahms-Saal Mary Neff signaled to Megan as she entered the auditorium. Egga had already gone backstage to join the other members of the quartet and tune up. There were still about fifteen minutes before the concert began.

"Good that you saved me a seat," Megan said as she joined Mary. "Thank you!" She looked around at the audience that was still pouring into the hall. "Who would have thought the auditorium would fill up so quickly!"

"I think any concert in the Brahms-Saal is guaranteed a full house. There are so many fans of classical music here in Vienna."

"Well, it's been quite a packed twenty-four hours since I last saw you," Megan said, stretching out her hands and feet and rotating her shoulders. She filled Mary in on the dramatic events of the day and they speculated on who the Mahler Bomber might be. Was he the same person who had planted the explosive at the opera house or was this a copycat incident? The Opera explosion had been given so much publicity that anything was possible now.

A hush fell upon the hall as the *Streicher Vier* entered from stage right with their instruments. The first violinist was Diane Radycki, a slightly-built brunette in her mid-forties with a winning smile. Behind her, also beaming at the audience, was the second violinist, Eric Forman, as tall as Diane was short and about the same age, then followed the violist, Marta Möller, a youngish blonde with long hair in a bun, and finally Egga, who immediately spotted her friends in the front row and acknowledged them with a quick nod.

After the quartet had taken their seats, Egga stood up, holding her cello with her left hand, and faced the public. She said a few words about the Haydn quartet they were about to play, asked the second violinist to play the major themes, sat down, gracefully straddled her cello, and waited for the nod from the first violinist. Then they were off and running. They played exquisitely and the audience was with them every note.

The same procedure occurred with the Mozart and Beethoven quartets, prefaced with Egga's short commentary and thematic exposition. The audience was immensely appreciative and applause, particularly after the Beethoven quartet, was loud and long.

Then, before the Schulhoff piece began, Egga stood up again and briefly recounted the gruesome stories of what happened to the bodies of Haydn and Beethoven after their deaths. The audience was appropriately surprised and shocked and now in the mood to listen to the Schulhoff quartet. It began with a savage *Presto con fuoco*. About forty bars into the piece, suddenly loud shouts were heard from the back of the auditorium. The audience wheeled around to see what was going on and the quartet stopped playing.

Two young men were yelling their heads off, shouting the threatening refrain "*No Jewish music in Vienna, no Jewish music in Vienna!*" Then, as quickly as they appeared, they disappeared.

There was a stunned silence. Egga stood up again and shouted with all her might: "*Yes, Jewish music in Vienna, yes, Jewish music in Vienna!*" Almost immediately the audience joined in and soon the entire hall was chanting fervently along with her. Without any prompting other than their own feeling of outrage, everyone in the room was standing up and applauding.

Egga nodded to the other players and they sat back down again, their bows poised to play. Immediately silence prevailed and the enthusiastic listeners took their seats again, many leaning forward to hear the first notes of what Erwin Schulhoff had to offer.

Only one audience member was missing.

Megan had left the hall.

49

Some forty minutes before the ruckus at the Musikverein, Karl Lueger had reached his goal out in the city's nineteenth district, the Grinzing Cemetery. Historically Grinzing had been one of the most popular Viennese places to live and to die. Consulting his web browser again, the would-be vandalizer marveled at the list of famous people aside from Gustav Mahler who were buried there. Gustav Klimt, whose last studio in the Feldmühlgasse was nearby, his fellow Secession artist Koloman Moser, and their mutual friend the architect Otto Wagner were all there, and from the music world, there was Alban Berg's grave. The next listing was a surprise: the Austrian fascist Chancellor Engelbert Dollfuss. Karl would have liked to take an admiring look at that assassinated politician's grave, but he needed to get down to business.

He pulled up a map of the cemetery, memorized the layout, revved up his cycle, turned left at the entrance, and rode to the middle section where Mahler's grave was. Hmm. Hard to miss. It was a simple gray cement triple plinth about eight feet high and surrounded by a verdant tall hedge. Thick lettering spelled out "Gustav Mahler" at the top in the center. No dates, no identification, just the name. As if everyone was supposed to know who he was! This was going to be super easy. Karl slowly drove his cycle between the two short entry hedges right up to the front of the monument. Aiming his spray can up toward the composer's name he squirted red paint on it in a circular motion. The name was completely obliterated. Nice.

Any other Jew tombstones around? The map on his cellphone showed a grave nearby for an "Alma Mahler-Werfel." Let's have a go. It was a pebbly granite slab with just those three words on it, again no dates. Karl squirted a generous dose of red paint on the words, unaware of the fact that Alma Mahler was not Jewish. Now, should he get out of there? He looked at his watch: still ten minutes before the cemetery closed. He better not take a chance. Two minutes later he was roaring out of the cemetery gates.

His third rush of adrenaline was the best of all.

50

"I think I'm having a stroke," Haim gasped, suddenly feeling dizzy and hiccupping violently. Grabbing the kitchen counter, he sought to regain his balance, leaning against Harry who had turned pale with concern. They were in the middle of preparing dinner.

"Let's get you to the couch," Harry said.

"Yes, I'd like to sit down," Haim said weakly. He grabbed Harry's offered arm and together they took short steps until they reached the living room/studio and the black leather couch against the studio wall. Haim gratefully sank down and Harry sat next to him, stroking his forehead. Houdini had followed close behind and lay at their feet, whining and looking up inquisitively. This was not the dinner routine.

Haim continued to hiccup and shook his head violently "no" when Harry asked if he should pound his back. Between gasps for air Haim tried to bat Harry away. He needed to handle this by himself. There was simply no room for intervention; all he could do was concentrate on trying to contain the hiccups. Finally the hiccups relented and Haim leaned back on the couch, taking long deep breaths. Everything had looked blurry when he began to hiccup but that seemed momentary and had already cleared up. Still unable to speak, he patted Harry's arm reassuringly while still staring unseeing ahead.

Finally he was able to gasp out a few words.

"I don't know what happened to me. I was fine one second and then all of a sudden I felt dizzy and started these horrible hiccups. Do you think I've had a stroke?"

"I don't know, my darling. Do you still feel dizzy?"

"No. Not any longer."

"I'm going to look up your symptoms online. Hold on." Harry literally ran over to his desk, grabbed his laptop, and returned to the couch with it already open. Seconds later he was staring at so many entries on stroke symptoms that he was paralyzed for a few moments. He studied the different topics and chose the least alarming looking one. It was about transient ischemic attacks, known as TIA. He tapped the URL and read aloud what it had to say about them. He was damned if he were going to look up "heart attack" with Haim at his side.

"Oh, good," he said. "If you've had a TIA then the effects shouldn't last more than twenty-four hours. How do you feel now?"

"I already feel much better, just tired."

Haim smiled in relief. He truly was beginning to feel better. The hiccups had left him tired, that's all.

"All right. That's wonderful. But even so I'm going to phone Abdul." Abdul Hassan was their wonderful family physician. He would know whether or not they should worry about what had just happened. Harry didn't want to talk to him in front of Haim in case alarm showed on his face while conferring with the doctor. He stood up and said he'd have to go find his cellphone; he'd left it in their bedroom.

Haim seemed to be comfortable with that.

Actually, Harry had the cellphone in his back pocket but he made his way to the bedroom and closed the door before calling their doctor at his home number. It was a few minutes after seven and he should be home by now. A recording immediately answered.

"You have reached Dr. Abdul Hassan. I cannot answer the phone right now but please leave a message. If your call is urgent, dial one-four-four. Thank you."

"Abdul, it's Harry Howell. I hope you are at home and will pick up. I think Haim has just had either a mini stroke or an actual heart attack. Won't you please pick up?"

Abdul Hassan did pick up. It was his custom never to answer his home phone in person. But he certainly did for Harry Howell.

"Yes, Harry, I'm here. Tell me exactly what's happened."

After Harry's detailed account Abdul was mostly reassuring.

"It could be nothing. Quite possible. But it's also possible that it was a TIA. I'd like you to take him to the hospital now."

"*The hospital!*" Harry almost yelled.

"Yes. If he's indeed had a TIA, we want to prevent another one from occurring, don't we?"

Reluctantly Harry agreed.

"But are you saying we should go the hospital *tonight*?"

"Let's not take a chance that his symptoms could return during the night. Take him to the Allgemeines Krankenhaus right away, go to the emergency entrance, and give them my name to call."

"Hell! Okay. You're the doctor."

"Yes, Harry, I am. And you were right to call me. If they find something serious I will come in."

"Oh, thank you Abdul, thank you!"

Harry opened the bedroom door and returned to Haim, affecting a reassuring smile.

"Honey, Abdul thinks it's nothing, but he does want us to have things checked out at the Allgemeines."

"Oh, no! This evening? We haven't even eaten dinner." Haim was grabbing at straws.

"We're going. I'll get the car and you come down to the street in about five minutes. Okay?"

"Okay." Haim knew Harry was right.

Virginia Dupuy was the physician on duty at the hospital that evening and she couldn't have been more efficient or simpatica. She checked Haim's blood pressure—it was a bit, but not alarmingly, high—and his cholesterol and amino acid levels, also a tad up.

"I'll tell you what, Haim. Since you're in your early seventies, and we don't want you to worry unnecessarily, I'd like to perform a TTE, a transthoracic echocardiogram. I'll be using a transducer. It is not invasive. I won't be putting anything into your body. I'll just be moving the transducer slowly across your chest. It will emit sound waves that echo off of different parts of your heart and we'll get an ultrasound image right away. All right?"

The procedure took less time than either Haim or Harry imagined and Dr. Dupuy was reassuring about the results. Everything seemed normal and they were free to go home. She would of course phone Dr. Hassan, whom she knew and report to him. The only caveat she issued to the two receptive men was that if something similar happened again, they would come to the hospital emergency room immediately. No delays. Relieved, they promised to do so and Harry settled Haim in the waiting room while he went to get the car. Another ten minutes and they were home. Houdini could hardly contain his joy. Haim was temporarily relieved, but Harry could tell he was churning inside. He decided to distract him.

"Haim, dear. I haven't told you because I wanted it to be a surprise, but I have something arriving in two days that is going to lift your and my spirits immensely. A fabulous addition to our home and a magnificent fiftieth anniversary gift."

"How exciting! Tell me what it is, please."

"No, I've told you too much already. But it's something really worth living for."

"Of course I'm going to keep living!" Now it was Haim's turn to reassure Harry.

"I feel completely myself again." He spoke the truth. And he felt happiness that he was home again with Harry and Houdini and that Harry had a surprise for him in the form of something for their very special anniversary.

"Won't you at least give me a hint?"

"I can say that you should only play music within the time frame of Mendelssohn and Schönberg...."

51

Thank goodness Erich Decker had answered his phone.

"Erich! It's me, Megan. I'm after him!"

"After who?"

"You can't have heard about it yet but at Egga's concert just now there was an anti-Jew demonstration! Two young men with shaved heads came into the back of the auditorium just as Egga and her friends were about to play music by a Jewish composer. They started yelling: 'No Jewish music in Vienna' over and over again. We were all stupefied. Then they left as abruptly as they'd appeared. And Egga led the chant 'Yes Jewish music in Vienna, Yes Jewish music in Vienna' and the audience stood and began shouting it with her. It was terribly exciting." Megan paused to catch her breath. Then she continued.

"But I wanted to confront the culprits and so I ran to the back of the hall and out onto the street. They were both there, on the other side of the Musikvereinplatz, talking to an older man who seemed to be paying them! I saw him giving what looked like banknotes to them both. Then they ran off and the man started to walk over to the Karlskirche. I'm following him. Now he's stopped in front of the church. He's looking around very slowly. Ah! Now he's going inside"

"Megan, do not do anything rash. Just wait outside the church. I'll be there just as quick as I can. And I'll call backup."

"No, I'm going inside. You don't understand, Erich. I can't lose sight of him. He has a round bald spot at the back of his head. *I think he could be the man who tripped in front of me at the Belvedere!*"

52

Someone else had also left the Brahms-Saal following upon the heels of the shameful disruption. Tonik Nektar had attended the concert for the sole reason that the work of a Jewish composer was part of the program of the *Streicher Vier*, a music quartet from Berlin. He had been looking forward to the performance with pleasure for several weeks. Schulhoff would have been seven years old when Mahler died, but perhaps there would be some trace of him in Schulhoff's work. That would be marvelous! He had a good view of the players from his center seat midway down the center aisle.

And now some ruffians had dared disrupt things. Tonik could hardly believe he was hearing what they were shouting in tandem over and over: "No Jewish music in Vienna!" His first instinct was to leap up, run right at them, knock them down. But just as he stood up the two hoodlums quit the auditorium. The concert was going to recommence. Should he stay and hear the music of a composer he had never heard of, or should he try to run after the hooligans?

He decided on the latter and discreetly but quickly left the auditorium even though it meant having to slip past the people in his row of seats. Running out to the front of the Musikverein he looked wildly around. The thugs were nowhere to be seen. No, wait! There they were across on the Karlsplatz, talking to an older man. They were holding out their hands to him. What? Was he *paying* them? It sure looked that way. So that was it. Probably those dumb kids didn't even know why their interruption of the concert with their wild yelling would be so hurtful.

And now they were walking away from the man they had met. Should he follow them? Or should he track the man and accost him. Ask him what the hell he was doing with two hoodlums who had interrupted a concert? Yes, he would do that. He quickened his footsteps, crossed over, and fell in behind the man as he walked past the Brahms Memorial without giving it so much as a look. He strode past the Wien Museum but when he got to the Karlskirche he paused, looked at the huge, shallow oval pond in front of it briefly, seemed to be studying the image of the church reflected in it, and then entered the church.

Nektar stood outside facing the great baroque church with its elliptical dome framed by two tall columns with spiral reliefs. The man wouldn't be able to leave without his seeing him exit. Tonik's febrile imagination was working overtime. Was the fellow planning to do some damage to the church because Gustav married Alma there? Perhaps the appearance of the Mahler Bomber on the scene last night was just the first act of vandalism. He'd better go inside the church and make sure nothing suspicious was going on. But first he had an idea.

He would call Rita Rausch and summon her to what might be the scene of a crime. She would have the first scoop.

53

¶In her small apartment on the Resselgasse, not far from her parents' home on the Dorotheergasse that evening, Adele Schmidt was studying a map of Tulln on her computer. The small town was only about twenty-seven miles away. She should be able to drive to the brass foundry there in less than half an hour come Wednesday.

Finishing her dinner she carefully folded up the black burqa she had worn that afternoon to the American Bar. The man who so desperately wanted to buy her Mahler bust had no idea who she was or what she looked like. And she intended to keep it that way. Her boyfriend Nicki who worked as a sales manager out at the Prater had reserved one of the closed cabins on the

Riesenrad for her on the evening she requested.

Tomorrow she would get to work early at the *Damen Repertoireschneiderei* before the others in the costume department arrived. Early enough to open the big floor safe where the sumptuous costume jewelry worn by the opera singers was kept. They were gorgeous pieces and, unknown to all but one of the staff, one piece was genuine. Adele was that person and she had stumbled on the object quite by accident. At the back of the safe she had discovered a locked mahogany wood box about the size of her two hands laced together. It had been ignored for decades. But one day, working late, and replacing the jewelry worn that evening, curiosity overcame her and she removed the box. She tried prying the lock, but no luck. When she turned the box upside down to see if she could push it in somehow, she saw a small piece of paper glued to the underside. The ancient cursive script read: "Property of Madam Anna von Bahr-Mildenburg."

Mildenburg! That great dramatic soprano of Wagnerian roles who worked with Mahler at the opera house during his ten-year reign there. Whatever was in that box had to be seen. Adele wedged a screwdriver tip under the top of the box and picked up a small brass hammer. On the sixth blow the box top sprang open and Adele gasped. There, sparkling before her eyes, was a diamond tiara the likes of which she had never seen! The stones were obviously real and there must have been some sixty of them in varying sizes. The largest diamond was about the size of her little finger nail and was set in the middle of the tiara. What an impression that must have made on stage! The tiara's refracted points of light could be seen from the highest balcony. How was it that the tiara had been left in the safe? Mildenburg lived through two world wars, surviving the second one by only two years. Perhaps, at her advanced age and with all she'd been though, she no longer remembered the treasure left behind at the opera house. Adele had reverently replaced it in its box at the back of the safe. But who knew? Perhaps the time would come when she might need the income it could produce.

That time had come.

54

Megan had not waited for Erich Decker to arrive at the Karlskirche. First, as she had done so many times, she shot an angry glance beyond the church to the Technical University which in 1907 had replaced the apartment house at Karlsgasse 4 where Brahms had lived and died. Megan had once written an article on the items in his three-room apartment entitled "The Visual Brahms: Idols and Images," and she still resented the fact that, because of the demolition of the Karlsgasse building, there was no museum to Brahms in the city, only a room dedicated to him in Haydn's museum. Well, maybe that wasn't too bad, as Brahms adored Haydn's music and helped to keep it known.

All this went through Megan's head before she turned and silently entered the church dedicated to Saint Charles Borromeo built by the architect Fischer von Erlach in the early eighteenth century. A concert was in progress. Antonio Vivaldi. She knew that the transplanted Venetian's music was frequently played at the Karlskirche and that he had been buried next to the church in a pauper's grave. The exact whereabouts were unknown now. Actually, the baroque composer had pretty much been neglected after his death until various troves of his manuscripts showed up in the twentieth century and the Viennese-born violinist Fritz Kreisler began performing him in public.

The musicians were gathered in front of the high altar and the many listeners were sitting under the great elliptical dome. Megan was unable to spot her quarry in the crowd. But she had an idea as to where he might be: in one of the several side chapels. The church's ground plan was well known to her from her first stay in Vienna in the 1950s when she lived just across the street from the beautiful edifice. First, she checked the two remote corners that stood at either end of the Greek temple-style entrance's long, narrow narthex ending at the two exterior campanile towers. Nobody in sight. Perhaps in one of the six small chapels off the dome area? She knew Gustav and Alma Mahler had married in a small private ceremony within one of the six chapels that gave off from underneath the dome, three on either side. Four were quite small, two were large. She checked the three chapels on the east side of the church first. Only a few worshipers in any of them and they were all women. She retraced her steps so not to walk between the audience and musicians and began searching the chapels on the west side. In the second, larger one she found her quarry.

The man was kneeling in the front-most pew with his head turned to the left. He was facing a colorful painting devoted to Saint Sebastian. Megan knelt in the back pew diagonally opposite and despite the live music in the main part of the church she could hear parts of what he was addressing in a low murmur to the martyred saint. Something about that although he was Protestant, not Catholic, he empathized with the saint whose body had been riddled with arrows, just as his own life had been pierced by barbs and shafts.

"Restore it to me, restore it to me," he kept repeating, unaware in his intensity that anyone else was in the chapel.

But that peace was not to last. The sound of racing footsteps startled both Megan and the praying man. Chief of Police Erich Decker stormed into the room, his pistol drawn.

"Megan!" he hissed. "Stand back. Stand back!" There he was. The man with the circular bald spot Megan had identified. And within a few feet of her. Was she out of her mind, following him into this side chapel?

"What's your name?" Erich demanded, pointing his revolver straight at the man who was still on his knees and had twisted to see who was addressing him.

"Ottokar Weininger. *Why*?" He stood up and faced Erich defiantly.

"Ottokar Weininger," Erich repeated somewhat incredulously.

"Professor Crespi, is this the man you saw at the Belvedere today?"

Ottokar stared directly at Megan as though challenging her to identify him. She returned his stare. There was a long, suspenseful pause during which only the strains of Vivaldi could be heard. Finally Megan spoke.

"I'm so sorry, Erich. I realize now where I saw this man before. It was not at the Belvedere I don't think, but at the opera house last night. He was in the orchestra pit, sitting behind the brass section and I could see the back of his head anytime he bent over."

"That's right," Ottokar answered before Erich could speak. "I am contrabass trombonist at the Opera." Erich lowered his pistol and returned it to his shoulder holster.

"You're part of the *orchestra*?" he asked. "We've been trying to contact you all day! You weren't there last evening when we were questioning all the other players. And yet my friend here saw you in the pit. How do you explain that?"

Relieved that the short older woman facing him had not placed him at the Belvedere, Ottokar regained his self-confidence and his prickliness.

"I left at intermission and I should hope you were trying to get hold of me in regard to my lost instrument! Somebody stole it during the opera last night."

"The Kärntner Strasse portier reported he saw you twice last evening. Each time doing something unusual."

"Really? Like what?" Ottokar hid his fury at the nosy old stage door man.

"I attend *every* opera performance, whether there's a part for me or not. So what's so unusual about that? The portier knows I do."

"He said he saw you first," Erich persevered, "just before *Fidelio* began. Just a few steps from the stage entrance, he noticed you exchanging instrument cases with a young man. He said you had to rush past him to make it to the pit."

"Your point?"

"Then the portier reported that right after the end of the first act you left the building and that you did not have your instrument case with you."

"Yes. That's correct." Ottokar was not about to proffer any explanation.

"So why did you leave your instrument behind?" Erich was irritated by the man's haughty manner.

"Because that was part of the bargain!" Anger overtook Ottokar and he blurted out information he would otherwise have kept to himself.

"What bargain? You must tell us if you want us to protect you."

"*Protect* me? Why should I need protection?"

"Because last night's explosion at the opera house was set off by an avowed anti-Semite who left a note threatening all Jews in Vienna and I have reason to believe that all the Jewish members of the orchestra could be in danger."

"But I am not Jewish! I am a Protestant." Ottokar was yelling now.

"But your surname is Jewish, is it not?" Megan asked.

She had quietly inserted herself into the interrogation, fascinated that the man's name, with the exception of the "kar" at the end of his given name, was exactly that of the weirdo early twentieth-century Viennese philosopher Otto Weininger. He too, had denied his Jewishness and converted to Protestantism. Ottokar remained silent, staring angrily at Megan. Erich tried to ease the tension.

"Well, we want to protect *all* the players of the orchestra, of course. Now if you would enlighten us on what the portier thought was peculiar about your movements last night?"

"That's easy enough. A few days ago I was approached by someone who wanted to trade instruments with me. Seemed that he absolutely loved my really old French contrabass slide and that he had a brand-new German-style Kühl, complete with a beautiful large case he was willing to exchange for mine. And I will tell you that in addition, he offered me one thousand euros. How could I turn down such an offer?"

"A bit unusual, wouldn't you say?" queried Erich.

"I didn't think so at the time. I was just excited! So last night, as arranged, he appeared at the stage door with the new contrabass trombone in its case and we exchanged instruments. My new one's case was locked. The man's one condition was that I take it with me unopened to my usual place in the orchestra pit and then leave it when I met him again during intermission to receive the case key and my payment. I admit it seemed odd, but I didn't care; I was eager to have both the instrument and the cash."

"Are you aware of what was in the case you left behind in the pit?" Megan asked.

"Yeah, I found out when I came back this morning to see if anyone knew anything about my missing bone."

"Bone? What's a bone?" Erich was not familiar with the term.

"Short for trombone," explained Megan quietly. Ottokar Weininger continued.

"Kerstin Jesse, the pit manager, accused me of playing a trick on the orchestra. She said when the police forced it open there were only bricks in it! *Gott!* I want my old trombone back! Can't you help me?" Ottokar's appeal was genuine. He had forgotten all about his anger at Megan.

"We'll do what we can, of course," Erich said, taking down his address and cellphone number. He was still doubtful about the man. What about the fact that he had been seen by Megan across the Musikverein apparently paying off the two hoodlums who had interrupted Egga's concert?

"Who were the two young men you were seen with opposite the Musikverein about half an hour ago?

"Those two kids? They were asking for a handout."

"And?"

"And?" Ottokar repeated defensively.

"You were seen handing them something."

"Oh, yeah. I was giving them back a petition they had asked me to sign. I didn't want to sign it." Erich looked at the man contemptuously. He was a very deft liar.

"So let's see. You were simultaneously asked for money *and* asked to sign a petition, is that it?

"No, you misunderstood me. I said I *thought* that's why they stopped me. For money. But, no, they tried to persuade me to sign some sort of petition."

Erich decided he would get no more out of the man at that time. He believed the story about the stolen trombone was true and that the Weininger man was sincerely surprised by the contents of the case he had left in the orchestra pit. What a stupid fellow, not to have verified that he had the new trombone as agreed.

And who on earth would want his old one?

"All right, Herr Weininger. I have just one more question for you and then you can go. Why are you here?"

"Here?"

"Yes. Here in the Karlskirche. You told us you are a Protestant. This is a Catholic church. Why are you here?"

"Why, for the Vivaldi, of course!"

"But we find you here in a side chapel. Not with the audience. Why is that?"

"I was just giving thanks to God for that wonderful composer." Erich had to resist rolling his eyes. Megan did not resist and Ottokar did not notice. He was much too eager to get out of the Karlskirche. So much for praying to a Catholic saint!

55

Rita Rausch had parked her Volkswagen behind the Technical University, then dashed into the Karlsplatz where she saw Tonik Nektar waiting for her in front of the church. She ran up to him.

"Has anything happened?"

"I don't think so, but I haven't gone inside yet. Didn't want to miss you."

"Let's get inside fast!" Rita ran ahead of Nektar and came to a stop inside the narthex scanning the people in front of her who were seated, listening to a concert.

"Do you think the man you saw is still here?" she whispered to Nektar, when he caught up with her.

"That's also why I stayed outside. I'm sure I would have seen him if he came out. What I'm worried about is that the man I saw came here because he wants to damage the church where Gustav Mahler was married."

"That's a pretty far reach, but anything is possible, I guess. What does the man look like?"

"I just saw him from a distance when he was with the ruffians who interrupted the Schulhoff music, but he looked old, short and hunched over."

"What about his hair. What color?"

"Um, black I think. Yes black. But sparse. Bald in back."

"All right. You take the right side of the nave and I'll take the left. We'll start from the back and end at the top of the transept. I see there are three small chapels on either side, so let's check them out on the way. Good?"

"Yes, fine." As they were separating they were passed by three people coming from behind them, who then headed for the narthex and the exit. Two were male, one was female. In their eagerness to scan the concert crowd in front of them, neither the newspaper journalist nor the Mahler worshipper noticed the exit of Megan Crespi, Erich Decker, and Ottokar Weininger.

56

𝐸gga was very surprised not to see Megan at the end of the concert. The applause had been overwhelming after the Schulhoff quartet, and the audience had begged for an encore. They did so, ending to roaring applause.

"Where is Megan?" she quizzed Mary after things quieted down and she had packed her cello in its case.

"Wish I could tell you. She sprinted out of here while you were leading the audience in that wonderful counter protest. I can't imagine where she was off to."

"Maybe she was feeling sick?"

"I don't think so. She was just the reverse of sick; quite sprightly and full of interesting comments on the Mozart quartet in particular."

"Which direction are you going in, Mary?" Egga asked after she said goodnight to the quarter's other members.

"I'm off to the Ring to take the D tram in the direction of the stock exchange building, the Börse. My apartment is nearby on Wipplingerstrasse. And you?"

"Different direction. Megan and I are staying at the Römischer Kaiser Hotel on the Annagasse."

"Would you like to have a drink before we part company?"

"Ordinarily I'd say yes, but after all the commotion and stress this evening the only thing I feel like doing is going to bed!"

"Of course. I understand. Just in case we don't see each other again, my compliments on how you handled the situation this evening. And I think your quartet is superb. I saw one of our best newspaper critics in the audience so be prepared for a good review in tomorrow's *Die Presse*."

The two women parted company and Egga walked back to the Annagasse feeling both tired and elated. It had been quite an evening. She thought about how Jew-baiting by right-wing extremists had risen alarmingly in her own city, Berlin, and how the newspapers had pointed out that the city's anti-Semitic incidents were double those occurring in Bavaria. Why, why? So many decades after World War Two, the Nazis, and the concentration camps. Why? Was it the constant coverage of explosive events in the Gaza Strip? Was it a resurgence of "Aryan superiority" in Germany and Austria? And what about in Megan's America? Megan had told her hate crimes against Jews were on a yearly rise. *Why was there so much hatred in the world?*

Egga really hoped Megan would be back at their hotel. She remembered how poignant her former teacher's coverage of the Holocaust had been in a far-away Dallas where so many of the philanthropists were Jewish.

She need not have worried. Megan was back, already in her pajamas when Egga entered their room.

"Hallo! Hey, why did you leave before we finished playing?"

"I left because I wanted to give those two demented youngsters who interrupted your performance a piece of my mind."

"Megan! That could have been dangerous for *you*."

"Common sense doesn't prevail when you're as angry as I was."

"Did you catch up with them?"

"No. They were already on the other side of the Musikverein when I got outside. But I did see something so interesting that I immediately phoned Erich Decker to come."

"What was that?" Egga called from the bathroom where she was changing into her pajamas. She reappeared for Megan's answer.

"An older man was conferring with them. He seemed to be handing something to them. After Erich arrived we caught up with the man inside the Karlskirche and Erich questioned him. And I realized that, with his bald spot, he looked familiar. Then I remembered why. I'd seen him in the orchestra pit last night at *Fidelio*. Turned out he was the contrabass trombonist and I'd noticed him because he was just sitting there, not playing."

"There's no part in Beethoven's score for a contrabass trombone."

"Right, Egga. But apparently he comes to every opera performance, whether there's a part for him or not. A real opera fanatic."

"Hm. That might not be all he's a fanatic about."

"That's certainly something to think about. You're a natural detective, Egga. Tell me, how did the Schulhoff go after the audience sat down and you began playing?"

"It went amazingly well. In fact the audience demanded that we repeat it!"

"How wonderful, Egga. Justice prevails."

With that comforting thought Egga fell asleep almost immediately. Megan was awake a little longer. The next day would be her turn to perform. Her lecture, "Egon Schiele in Prison," would be in the town of Neulengbach where the artist had been incarcerated in 1912. Should she get up and go through her riveting PowerPoint images one more time? No. She, too, needed her sleep.

57

"How do you feel this morning, love?"

Harry had brought two cups of hot coffee and toast covered with cream cheese into their bedroom where Haim was still half asleep. Houdini was beside him and not stirring.

"Good morning, dearest!" a smiling Haim greeted his friend and partner.

"And thank you for supplying me with my favorite breakfast. But I really could come to the dining table." He made a motion to get out of bed and Houdini, reading his every movement, sat up.

"Don't you dare! Stay right where you are. I command it," Harry urged and Haim happily complied as did their canine buddy.

In between sips of coffee and bites of toast they discussed yesterday's medical emergency.

"Above all, I don't want you to let the kids know about it," Haim declared firmly.

"Are you sure? I think they should know."

"Absolutely not. Our whole relationship could be affected. They would think of me as a fragile old man."

"Well, are you not?" Harry asked gently.

"If I am, then you are, too," Haim pretended to pout. He was actually feeling quite well. The scary episode of yesterday evening seemed so long ago.

"Won't you tell me what your surprise is for our anniversary?"

Harry laughed as he shook his head no. Haim really was better.

"I could have had another TIA by then. Tell me now."

"Don't even joke about that!" Harry was spooked by what was meant as a jest.

"I'm sorry. But give me another hint at least. Last night you said I should limit my music playing to between Mendelssohn and Schönberg. What did you mean by 'between?'"

"Just that. Between. Don't play anything today that predates Mendelssohn or was composed after Schönberg."

"I was going to take up Fauré's second cello sonata again. It's been so long since I've played it. Is that permissible, maestro?"

"Yes, that's permissible."

"How this throws any light on what your surprise for me could be is beyond me."

"And that's exactly how it's supposed to be." Harry threw his partner a loving, teasing glance and carried the coffee cups and empty toast plate back to the kitchen. Houdini looked from one of his humans to the other, yawned, then decided to stay with Haim.

Harry could hardly wait for the strange parley that would take place atop the *Riesenrad* in the sight of all Vienna. Just two days to go.

58

Adele awoke a few minutes before the time she had set her alarm: six o'clock that morning. She dressed hurriedly in her running shorts and tank top, hardly taking time to drink her cup of green tea. She cut through the Rosa-Mayrader-Park, and was at the Opera's repertory tailoring department well before seven. The cheerful portier at the Operngasse was accustomed to seeing her arrive early and waved jovially at her as she passed by him.

There was no one in the tailoring room. And it would be empty until nine o'clock if things went as usual. Plenty of time to open the floor safe in private. But she could tell she was nervous when her two turns and counter-turns of the dial failed. She tried again, this time with success. Brushing aside the costume jewelry, she pulled out the mahogany box at the back of the safe and checked to see that the tiara was in it undisturbed. Yes, all was well. She locked the safe and placed the box in her shoulder bag. She would take the Kärntner Strasse exit so the other portier would not notice she had left the building again so soon. Then she walked briskly back to her apartment, changed into the garment she had sewn together at the Opera tailoring department, and headed for her Volvo which was parked, for once, uncharacteristically very nearby. She drove south toward Vienna's heavily populated Favoriten district—once in Russian hands after World War Two—and its famous Dorotheum pawnbroker shop.

Adele had done her homework well. Although she had at first thought it would be wise to go to a pawnshop outside the city, what she had read online about the Dorotheum convinced her she would be best served there. Not to be confused with the downtown auction house of the same name, the pawnshop advertised itself as offering a "quick and unbureaucratic financial service that enables you to take up loans on a temporary basis." The clincher was when she read the end of the pawnshop's self-description: "At the Dorotheum you will receive cash in an instant: in a simple and secure way, without incurring debts, without involving your bank."

As Adele drove down the long Erlachgasse searching for number ninety she was pleasantly surprised at the large number of Muslims on the street and in the stores. The women were in either full-length black burqas that revealed only their eyes or wearing hijab scarfs of different colors and lengths. Perhaps I'll buy a colorful burqa, if they come in any other color but black, for my assignation at the Prater, Adele laughed to herself.

She sighted the pawnbroker shop, adorned with the traditional symbol of three spheres suspended from a bar. Now to find a place to park. After some searching Adele found a tight but manageable place on a nearby side street two blocks down.

When she walked into the Dorotheum she entered a different world. A square show room presented its magnificent wares. Glass show counters were loaded on top of glass show counters to shoulder height and they were filled with jewelry and samples of precious stones. An older man dressed immaculately in a dark gray suit looked up from behind a desk in the back of the showroom. He rose and walked up to the sales counter and smiled at her, apparently unsurprised by the burqa she wore.

"Good morning Madame. And how may I be of service to you?"

"I want to pawn this," Adele said, affecting what she thought sounded like an Arabic accent, with her "p" sounding like "b." She drew the mahogany box out of her bag and deliberately turned it upside down on the counter so the label could be read by the man.

"Let's see. 'Property of Anna von Bahr-Mildenburg.' The great opera singer? My, my, what have you here?" The man turned the box over with fastidious care. The top slid off easily. Too easily. It seemed to have been recently forced open. Lying inside on black velvet was a large, lustrous, diamond tiara. This was not costume jewelry. The tiara appeared to be made of a collection of the very finest diamonds. Could this be so?

"Do you mind if I take my magnifying glass to these jewels?"

"No, not at all. I expect you to."

The man slipped a small two-ended loupe from the breast pocket of his jacket and applied one end to the large diamond in the center of the headband. Had Adele been looking at him rather than at the tiara she would have seen him blanch for a mini-second.

What he had seen was, if verifiable, something truly rare. He flipped his magnifier and looked again at the gem, this time through a much more powerful magnification. The stone looked genuine and the color it reflected was an intense pink. Dare he think what that signified?

"Madame, I am the manager here, Fritz Schauer, and I would need to look at this tiara under my laboratory microscope, if you will allow."

"But of course."

Gingerly, Herr Schauer lifted the tiara up from its black velvet nest and carried it back to his desk where he thoroughly cleaned the stone. On the nearby worktable he kept his private trinocular stereo zoom microscope. The binocular eyepiece had two Barlow lenses of 0.5X and 2.0X and a magnification of 0.7X to 4.5X zoom, as well as adjustable inter-papillary distance.

Before using the microscope, however, he applied the primitive but reliable test traditionally used by jewelers and amateurs alike: the "fog" test in which one holds up the heat-conducting stone under inspection and, exhales on it. If the jewel is genuine, the fog disappears immediately. If not, the fog lingers.

The fog dispersed right away. Now Schauer was excited, although he chose not to show it. He placed the tiara under the microscope and focused on the huge center Marquise diamond. There was that inescapable, intense pink light again. It was what in his profession was called a "red" diamond, the rarest of all diamonds. And it was absolutely genuine as were the smaller diamonds in the tiara which he then examined one by one through his microscopic lens. He turned to the woman in the black burqa. She could not possibly know the value of what she had.

"Madame, you have a classic nineteenth-century sunburst tiara here."

"Yes, I know. And I also know it must be extremely valuable." Adele had done her own research.

"Relatively valuable, it is. And for how long would you want to pawn the piece?"

"Thirty days."

"Thirty days it is then. We can issue you an immediate loan of twenty thousand euros and there would of course be the added interest at fifteen percent for the payback. Is that clear?"

"Quite clear." Adele had no intention of returning for the stolen piece, despite the trouble she had taken to be unidentifiable. Twenty thousand euros was far more than she had guessed. She would now have the funds to pay for the surmoulage being cast for her at the Tulln bronze foundry. All thanks to Madam Anna von Bahr-Mildenburg.

"Now there is just one last item to cover, Madame. *We of course need proof of ownership.*"

59

All morning Ottokar had pouted over what had happened in the Karlskirche the evening before. That damned old woman with the police officer asking if his surname wasn't Jewish! He'd *told* them he was Protestant.

All right. Let's see what his namesake Otto Weininger, who had also converted, had to say about being Jewish. Ottokar looked him up again on the Internet and found a transcript of his *Geschlect und Charakter*. Chapter 13 was entitled "Judaism" and he turned to it first. Its themes and its thoughts were parallel to his own! Sections were devoted to personality and self-worth, amorality without anti-morality, soullessness, and therefore deficiency in the desire for immorality, lack of humor of the Jew, the Jewish woman, want of belief and inner stability, inner lack of dignity, Christ as the subduer of Judaism, Christianity and Judaism as ultimate contrasts.

Ottokar read these sections with the greatest of attention and satisfaction. What a soulmate he had found! No wonder he was an anti-Semite!

Tonight at the Musikverein where Jewish music was being directed by a Jewish conductor he would act on his beliefs.

60

This morning, their schedules finally coordinated, Megan and Egga were enjoying a long, relaxing breakfast downstairs at their hotel. They had both ordered scrambled eggs in addition to the cereal they had begun with. Egga had taken to Megan's manner of topping cereal with blueberries, strawberries, banana slices, and yogurt and she had already decided to serve the aggrandized concoction to her boys at home.

"I'm so glad you can drive out with me to Neulengbach," Megan was saying. Before they came down to the breakfast room, she had run through the PowerPoint for her Schiele lecture, and she was feeling relaxed and ready to take on the day. Egga's quartet concert last night was the final one, and she was now free to join Megan for the rest of the week they had together before both flew home. The only fly in this morning's ointment had been the TV news concerning the occurrence of three new anti-Semitic acts in the city: hate note postings in the University, the spray painting of the Sigmund Freud statue at the Medical University, and the red paint smearing of both Gustav and Alma Mahler's gravestones at the Grinzing Cemetery.

"Let's try not to talk about these distressing events over breakfast," Megan had urged herself as well as Egga. They turned instead to their plans for the day.

"It will be a first for me to visit the little village where you discovered Schiele's cell. How many years ago was that now?"

"You do the math, Egga. I found it in when I was twenty-eight years old and I'm in my mid-eighties now."

Egga did the math in her head and was suitably impressed. Megan's discovery had become part of Austrian history. And she knew Megan, with her rigorous morning exercise routine, was keeping herself fit. She uttered an amazed "wow" before continuing her questioning.

"And you really had to *sneak* into the building that had once been the town prison?"

"That's right. You'll hear about that episode in the lecture, but I can tell you this much: it was the second time in my life that I realized it is sometimes better to beg forgiveness than to ask for permission."

"Ha! Great motto. I must remember that. What was the first time?"

"The first time was when I was eighteen and sent to Italy by my parents to learn 'adult' Italian. I did so, at the University of Perugia, but I also bought a small motorcycle, a Paperino—gosling—and drove around Umbria with it. Finally I drove all the way to the little medieval-walled republic of San Marino which is high up on Mounte Titano and surrounded on all sides by Italy. It's just about six miles from Rimini on the Adriatic Sea, so it was a long ride from Perugia, but worth it."

"It must be thrilling to be looking down on Italy from there!"

"Oh, it was. I crawled out on a precipice overlooking a twenty-four-thousand-foot drop and had a friend photograph me. It was a crazy thing to do, and when my parents back in Texas saw the photo they wired me to come home. And that was my first occasion learning that sometimes it's better to beg for forgiveness than ask for permission."

"What a story!"

"Well, it's true and I have the photo to prove it. In fact I reproduced it in an autobiography I was asked to write by the genial New York publisher George Braziller."

"Megan! I am the proud owner of *In Passionate Pursuit*. You sent me an inscribed copy many years ago and I treasure it."

"Woops, I'd forgotten. Thank you, Eggalina."

"And I remember exactly what you wrote. You wrote 'May your musical career reach the same ascent as the Monte Titano in this book.'"

"Oh, so I did. And just look how you have succeeded. I'm so proud of you."

"Thank you, Megan. I plan to make you even prouder."

"How so?"

"I'm working on writing a sonata for cello and piano."

"How marvelous! Will it be melodious or densely modern?"

"Both."

"Will there be anything else, *Frau Professor*?" the waitress had stopped at their table. She and Megan had known each other for a long time.

"*Nein, danke*," answered Egga for them both.

Megan looked at her Apple Watch. The time had passed by so quickly. It was already ten o'clock. She wanted to get them back from her Neulengbach lecture in plenty of time to rest before the concert they were attending in the evening. It was going to be a real treat: the brilliant, self-taught conductor American Gerald Chaplin conducting the Vienna Philharmonic in Mahler's Second Symphony, the "Resurrection" Symphony, with its enormous orchestration and choir.

After a quick trip to their room they exited their hotel and walked the few blocks to the Hertz car rental on the Kärntner Ring. Their glistening white Audi A3 was waiting for them.

61

"But don't you see, *Liebchen*, something like that could happen *again* during your performance tonight?"

Michael Hüttler, a second-year student at Vienna's Medical University— MedUni—and president of his class, was urgently trying to persuade his friend Theresa Canales, bass drummer for the Vienna State Opera orchestra, to call in sick for this evening's performance of Mahler's Second Symphony with the Vienna Philharmonic.

Unconvinced, Theresa had remained silent, although she was touched by her boyfriend's concern. She was extremely proud of the fact that, as a five-year member of the Vienna State Opera orchestra, she had been accepted into the private association of the Vienna Philharmonic which only accepted players who belonged to the Opera orchestra and had been in it at least three years. But Michael pressed his case.

"Just look at the spate of anti-Semitism that's broken out all around the city since the Mahler Bomber! His tomb desecrated and his effigy at the Belvedere vandalized. And then the hateful messages about Freud posted all over Vienna

University, and the spray-painting of Freud's statue at my university!" These outrageous incidents had dominated the media all morning.

Theresa, however, was more concerned with how important her instrument was for tonight's performance. In fact, for her whole percussion section. Mahler's immense orchestration included not only her crucial bass drum—in fact two of them—but she was first desk. In addition Mahler's score called for two sets of three drums, two military drums, cymbals, triangles, both a conspicuous high tam-tam and a low tam-tam, a glockenspiel, bells, and a rute, constructed from a solid rod and thinly split partway down with multiple thin birch dowels. She would be tapping it rhythmically to the center of her bass drum head. Mahler's employment of the rute in the symphony's third movement broke with tradition and focused on its coloring possibilities rather than on traditional military rhythm for the Turkish rute that Mozart had used in his opera *The Abduction from the Seraglio*.

Theresa tried to explain all this and that there was a lot to consider before she could even consider bowing out. The thought of a fortified percussion section such as that required by Mahler excited her enormously and she tried to convey this to her dear Michael who was unnecessarily obsessed for her safety.

"No, Michael, I'm sorry but I cannot abandon my fellow percussionists, especially tonight of all nights with Mahler." Michael studied her closely. He knew once she made up her mind nothing could change it.

"All right," he said smiling at her, "in that case I am going to protect you." Theresa laughed.

"And how are you going to do that, *Liebchen*? Only players are allowed on the orchestra stage of the Musikverein's grandiose auditorium."

"Did I say anything to you about being on stage with you? No, I am going to protect you and your fellow players by staging a pro-Jewish demonstration outside the Musikverein that will take place half an hour before, during, and after the concert."

62

ℋarry Howell was angry with himself. Angry and frustrated. Haim had been working on the Fauré second cello sonata all morning and so he had felt secure that Haim wouldn't know what he was researching on his computer in their study. He had decided to read up about Rodin's modeling of Mahler's head. The data was interesting. In her published diaries and memories of Mahler, Alma Mahler described the sessions her husband had had with the famous French sculptor, both at the height of their fame. The sittings took place in April and again in October of 1909, as Rodin had "fallen in love with his model," even if it did involve his standing for well more than an hour at a time. The edgy composer was unable to remain still during the one-and-a-half-hour sessions and felt it was a "waste of time" to be away from his work. Harry smiled at that. So typical of Mahler!

But what he read next totally confounded him. It seemed that Rodin had made *two* preliminary studies: a "rough, expressionistic" one and a "smooth, more naturalistic one." They became known as Model A, and Model B, but Model B seems to have been earlier than Model A. Confusing.

Valiantly Harry read on. It was Model B that was preferred by Mahler's family. Well, that was interesting. Which was the Model that had been at the Vienna State Opera? He and the family had seen it dozens of times over the years but they had never really gone up close to examine it. He was reading a URL text he had opened about Rodin; perhaps he should look up one on Mahler and see if he could learn more. Just as he was about to do so, Haim came in holding his cello high up with his left hand. Harry quickly clicked to his screen's homepage. It was good he did so because Haim came right around his desk, bent over, and stared him in the face. Then he plucked each of the cello strings close to Harry's right ear.

"Tell me the truth," he demanded. "Does my cello sound out of tune?"

"Uh, no, not that I can tell. No."

"I want the truth, Harry! I think I don't seem to hear as well as I used to."

"Did you use that Korg cello tuner I gave you last Christmas, hon?"

"Oh. Right. I forgot about that. Wonder where we put it?"

"Where 'we' put it is next to your cello bow stand. Remember? You liked the way the needle moves to tell you if your strings are flat or sharp."

"So you don't think I have any hearing loss?"

"We both probably have some at our age. But I wouldn't worry about it. Just get the cello tuner."

"Yes, but I hate to think that I *need* one."

"What?"

"You didn't *hear* what I said?" Haim was amazed.

"Of course I did, darling. I'm just making fun of you, of me, of us."

Morosely Haim shuffled away. Harry could hear him murmuring to himself and to Houdini who had followed him in and out of the study.

Enough of research, Harry decided. He would go to the kitchen and make Haim's favorite lunch: smoked salmon on a toasted bagel with cream cheese and capers. And a slice of lemon on the side.

63

"We of course need proof of ownership."

The pawnshop manager's words rang in Adele's ears. She had not prepared for that. But she was an excellent improvisor, albeit in a Middle East accent.

"Oh, yes. 'Proof of ownership.' This tiara was among my husband's belongings after he died last month. My husband was Austrian, Engelbert Mildenburg. He was the grandnephew of the opera singer whose name you see on the back of this box. I do not know about any 'proof of ownership' except the fact that I now own it. I am not a musician. I cannot tell you anything more."

Herr Schauer was silent. He looked at what he could see of the completely veiled woman whose eyes were covered by an eye mesh and enormous sunglasses. He looked again at the tiara. He was offering to lend the woman in a burqa only one third of what it was worth. Then he spoke.

"All right, Madam Mildenburg. We will make an exception in your case as you are a widow and coping with many things you had not anticipated."

"Thank you. Thank you." The sunglasses covered the glow in Adele's eyes.

"If you will wait here I shall go upstairs and procure the amount of money upon which we agreed: twenty thousand euros. And in the meantime, will you be so kind as to fill out this ticket with your name, telephone number, and address.

"But, of course."

Adele waited until the man had disappeared. Then she carefully printed out a very legible fictitious name, telephone number, and address.

Herr Schauer returned with a large envelope. It was unsealed.

"You will count and confirm that the number of bills is correct, please."

Adele counted the crisp new notes, yes they added up to twenty thousand euros.

"Now please sign and date here where it says 'signature' on the ticket." Adele fabricated a wildly cursive, large signature that seemed to spell out the name "Mildenburg."

"Take care not to lose it. You cannot reclaim your property in thirty days if you misplace or lose the ticket." Adele nodded vigorously, turned, and left the pawnshop, Herr Schau watching her with a mixture of incredulity and amusement.

At least one of them knew the ticket would never be returned.

64

ℋenri-Claude de La Granger checked into the Römischer Kaiser Hotel just before noon. It was his preferred residence when visiting the city that had hosted the composers Haydn, Mozart, Beethoven, Brahms, and Mahler. He had come on the spur of the moment and specifically to hear Mahler's Second as conducted by his American friend Gerald Chaplin. Although the concert at the Gold Hall of the Musikverein had been sold out weeks ago, Gerald himself had arranged to secure one of the additional seats for him. After the concert they had planned to meet at the Hotel Sacher to wind down with some delicious chocolate cake—the famous *Sachertorte*.

Relaxing in his room after unpacking his few travel items, Henri-Claude took a look at the newspaper he had picked up at the airport before taking a taxi into town. He was horrified to read about the spate of anti-Jewish happenings around Vienna, apparently centering on Mahler but other Jewish cultural figures as well. He remembered that one member of the New York Philharmonic—a Scottish trombonist—had severely criticized his friend's conducting of the Mahler Second at a performance in 2008. He pulled up the review on his cellphone and read it again:

> Having not previously heard either of Mr. Chaplin's two recordings of the symphony, nor having seen him conduct, I came to our rehearsals with an open mind. My initial impression was that Mr. Chaplin displays an arrogance and self-delusion that is off-putting. As a conductor, he can best be described as a very poor beater of

time who far too often is unable to keep the ensemble together and allows most tempo transitions to fall where they may. His direction lacks few indications of dynamic control or balance and there is absolutely no attempt to give phrases any requisite shape. In rehearsal, he admitted to our orchestra that he is not capable of keeping a steady tempo and that he would have to depend on us for any stability in that department. Considering his Everest-sized ego, this admission must have caused him great consternation upon reflection. Mahler's wonderful use of the off-stage brass in the fifth movement gave Chaplin much tribulation. One would think that after more than fifty performances of the work, even the most plebeian of conductors would have some understanding of how to bring together musicians that are separated by great distance. In the performance, these haunting moments of the symphony slipped away like some wayward musical slinky.

I have to take extreme exception to the many reviews I have read of his performances. Some critics have written that he brings the finest details of the work to the surface. If his past performances were anything like ours, Mr. Chaplin excels in ignoring the blizzard of Mahler's performance direction.

Much has been written about Mr. Chaplin's passion for Mahler's great symphony as if this emotion is unique to him. This assertion is an insult to all professional musicians who have dedicated their entire lives and have sacrificed much toward the preservation of all the great works of history's finest composers. His continued appearances are also an affront to all "real" conductors who have toiled relentlessly for the recognition they duly deserve.

Henri-Claude was extremely sorry he had elected to reread the trombonist's hateful review of his friend. It called up all sorts of the anti-Semitism Mahler himself had suffered during his career. And it made him think of Alma Mahler who, in spite of having been married to *two* Jewish cultural figures—Gustav Mahler and Franz Werfel—was scornful of Jews in her writing and in her speech. Such a conundrum! She was rather like Vienna's mayor Karl Lueger in her inconsistent relationships with Jews.

Feeling depressed rather than elated that he was back in the music capital of the world Henri-Claude decided to leave the hotel and say hello to the friend

Megan Crespi had introduced to him years ago, Hanskarl Klug at the Christian M. Nebehay Antiquariat. The venerable establishment was practically next door and on the same side of the Annagasse as the hotel.

He entered the shop just as Hanskarl was walking from the back room into the front gallery and they both smiled in happy recognition.

"Why if it isn't Henri-Claude! What are you doing here in Vienna?"

"That's simple. To attend a performance of Mahler's Second this evening."

"Wonderful! I tried to obtain a ticket, but it was already too late."

"What a pity."

"I have only myself to blame."

After discussing the spate of vandalism inspired by what was being called the Mahler Bomber attack that had happened two evenings earlier at the Vienna State Opera, they moved on to more pleasant things. There was a Gustav Klimt exhibition opening at the Belvedere and there was an Egon Schiele show that was just about to close at the Albertina Museum.

"And our very own Megan Crespi will be speaking about him there this Thursday evening," Hanskarl said proudly.

"What? *Megan is in Vienna*? But she didn't tell me!"

"I didn't know either until she walked into my shop yesterday. She's still the same. Bouncy and full of curiosity about everything."

"Wouldn't expect anything less. You should see how energetically she plays with Vito when she visits me in Toblach."

"Who is Vito?"

"Vito is my marvelous German Shepherd dog. I take him with me every summer when I stay in Mahler's summer retreat in the Italian Dolomites, Dobbiaco, or as it was called when that part of Italy belonged to Austria, Toblach. You know, I rent the house that is closest to the little Hotel Trenkenhof—actually a large farm house—where he and Alma stayed the last three summers of his life. He found it peaceful and inspiring. It was there he composed *Das Lied von der Erde*, wrote his Ninth Symphony, and began his Tenth there. Alma, on the other hand, found it utterly boring. Nowadays that large old farmhouse is the 'Gustav Mahler Stube.'"

"Isn't one of the 'composing' huts Mahler had built for himself in Toblach?"

"Yes, but it's shamefully preserved. It's on property belonging to the descendants of the family that rented to Mahler but they've turned the land around it into a 'Wildpark' and so right next to you as you approach the composing hut are pigs and ostriches. It's a travesty!"

"Henri-Claude, I think you should know. I am going to be closing down the Antiquariat next month."

"No! Why?"

"Because of our new cyber world. Lots of art galleries and rare book bookstores are closing because of the ease of shopping online. I've updated of course, but I simply can't keep up with all the email correspondence that comes in every day. And, frankly, Henri-Claude, I am tired."

"*Alors*, I do understand, my friend, but it will be so sad not to have your shop to visit anymore."

"Thank you for that. I was just going up the street for lunch. Would you like to go with me?"

"Yes, indeed. I haven't eaten since breakfast on the plane early this morning."

Hanskarl locked up and they began walking the Annagasse toward the Kärntner Strasse. Just before they got there, Hanskarl turned to the right at Annagasse 3 and Henri-Claude stopped in amazement.

"You're eating at a Burger King?"

"I know it seems odd, but the service is fast and the food is actually quite good. Plus it's cheap and there is no one to tip. Except for cleaning the tables, the staff is all behind the serving counter."

Henri-Claude had never been inside a Burger King but he gamely followed his friend inside and, tasting the cheeseburger that was ready in under forty seconds, he became an instant convert. Heaven could wait!

65

$\mathcal{U}$nable to fall back to sleep that morning, Karl Lueger pulled his laptop over to his bed and began making a list of further locations where he might post or paint his "statements" around the Austrian metropolis's inner city. Ideas were popping in and out of his head so fast he could hardly keep track of them.

The Jewish Museum on the Dorotheergasse in Vienna's first district was the most obvious target, but he would have to be careful. TV coverage of his ubiquitous activities yesterday was being sensationalized and endlessly repeated on television and there was every likelihood that the elegant but small street entrance at number eleven was under continuous surveillance. But that museum had a branch, the Misrachi-Haus, which was located in the nearby Judenplatz, an area associated with Jewish immigrant settlers ever since the early middle ages and site of the famous pogrom of 1421. The archaeological remains of the original synagogue there had recently been discovered and artifacts could be viewed in the museum. Complicated. The small Misrachi-Haus museum was not a good candidate, Karl decided.

Nor was the new Holocaust Memorial that sat ostentatiously in the Judenplatz Square in the middle of any traffic. It wasn't a statue, it was a huge, ugly cement cube, twice the height of a person, designed to look like a library's overcrowded shelves. But there were no shelves or even corners. The crammed books stood eleven "shelves" high. But their pages, not their spines, turned outward. Go figure! How did that make any sense? You couldn't even read the titles of the petrified books. A double door was in one wall, but it too was concrete. There was no entry, no interior. Who was the crazy person that designed this obnoxious impenetrable concrete box? Karl looked it up on his Firefox browser and read the name: Rachel Whiteread. Hmm. "Rachel?" "Whiteread?" Hell, he should have known.

Maybe there was something else in the Judenplatz he could address swiftly. What's that over there? A larger-than-life statue of someone named Lessing. Plunked down on one side of the large square. On his laptop Karl opened one of many URLs he found on Lessing. Ah, here was the connection. He was an eighteenth-century Enlightenment author whose play *Nathan the Wise* preached liberal views toward Muslims and Jews. Typical. They couldn't even find a Jewish hero to make a statue of for the Judenplatz. Karl read further and came to a stop. Wouldn't you know it, the man was a close friend and supporter of the Jewish philosopher Moses Mendelssohn. So he was buddies with a Jew. Now where the hell had he heard that name Mendelssohn before? He read further. Oh, yeah. He was the grandfather of the nineteenth-century composer Felix Mendelssohn.

Now Karl was getting somewhere. Here was something he could do in minimal time he realized as he studied a closeup image of the statue. The figure stood with one foot on two books. What was that supposed to mean? Lessing's taller-than-life lean body was wrapped in a ridiculously long frock coat and his head was the smallest thing about him. Well, the sculptor, whoever he was, got that right! Let's see what Wikipedia says about the artist. The man was a certain Siegfried Charoux, a Viennese sculptor who ended up in England. He had created the bronze effigy for the Judenplatz in the 1930s. But the statue was destroyed by the Nazis—ah ha, *they* obviously knew about the Lessing-Mendelssohn connection. But then in the 1960s Charoux was commissioned to cast another bronze copy and that is what's in the Judenplatz today. All right! Made to order. But how to vandalize it? He magnified and studied the online photographs of the cocky statue with its right foot on two books. Unfortunately, it stood on a double-stacked white plinth making the statue too high for him to reach easily. He looked again at that right foot. It protruded from the plinth and the books. Perfect.

Karl made himself breakfast and talked with his parents briefly—told them he was studying Lessing and they beamed in approval. After returning to his bedroom/study he laboriously printed eight words in thick black capital letters onto a very large piece of white cardboard. Then he attached four interlocking large bungie cords to the poster and strapped the ensemble to his back, securing it by donning an oversize black T-shirt. Unseen by his parents he walked down to the apartment house courtyard where his motorcycle was parked. He was ready.

66

By noon Ottokar Weininger had scraped together a decent sum of money. He boarded a tram for the long ride to the tenth Favoriten district and the Dorotheum pawnshop on Erlachgasse. His mind was working overtime. Those two street ruffians he had paid to disrupt the *Streicher Vier* last night must have run out of the Brahms auditorium just seconds after shouting the chant he required of them: "No Jewish music in Vienna!" Cowards! And then they wanted more money than he had told them he'd pay for three minutes of work. The cowards had complained it was "dangerous" work and that they deserved to be paid more. In the end, to get rid of the haggling cowards and in case the police had been called, he paid them the extra money. Then he had taken shelter in the nearby Karlskirche where some repetitive Vivaldi was being played at top volume. He slipped into a chapel on the left side of the church where there was a reredos of Saint Elisabeth of Thuringia and stood trying to calm his nerves. Realizing he should look like a worshipper, he knelt in the front pew. He noticed an image of Saint Sebastian to his left and, feeling empathy with the cruelly martyred saint, he turned and faced it. He thought about his lost trombone and decided saying a prayer or two wouldn't hurt. He commenced, out loud, and this was when that hateful old lady and the policeman came upon him. He almost buckled under their questioning but managed to carry things off successfully.

The tram had almost arrived at the Erlachgasse. When it stopped, Ottokar went straight to the showroom section of the pawnshop where all makes, shapes, and sizes of musical instruments hung on the walls, or were displayed in the showcases below. The brass section had a wonderful array of trumpets, trombones, and even two tubas. But Ottokar was more interested in the cases for trombones which were lined against one wall. He found the largest one, in good condition and obviously made for a contrabass, and turned to the clerk who had been watching him with mild interest.

"Where is the instrument for this large case?" Ottokar asked, affecting ignorance. He pointed to one in a group of cases leaning on the wall in a row.

"Well, that's a contrabass trombone case and unfortunately we don't have the matching instrument. Never have."

Ottokar couldn't believe his ears. Exactly what he was hoping for! He should certainly be able to afford the empty case. It all depended upon how he phrased his next question.

"You know, I have a rather large old trombone at home, and I've never had a case for it. But now that my son has taken up playing it in his school band he is embarrassed to be the only one in the band not to bring his instrument in a case. In fact the other children are beginning to make fun of him. He has to carry his mute separately and they make fun of that too. So I'm wondering. I don't want to invest too much in a case, but I don't want my son to be the object of cruel teasing anymore. What could be your lowest price on this case here?"

"Let's see what the asking price on it is," the clerk said obligingly, walking over to the case that was leaning against several others and lifting it up. He examined the bottom.

"Here's the price. Ninety-five euros. But for your son we could make it, say, sixty-five euros."

Ottokar's narrative had worked. He had just enough to cover the price. Moments later he was on a tram heading back to downtown. Standing up next to his seat was the empty case.

Early this evening it would be his ticket to getting inside the Musikverein.

67

The white Audi was more than comfortable, the highway uncrowded, and Megan and Egga had a chance to talk at length about the exciting concert the Vienna Philharmonic would be performing tonight.

"I so wish I could sneak into the Musikverein ahead of time and play with the cello section," Egga sighed.

"Wish you could too," said Megan. "But it's the same as at the opera house: the musicians all have to insert their ID cards into a chip reader before they're allowed inside."

"Boy, oh boy, are they going to have a lot of ID cards to process tonight!" Egga exclaimed, thinking of the mammoth orchestration of Mahler's Second Symphony.

"Do you know the score's instrumentation, Megan?"

"Certainly not off the top of my head. I know it's massive and that there are a lot more doublings even tripplings of the standard orchestra sections size."

"Well, I looked it up yesterday and can give you the instrumentation, if you like."

"Definitely. Tell me. I know there are two harps but I couldn't specify the other multiplications."

"Okay. This will only take half an hour," Egga seemed to be joking but actually she knew that citing the instruments and how many in each case would take quite a while. Loving to talk about this sort of thing she jumped in.

"First off, since I'm a cellist, I'll give you the disposition of the string section. And although it's not used much in today's orchestras, especially your American ones, what's called the 'Mahler Order' is still used by the Vienna Philharmonic. That means the placing of the two violin sections is done antiphonally, with first violins on the conductor's left, and second violins on her, or his, right. Could be the same this evening with the two harps called for in the score—one on the left, the other on the right side of the stage."

Megan was grinning at the nice feminist sequence she had just heard— "on her, or his, right."

"So where are the violas, cellos and basses?"

"They are fanned out on audience left, back where the second violins are usually seated today, and the cellos are right in front of the conductor while the string bass players stand fanned out in the back of the orchestra in the Mahler grouping."

"That's certainly different from how orchestras look today. So how many players are in each section? I know there are a lot more than usual in that Second Symphony's immense orchestration."

"Between sixteen to twenty violins, fourteen or so second violins, maybe twelve violas, ten cellos, and between eight and ten string basses. Now some of those string basses have to have that fifth string for low C."

"I thought string basses had a low B string, not C."

"Listen, we're talking about *Mahler* here. Do you dare question him?"

"Okay. How about the woodwind instruments? How many of them in Mahler's score?"

"This is where it gets really wild. I don't remember the exact numbers so wait a sec until I find it on my cellphone."

Megan sighted a sign. Still twenty kilometers, or twelve miles to Neulengbach. Egga held up her phone.

"Okay, here's the orchestration. I don't know why they haven't specified the number of strings. It only says 'usual strings.' Let's just presume Mahler used the outer numbers I just gave you. Let's see. You wanted to know first about the woodwinds, right?

"Yes. As a flutist, that's what I find interesting."

"Listen to this! Four flutes and all four of them doubling on piccolos; four oboes with the third and fourth ones doubling on the English horn; three B flat, A, and C clarinets with the third one doubling on bass clarinet. Then, get this, two E flat clarinets with the second doubling the fourth clarinet, and both doubling fortissimo where possible, and finally four bassoons and the third and fourth are supposed to double on contrabassoons."

"That's a lot of wind," an awed Megan allowed.

"Sure vies with the brass section. Here we go: *ten* French horns, but the seventh through the tenth are only used in the fifth movement and are partly offstage."

"Yes, I do remember that Mahler has two small bands that are supposed to play on either side of the auditorium. That should be interesting to see how they do it in the Musikverein auditorium!"

"Right. Ten trumpets, and like the horns, the seventh through the tenth are only used in the fifth movement and are, again, partly offstage. Then there are four trombones—no mention of a contrabass one—and, oh, how sad—only one tuba."

"Just plain unfair," Megan took up Egga's fake lament. "Okay, I'm ready for the percussion section. I know it's enormous, but what's the division and the selection? I know there are some extra things called for. What would Mahler be without his percussion instruments? I remember one jabbing contemporary cartoon that shows him standing looking perplexed before an array of bells and drums."

"Let's see. Here we go. The score calls for seven timpani manned or womanned, by three players and the seventh kettledrum only sounds offstage in the fifth movement. Same with the two bass drums, with the second one being used only in the fifth movement. Now also in that movement and *only* in that movement are: several snare drums, and three untuned, deep bells. In addition, of the two pairs of cymbals called for, the second is only used in the fifth movement and offstage. Hmm, exactly the same with two pairs of triangles. Now here's something interesting: there are two pairs of tam-tams—one is high and the other is low. And this is even more interesting. There is a rute brush stick scored for the third movement. And to end it all, there is, *of course for Mahler*, a glockenspiel."

"Ha! You've left out an instrument, Egga."

"Nope. I've got the list right here."

"Well, spool down to keyboard instruments. There's an organ!" Megan's voice sounded urgent.

"So there is. Forgot that. It's in the fifth movement."

"And then there's the little case of the voices used in the symphony. I think it's supposed to have, in addition to a soprano and an alto solo, a mixed chorus of two hundred voices 'if possible.'"

"I can't see them stuffing that many singers into the Musikverein, can you?" asked Egga.

"Definitely not. I do know the great hall seats around a thousand, seven hundred people and that there is standing space for three hundred more. That's a lot, huh? For chorus space, you can be sure they'll have as many singers as possible standing on the balcony above the stage at the organ level, and perhaps even along some of the boxes close to the stage. Although some of the brass might be put there. We'll just have to wait and see."

"Speaking of 'wait and see,' Megan, we're here! See that sign? We're in Neulengbach."

"How did that happen so fast?" Megan had been totally immersed in Mahler. That was the magic about him.

68

On his blue BMW cycle Karl Lueger easily zoomed in and out of traffic. He had decided to go to the Judenplatz by way of the Schottenring and then along the Wipplingerstrasse in the direction of Saint Stephen's Cathedral. He would turn right onto the short, narrow Futerergasse and that would bring him right into the square with the idiot concrete "book" monument on his immediate right. Slowing down to a walking pace, he drove his bike around the box once, sizing up the pedestrians in the square. Very few, and all of them tourists. Most people this time of day were having lunch. The café on the street was filled inside and out with people. The Lessing statue was on the far side of and facing the hideous cement box. Karl steered his bike to the front of the statue, came to a standstill and parked, his kick stand securely in place. One last glance around, then he raised his T-shirt high, unhooked the bungie cords across his chest that cupped the poster around his back, pulled his cardboard poster around to the front, then up and free of the shirt. Yanking a roll of duct tape out of his trouser pocket, he positioned the poster squarely above the jutting cement band with the name Lessing incised in black on it. He secured the poster with four strips of tape. Ten seconds later he was speeding back up the Wipplingerstrasse.

The sign hanging below Lessing's extended right foot read:

**LESSING
AND THE JEW MOSES MENDELSSOHN WERE LOVERS**

69

There was still an hour to go before Megan's lecture. After trying out the auditorium mic and testing the PowerPoint onscreen, Megan had asked that she and Egga be given some down time in the small room behind the stage. They had just visited Schiele's prison cell and Egga had marveled at how the basement corridor and cell had been turned into a heavily visited museum.

"And all because *you* discovered it!"

"Ha! As you'll see in my lecture, this was the second time I used that maxim: 'it is sometimes better to beg pardon than to ask permission.'"

"I can't wait."

"Thank you. You're very kind. But now I'd really like to run through my German text with you if you're up to it."

"Of course!"

This would not be the first time Egga had been requested to lend her critical ear to Megan's German pronunciation. She had once accompanied her former teacher to Leipzig when the city was still in Communist hands and where Megan was to give a lecture for one of conductor Kurt Masur's biannual symposia. If anything, Megan's German had sounded Italian. Both times, then and now, Egga had found only a few pronunciation "defects," as she called them. And Megan was gratefully open to correction. One thing for sure, her lectures were always riveting. This one, titled "Egon Schiele in Prison," was devoted to the meticulous drawings he had made of his prison cell, the cellar hall outside which he was forced to clean, and the heavily bolted cellar door which, in the title he gave the drawing, was signified as "The Door into the Open."

At five minutes to two, when the lecture was scheduled to begin, they left the small room and went around the side of the stage. The auditorium was packed. Egga took the front row seat upon which a "Reserved" sign had been placed while Megan joined her genial host, Dr. Günter Wagensommerer, the devoted architect who had turned Schiele's prison into an extraordinary museum where proven artists were occasionally permitted to spend one night creating work in Schiele's cell. Together, Megan and Günter walked to the stage and stood to one side of the lectern. After his introduction and as Günter started to leave the stage, Megan stopped her friend and announced to him and to the audience that she had a small gift for his Museum. She held up a white feather pen more than one hundred years old. It was the last of Schiele's several drawing pens that his sister Melanie had given to her as mementos of her brother. The audience and the recipient were enthralled.

Megan's lecture was indeed riveting as she described what had happened after she located the only building in the small village of Neulengbach where, fifty-one years previously, there could have been a basement cell. It was the district courthouse. No European Schiele scholar had ever bothered to identify or visit it. The cellar cell that had so impacted the artist's life was forgotten. Megan knew Schiele's twelve prison drawings of his dreadful environment by heart, as she had spent hours in the Albertina sketching copies of them to the best of her ability. From eyes to hand to permanent memory. The images were burned into her mind that day as she approached the building.

A sullen bureaucrat at the courthouse entry door prevented her from entering the building however, even after she showed him an enthusiastic letter of recommendation from the director of the Albertina Museum in Vienna. It was the very mention of the big city, it seemed, that ignited the official's ire.

"*But I've come all the way from Texas!*" Megan had protested.

"You cannot enter. There are important government papers inside," the man had answered firmly. There was nothing that Megan could say to change his mind. Sadly she walked away, but not very far away. She stood behind a tree and tried to think of a solution. Then all of a sudden the noon bell rang and people began walking out of the building, including the pompous bureaucrat. This was her chance! She discreetly joined the exiting group of people, but while they were walking forward, she was walking backward. Within moments she was inside. Almost immediately, she spotted the narrow stairway leading down to the dank, dark cellar. It looked exactly as it had in Schiele's drawing of 1912, fifty-one years earlier! Breathlessly, Megan held up her Rolleiflex 2.8 F and photographed the view the artist had drawn, with standing mops and floor bucket still in place.

There were doors to six cells in the cellar corridor. How would she be able to identify in which cell the artist had been locked up? Again, her precise memory of one of his drawings came to the rescue. It showed the initials a previous prisoner had carved into the interior of the closed wooden door: "M H". Megan opened the first cell door. No initials. She pushed open the second door: *there they were!* The initials "M H"! She could feel her heart beating as she raised her camera to take a closeup shot. This was the most important moment of her life! She had discovered Egon Schiele's forgotten prison cell. She turned to glance at the "important government papers." There were none. Instead, stacked firewood. The same in the other five cells—firewood! Her photographic documentation completed, Megan slipped out of the courthouse and into Schiele history as the young American scholar who had discovered the Austrian artist's neglected prison cell. As she told her fascinated audience in conclusion: "Sometimes it is better to beg forgiveness than to ask permission." The audience howled and applauded enthusiastically, finally standing up. Egga smiled to herself: so this was the second time Megan had put into practice her wise adage!

By four o'clock, after an exhausting wine and cheese reception, the two friends were on their way back to Vienna and, for Megan, a well-deserved rest.

70

After demolishing his cheeseburger at the Annagasse Burger King, Henri-Claude de La Granger accompanied Hanskarl Klug back to the Nebehay Antiquariat and said goodbye. He returned to the Römischer Kaiser long enough to leave a note for Megan telling her he was in Vienna. After that he walked down to the end of Annagasse, turned right at the Haus der Musik and onto the long Schwarzenbergstrasse. He continued past the familiar equestrian monument to Karl Philipp, Prince of Schwarzenberg, and arrived at his destination, the Arnold Schönberg Center. It took up half a story in the renovated palace at Schwarzenbergplatz No. 6. In the late nineteen nineties, the Vienna city council had voted unanimously to pay over two million dollars for start-up costs and some 652,000 dollars a year for rent and upkeep.

Although the center was devoted to Mahler's younger colleague, a number of Mahler manuscripts were kept there. Henri-Claude had last seen them in California when they were still in the Schoenberg Institute at the University of Southern California. To the French scholar's irritation, the university had followed the composer's American spelling of his surname. It was actually Megan Crespi who had introduced Henri-Claude to the director, noted musicologist Leonard Stein, and he had been given full access to

Mahler's papers there. But since then everything pertaining to Mahler had been transferred to the newly built Schönberg Center in Vienna, and Henri-Claude wanted to see the additional material since acquired. He was welcomed with open arms and given a private room in which to study the manuscripts. Three fruitful hours fled by and when Henri-Claude looked at his watch he was astonished to see it was four-thirty. He wanted to return to his hotel, rest a bit, and try to connect with Megan. It would be wonderful if they could have dinner together before the Mahler concert this evening.

71

There was one more item Ottokar Weininger needed for this evening's performance of Mahler's tortured symphony. It was his father's service pistol, a Glock 19 with a four-inch barrel, smaller but just as effective as the popular Glock 17. The only problem was retrieving it from his mother's apartment without her knowing. He hated visiting his widowed mom. All she could talk about was the past, and she kept asking the same questions over and over again. It had been over a year since he last saw her. He would make the visit as short as possible and there was always the chance that she might be at the grocery store—the only place she went now that she was on a walker. She lived out in Heiligenstadt, where Beethoven once lived, in a rundown building on the Grinzinger Strasse. From the convenient Opera stop the D tram took Ottokar straight out to the northern nineteenth district and within a block of his mother's apartment house.

The elevator was out of commission. That was a bad sign. Mutti would be homebound. He climbed the four flights of stairs and knocked loudly on his mother's door. He heard a slow progression of footsteps and then his mother's voice asking tremulously who was there.

"It's me, Ottokar, Mutti."

"I'm not at home."

"What do you mean you're not at home? I'm *talking* to you."

"I'm not at home to *you*. You never visit me anymore. You've forgotten all about me. You're not my son.

"Mutti! That's why I'm here. To visit you."

"How can I know it's you?"

"Just open the door and you'll see it's me." He was about to pull out his own key to the apartment when the sound of a bolt being pulled back reached his ears. A moment later the door opened and his mother stood on the threshold looking up at him suspiciously.

"So it is you."

"Let's go inside, Mutti." He put his arm around her frail shoulders and turned her gently around, walking them into the small room that served as her bedroom, dining room, and living room. He sat her down and faced her.

"I came to talk to see how you are and to talk to you about Papa."

"Papa? He's not here right now."

"Yes, I know. Where does he keep his things?"

"He wouldn't want me to tell you. He's not here. He's at the grocery store."

"Yes, I saw him there. He wants his box. You know, the box where you put all his things when he went, um, goes away. He wants me to get something for him out of the box."

"That box was his father's, you know."

"Yes, you've told me many times. Where does he keep it?"

"Under the couch where you're sitting. Where it's always been. You say he's at the grocery store?"

Ottokar didn't answer his mother. He was on his knees sweeping the space underneath the couch with his right arm and hand. There was nothing.

"Mutti, there's no box here."

"I know. Papa took it with him to the grocery store. Did I ever tell you what he most likes to have for breakfast?"

"Yes, you have. Where does Vati put his box when it isn't under the couch?"

"With his gun."

"With his gun?"

"Yes. Do you want me to show you?"

"Yes. Please." His mother reached up for her walker, hoisted herself and made her way to a closet by the door. She opened the door. There were only two items in the closet. Her winter coat and her husband's winter coat."

"Where's the pistol?"

"In the pocket of the coat."

Ottokar pulled his father's coat out into the room and thrust his hand in the pocket closest to him. The other pocket. Nothing.

163

"It's not here. There isn't anything in these pockets."

"That's true, dear. Not since your father left for the grocery store."

Ottokar resisted the impulse to strangle his mother then and there.

"Here," she said, reaching into the front pocket of her own winter coat.

"Is this what Papa wants to have at the grocery store?"

She held up the Glock 19.

"Yes! I have to take it to him right away." He grabbed the pistol and jerked open the front door with never a backward glance at his mother.

"I enjoyed our visit," he heard her say as he galloped down the stairs. Now he had everything he needed for what should be a heart-stopping performance of Mahler's Second Symphony.

72

It had happened again. Harry was out—said he had an errand—and Haim was just about to water the large plants in the salon when he began hiccupping violently. Choking for breath, he sat down as fast as he could, grabbing his throat. The watering can fell to the floor. Then the spasms stopped as abruptly as they had begun. Haim felt his pulse. It was racing. He pressed his hand over his heart. It was racing as well but there was no pain. Houdini had put his muzzle on his lap, looking up at him with great inquiring eyes. He had seen his master act like this once before.

Haim self-diagnosed. If this was a mini-stroke, so let it be. He felt fine now. And there was no need to tell Harry. He worried so about things. And this evening they were attending a dream concert. Mahler's Second Symphony with Gerald Chaplin conducting. Nothing could make him miss that! And it would break Harry's heart if they couldn't go. Haim mopped up the water from the floor, refilled the watering can, and continued taking care of his beloved plants, exact duplicates of the ones shown in paintings of Makart's studio.

About half an hour later he heard the front door open. It was Harry. He had a briefcase with him.

"Where have you been, honey?"

"To the bank. Needed to get something done and it took much longer than I thought it would."

"I was beginning to think you'd forgotten about tonight."

"How could I forget? It's practically a dream come true."

"We are so very lucky," Haim smiled and looked deeply into his partner's blue eyes.

"Yes. Makart and Mahler. Callas and Bell. Houdini. Who could ask for anything more?"

73

A curious and noisy crowd had begun gathering in front of the Lessing monument in Judenplatz. Soon the press was there as well with photographers snapping closeup views of the cardboard-printed message taped on the statue's pedestal with its weird claim. Most of the gawkers had no idea who either Lessing or Moses Mendelssohn were, but the hatred emanating from the sign was unmistakable.

"Did they even *have* homosexuality in those days?" asked one naïve teenager.

No one thought of removing the weird poster until the police arrived on the scene when it was instantly taken down and plastic-wrapped for fingerprinting.

Callas, who had been visiting the Judenplatz branch of her museum, was one of the first to run to the increasingly raucous scene. As the daughter of a Jewish father who was also gay, she was outraged. Why would anyone tape such a hateful message onto the statue pedestal? It had to be someone well-educated in the history of German literature. Or did it? With today's instant online education anyone could have learned about the two cultural figures. But there was nothing about either of the historic figures' personal history that indicated homosexuality. And even had one or both of them had been gay, so what? And yet the animosity of the brief, six-word message was blatantly purposeful. Meant to demean a Christian Lessing and a Jewish Mendelssohn. Who would want to do this? Was this yet another instance of hatred simmering in the city that had begun with the Mahler Bomber? She only knew that the hateful poster made her feel physically nauseated. How she hoped her dads would not learn of the incident. She, her brother Bell, and their dads were all attending a concert tonight that could certainly be the target of additional Jew-hating focus. The music was written by a Jew and the conductor was Jewish.

But why was it *necessary* to know whether a composer was Jewish or not? Or a musician or an artist or an author? Why was it important to know that a conductor was Jewish? Was it really necessary to know if one of your friends was Jewish? Or Muslim? Why is there so much racial hatred in the world? Walking back to her museum as the crowd began to disperse, Callas tried to find any plausible answer to her questions. She did not.

74

It was customary for symphony players at the Musikverein to arrive a full hour before performance and this evening was no different. In fact instrumentalists and singers alike began arriving even earlier, as the logistics were quite complicated and the American conductor Gerald Chaplin had asked that they be in their places onstage and in the front balconies and long balcony on either side of the organ with its great row of pipes by six-forty at the latest. As the performers gathered, one topic was discussed with excitement: the ring of upbeat protesters that had gathered outside the building yelling their support for Jewish music and Jewish conductors. What an extraordinary preamble to their performance of Mahler! The excited instrumentalists and vocalists were at their most appreciative and attentive. And they were right to be so. Eager anticipation was the emotion felt by all who entered the Musikverein building that evening, whether performers or auditors.

All except one.

Ottokar Weininger had timed his entry into the Musikverein perfectly. Casually carrying his pawnshop-acquired case for a contrabass trombone—for which ironically there was no role in Mahler's vast score to the giant symphony—he joined two trumpet players he knew and they entered together, inserting their ID cards into the chip reader at the stage door entrance. Instead of walking to the back of the stage where his colleagues were going, however, he broke off and headed toward the dressing rooms, looking for one in particular. After that he entered the auditorium balcony on audience left where one of the two small brass ensembles was gathering. He took a seat behind and above the two trombonists and smiled at them as he laid his case down.

"Yet another free symphony ticket, for you, huh, Ottokar?" one of them said jokingly.

"I wouldn't miss it for the world."

From his position Ottokar had a perfect, unblocked view of the conductor's raised podium. Let the symphony begin. *He knew exactly what his musical cue would be.*

75

Michael Hüttler had kept his word. From six o'clock on, a large, enthusiastic group of students from MedUni had formed a linked-arm ring around the large Musikverein building and were chanting the refrain: "*We say yes to Jewish music in Vienna, we say yes to Jewish conductors in Vienna!*" Other young people joined their ranks as did some surprised individuals who happened to be passing the Musikverein. A few policemen were present but they made no move to silence the chanters. Members of the press also began to gather. Rita Rausch was one of them. Leaving her photographer to shoot any events, she entered the building and took her standing spot in the back of the second balcony. It faced the orchestra stage. Chief of Police Erich Decker was also on hand. He had chosen to stand next to the organ on the balcony where he had a full view of the audience on all levels from ground floor up to the highest back balconies. At precisely seven o'clock when the concert was scheduled to begin, the chanting would stop on Michael's signal. The demonstrators would remain silently in place during the entire concert. Press photographers and TV interviewers recorded their presence. What a wonderful statement from Vienna's citizens! This was the true Vienna.

76

"It's just too good to be true!" Megan was hugging Henri-Claude as they met in the lobby of the Römischer Kaiser. She had gotten his message and called his room. Dinner together would be wonderful. She, too, was going to the Mahler concert and someone he had met at one of the Gewandhaus symposia in Leipzig would be with her. When Henri-Claude saw Egga approaching him alongside Megan, he exclaimed in recognition and gave the grinning cellist a hug as well.

"But why didn't you tell me you were coming to Wien?" Megan asked reproachfully.

"It was a last-minute decision. Vito has been quite sick and I didn't want to leave his side. But these past two days he's seemed much better so at the last minute I decided to fly here. And Gerald, bless his heart, got me a seat."

"Singing tenor in the choir." Megan added playfully.

"Where shall we eat?" Henri-Claude asked the two women, ignoring Megan's silliness.

"Just down at the end of the street," answered Megan, "there's a really good Italian restaurant, Salieri. We'll be close to the Musikverein and won't have to rush dinner."

"Excellent. After you, ladies." They exited the hotel.

Megan was delighted when they entered the restaurant because her favorite table was free. It was separate from all the other tables in an alcove of its own just to the left of the entrance. They would be able to hear each other talk. She chose gnocchi, her friends both chose vitello tonnato. They ordered a Nero d'Avola Sicilian red wine which Megan ruined by squirting some strawberry kiwi Dasani drops into her glass.

"I love the health benefits of red wine," she explained to her horrified friends, "but I don't like its taste. This is my solution." Henri-Claude was indignant.

"I suppose you also castrate male dogs?"

"Yes. My little Button was neutered. Why do you ask?"

"I ask because I find it a barbaric American custom. I would never, ever castrate my Vito."

"Well, maybe if you had, he wouldn't have attacked me and nipped my arm when I entered your guest room four years ago."

"That was because my previous guest there had been a man, and Vito was surprised." Henri-Claude had been dismayed that his dog had attacked Megan and had rushed her to a walk-in clinic where she was treated.

"You know how sorry I am about that, dear, dear Megan."

"Of course I do. Let's forget about it." They spoke for a few minutes about the curious case concerning a stolen Klimt work that had brought her to Europe.

"Would anyone like an espresso before we walk to the Musikverein?" Egga asked, changing the subject.

"Yes!" Megan and Henri-Claude said at the same time.

They had plenty of time still so they lingered over their espressos. Megan recounted for Egga's amusement how she had played a "Mahler" trick on Henri-Claude when he was visiting her once in Texas. With the compliance of a student music composition major, she created a musical score page with orchestration written out in a Mahler lookalike script. Then with a few drops of water they "aged" it in a microwave and secreted it in the drawer of a gift that had been made to the Music Department of SMU decades ago: the wooden desk Mahler had used during his summers at Toblach. Touring the university the next day with Henri-Claude, Megan led him through the music library to the inner office where the Mahler desk was kept. As he eyed it reverently, Megan said, equally reverently, "Wouldn't it be amazing if Mahler had left something in the drawers?"

"Ha! That would be something." Megan persisted.

"I wonder if anyone has even ever opened them." She pulled open the top drawer and pretended surprise.

"Look! There's something in the back!" She pulled out a balled-up sheet of score paper and handed it to Henri-Claude. Dubiously, he unfolded the paper, looked at the freshly-penned orchestra score page for a mini-second, then chortled heartily and accused Megan correctly of playing a trick on him. The two friends laughingly relived the moment of deception.

Egga reminded Henri-Claude how they had met at one of conductor Kurt Masur's symposia in the early 1970s. She had traveled there with Megan who, even then, treasured her help with complicated German pronunciations. They had all posed for a jolly photograph at the end of the symposium which that year was on Brahms. Masur had heard Megan lecture on the composer during a guest appearance at her university in Dallas and that was why she had first been invited to Leipzig—to repeat her lecture on Brahms there. She had returned twice to give lectures on Beethoven and on Bruckner. Ah, those were the days!

Megan recounted how, during that period when East Germany was still under Communist rule, Kurt had regularly worn, in silent protest of the regime, a bolo tie he had acquired in Dallas. They all lamented his recent death from complications of Parkinson's disease. Henri-Claude had many charming stories to tell about the magnificent conductor who was especially known for his masterful interpretations of composers as different as Beethoven, Tchaikovsky and Prokofiev. And yet performing Gershwin was not beneath him. And Megan remembered how Masur told her about the abrupt end of what might have been a promising piano career because of the development of a shortened tendon in the little finger of his right hand. Later, in the full glory of his fame as a conductor, he used to laugh and give thanks to the little finger that had propelled him into the right profession.

Henri-Claude became serious as he recalled and related how sensitively Masur had conducted the massive five-movement "Resurrection" symphony they were to hear this evening.

"So what do you think of the American conductor's treatment of Mahler we're going to hear, or shall I say, see tonight?" Egga asked. She had her doubts about a self-educated man whose conducting was limited to one symphony. Henri-Claude spread his hands and smiled benignly

"*Alors*, Gerald Chaplin is a phenomenon unto himself. There may be arguments as to his rhythmic command—you know how constantly Mahler's inner rhythms can change—but there is no argument as to the knowledge and passion with which he leads an orchestra. Gerald has conducted just about every major orchestra and he has learned as well as given. So I would definitely give him a high passing grade."

His two listeners knew he was speaking sincerely. But neither one of them was totally convinced. After all, Henri-Claude and Gerald Chaplin were friends. As if sensing what they were thinking he added: "He *is* a womanizer, this can't be denied. There was a sizzler of an infamous affair in Berlin with a member of the Berlin Philharmonic orchestra when he was conducting there, I remember. In fact Gerald's left broken hearts on several continents."

"I'd heard as much," Egga acknowledged with a roll of her eyes. Megan decided to change the way the conversation was going.

"How do you yourself see the structure and the meaning of Mahler's symphony?" Megan asked the great Mahler biographer and expert.

"How much time do we have?" Her French friend smiled ruefully, spreading his hands open to suggest the immensity of such a task.

"You both know it deals with the greatest questions of life, death, and a belief in life after death. You may be aware that it was Mahler's favorite of his ten symphonies. And that he was well aware listeners would think he was imitating Beethoven's Ninth Symphony which had first introduced voices in a symphony. But this did not stop him: the final two movements have, as you know, solo voices, a mixed chorus, and sung verses."

"Oh yes," Egga exclaimed and sang: "*O Röschen rot! Der Mensch liegt in größter Not!*"

Megan repeated the words in English: "Oh, little rose! Man lies in greatest need!"

"*Ich bin von Gott und will wieder zu Gott!*" Egga jumped ahead to the symphony's hard-won, comforting conclusion.

"I am from God and will return to God," Megan translated quietly to herself. Henri-Claude continued.

"But before we get there we must first endure the startling, explosive, huge first movement, the *Allegro maestoso* that dares to search for the meaning of life."

The two women nodded in agreement.

"Did you know Mahler wanted a five-minute *pause* after the first movement before the symphony continued?" he asked.

"That's something certainly not done in modern performances," Egga smiled. Henri-Claude continued, warming to his subject.

"One could understand the middle three movements—basically a dance, a waltz, and a child's song—as preparation for the final movement's revelation and eventual resurrection. The *Andante moderato* communicates bliss and sad recollections; the *Scherzo* articulates a negative, despairing of self and of God with its climaxing cry of despair, and the fourth movement, with the alto solo, *Röschen rot*, is a naïve child's song." Henri-Claude paused, then asked his friends another question.

"Did you know that the final movement, in *Tempo des Scherzo*, with chorus and verses by both Klopstock and Mahler, lasts thirty-eight and a half minutes?'

"I knew it was well over half an hour," Egga confirmed and Megan nodded.

"Mahler's reason for this was to allow the terrified, and terrifying music to have time to sound and encompass all the emotions of life, all stages of doubt, fear, and triumph. Every now and then we hear the four-note quotation from the thirteenth-century hymn that Berlioz also used, the *dies irae*—day of wrath. The symphony has crashes, timidity, hopeful fanfares, quivering misgivings, funeral dirges, hushed expectancy, and an at first barely audible a cappella chorale that climaxes in that triumphant mix of chorus and soloists singing Mahler's own words '*Sterben werd ich um zu leben*—die shall I in order to live'—one of the most glorious and powerful endings in the history of music."

"Yes, and all that is amplified by Mahler's gigantic percussion section, the offstage brass, and the vast sound of some three hundred or more players and singers," Megan added reverently.

Time passed so quickly that they were surprised when the waiter presented their check. Only then did they realize it was high time to get moving. Since they were already at the end of the Annagasse they turned into the broad Schwarzenbergstrasse, crossed the Kärntner Ring to the Hotel Imperial, then down the short Canovagasse to the Musikverein. They were astonished to see a large throng of university students with linked arms surrounding the building. They were yelling a chant: "*We say yes to Jewish music in Vienna, we say yes to Jewish conductors in Vienna!*" Other people were spontaneously joining the students and the excitement was almost palpable. The demonstrators, who had linked arms, courteously broke their circle any time concert goers approached, then linked ranks again. Once Henri-Claude, Megan, and Egga had entered the auditorium they went their separate ways—the two women to aisle seats on stage left and right of the same row half way down the auditorium, and Henri-Claude to the front row seat provided by the conductor of this evening's performance.

What a treat was in store for them all at the Musikverein this evening!

77

The entire Schmidt family, including Stefan, who was proudly playing first desk cello in the orchestra, were at the Musikverein that evening. They had come quite early because of Basileus's poor health and were amazed to see the pro-Jewish demonstration staged by dozens and dozens of university students who were in the process of forming a ring around the building. There was no menace, just enthusiasm and a camaraderie that was infectious. Even though, because of the discrimination his son had received in the opera house orchestra, Basileus Schmidt did not care for Jews in general, he was certainly willing to accept individual Jewish artists like Mahler who was, after all, a convert to Catholicism. Or someone, say, like the brilliant British politician Benjamin Disrali, who became an Anglican at the age of twelve.

He thought about the treasure he had discovered in the Vienna National Library so many years ago which was locked up in his safe at home. The mere thought of it made him all the more eager to hear tonight's concert in which music would convey the great questions of life and death. An orchestration that included the human voice was very much a reflection of the composer's high-strung, nervous, persevering, fearful, critical, demanding self. Never had Mahler forgotten the criticism given by revered Wagner conductor Hans von Bülow when he played for him on the piano his *Totenfeier* march for the Second Symphony: "If that is still music, then I do not understand a single thing about music!"

Having become, because of his find, an avid Mahler fan, Basileus was familiar with all the biographies of the man and even found himself sympathizing over the often hateful critiques of his music, both during his lifetime and even now. Certainly Bülow's rejection was one of the severest.

Because of his connections, Basileus, Sabina, and Adele had front row seats behind the conductor in the great golden auditorium hall. They had no idea that the handsome, white-haired man seated next to them on the aisle was the world authority on Gustav Mahler.

78

A contingent from the International Mahler Society had made its way through the ring of welcome demonstrators. They were Berta Zuckerkandl, the local doyenne, Ben Geistert, the society's president, and Tonik Nektar, the despair of the society. Nektar had made sure he had a seat downstairs where he thought the acoustics were best but the other two climbed the stairs to the second balcony. Heaven knows it was worth the climb. Their subscription seats were in the front row center and their long view down the hall gave them everything: the audience, the boxes, the orchestra, the conductor, the choir, and the mighty organ. Zuckerkandl looked around approvingly, then quoted to Geistert what her legendary grandmother once said of her famous society parlor: "*In meinem Salon ist Österreich*—In my salon is Austria."

79

Haim and Henri were dressed in their best as were Callas and Bell. As they approached the Musikverein they were amazed to see and hear the demonstrators ringing the building and chanting their support of Jewish composers and Jewish conductors. What a first for Vienna! Haim was deeply moved. He had seen nothing like it during his many decades of living in Vienna. He thought about how his parents, by emigrating to America in the early 1940s, had narrowly escaped the notorious roundup of Romaniote Jews in Ioannina during the final months of Nazi control of Greece. Almost two thousand Romaniote Jews were deported to Auschwitz and murdered. Haim knew that only about fifty elderly Jews now lived in Ioannina. The small city had recently constructed a monument in its thirteenth-century Jewish cemetery to honor the thousands of Greek Jews who had perished in the Holocaust. A small comfort. And Haim also knew that in 2003 the memorial was vandalized and that since then, the Jewish cemetery itself had been repeatedly vandalized. *When would it ever stop?*

Harry gently touched his hand as they pressed through the friendly ring of activists. He knew what his dear one was thinking. Callas and Bell had stopped to talk with two of the demonstrators they knew. Why don't you join us, they asked. If we didn't have tickets to this super rare concert we would join you, was their answer.

Their four seats were downstairs in the front row of the second section to audience left. The orchestra was already in place and spaced out on the stage with its five raised ramps forming a seating arc across the stage. Bell got a kick out of spotting some of the trombonists he knew in the orchestra. He glanced up at the four balcony boxes on his side nearest to the stage. The boxes were only partly occupied by audience members. The other half, further back and closer, to amateur trombonist Bell's delight, was occupied by one of the two "distant" brass bands called for in Mahler's score. They stretched to the first exit's flight of descending stairs below that led directly to the street. The second brass band was disposed in exactly the same way in the boxes opposite.

Callas also saw several people who she knew were connected to her work at the museum. One of them, an American country music fan, told her that they were about to hear the maxi-equivalent of Eddy Arnold's contented last song, "To Life." Callas smiled politely but was inwardly nonplussed. Certainly not, she thought to herself. Mahler's ode to eternity was wrested from doubt and despair! She settled down for the mighty musical experience awaiting them.

80

Mary Neff had stopped to talk to one of her Opera vocalists whom she spotted linking arms with the students outside the Musikverein. She was delighted to see the woman's activism but cautioned her not to join in the chants at full voice; it could damage her vocal folds. It was fifteen minutes to seven. Mary entered the stage door that gave on to the Dumbastrasse and joined the chorus singers backstage. The two-hundred voice choir would not take its position in the balcony on either side of the organ until that eloquent five-minute pause after the first movement. The symphony itself lasted between eighty and ninety minutes. The less standing the better.

81

It was now four minutes after seven. The audience's murmuring had increased and all eyes were on the orchestra. Everyone awaited the entrance of American conductor Gerald Chaplin.

Finally the figure of a man appeared on audience right and a few people began to clap. But this was not the conductor! He was not dressed appropriately and he was not making his way to the front of the orchestra and the one-step podium. Instead he stood where he was, a microphone in his hand, faced the audience, and jerkily signaled for silence.

"My honored ladies and gentlemen," he said in a piercing high-pitched voice, looking agitatedly left and right.

"I am general manager of the Musikverein, Albert Vogt. I have to tell you that *a death threat against Maestro Chaplin has been found in his dressing room.*"

Everyone in the auditorium and on stage gasped as if one.

"The police have thoroughly searched backstage and everything is now secured. But, given the circumstances..."

A huge collective sigh of disappointment filled the auditorium.

Then suddenly a second man appeared on stage. Dressed in black with a white collar, he was walking straight up to general manager. People recognized him. He was Gerald Chaplin. The audience and players began cheering and applauding.

Chaplin held up his hands. There was an immediate hush.

"Yes, It is true. A crazy, deranged threat was found in my dressing room. But . . . if you feel as I feel, *Mahler cannot be intimidated.*" Loud shouts of support sounded from all sides of the auditorium and many people stood up.

"So if it is your wish, Mahler's Second Symphony will be performed this evening!"

Every single person present stood up and a chant began: "*Play, maestro, play!*"

Chaplin bowed his head and stood silent for a full minute. An appreciative hush fell over the audience.

Then he turned energetically to the orchestra, looked left, center, and right, seeming to make eye connection with each player. He raised his baton. It appeared to stay poised in the air for an eternity, but in reality, it was only a few seconds. Chaplin gave a swift upbeat, then came the downbeat and the initial rapid notes of the first movement of Mahler's *Resurrection Symphony* sounded.

The opening measure of the *Allegro maestoso* was a unison G tremolo in the upper strings that began with a double fortissimo followed by a swift decrescendo to piano in just one measure. Then came the cellos and string basses in the fleeting second measure with four rapidly moving eighth notes—C, B-natural, C, D—culminating in an E-flat quarter-note that made the music sound as if it were in the key of C minor. This was Mahler to the core, masking tonalities. Actually the symphony so far was in the relative minor of the key signature E-flat major, although both keys have three flats. Thus, the listeners did not actually know what the first measure's tonality was—a puzzle. It epitomized the conundrum of human existence, something that Mahler would obsessively explore throughout the five movements of a symphony that took seven years to write—he was thirty-four when he completed the mammoth work.

During the five-minute pause that followed the conclusion of the symphony's first movement, utter silence prevailed. The two soloists and the almost two hundred singers assembled for the chorus entered the auditorium soundlessly and took their places three deep on either side of the organ and in the balcony closest to the stage. Chaplin stood motionless with his head down, eyes closed in concentration. Then he lifted his baton in upbeat and with the downbeat the second movement began.

It was in three/eight time, sounding like a genial country Ländler or even a slow waltz. Chaplin lightly emphasized the first beat throughout and the rectangular auditorium with its boxes, U-shaped continuous balcony and sculptures allowed numerous sound reflections. But wait, that darker tone. Was it all just joy or were there some sad reminiscences in the darker passages? The audience was left to decide for itself.

The third movement was in a sinuous *Scherzo* format and alternated carefree moods with declarative brass flourishes, sudden ascending screeches of reed and wind instruments in what Mahler himself called "death shrieks," and occasional reminiscences of Jewish folk music. At least one of the Mahler experts listening thought that if ever there were an anti-Semitic moment for fulfilling the death threat against Gerald Chaplin's life, this was it. Praise God, nothing happened.

The fourth movement, marked *"Urlicht—Primeval Light"*—brought the alto soloist forth with the child's naïve song *Röschen rot* and its reassuring declaration *"Ich bin von Gott und will wieder zu Gott—I come of God and will return to God."* There was no pause between the fourth and the vast fifth movement, marked "in the tempo of a scherzo." It began with a startling crash of instruments—the death shriek—joined later by the offstage brass sounding the last trumpet call and braced by the visceral presence of massive percussion instruments at tremendous volume. There were times when the brass, especially the French horns, sounded idyllic and welcoming, then abruptly menacing. One heard motivic references to the *Dies Irae—Day of Wrath*. One heard welcome calmness, hope, then doubt, fear, shuddering. The constant variation at staggering pace within a prevailing tempo suggested to knowledgeable Mahlerites in the audience the manner in which Mahler actually walked, lurching forward and constantly changing his stride. Then, just past the halfway point of the movement, after an idyllic welcoming from the high winds, one of the quietest choral entrances in the history of music occurred: Friedrich Klopstock's ten lines beginning with "*Aufersteh'n, ja aufersteh'n—Rise again, yes rise again*"—followed by twenty-six lines of Mahler's own words with the final hard-won, prospect of resurrection—"*Aufersteh'n.*"

When the orchestra and vocalists got to Mahler's first word of the fortissimo fifth measure before the end of the symphony—"*Die* shall I in order to live," something unimaginable happened.

Two pistol shots sped inaudibly through the mighty musical apotheosis across the auditorium. The bullets came from different directions and landed on the left and right side of Gerald Chaplin's head. He fell over dead.

82

Sheer bedlam broke out onstage and in the huge auditorium. From his post in the balcony next to the organ a horrified Erich Decker was desperately scanning the vast hall as he called for both an ambulance crew and a forensic analyst. There was suspicious movement in one of the balcony boxes close to the stage. It was the fourth one back. The brass players there seemed to be turning around and shouting at each other, pointing to the exit stairs underneath and next to them. Stairs that, from their site, one would have had to jump over the box railing to reach. Decker saw a tall, boney man from the audience come racing down the aisle to the exit staircase and disappear down it. Was he in pursuit of the suspect, or was he the shooter? The man must be caught. He issued quick commands on his cellphone while keeping a vigilant eye on the auditorium and stage.

The orchestra members seemed to be in shock, frozen and holding on to their instruments protectively. Decker scanned the players and singers below him. It was impossible to judge each face, each movement. He called his second in command who assured him all exits were being closed. Decker issued further instructions and then hurried down to the orchestra level. Switching on his handheld mic, he gave instructions to all those present. No one was to leave the building. Audience and orchestra members were to remain in place. It was possible that body searches would have to be carried out. God! This was like a repeat of the opera house explosion! Only this time someone had been murdered.

He watched as an ambulance crew, and then the forensic analyst arrived. She knelt over the body of Gerald Chaplin. He was on his back, limbs splayed outward, and with what was left of his massively bleeding head showing two entry holes, one at the temple, one below the ear. There was nothing to be done.

"What have you found?" Erich asked, identifying himself. The physician answered.

"There are at least two points of bullet entry. One is on the left side of the head, the other is on the right side. We'll have to wait for the autopsy to know everything."

"Of course. But in the meanwhile I do ask you to send over the bullets as soon as they are removed. We hope that identifying what make of the pistols used will be helpful. We may be able to trace the owners. It's a small possibility but we can't overlook it."

"Gotcha!" the medical analyst said.

"Erich!" He heard his name called out and saw Megan and Egga racing from their aisle seats toward him despite his instructions that audience members remain in place.

"It's not possible!" Megan gasped when she reached him.

"Incredible," murmured Egga, staring at the body on the stage floor to which the medical examiner had now returned. A police photographer was taking close-up shots.

"What is incredible is that there were *two* assassins shooting simultaneously from opposite sides," said Erich.

"What? But how could such a thing even be possible?" Megan was having trouble visualizing such an act.

"Do you have any idea who the assassins could have been?" Egga asked.

"Right now, no. We're still trying to establish precisely where the two shots came from. Our forensic analyst is taking measurements as we speak."

"That should tell us something. But where do *you* think the shots came from?" asked Megan, still trying to wrap her mind around an apparently simultaneous double shooting.

"Again, right now I just can't say. They could have come from either side of the orchestra or chorus, or even audience. If from the audience, probably from one of the front boxes or balcony as it circles the stage. But anyone doing that would surely have been noticed. I was standing right by the organ and I saw nothing suspicious on either side of me." Erich shook his head in frustration and continued.

"And how could the shots have occurred at precisely the same time? It has to mean we have two assassins who must have been in cahoots. All the singers were performing at that moment so I'm thinking there could have been a key word in the text when they were singing, since the timing was so incredibly precise." Erich wiped his forehead with his handkerchief. He was thinking out loud.

"So it had to be two persons who know the symphony extremely well. In all likelihood two musicians—maybe one vocalist and one instrumentalist. And even not necessarily someone in the orchestra or chorus. It could be a musicologist or someone well acquainted with the particular symphony played this evening. That the shots were simultaneous points to a musical cue." Megan nodded her head vigorously and touched her friend's arm.

"Absolutely right, Erich. I can give you the cue right down to a single word. The vocalists were all singing the same word: 'Sterben.'"

"Right! 'Die'! That's when it happened. Insidiously clever," said Egga, "and so satanically mean."

"Oh, yes, the assassins must have been very proud of themselves," Megan pronounced sarcastically.

"But at least they've left the clues that both are very knowledgeable about Mahler, and this narrows it down somewhat . . . I hope," sighed the police chief.

The forensic analyst had just finished her first reading of the blood spatter patterns. She turned to Erich.

"Okay, we can give you a pretty good idea now of where the shots came from. When the shots took place, the victim had just turned his head slightly to audience left. The shot that hit the maestro's left temple most likely came from the third or fourth balcony box at the end of that row over there closest to the stage." She was pointing to audience left.

"That substantiates what I actually saw from where I was standing near the organ," Erich confirmed. He spoke to all of them.

"There was great commotion in the fourth balcony box where the brass players were sitting and standing. They were all turning and pointing to the exit stairs just below them. Presumably the shooter. Then I saw a man from the audience—he was quite tall and thin—come racing down the aisle and disappear down the same staircase. Don't know if he was chasing the shooter or if he was somehow in cahoots with the shooter. I called my men and told them to hunt them both down. They exited on the Dumbastrasse side. I haven't heard back from them yet."

"And the other shot?" Megan asked the physician who was listening with interest.

"Here's where we have something really definite. At first we thought it might have come from the balcony overlooking the stage on audience right. But the blood spatter pattern indicates the shot came from much lower and much closer to the maestro. From the back of the stage over there." The physician turned and pointed to her right and the uppermost ramp on the stage.

They turned in the direction she was indicating. They all were looking at the same thing: a harp. The player of the harp—a woman—was sitting on the far side of the instrument. They could see her body but not her face from where they stood. Erich, Megan, and Egga looked at each other all with the same thought.

"You want to know who the harpist is on audience right?" they heard a voice ask from behind them. It was Mary Neff who had discreetly followed Erich down from the organ balcony and was standing with them.

"I can tell you exactly who. I was standing just above her. It's Paloma."

83

With his wiry physique and long legs, Tonik Nektar was a fast runner despite being in his mid-fifties. Exiting the Musikverein building on the Dumbastrasse, he looked left and right and witnessed the tail end of an angry argument between some of the demonstrators who had linked arms and a thin, stoop-shouldered man clutching a large musical instrument case who was trying to press his way through their line. Tonik almost caught up with the man as he crashed through the demonstrators' line. What was left behind however was the black instrument case the fleeing man had thrown to the ground.

"Take that case to the police!" Tonik commanded as the demonstrators, realizing he was trying to catch the man ahead of him, parted to let him through.

Tonik ran to the Ringstrasse. Frustratingly, the man he had almost caught had blended in with the pedestrians who were out and about at that time of the evening. It was eight-thirty. Cursing his luck, Tonik decided to run up the Ringstrasse to the underground Opera Passage. Perhaps the man was going to take the escalator or stairs down and try to blend in with the crowd of tourists who were always to be seen ogling the shops in the elegant subterranean passage. His quarry would be dressed differently from the usual tourist. As one of the instrumentalists he would be in the standard formal black apparel worn for orchestra events.

Tonik's search was in vain. Exhausted and exasperated, he decided to return to the Musikverein and learn what he could about the terrible tragedy he had witnessed. What was the motive for the murder? Could it be anything other than a terrible hate crime directed not only at the greatest Jewish composer who ever lived, but a renowned Jewish conductor as well? There could be no other explanation. But why does anti-Semitism continue to exist? Is it because we are seen as "the other"? But to Westerners, aren't Asians "the other"? Aren't Muslims "the other"? Why can't we all just simply get along?

84

The orchestra and audience had been told to stay in their places and, with the exception of Megan and Egga, so they had. Seated in the front row facing the orchestra, Basileus, Sabina, and Adele Schmidt were exchanging worried glances with Stefan, who was holding his cello far out to one side in an effort to watch the medical team surrounding the body of Gerald Chaplin. Now and then he would look out at his family and send them baffled shrugs as to what was going on. As principal cellist, he felt it his duty to calm the other cellists while they obeyed the police orders to stay where they were. He wheeled around in his seat and caught the eye of the youngest cellist. She was also the furthest away.

"Everything okay back there, Julie?"

"Not really." She leaned forward and cupped her hand to her mouth. "I think I witnessed something the police should know about."

"Oh? What?"

"Over my right shoulder I saw the harpist over me there stand up suddenly just before the maestro fell to the floor. I couldn't see what she was doing because her right hand was blocked by the harp, but she was looking straight at Chaplin when I saw him collapse to the ground."

"The police should definitely know about that, Julie. Let me see what I can do." Stefan stood up and waved his right hand wildly at the policeman in charge who had used the podium mic to issue orders to stay in place. Erich Decker saw the commotion out of the corner of his eye and turned toward the agitated orchestra player. He had planned to interrogate each member personally, but this young man seemed eager to talk to him now. Rather than have the cello player come to him, Erich strode over and up the first ramp.

"What's up?"

"It's what the cellist in the back row saw. We both think you should know. She says she witnessed the harpist, the one nearest her there on the right, stand up suddenly and stare at our conductor just before he was shot."

"Is the harpist she saw named Cristina Paloma?"

"Yes, that's the one. Cristina Paloma. See, she's back there sitting behind her harp and looking glum."

"All right. Thank you and thank your colleague for me."

Without another word Erich signaled Megan to join him. They climbed up the five low stage ramps, turned right at the top one and walked straight over to the harpist. They were both well aware of who she was and what type of explosive personality she possessed from their interview with her the evening before when the Mahler Bomber interrupted *Fidelio*. She was that self-important Italian drama queen.

"*Frau* Paloma, we need to interview you concerning what you were doing during the last few minutes before Maestro Gerald Chaplin was shot."

"It's not 'Frau,' it's 'Fräulein.' Actually *Signorina*. And I had just stood up to stretch. It's a long symphony. We still had sixty-nine measures to go. Is stretching now a crime?"

"I think we can do without the sarcasm, *Fräulein* Paloma. We've just had a murder in front of well over two thousand people."

"Let me see if we have this right," Megan cut in abruptly without concealing her disbelief. "It was a few minutes before the end of the symphony and you suddenly needed to *stretch*?"

"*Sì*. What's wrong with that?"

"Wrong?" Megan almost shouted. "You stood up to stretch just at the very moment Chaplin was shot? I'd say that was pretty convenient if you were holding a pistol in your right hand and you intended to use it."

"How *dare* you?" The two women glared at each other.

"*Fräulein* Paloma," announced Erich Decker, "you are under arrest on suspicion of murder."

85

Henri-Claude could not help overhearing the lively conversation going on between the family members seated next to him in the front row of the auditorium. They were discussing whether or not the text Mahler had written for the conclusion of his Resurrection Symphony was his true belief and if the murder of the conductor at the exact time the final thought of death and resurrection was being literally voiced was calculated or not.

"It has to have been an accident," said a young woman, obviously the daughter. Her mother was not so sure.

"I think any of the really loud parts of the symphony could have served as cover. No one would hear the shot. Maybe the shooter wanted to have his own 'finale' and that's why he waited to almost the end for that reason. He might have known that the symphony was going to be deafening at the end." Henri-Claude could contain himself no longer. He turned toward the three family members.

"May I offer my opinion? I am absolutely certain that the shooter timed the shot to coincide with the first word of Mahler's last vocal phrase, '*Sterben*'."

The Schmidt family looked at the distinguished older man who had addressed them so earnestly. Baselius looked at their polite interrupter and saw the correctness of his analysis. He spoke German with a slight French accent and Baselius had the sudden thought that an elderly Frenchman whose much-coveted front-row seat was just behind the conductor could only be one man: Henri-Claude de La Granger. He turned to the stranger sitting in the aisle seat on his left, studied him for a moment, and asked a question.

"Are you by any chance Henri-Claude de La Granger?"

"I am. And I cannot believe what has just happened!"

"Yes, it is devastating. And while Chaplin was *conducting*. Ah, Monsieur de La Granger, I have always wanted to meet you. But now, under such tragic circumstances!"

"It's shocking, shocking. And you are?"

"I am Basileus Schmidt, director of the Austrian National Library."

"Ah. I am an avid Internet frequenter of your noble library. Strange that we have not met. Online at least."

"That must mean none of your requests were subject to review and permission." Both men allowed the briefest of smiles to flit across their faces.

"Do you have any idea what maniac could have done this?" Henri-Claude asked, noting that the man he was now addressing also spoke German with a slight accent, but one he was unable to identify.

"I am absolutely sure it has to be the same person who set off an explosive in Rodin's bust of Mahler at the opera house Sunday night. Who else could it be?"

"Ah, the so-called 'Mahler Bomber,'" Henri-Claude answered. "Yes, I've heard about him and also about the desecration of Mahler's grave and the vandalization of the Lessing monument in the Judenplatz. I don't know why they aren't calling him what he is, 'the Jew-Hater.'"

"I agree! Did you also hear about yesterday's spray-painting of our newly-installed Sigmund Freud statue?"

"Good lord, no!"

"The police have been trying to decide whether these three acts of vandalism are copy-cat incidences or whether all of them, including the destruction of the Mahler bust, were by the same crazed person."

"Well, and I should think what has just happened here—this is by the same madman." Henri-Claude paused for a moment, then looked Basileus straight in the eye almost beseechingly.

"Why, why has anti-Semitism come to the fore again in Vienna? This is exactly what Mahler fought against all his life! And now here we are, after two world wars in the last century, and after so much assimilation of so many ethnic groups and mixture of so many races. Why is this occurring again?"

"I ask the same question, Monsieur de La Granger, but I have no answer. In my own childhood I too experienced hatred toward my ethnicity. Both my parents and all my siblings were killed in the Gaza Strip bombings during the

Arab-Israeli war and I was adopted by a kindly neighbor's family."

"I am very sorry, Herr Schmidt. Hatred and senseless killing have taken place since the beginning of time, what can one say." Henri-Claude was genuine in his condolences.

"It was very, very touching to see so many young people outside the Musikverein forming a protective ring around the building and holding up their posters and chanting such a welcome to Jewish composers and conductors," he continued.

"It's a first for this city. And it comes at the right time." Basileus then introduced his wife and daughter to de La Granger and proudly pointed to the first cellist stand in the orchestra where his son was sitting.

"Actually both our children work for the Vienna State Opera: Stefan as cellist, Adele as the lead seamstress on performance nights."

"How proud you both must be," Henri-Claude sent an admiring glance toward the young first cellist of the evening's orchestra. Basileus handed the renowned Mahler expert his business card and Henri-Claude obliged with his own.

An ear-splitting announcement over the loud speaker suddenly halted conversation. It was the voice of Erich Decker, Vienna's Chief of Police.

"Ladies and gentlemen. As you know Maestro Gerald Chaplin has been brutally murdered. We have reason to believe two persons were responsible for this heinous act. A suspect has been arrested but a second suspect seems to have escaped. Therefore you will be at liberty to go as soon as you pass through a brief, non-invasive body search for weapons. Scanners are now in place at all exits. Please leave in an orderly fashion, both sides of the auditorium, ground floor first, left and right, then balconies beginning with sides, then back. Thank you."

In the silence that had fallen during the announcement one could just hear the, now so very moving, stubborn chanting of the students outside: "*We say yes to Jewish music in Vienna, we say yes to Jewish conductors in Vienna!*"

86

𝒦arl Luegar was glued to the news coming in on his cellphone. A sensational murder at the Musikverein! About ten minutes ago! A reporter,

Rita Rausch, was speaking from inside the auditorium. She had witnessed the killing. During the final movement of the symphony being performed, Mahler's Second, someone had shot the conductor. He died instantly. His name was Gerald Chaplin.

Ah ha! It was a *Jewish* conductor who had been shot to death. Now why hadn't he thought of such a brilliant idea? Of course he wouldn't have had the money to buy a ticket to such a fancy event. But still, he could have waited outside the stage door entrance. But which one? He knew the Musikverein had two stage door side entrances. They gave out onto two different streets. No, it would have had to have been, as they called it, an "inside job." He laughed at his own witticism. Then his thoughts took a serious turn. He was inspired by an unknown comrade's bold act. It was a challenge. He would have to think of a similar audacious deed. In fact he would strive to outdo his predecessor. Perhaps, like his great-uncle, his name would be in the history books.

87

Ottokar Weininger had never run so fast in his entire life. But he had outrun the man who was chasing him, shouting at him to stop. It had been hard enough to get past the harebrained students who had locked arms and tried to stop him. Someone had ripped his empty instrument case from his arms. They had been yelling some idiotic refrain about saying "yes" to Jewish music and conductors. Totally weird. Wasn't Vienna already too full of Jews and Jewish music and conductors? What in damnation was going on?

Free of the instrument case and with the recently used pistol tucked securely in his belt back, he had galloped swiftly along the Ringstrasse, then down the stairs into the Opera Passage. He ran past the shops and to the far end of the Passage where the exit opened onto the street nearest the Secession building. Using back-streets he worked his way over to the University, took the tram back to his small apartment in Leopoldstadt, and collapsed on the lumpy bed in his attic room. Only then did the shivering begin. He had just rid the world of a Jewish conductor. And a Jewish conductor who traveled the world conducting just one symphony by one Jewish composer. The world owed him a debt of gratitude. But why was he shivering? Was it because as he broke through the ring of chanting student idiots he had been forced to leave the contrabass trombone case behind? The yawningly empty case he had successfully bargained for at the Dorotheum pawnshop? But if the police got hold of it, the thing could be traced back to him since he had carried it with him in order to gain unquestioned access to the Musikverein. He forced himself to think of something else.

By now the news media must be heralding the news. Ottokar turned on the small television set that faced his bed and lay back on his yellowed pillow to soak it all in. There it was. His act of courage dominated the news cycles. The murder of the conductor of that evening's performance at the Musikverein. On one channel a woman named Rita Rausch was being interviewed. Apparently she was a newspaper reporter who had actually been in the audience and seen maestro Chaplin abruptly fall to the floor. She was discussing what the on-site forensic analysist had told her. Ottokar was jerked up from his pillow to a sitting position when he heard the woman utter the words: "the second shooter was to audience right." *A second shooter?* How dare they ascribe his brilliant assassination to a second party?

The shivering ceased as righteous indignation took hold of him. Five minutes later he was sound asleep.

88

"Did you receive the same email I did?" Henri-Claude asked Megan and Egga as they were having breakfast at their hotel. They had appropriated Megan's favorite corner table and were enjoying the privacy it provided. It was eight o'clock and they were almost the only people in the room.

"Which one is that?" Egga asked. Megan, whose mouth was full of yogurt-and-fruit-enhanced cereal, looked at Henri-Claude inquiringly.

"The one announcing a noon march along the Ringstrasse in support of the city's Jewish residents. People are urged to wear black as a sign of mourning for Gerald Chaplin."

"No, but I only looked at ones from my family. What a wonderful idea!" Egga exclaimed.

"I haven't had a chance to look at email this morning because I was doing my exercises, but let me look now," said Megan, turning on her iPhone. Egga did likewise. The email Henri-Claude had asked about showed up on both their phones. The sender was identified as a "MHüttler."

"I have no idea who this person is, but I applaud his initiative," Megan said after reading the rousing email. Egga was visibly excited and read the message out loud:

To all those who mourn the murder
of Maestro Gerald Chaplin at the Musikverein last night
and to all those who wish to show
our Jewish neighbors they are welcome in
Vienna
JOIN US IN BLACK
ON THE RINGSTRASSE
TODAY AT NOON

"We *have* to do it!" Egga looked at her two friends.

"You bet," agreed Megan. Henri-Claude nodded in vigorous agreement.

"It means adjusting my day a bit, but I will be there," he said. "At noon. Where shall we meet?"

"If the crowd is big, and I think it will be, we might not be able to find each other. Shall we meet in our hotel lobby and walk over together?" Megan's question was answered in the affirmative.

"I better get cracking," Henri-Claude said, standing up. "See you here at noon. At least I have a black necktie with me."

"Hmm, I don't have anything black with me," Egga told Megan after their French friend had left. "I know *you* do, but I'd better go buy a black scarf." She was referring to Megan's standard lecture outfit: black slacks, elegant black vest, and red, white, and black blouse. Because her Leopold Museum book-signing was scheduled for five that afternoon, she had already dressed for the event.

"I'll go with you when we get back from Tulln this morning," Megan said. "I know a tourist store one block from here on our side of the Kärntner Strasse where they sell gorgeous long black scarves with white music staves and notes on them. You'll love their looks." The enthusiastic expression on Megan's face changed suddenly to a frown.

"What is it?" Egga asked.

"I'm just thinking. *How* did your, my, and Henri-Claude's email addresses get cyber-outed?"

"Oh, I wouldn't worry too much about that. Some bright techie hack probably swept through all Vienna hotel guest lists. After all, everything's online nowadays."

"I understand. But it gives me a creepy feeling."

"Right. So welcome to the world of cyber white hatting."

"Huh?"

"White hats."

"You've lost me." Megan thought her friend was suddenly speaking gibberish.

"To white hat someone is the term used in regard to what conscientious hackers do. In this case the hacking is for a good purpose, for the social good. Like our email telling us about the noon demonstration. And to black hat is just the opposite. Then you are being hacked in order to steal or destroy your data, or sometimes the hacker demands a ransom for not doing so."

"Stop, Egga! You're beginning to scare me." Megan was half-serious.

"Then I won't tell you that there is gray hatting too, right?"

"Oh, please stop it!" Megan was serious now. "We have to pick up our car at Hertz and get to Tulln and the new Schiele museum early enough so we won't feel pressured about getting back in time now for the noon demonstration."

Another twenty minutes found them happily chatting in their white Audi rental car—they had specified wanting it again—as Egga drove them the twenty-seven miles to Egon Schiele's birth town. The museum there devoted to the artist had been completely refurbished and the initial exhibition had just opened. Megan was eager to see both the building and the show. The director had told her she would be surprised. What did that mean? Had they discovered other Schiele works?

"And let's try to make a quick visit to that *Kluger Guss* outfit. You know Doblinger's has sold out of its Mahler busts from them and maybe, just maybe they have a leftover I could buy for my boys."

"So, Egga, you are developing a love of Mahler, even though he wrote nothing special for cello?"

"That does not have to be a criterion for loving Mahler, you silly art historian, you. No, David and I have acquired several busts of composers as inspiration for the boys, and after our unforgettable experience with Mahler last evening, I should very much like to bring home a bust of him for the family."

"All right. We'll try to fit that in after the museum visit, but keeping the noon demonstration on the Ringstrasse in mind."

"Don't worry. I wouldn't miss that for the world."

89

Another car had left Vienna for the small town of Tulln that morning. At exactly nine thirty, Adele Schmidt was placing her empty rolling tote in the back seat of her gray Volkswagen, parked one street down from her apartment on the Resselgasse. Then she was off to the nearby town. The bronze foundry *Kluger Guss* had promised to have the surmoulage she had ordered ready by ten o'clock and she was eager to pick it up as soon as possible. But when she arrived at the foundry she was told there had been a "slight" delay in the drying stage of the casting process and that the surmoulage would not be ready until eleven o'clock. And please to remember that there was a four-thousand-euro extra charge for her rush order. Adele hid her anger and decided not to cool her heels at the bleak building. She would find something to do while waiting. As she had driven into town she had noticed colorful yellow and black posters calling attention to a new exhibition at the local Egon Schiele Museum. She had heard of Vienna's shocking Wunderkind, still famous well over one hundred years later. Okay, that is where she would spend her time. The museum was only a few blocks away, facing the Danube, and with plenty of parking in an area designated as museum parking. As Adele walked the few steps to the museum she encountered a larger-than-life bronze statue of the artist on a high cement plinth. He was standing, hands raised to his chest, and with outspread fingers in one of his famous enigmatic gestures.

The museum entry was through an open gray gate next to a magnificent pair of towering iron gates, the upper two thirds of which spelled out the artist's name in a gray iron font that suggested his printed signature. His dates, 1890-1918, were on the sides.

Inside, after buying a ticket, Adele walked into a hall that displayed on the left a Tandberg tape recorder, a Rolleiflex 2.8 F camera, didactic placards, and photographs of a young American woman who, half a century ago, had discovered the prison cell in which the artist had been incarcerated for twenty-four days on charges that included pornography. From there Adele turned into a very long hall that had been subdivided into six cubicles, each one of them presenting in shadow figures the course of the young woman's interviews with Schiele's two surviving sisters and sister-in-law. Hardly anyone was in the museum at this early hour. Only two women who were at the farthest cubicle watching the shadow figures pantomime and quietly speaking in English to each other. Opposite the cubicles were desk nooks where one could sit and listen to the full recordings. Adele sat down in one of them and put on the earphones provided. Listening to the exchanges between the elderly Viennese women in their old-fashioned patois and the inquisitive young American researcher, time went by very quickly. It was now almost eleven. Adele realized she would not have time to visit the top floor of the museum.

As she was about to leave the building she encountered the two women she had seen in the museum. They were laughing and pointing to the Rolleiflex camera on exhibit as they walked toward the exit. The voice of the older woman sounded remarkably like that of the young American researcher she had seen as a shadow figure interviewing Schiele's relatives. This was verified when the younger woman addressed her as "Megan." Adele slipped by them, not wanting to attract attention to herself, and once outside she ran over to her car, glancing at her watch. Five minutes to eleven. *Kluger Guss* was only four minutes away at the most.

90

What would be the best vantage point from which to observe a probably rowdy, ever-growing public demonstration along the resplendent U-shaped boulevard known as the Ringstrasse? Rita Rausch pondered the question as, several hours before the noon rally was to take place, she walked toward the Ringstrasse from her small but marvelously situated apartment on the Fichtegasse. Her front window overlooked Caspar von Zumbusch's spectacular 1880 bronze monument to Beethoven. And that part of the boulevard called the Schubertring was only two short blocks away.

But once Rausch reached it she realized there was not enough open space among the buildings facing the tree-lined boulevard for crowds to gather. Looking northwards up the Ring to that part running along the vast city park called the Parkring, she doubted that many people would be able to assemble in front of the steep wall of trees fronting the boulevard along the length of the park. Looking further up at that part of the Ringstrasse fronted by the famous Museum of Applied Arts, the Stubenring, Rita recognized there were just too many buildings there for a probable boisterous bevy of bystanders. And it was the same way all the way eastward up to the Danube Canal.

The east Ring, then, was not a good option. And as a journalist and television reporter Rita wanted to be at the very heart of the protest rally. Her television crew was ready to assemble at whatever Ringstrasse point she designated. She crossed over to the north side of the Ringstrasse and began walking west on the two long blocks of the Kärntner Ring—large buildings and tall trees on both sides of the boulevard, but no open spaces where people might possibly gather in the hundreds. Well, this brought her to the Opernring and the opera house. It was one very large building fronting the Ring and not set back much from it. Of course, crowds could surround the entire edifice, but that did not seem very likely as people in the back of the building would not be able to see what the people in front were doing, and vice versa.

Rita reluctantly nixed the heavy Italian Renaissance style opera house as the coming demonstration highpoint, tempting and as important for pedestrian traffic as it was. She walked westward along the north side of the Opernring which soon became the Burgring. Heading past the marble Mozart Memorial on her right she came to a stop at the Burgtor beyond it. Ah. Here was a rather large rectangular space with a huge open area behind it—the Hofburg—situated in front of the Habsburg Palace. It was from a balcony on that palace front that, right after the Anschluss, Hitler had addressed a receptive crowd of several hundred thousand people in March of 1938. What a terrible moment in history. But Rita saw that because of the great trees lining the Ring, any crowd who gathered here would be almost inconspicuous as seen from the Ringstrasse. And it was *on*, therefore *along*, this boulevard that the call to demonstrate at noon had specified. Not within a park or in front of one specific building.

Rita crossed over to the other side of the Ringstrasse to the Maria-Theresien-Platz. Its two enormous museums of natural and art history faced each other across the buoyant twenty-four-bronze-figured monument to the eighteenth-century empress by the same Caspar von Zumbusch who had created the Beethoven Monument. Composers Gluck, Haydn, and the boy Mozart were among the figures at the empress's feet. The space of this square was almost as large as that of the Hofburg. It was here that Hitler stood on a reviewing stand to watch his military units, artillery, and tanks parade before him. Certainly a darn good place to address large crowds. And there was an equally large open space behind it where additional crowds could gather—the Museum Quarter with its new Leopold Museum. But the area did not look out onto the Ringstrasse. And from the Ring point of view there still remained the line of tall green trees on both sides of the boulevard to contend with. Same problem as with the Hofburg square. And what if the crowd were in the thousands? Hardly likely, considering the call to assemble only came out this morning. Nevertheless, what had begun as an email blitz early this morning had been picked up by television and was now being broadcast to thousands of viewers.

Staying on the south side of the Ringstrasse and heading west, Rita walked the one block to the next imposing public building, the Parliament. Designed as a temple in the Greek classical style it was fronted by an immense fountain crowned by a monumental sixteen-foot high statue of Pallas Athena atop a pedestal of life-size figures. And here there were no trees! Well, here at least there was quite a bit of open space for surplus Ringstrasse demonstrators. Should she choose this as her reporting site?

After some rapid calculations Rita decided against it. She wanted to check out the next imposing building on her side of the west Ringstrasse, the Town Hall, set a full block length back from the Ring. The cathedral-like Rathaus with its single spire had a long rectangular open space in front of it opening onto the Ringstrasse. But was it wide enough? Hardly. On either side were two parks, each with as much arboreal girth as the Gothic Rathaus. Again Rita rejected the site as being suitable only for excess demonstrators and therefore not practical for the reporting she planned to give.

Determined to walk and scan the entire Ringstrasse length to scope out a possible crowd climax point, she walked past the vast green Volksgarten on the other side of the Ring with its Theseus Temple and the Empress Elisabeth Memorial. Both, however, were screened from the boulevard by a double row of trees that stopped only at the huge, neo-baroque Burgtheater, the last of the magnificent public buildings to be added to the Ring. When Rita got to the world-famous theater with ceiling paintings by Klimt, she saw from the placards that Lessing's formerly, and now newly, controversial play *Nathan the Wise* was being performed. How timely in this week of anti-Semitic outbursts! If only there were more space in front of the theater, this would be a super-logical place for the demonstration center. But its façade was as close to the Ring's streetcar tracks as was the opera house, so neither building was optimum for an event that could possibly attract hundreds of people.

What came next was a building well known to the reporter, as she had frequented it almost daily a decade earlier. It was the University of Vienna where she had majored in science-technology-society. No point even considering it and its fronting Universitätsring as a primary assembly point. The huge building's façade was quite close to the boulevard. Only a single row of trees separated it from the street. Too bad, as probably it was going to be mostly students who would form the majority of the demonstrators.

However, and Rita was smiling at the obviousness and simplicity of it, there was plenty of space for people to gather just across the street to the west of the university—a very large park facing the Ringstrasse and not, for once, rimmed by trees. And, irony of ironies, its name was *Sigmund-Freud-Park*! It stood directly in front of the famous church, the Votivkirche, built in thanks for Kaiser Franz Josef's life having been spared during an assassination attempt in 1853. The Sigmund-Freud-Park faced one of the great transit hubs of the inner city, the Schottenpassage, a vast underground interchange site between the U-2 metro train and a number of tram lines. So there was easy transportation to the site from a number of directions. This was it! This had to be Rita's onsite report point. No need to follow the northwest course of the Ringstrasse past the Stock Exchange on its way to the Danube Canal. Rita immediately phoned her waiting crew and instructed them to gather on the topmost floor of the high building on the Ring opposite the University. From there were unobstructed views of the Votivkirche, the Freud park, the University, and the Ringstrasse. What better coverage site could one ask for?

91

Ottokar Weininger had shivered the night before in the wake of outrunning his unknown pursuer from the Musikverein. Honorable indignation, however, had overtaken him at the ridiculous suggestion on television channels that a *second shooter* had been involved. His sleep had been sound and refreshing.

But when he woke up that morning he had cause to shiver again. Instead of concentrating on his brilliantly timed assassination of Gerald Chaplin, all of the television channels, both liberal and conservative, were touting something truly outrageous and idiotic. *A noon all-city demonstration sit-down on the Ringstrasse in honor of the conductor!*

Could he shiver and feel indignation at the same time? It would seem so. Try as he might, he could not shrug off what became a heavy, heavy depression. He had suffered black moods before but they were nothing compared to this darkening of the spirit. He could not get up, could not eat any breakfast. Instead he sat propped up on his bed switching from channel to channel, becoming increasingly dispirited as he watched one "honorable" politician after another testify to the city's love of its Jewish citizens. And the cheap showmanship of holding a demonstration honoring both Gerald Chaplin and Vienna Jews! How maudlin could one get? Where were the *anti-*Semitic celebrations? Where was the brilliant Mahler Bomber? Where was the amateur spray painter of the statues of Freud and Lessing? The copycat despoiler of Mahler's grave? They damn well had better show up at this noon demonstration. Would he be the *only* one brave enough to act on his principles, his beliefs?

This last thought galvanized Ottokar. His depression lifted and he sprang into action. He dressed for the day and wolfed down an energy bar. Then he searched his small desk for the leftover item he had bought at that snazzy toy store downtown. He finally found what he was looking for and tucked it into his shirt pocket. It would be a minor weapon but the assault he now pictured would reap major press coverage and further demoralize the city's Jews.

He caught the D tram into the city center but before it even got to the University station, it was forced to come to a stop. A huge crowd was in the street and sitting on the tracks in both directions. Many of them were wearing black. The crowd was increasing every minute. And slogans were being shouted. *"Jews are welcome in Vienna"* and *"We reach out to our Jewish neighbors!"* Ottokar jumped off the street car and walked briskly down the Ringstrasse to the opera house, pushing his way through throngs of people fanning out onto the boulevard. Nodding to the day portier on the Operngasse side of the building, he slid his ID card into the chip reader and took the stairs to the lobby floor overlooking the front of the building and its portico from which he could look out on the people below who were already gathering. Then he paced over to the Schwind Foyer windows that gave out onto the Karajanplatz, the square so renamed despite Herbert von Karajan almost bankrupting the Opera in seven years of ostentatious excess. It wasn't even eleven o'clock yet and dozens, no, hundreds of people were joining the throng around the opera house. For Christ's sake!

Riveting as the growing spectacle was, Ottokar turned his back on it temporarily and walked back to the Operngasse side of the building and to what had in recent years been designated the "Mahler Hall." So named under the pressure of a certain whining Gerald Chaplin—oh god, that man again—who, upon being invited to join a centennial Mahler ceremony at the opera house, had at first proposed that a *statue* of the composer be placed in the building's forecourt. Fortunately that was turned down, Ottokar remembered with a smirk. Determined to win, Chaplin commissioned and funded an American Jewish artist who lived then in London to create a giant portrait image of the composer. What was that conniving artist's name, again? Ottokar walked over to the wall didactic being studied by a few tourists and read the name: "Ronald Brooks Kitaj, 1932-2007." Dead now. Good. An atrocious artist.

Ottokar stepped back to take in the five-foot high, gold-framed, brightly colored pastel portrait of Mahler that hung over a small, black, glass-encased piano that had belonged to the composer. Ottokar looked at the maudlin portrait with contempt. It showed the temperamental little Jew, who had reigned for ten years at the opera house until 1907, from chest up and in left profile. His mane of black hair was receding, a glittering pince-nez sat atop his prominent nose, his lips were tightly closed, and the chin was laughably enormous. In an effort to convey what Ottokar sarcastically decided was supposed to be great "suffering," the artist had painted the face and neck a hot pinkish red, with black brush jabs up and down the face. As if that weren't enough, the artist had deposited Mahler by the shore of the Attersee lake where he had composed part of his sniveling Second Symphony. Across the lake on the far shore was what looked like the Föttinger Guesthouse where Mahler stayed and had to have a composing hut built for himself. Guess the temperamental hermit couldn't work under normal circumstances? And anyway, what the hell was he doing composing when he was supposed to be conducting operas? That he was taking too much time composing was one of the many complaints that drove him from the Vienna Opera. That and an animated local press which knew a Jew when it saw one. Nowadays the press and television were such sniveling cowards with their fake political correctness.

Ottokar felt his breast pocket. Yes, his tool was there and ready for silent action. But this was not yet the moment. He would wait until all eyes were on the noon spectacle. Until any tourists on the foyer floor with him had joined the crowd assembling at the tall windows overlooking the Opera Ring. It was ten minutes after eleven. It wouldn't be too long now.

92

¶It was ten minutes after eleven. Egga was looking at her watch and gauging the time. She glanced over at Megan, who was in the passenger seat taking in the Tulln streets she remembered so well.

"I think we have time to see if that foundry here has one of their Mahler busts still in stock," she said.

"Oh, do you think so, really?" Megan hated being late with a passion and they had promised Henri-Claude to meet him at the hotel before walking over to the opera house to see how large the crowds were for the Gerald Chaplin sit-in.

"Sure. I'll just run in and ask. You don't have to leave the car."

Egga checked the map on her cellphone and took a left at the next turn.

"Here it is. Look, that building there!" Megan had spotted the modest sign that read *Kluger Guss*.

"Okay. I'll stay in the car. Have fun."

She watched her sprightly younger companion gallop to the foundry entrance and disappear through a large swinging door.

Within less than a minute, however, Egga reemerged, grinning broadly and beckoning to her that she should come inside. She looked very excited.

Megan suppressed a groan and slowly exited the car. Why did such a simple act seem difficult now? Why didn't her daily exercises seem to count? Of course she knew they did and that she was impressively limber for her age. Maybe she was just tired. They had done a lot of standing in the Schiele Museum.

Egga was holding the door open for her and as soon as she entered she saw why her friend was so excited. There in the small front office a smiling employee stood with a Rodin bust of Mahler in his hands. It was a Model B. Feeling just as excited as Egga, Megan immediately examined the neck. There it was, the fonderie Alexis Rudier's mark on the back of the neck. This was a legitimate cast. One from which copies could be made. She nodded confirmation at Egga.

"And what is the asking price for a surmoulage?" Egga asked.

"Funny you should be interested in our Mahler bust. We just had a client from Vienna pick up a copy we made for her. It was a rush job and it came out just beautifully."

"So how much would another casting . . . "

"We *really* have to get going!" Megan interrupted.

Silence reigned after they were back in the car and on their way again. Egga was obviously angry and drove without making conversation. Megan tried to make amends.

"If you really want to know what *Kluger Guss* charges for its Mahler busts you could go online, or simply call them."

"Well, Megan. You're just sitting there. Why don't you go online for me and find out?"

"Okey dokey. Anything for you, my dear. And I'm sorry for being such a worrywart." Egga reached over and patted her friend twice on the shoulder. All was forgiven. Megan pulled out her iPhone and began researching. Occasionally they drove through areas where there was no cell service but she was able to find out enough to demonstrate that *Kluger Guss* did not address pricing on its very modest website. But they did give a telephone number. Megan called it with speaker on so they both could hear.

"Hello. I'm one of the two ladies who entered your shop just now. We are very interested in ordering a Mahler bust from you. Can you tell me what such a surmoulage would cost?"

"Our standard casting price in the case of our nineteen-twenty-six Rodin cast of Mahler Model B is sixteen thousand euros. Orders take two weeks to complete."

"Thank you and we'll get back to you," Megan said, hanging up quickly before the clerk could hear Egga's indignant outburst.

"That's outrageously high!"

They had reached Vienna and the Alser Strasse. Now they were on the Währinger Strasse heading for the Ringstrasse. Traffic seemed uncommonly slow and they happily chalked it up to the noon sit-in. Some twenty blocks later they and the vehicles around them were at a standstill. The University was only a few blocks away. Packed tight, no cars were moving and people were getting out of them, asking questions of each other, and making calls.

"Shall we leave the car and walk to the Universitätsstrasse?" asked Egga. It was pretty clear that the people around them were doing just that.

"I guess that's the only thing we can do right now. This jam isn't going to break up anytime soon. But what about meeting Henri-Claude? He must be waiting for us at the hotel."

"Text him."

"Right. I keep forgetting we're in the cyber world of instant communication." Megan obediently sent a text telling Henri-Claude where they were. He texted back immediately, saying that given the enormous crowds swarming into the inner city he wasn't surprised and not to worry about joining him. He would head for the opera house immediately and they should text each other what they saw during the sit-in. Megan read his message out loud.

"That sounds good. Let's do it. The only thing I don't feel good about is leaving a rental in a crowd of cars."

"I was thinking the same thing. But we can't move and the standstill is spreading. So I vote we walk over to the Ring." Megan was now eager to leave the car.

No sooner said than done. Megan put the catalogues she and Egga had bought at the Schiele Museum out of sight under her seat, they locked the Audi, and followed the growing crowd. It was obvious everyone was heading in the same direction.

If Megan had become a slower walker in her eighties it was not apparent now. She not only kept up with Egga, she actually outpaced her for a few moments when they caught sight of the Votivkirche's spire. The crowd of sit-ins extended almost to where they were. Masses and masses of people, most of them young, most of them students, but also many older people, and as many women as there were men. Some of them held homemade signs aloft, waving them strenuously for the various television crews surrounding them. And black clothing was everywhere in evidence.

The two friends made it as far as the crowded Sigmund-Freud-Park and plunked down beside some simpatico-looking boys, all in black with long hair, beards, and tattoos. Megan wondered how it was she could feel a bond with what in her Berkeley days at the University of California she would have considered as drugged-up hippies. But here, in this charged environment of pro-Jewish posters and chants, everything had changed. How heartening that so many people had been bestirred enough to take a stand, or rather, take a *sit* against prejudice. Megan was thankful and proud to be demonstrating with them, grateful that she was still around and could join their chants. Chants that could be heard in several languages. How heartening. Vienna, this Vienna she was experiencing right now, was not anti-Semitic. It was declaring one of the great virtues: tolerance and open-mindedness. The Mahler bust mayhem was forgotten. She joined the chant.

"Welcome Jewish sisters and brothers!"

93

A bewildered Karl Lueger was just as surprised as everyone else in the city that the sit-in turnout was becoming so large. He hadn't been able to ride his motorcycle down the mobbed Ringstrasse as he did normally and it was only by taking backstreets that he was able to reach his destination. Situated just two blocks from the Ring and not far from the Secession building, the large Schillerpark was his goal.

It wasn't because, unlike Lessing, the multi-faceted German philosopher, physician, and playwright had a fervent tolerance for Jews.

And Karl didn't give a damn that Friedrich von Lessing was a friend of Germany's greatest luminary, Johann Wolfgang von Goethe, or that together they founded the Weimar Theater. Who the fuck cares now? No, why Karl Lueger was visiting the Schillerpark now was to locate a minor monument erected there in more modern times. It was a memorial to Franz Werfel, the Jewish writer from Prague and friend of that other Jew from Prague, Franz Kafka. Werfel had written that maudlin book *Song of Bernadette* and an account of something called the 1915 Armenian genocide, whatever the hell that was.

Karl knew from going online he was looking for a granite pillar with a circular indentation for what would probably be an ugly bust. He'd seen a photo of the man with his wife, and he was short and stocky with receding hair. The fact that the photo identified the wife as Alma Mahler Gropius Werfel had triggered his memory. Hers was the grave at the Grinzing cemetery he had applied red paint to after defacing the Gustav Mahler tombstone. Yeah, everything was falling into place. Super weird, though, how that Alma broad kept marrying Jews even though she was known for anti-Semitic outbursts. Well, no accounting for tastes.

He parked his cycle by a tree in the center of the park which took up an entire city block and set off on foot to find the Werfel thing. Yeah, there it was, just like the online photo he'd seen. A tall gray slab with a man's head two-thirds of the way up and his name underneath. His receding hairline ended in thick waves of hair. Sculptural liberty? Underneath was the information that the man was born in Prague in 1890 and died in Beverly Hills in 1945. A two-line inscription near the ground read: "In gratitude and respect, the Armenian people."

Well, this is *my* sort of respect, Karl said to himself after he scanned the park for any bystanders. All clear. Everyone was at the sit-in. He took his can of spray paint, black this time, and squirted it generously at the bust, the name and dates below, and the Armenian inscription. Who the hell were Armenians, by the way?

It was almost noon and he could hear the increasing volume of shouts and chants coming toward him from the Ringstrasse. Locking up his cycle, he walked over to witness the sit-in. What sort of mushy speeches would there be and who on earth would be giving them?

94

Blending church bells were ringing in the noon hour. For a moment they were the only sound that could be heard on the Ringstrasse. Then there erupted a sound louder even than the great bells. It was hundreds and hundreds of voices shouting in organized unison: "*LIEBE NICHT HASS*—LOVE NOT HATE." The chant went on for some fifteen minutes.

The amassed demonstrators, who were now standing, flooded out of a completely closed-down Ringstrasse and into the adjoining streets. Their mantra stopped abruptly upon the sound of a man's voice booming over loudspeakers set around the Ring. It was the voice of the mayor of Vienna.

"Friends! Christian and Muslim friends! Children, women, men! All friends of Jews. Listen to our chant. Hear the sound of our love and friendship. And *believe!*"

At this last word a new chant was taken up: "Believe, believe!" Strangers embraced strangers and children yelled and ran with excitement.

Standing and looking down at the animated crowd surrounding the opera house, Ottokar Weininger stood behind the small throng of tourists who had paused with their tour leader to watch what was happening. They were totally engrossed. This was the moment Ottokar had been waiting for.

Turning rapidly, he strode to the giant Mahler portrait on the wall, slipped the toy store squirt pen filled with black ink out of his shirt pocket and silently orbed the word "JEW" over the portrait face. Task completed, he automatically kicked the discharged pen underneath the Mahler piano display cabinet and rejoined the gawking tourists.

Loud speakers were blaring the voice of the mayor of Vienna: "*Hear the sound of our love!*"

No more speeches were needed. The exhortation rang as clearly as the noon bells.

95

"*O*h! *Professor Crespi*! Hallo!"

Bell, the affable guard at the Upper Belvedere who had photographed Megan in front of the "selfie" Klimt *Kiss* painting just before the museum attack, was beaming at her. She, along with all the other demonstrators, had stood at the sound of the noon bells and it was then that Bell, also in the Freud park, had recognized the American professor.

He was all grins as he proudly introduced his sister Callas and their parents Harry and Haim. He had to speak very loudly to be heard over the din of the excited crowd around them.

"We're here in force at this incredible demonstration because one of our dads is Jewish," Bell said, pointing to Haim. Megan introduced Egga, and over the crowd noise they discovered that there were two cellists in their group. Haim had Egga's French Romantics CD and they eagerly talked shop while Harry fell into animated conversation with Megan as they learned they had many things in common. Harry was an admirer of both Klimt and Schiele and he knew of Megan's books on them; in fact he owned the one about Schiele's imprisonment. He was devastated when he learned that Megan had so recently lectured on just that at Neulengbach.

"Well, as a matter of fact I am speaking partly on that tomorrow evening in a lecture on Schiele collectors at the Albertina Museum. And the following evening, Friday, at the University I'll be giving a lecture on what I call 'The Two Gustavs,' meaning Klimt and Mahler, of course. So perhaps you and your family might be free for one of those?"

"We'd be free for *both* of them," Harry answered, looking quickly at his family. "Wouldn't we?" Haim, Callas, and Bell all nodded an enthusiastic yes.

"That's marvelous. Both lectures begin at seven o'clock so I'll look forward to seeing you there." Megan was smiling.

"Are you by any chance free this evening?" asked Haim suddenly, looking at his fellow cellist. Egga glanced at Megan and they both said yes. It was their only free evening.

"Then we should very much like to invite you to dinner, correct, Harry?"

"Yes, correct." Harry was tickled to see his fragile partner so full of enthusiasm. He expanded on Haim's invitation as both their children nodded in enthusiastic accord.

"I think you would find our home very much to your liking," Harry continued. "It takes up the entire third floor of the building on the Liechtensteinstrasse where both Zemlinsky and Schönberg lived. We live in what was once their two adjacent apartments, only we had the dividing walls taken down and now we have the entire third floor to ourselves."

"Oh my god, how exciting!" Egga's eyes opened wide.

"What a treat," Megan joined in. "When would you like us to be there? I've passed that historic building many times."

"Shall we say seven o'clock?" Haim glanced at Harry for approval and received a vigorous nod.

"Perfect. We'll be there. Is there anything we can bring?"

"No, just bring yourselves," Haim answered.

He paused, then looked at Egga mischievously.

"Although you could bring your cello. . ."

". . . and we could play duets," Egga finished the sentence with a happy smile.

"Is there anything you don't eat?" Henri asked with concern.

"*Mushrooms and liver.*" Megan's answer was instantaneous. She spoke from an embarrassing situation she had found herself in decades ago when she was first beginning to research Schiele and was visiting a famous collector and his family in Graz. They got along so well that she was asked to stay for dinner. At the dining table a full plate was placed in front of her. On it, in addition to rice, were two servings. One was liver, the other was a generous supply of mushrooms. Megan had been forced to confess that there were two things she could not eat: liver and mushrooms. They made her throw up. She did not share the latter with the family. The father rose, went to the kitchen, and singlehandedly prepared an omelet for Megan. She was grateful to this day and the Graz family had remained her cherished friends. She saw them every time she visited Austria and they met in the atmospheric Vienna restaurant owned by one of the daughters and memorably-named *Zum weißen Rauchfangkehrer*—At the White Chimney Sweep.

The crowd was beginning to thin and Megan suddenly pictured to herself their Audi stranded in the middle of the street where they had been forced to leave it, surrounded by other abandoned parked cars. She expressed her worry.

"I'm sorry to break this up, but we had to leave our rental car in the middle of a crowd of other temporarily abandoned cars. They might be thinning out, now that the demonstration seems to be over, and I think we better get back there."

"Right! Here's my card," Haim said, "and we'll see you at seven this very evening at Liechtensteinstrasse sixty-eight-dash-seventy." Megan quickly gave the two charming men her business card as well.

A few minutes later six very energized people parted company on the historic Ringstrasse where traffic was finally beginning to flow again.

96

Back from Tulln with her Mahler bust surmoulage and after a stint in the opera house costume sewing room, Adele Schmidt was diligently preparing for two events. First she was going to make a visit to her parents' home while her father was still at work at the National Library. She knew her mother would be at the hairdresser for her weekly three o'clock appointment so she was timing her arrival at Dorotheergasse that afternoon for about ten minutes after three. With her parents' apartment empty, she would be able to slip in with the surmoulage, run up the narrow staircase to her father's study in the attic and place it where his Mahler surmoulage had been kept. Her father had been too weak these past two weeks to attempt the staircase and it was because of this that Adele's borrowing of the bust had not been noticed. The bust switch she had made at the Schwind Foyer had, of course, demolished her father's Mahler bust. Now she was going to right the situation. With the fortune she would receive tomorrow evening at the Prater, she would also be able to help finance the operation and the outrageously expensive medications her father needed.

After that she had a very important appointment. That crucial meeting at a place "both public and private." The *Riesenrad* meeting was set for six o'clock. Adele's burqa was already laid out on the bedroom chair. She would be wearing it again for the last time in just twenty-four hours.

97

The white Audi was completely encompassed by five other cars, the owners of which had not yet returned for them. So Megan and Egga caught up on email in the car as they waited. One of Egga's emails from her husband announced that their son Jacob would be playing with twelve young cellists in a program of the Berlin Philharmonic. The two women were delighted, reminiscing how young the boy had been when he first declared he wanted to learn the cello. Amid enthusiastic exchanges, people were returning and starting up their cars. Soon Egga was able to propel the Audi toward the Ringstrasse and the Hertz car rental. Megan was on her iPhone with Henri-Claude and they agreed to meet at Salieri's for a late lunch. They were eager to exchange accounts of the amazing sit-in. Caught up in the excitement, both had forgotten all about texting each other.

The Frenchman was first to arrive and he picked the table they had before. A waiter recognized him and brought three menus at Henri-Claude's request. Some five minutes later Megan and Egga entered, automatically glancing at the table in the alcove to their left and delighted to see their friend had already commandeered it. After a quick menu study they settled on three varied small pizzas and began to exchange reports on the exciting sit-in as experienced from their respective vantage points. They agreed that the turnout was amazingly successful and the mayor's brief exhortation extremely moving and just what was needed.

"It is unthinkable there is still so much anti-Semitism that we need to demonstrate against it," Egga said with passion. "That a Jew conducting music by a Jewish composer in this day and age would be murdered because he is Jewish!"

Looking at Egga, Henri-Claude smiled ruefully. "Anti-Semitism has existed since ancient times. It's not something new. But it does seem as if it is on the rise once again."

"Certainly it has been in Berlin because of the influx of Muslim refugees. They seem to take out their anger on our Jewish population. There have been some beatings of men wearing kippahs, and a synagogue bombing attempt."

"I've read about that!" Megan was intrigued. Egga nodded sadly then looked at Henri-Claude.

"I know about Wagner's hateful pamphlet on Jewishness in music—can you tell me if his operas are also anti-Semitic?"

"Oh, that's a biggy. You do know Megan's book signing begins at five, don't you?" They laughed then became serious.

"Well, let me put it this way. He drew on nineteenth-century clichés concerning the Jews whom he and so many others considered responsible for society's corruptive materialism. He gave the villains in his later operas some of the racial traits commonly ascribed to Jews: pallid complexions, a tottering, unsteady, walk, and a high, slurred, whining voice. These assigned characteristics can be recognized in some of his unsavory characters. Think of Beckmesser in *Die Meistersinger*, of Klingsor in *Parsifal*, and in the *Ring*! Oh, in the *Ring* you have, Mime, Alberich, and Hagen. It's downright creepy and yet so characteristic of how people thought in those days."

Henri-Claude flinched suddenly as a man in a black shirt who had abruptly appeared by their alcove table touched him lightly on the arm.

"Monsieur de La Granger? You were identified to me when we were in the sit-in crowd in front of the opera house. I am Homer Bläser, principal French hornist with the Opera Orchestra. It is an honor to meet you sir."

"And who identified me to you?" Henri-Claude was slightly taken aback.

"Our music librarian Janis Bergman. She worships you and your four-volume biography of Mahler."

"That's very nice. Please give her my regards." Henri-Claude nodded a polite dismissal as a small pizza was placed in front of him. Homer Bläser was undeterred.

"I am thrilled to speak to you in person, Monsieur de La Granger, because I have something concerning Mahler that I think you will find most interesting.

"And that would be?"

"My grandmother died recently and in clearing out her attic I came across what I swear is a portrait of Mahler. I took a shot of it. Might you kindly look at it?" Homer Bläser thrust his cellphone in front of a pizza-deprived Henri-Claude.

The Mahler biographer's eyes opened wide. He said nothing for a minute, then addressed the dark-haired man who seemed to be in his forties.

"I have my own reaction to this portrait and I will tell it to you. But before I do so, I should like you to show the image to my colleague here, Dr. Megan Crespi. She is an art historian and an expert on Viennese painters."

"Oh! How wonderful! I'd be thrilled if you took a look, Dr. Crespi."

He handed his cellphone across the table to Megan. Egga leaned in from her seat to see. As with Henri-Claude, Megan's eyes grew larger. Silently, she studied the image, magnified it on the screen, and studied every corner of the work, then sized it down again. What she saw was a three-quarter profile portrait of a man with dark hair dressed in black, his back to the beholder, face turned to his left, and right hand raised, holding a baton. Finally, with a quick affirmative glance at Henri-Claude, she spoke.

"Herr Bläser, what you have here is very likely an early work by the Expressionist artist Oskar Kokoschka, and yes, the portrait is definitely of Mahler. I would, however, have to see the painting in person to be absolutely sure about the painter."

"Oh my God!" Homer Bläser almost shouted in excitement. "To think that not only is this portrait positively of Gustav Mahler, but that it could be by a famous artist!"

"Where is it now?" Megan wanted to know.

"Oh, I have it at home. I live not far from here, just behind the Stefansdom."

Megan looked at her lunch companions quizzically.

"It's several hours before my book-signing event. How are you for time right now, Henri-Claude?"

"This afternoon I still have time, but I do have a dinner appointment this evening. Sorry to miss your Leopold Museum event, Megan."

"Don't give it a thought, Henri-Claude. It's just a book-signing thing after all. And you Egga?"

"I'm with you for the day and evening."

"All right. Herr Bläser. If you are free, we could accompany you back to your home and take a look at the painting now."

"Absolutely I am free, you better bet I am!" Bläser was thrilled. What incredible luck! He could just kiss that music librarian.

"Just allow us to eat our pizzas while they're still warm," commanded a suddenly very hungry Megan.

"Do sit down and join us," Egga invited, happy to speak with a fellow professional musician. They quickly fell into orchestra talk when Homer learned that she was a cellist. Soon she was showing him images of her cello-playing son Jacob and her violinist son Phillipp. Henri-Claude and Megan smiled at each other.

They skipped espresso, paid the bill, and stood up with lifted spirits, ready for this unexpected Mahler adventure. Not everything was distressing in the world of Mahler mayhem.

98

From their post overlooking the Universitätsstrasse and the Sigmund-Freud-Park Rita and her crew were wrapping up. The broadcast had been live throughout the demonstration and she was more than grateful that nothing disastrous had happened. That no one had attacked the sit-in. She wouldn't put it past the Mahler Bomber and his like to strike such a tempting target. The resulting publicity would have been enormous. But as it was, the publicity had been vast, televised not only in Austria but throughout Europe.

Her cellphone rang.

"Rita Rausch here."

"Rita! It's Hans. There's been a vandalism of the Opera's portrait of Mahler! Can you and your crew get over right away?"

"I'm on it." She signaled to her team not to disband and told them what had come up. Traffic was almost back to normal on the Ring and they reached the Opera building in quick order. Taking the Operngasse side entrance, a waiting guard led them up to the Mahler Hall. There it was. The giant portrait of the composer, black ink across the face spelling out in three fat letters the word "Jew." What a travesty!

As the crew started to set up its digital broadcast cameras a tall woman with short blonde hair approached Rita.

"Are you Rita Rausch?"

"That I am."

"I've read your reporting and seen you on television many times. Glad to meet you in person. I'm Harriet Hausmann, associate director of Opera properties. We have a very crude and cruel hate action here."

Rita assessed the vandalism, ticking her tongue in disapproval.

"This is terrible, just terrible."

"Fortunately, not as terrible as it might have been," Hausmann said quietly.

"What do you mean?"

"We feared that this controversial portrait might possibly be the target of some mayhem and therefore we had it covered with non-glare, bulletproof glass. The heinous graffito can easily be wiped off. We were just waiting to show it to the press and television."

"Why, that's wonderful." A thought occurred to Rita. "How many people know about this?" she asked.

"Right now, just you and your team. We called you first."

"Then I have an idea. This could be the work of the Mahler Bomber who struck here before. Obviously he craves publicity. And his example has set off a number of copy-cat defacements of Jewish memorials around the city, as you know."

Hausmann nodded sadly.

"What would you say if I asked you to downplay what has happened here? If we and the other channels do *not* televise it with the damage on it?"

"Oh?"

"Look. The party responsible for this damage *craves* publicity. If we cover the story as the portrait looks now, he and his imitators will be inspired. Especially since it happened *during the sit-in demonstration*."

"I see what you mean! Yes. I'm agreeable to that. Let me get our restorer up here right away and we'll remove the ink. Good thinking! But what about the other news outlets? We called you first, but we also contacted the others. People should be arriving any minute."

"Leave that to me. I'm buddies with most of them and I believe they will approve of what we might call a countermeasure."

"Perfect. And I'll have them admitted only to this side of the building so you can meet them just outside the Mahler Hall and explain that the damage has already been removed." The two women shook hands conspiratorially.

Everything transpired for the best just as Rita had hoped. Her colleagues immediately understood the idea and need for underreporting the event and when they entered the hall there was indeed no visible damage to the Mahler portrait.

"Were there any witnesses?" one reporter asked Hausmann.

"Not that we're aware of. Everyone's attention was on the demonstration which they were viewing from the front windows over there." Hausmann waved her hand toward the great outdoor loggia that fronted the building.

"So it was just black ink on the portrait?" one photographer asked.

"Just black ink," affirmed Hausmann. She was careful not to suggest any text had been affixed to the glass protection shield.

"Any damage to the Mahler piano just below the portrait?"

"No. As you can see it is encased in protective glass. And that glass is shatterproof."

"Did the vandal leave a squirt pen or something like that behind?"

"We have thoroughly searched the room."

"Was a note left?" a man's voice asked.

"No note."

"Do you think the Mahler Bomber has struck again?" The questioner continued.

"There's no comparison between the sophistication of that tragic happening and the awkward, amateur act of vandalism committed here. A naughty child with a squirt pen could have done it."

Video teams began packing up to leave and only one journalist seemed eager to ask for more information.

"Do you have any suspicions as to who might have done this mischief?"

"No, and I think that word, mischief, is a good word to describe this event. 'Malicious mischief.'"

And that is how the event was reported on television and in the newspapers and online that day. A wacko case of malicious mischief.

99

"Adele? Is that you up there?"

Sabina Schmidt had returned from her three o'clock Salon early as the water had been turned off due to a plumbing problem. She saw her daughter's purse on the living room couch and her work roller tote next to it. How nice. Where could she be?

"Here I am, Mutti," said Adele, as she came trotting down the staircase to her father's office.

"Hello, love. What were you doing up there?"

"Oh, just looking for a book I thought Papa might have."

"And did he?"

"No."

"What's the book? Perhaps I have it, *Liebling*."

"It's not important."

"Of course it's important."

"It's a new book on Mahler and I thought he might have it. I can't remember the title but I thought it might jump out at me if I looked."

"He ought to have all the latest books on Mahler. You know how he collects anything to do with him."

"How is Papa, I mean really?"

"He's in a lot of pain and it's continuous, all the time, Adele. I know, even though he's very good at hiding it."

"Yes, I could tell at the concert last night. And the assassination of Gerald Chaplin! That's painful for us all."

"Did you know that Chaplin was scheduled to visit the National Library this afternoon?"

"No. How sad."

"Yes, your Papa was so looking forward to meeting him in person. Said he had something to tell him about Mahler."

"Wonder what that was?"

"You can ask him when he comes home. Can you stay for dinner?"

"Um, not tonight. I've got a dinner date."

"Anyone I should know about?"

"Come on, Mutti. I have to have *some* private life."

"Sorry. Didn't mean to push."

Adele walked over to the couch and picked up her purse and grabbed her roller tote.

"That's okay, Mutti. Rest assured, I'll tell both of you if I should find the right man."

Sabina walked her daughter to the front door but stopped midway down the hall.

"Oh! I haven't told you yet. We just learned your grandfather is flying in from Palestine this evening. He is worried about your dear Papa. I know both you and Stefan are busy at the Opera this evening so not to worry, we're taking an Uber out to the airport to pick him up. But we expect you two to be here tomorrow at noon for lunch with him."

"Wonderful! I remember Opa was here once but I was only three or four then. I can't picture him but I do remember how deep his voice seemed."

"Actually you were five, *Liebling*, but he was here such a short time I can understand you don't recall much about him. But you and Stefan will be here for lunch at noon, yes?"

"Yes. I wouldn't miss it for the world."

Adele left her parents house feeling both happy and relieved. One of two major operations was completed. Her father would never know the difference between the Mahler bust surmoulage he previously owned and the new one she had left in its place.

When she got back to her Resselgasse apartment she gave Stefan a call. Yes, Mutti had just called to tell him the good news about Opa, and yes, of course he'd be there for lunch tomorrow. Punctually! But her brother didn't sound very happy. She told him so.

"You could hear it? Well, you're right, I am *not* in a very good mood. When I got to the Opera today all of the cellists were told that Maestro Alexander is planning to hold auditions for first principal."

"*What*?"

"You heard what I said. That old Jew buddy of Jared Bogenstein has it in for me. And this is his way of maybe getting me out of his sight and into a back row."

"I can't believe this!"

"Well, it's true. Everyone in the cello section knows I'm the best cellist.

I've *earned* first stand. I deserve it rightfully. And frankly, I'm sick at the stomach over this."

"Look, Stefan, if there are going to be auditions, so what? We know, they know, that you're the best. And if Maestro Alexander pretends someone else is and promotes that person, there will be hell to pay. Both within the orchestra and outside."

"What do you mean 'outside'"?

"Well what do you *think* I mean?"

"Explain. I'm in no mood for games, Schwesterlein."

"Just look what an 'outside' person did to damage Jewish standing within the Opera orchestra for you?"

"How could I ever forget, Adele! So incredibly ingenious and brave of you. I will never, ever forget what you've done for me."

"So be of good cheer, Brüderchen."

"It's just that I'm so depressed. I've worked so hard, Adele, and I *know* I'm a fine cellist. When I play with the Philharmonic at the Musikverein there's no problem. I'm de facto principal, but in my own Opera orchestra suddenly there is the need to hold auditions!" Stefan was becoming agitated.

"I have to tell you, Adele, I think I hate Jews. They're always taking, taking, taking."

"Listen, please calm down. We'll think of something should the impossible happen and you don't win that audition. Just put it out of your mind for now."

"Okay sis, I'll try." He hung up.

Adele looked around her apartment. The rolling tote bag would, in just twenty-four hours, once again hold the original Rodin bust of Mahler she had briefly shown photographs of to the man who had called himself "missingmahler" in the newspaper two days ago. Gosh. Was it just two days ago? It seemed so much had happened since then. The American Bar scene with a man willing to pay an unknown woman in a burqa fifty thousand euros for the Rodin bust, the tiara, the pawnshop, the foundry, the surmoulage pickup, the substitution in her father's office, and now the news that grandpapa was arriving in Vienna. Too much, too much.

But now she must steel herself for the second and major operation of tomorrow: selling the original Rodin Model B bust of Mahler to Herr "missingmahler" at the princely sum of fifty thousand euros. Selling what, at shortly before four in the morning three mornings ago in the Schwind Foyer, had become her possession. The full-length black burqa was waiting on her bed. And one of the private closed cabins on the *Riesenrad* had been reserved.

All was in readiness. But why did she feel so nervous?

100

Homer Bläser's apartment was indeed just behind the Stefansdom in the same building on the Schulerstrasse as the Mozart Museum. They walked down the Kärntner Strasse and the length of the cathedral to the corner building.

"Here we are, but please follow me around the corner," Homer said. "To avoid the perpetual lines of tourists waiting to enter the Mozart Museum, I always enter from the side of my building."

His apartment was only on the second floor so they took the steep staircase rather than wait for the elevator. Something Megan would not have minded doing. Homer held the door open for them and they entered a different world. This was certainly not your everyday apartment. The walls of the large living room were painted with green palm trees against a sand colored beach and light blue sky. The shelves of a high cabinet were painted a rosy pink and laid out on them were at least six different oboes and two bassoons.

"But you said you play French horn!" Egga was mystified by the collection of double reed instruments.

"I do. These are instruments I inherited from my late parents. They were both double reed players, and it is comforting to have their instruments with me. And I did start out as an oboist but the development of a trigger finger sent me off into another direction—one I've never regretted. I see you are looking at my walls. My parents had always wanted to go to Jamaica, so I painted this beach panorama to make their journey come to pass, at least for me."

His visitors were obviously moved by his explanation. After a moment he spoke again, this time more upbeat.

"But you are here to see the Kokoschka! Let me bring it to you. Please do sit down."

Egga and Megan took chairs on either end of a small couch which Henri-Claude had immediately requisitioned. They continued looking around at the picturesque walls.

"Here it is." Homer was carrying an unframed canvas on wooden stretchers and holding it face front toward them. It was larger than any of them had imagined. In fact it was almost life size. Carefully placing the picture on a straight-back chair facing them, Homer stood far to one side so as not to block anyone's view. His guests studied it in silence. Finally Megan spoke.

"May I see the back, please." Homer looked surprised but immediately obliged. Megan stood up and studied the old canvas carefully. She touched it lightly in one place with her right forefinger, then nodded.

"Why are you looking at the back, Megan?" Egga was curious.

"I'm verifying the approximate age of the canvas, looking for any signs of a first sketch, any gallery stamp, and of course, a date, even a signature."

"Do artists ever sign their paintings on the backside?" Egga asked.

"Artists have put all sorts of informative wordings on the back of their works. Like a long title for instance."

"Hm. I hadn't thought of that." Megan looked from her to Homer.

"And now if I could look at the front again and examine the brushwork close up." Homer turned the picture around carefully and held it against his chest.

The controlled swirls of paint building up to a three-dimensional figure were agitated yet precise, just as they were in Kokoschka's early works done in Vienna from around 1910 to the outbreak of World War I in 1914. After a dramatic break with his lover, the recent widow Alma Mahler, the artist had volunteered as a dragoon in the Austrian army. In this portrait of Mahler, seen in left profile, his one visible eye imperiously commanding attention, the figure vied with the background for painterly attention. The development of style suggested a date of about 1913. There was no specificity of locale, no hint of an orchestra as suggested by the raised baton. What there was plenty of was pictorial tension. The figure in the painting both escaped and yet was tied down by his seething environment. The erupting bleak colors of midnight blue, gray, and black were Kokoschka's, the dramatic projection of the figure toward the viewer despite tethering brushstrokes, and the tension of a psyche being revealed in paint were all Kokoschka. But Megan did not yet say so.

There was one problem for her. When did the painter ever meet his subject? A terminally ill Mahler died at the age of fifty in Vienna in 1911. In that year Kokoschka was twenty-five. For the previous four years, 1908–1911, Mahler had been in New York as conductor first of the Metropolitan Opera and then of the New York Philharmonic. Did a very young Kokoschka ever attend one of Mahler's performances in Vienna during the years 1897–1907 when he held sway over the city's opera house? Highly unlikely. The fledgling artist was too busy outraging society by his outrageous public conduct and his artwork.

Suddenly the answer to the enigma presented itself to Megan. Of course! Kokoschka never met Mahler. But during the torrential love affair he had with his widow, he had objected to the fact that Alma kept a photograph of Gustav on her bedside table. This was it. Close proximity to that haunting black and white image and the fact that Kokoschka proudly boasted he didn't have to paint a portrait from life, he only needed to see the room in which the person lived; all this explained the incongruous later date of a portrait painted when the person portrayed was deceased.

Megan turned to the persons watching her in suspense.

"This is, without a doubt, a genuine work by Kokoschka."

Exclamations of delight filled the room.

"However," she continued. "it was not executed in Mahler's presence. Stylistically, it dates to the period between nineteen-twelve and nineteen-fourteen. Thus, after Mahler's death. Not from memory but rather coerced by a remembered and resented photograph Alma Mahler kept by her bed."

Excitement animated her small audience.

"Homer, do you have anything else that might connect to this portrait? Did your grandmother have any pertinent letters or a diary perhaps?"

"I don't think so. She just mentioned once that she had a painting in her attic that had belonged to *her* mother. No one was interested at the time. And it is only now that I've cleared out her attic."

"Do you know anything about your great grandmother?" asked Megan.

"I know that as a young girl she worked for a time as a model at the Wiener Werkstätte." Megan's eyes opened wide.

"The Vienna Workshop?" As a student at the Kunstgewerbeschule—the School of Applied Arts—Kokoschka designed some postcards for it! They might have known each other. He could have given her the portrait when he left Vienna for Dresden, where he stayed for almost ten years. Homer, do you by any chance remember the name of your great grandmother?"

"Oh yes. I did an ancestor research online and that was one of the results. The names of my great grandparents on both sides of the family. Her name was Lilith Lang."

"Bingo! That has to be the connection. Kokoschka fell in love with the sister of a fellow student, Erwin Lang. He had a sister named Lilith. In fact, Kokoschka's first important work, a so-called children's book with eight color lithograph illustrations that convey adolescent sexual anxieties, ends with a depiction of what he called 'The Girl Li and I.' It shows them in nature, each in their own extended 'bubble,' and completely nude. Lilith is sure of herself; Oskar is the timid, confused one."

"You're saying that my great grandmother is depicted in a book and that she was the girlfriend of Kokoschka?" Homer was incredulous.

"Everything points to that. So it's even more likely that she was the person to whom he gave the Mahler portrait when he left Vienna."

"That's really awesome."

"Homer, what would you like to do with this portrait?" Henri-Claude was already thinking of his _Médiathèque Musicale Mahler_ archive in Paris. What an addition this portrait image would be!

"I haven't thought that far ahead," Homer answered truthfully. "I suppose it should be in a museum somewhere. Or perhaps in the Mahler Hall right here in Vienna?"

"That is not a secure enough venue for such a painting," Megan warned.

Homer was looking indecisive and unsure. Henri-Claude made a proposal.

"Look here. The portrait is unique because of its biographical surround. The _Médiathèque Musicale Mahler_ in Paris is visited daily by scholars from all over the world. The archive would be more than willing to pay you a fair price for the portrait. Why don't you think it over? There is no need for haste. Except, perhaps, for its _security_."

This last remark had its effect. Homer looked worried. His first impulse had been to show it to all his orchestra friends. Now perhaps he should not let anyone know he possessed the valuable portrait.

"An alternative would be to place it for sale in the next Dorotheum auction," Megan said gently. "But doing that would probably mean the portrait would end up in a closed private collection remote from the musical life of Europe. You'd be surprised how much auctioned art is successfully bid for by Russian and Chinese collectors."

Egga was listening to the interesting back and forth and only wished there were a Mahler Foundation in Berlin. The portrait was so commanding, so unusual! You might even call it a portrait of hate, of envy, or of fear, since even the dead Mahler was a threat for Kokoschka. Perhaps the Berlin Philharmonic could acquire it. Ah, but symphony orchestras had no money to spare. That she knew for sure. Suddenly Homer's face lit up with excitement.

"If your Mahler archive can buy it for, as you say, a fair price, then I think Paris would make a fabulous site for it."

"And of course with the stipulation that it be on permanent display," Megan added, looking at her French colleague for confirmation.

"But of course!" Henri-Claude was thrilled and already knew where best it could be hung as to receive maximum attention. "We shall research the portrait's value in today's market and absolutely make you an equivalent offer."

"All right. This sounds more than fair. Do I have to get a frame for it, or anything like that?" Homer looked worried.

"Definitely not," Megan assured him. "It is better for the canvas not to be framed right now since it might be necessary, for example, to have the painting cleaned—something the curator of the Mahler archive would most certainly recommend having done. Right, Henri-Claude?"

"Correct. It does not need heavy restoration at all, just the requisite cleaning." He was quite thrilled at the idea of displaying an image of Mahler that had such an intriguing history.

Another thought occurred to Homer.

"You know what? Before the portrait leaves Vienna I'd like to invite my fellow instrumentalists over to see it. They'd be so interested. Would that be all right?"

Megan instinctively felt cautious about such an idea. The fewer people who knew about the existence of such a historic portrait the better. Imagine if a covetous colleague broke into his apartment to steal it! She told Homer her fears and he nodded sadly.

"What we could and would do is have a color photograph of the exact same size made up for you to display," said Henri-Claude. "We could frame it for you gratis. Would you like that?"

"I'd *love* that! What a perfect solution. Yes, yes, let's go ahead with your proposal."

Megan asked if she might photograph the portrait and Homer readily agreed, immediately understanding the request when the American professor in her haste merged the term "Photo" with "iPhone," resulting in "iPhoto."

After more animated conversation the visitors rose to go and an excited new Kokoschka owner walked them down the stairs and out onto the street.

As they parted company, Megan put a hand on Homer's arm and quietly repeated her warning.

"Do remember, keep the existence of your painting hush-hush for now. Considering what happened to Rodin's bust of Mahler at the opera house the other night, it is best that no one knows this painting exists."

101

The idiotic sit-in demonstration had taken hours to clear out. It was as difficult to get public transportation back home as it had been to reach the opera house for an indignant Ottokar. Only the thought of the sensational damage he had done to the Mahler portrait kept him from cursing out loud. "Jew." That was the only word needed. Writ large right across the man's profiled face. Now both public images of the man who had defiled the Opera building were themselves defiled. Whoever his unknown partner was—the man who blew up the Rodin bust in the Schwind Foyer—he would soon be applauding.

The news must already be on television. Running up the stairs to his attic apartment Ottokar flung open the door, turned on his set, and threw himself on top of his moldy bed. The round of international news was just beginning to wind down and local news would be next. Just time to grab something to eat. Dashing past the refrigerator in his kitchen reminded him that he should dispose of the emptied squirt pen he had kept there. He reached into his breast pocket and felt only his own chest. Where was the pen? Had he forgotten to replace it in his pocket? He felt his pants pockets. Empty. Damn! His fingerprints were on that pen. And his ID entry card via the red chip reader could be traced back to the precise time he'd entered the Opera. And exited. But would they suspect a member of their own orchestra of doing something so, to them, outrageous?

That overwhelming feeling of depression Ottokar had experienced last night took hold of him again. Forgetting he was hungry, he walked back to his bed, propped up his pillow, and waited for the news to turn local. It should be the first item.

And it was. A view of the Mahler Hall appeared with Mahler's portrait and piano below. The anchorman began speaking.

"At the opera house today just as the sit-in demonstration reached its high point at noon some mischief-maker was carrying out his own demonstration. The person squirted the portrait of Gustav Mahler with black ink while people were watching the sit-in. Fortunately, the picture is completely protected with non-glare glass so the vandal had no idea the ink had not reached its target. Police have no suspects in this case of malicious mischief."

"*Malicious mischief?*"

What the hell? They don't think spraying the word "Jew" on a hypocritically converted-to-Catholicism-just-to-get-a-job Mahler face is major defacement? How disingenuous of them. Was it the media or was it the Opera itself that termed the defacement of Mahler "mischief"?

Ottokar sat down in a slump. He realized he did not feel up to another Mahler attack. It all seemed to be so in vain. His genius murder of Chaplin last evening in which he'd put himself in real danger had been answered not by jubilation but rather by a city-wide demonstration in *support* of Viennese Jews! Won't these people ever learn?

The inspiring words of his namesake Otto Weininger came to mind. Here was a genius who, writing at the same time as Mahler was conducting at the Opera—1903—understood what a blight on society Jews were. And yet he committed suicide. Two shots through the chest. Died the next day. Suddenly Ottokar realized why the man chose to kill himself. His message was not received, yes, but there was another, even more compelling motive aside from bitter disappointment at the reception of his book.

Otto Weininger's suicide in the house where Beethoven died was a supreme act of publicity. After his sensational death, *Sex and Character* became widely read throughout Europe. Even the Swede August Strindberg read and was affected by the book's rousing message.

And so it could be the same for him. He had risked imprisonment, perhaps even his life, in response to the Mahler Bomber's inspiring precedent. And what he had done today was simply described as "malicious mischief." But now he knew how to override that.

Ottokar knew what he had to do. He would do it at Schwarzspanierstraße 15. Tomorrow.

102

"I told you attending the demonstration sit-in would be too much for you!"

Henri was looking at Haim with concern. They had returned to their apartment building on the Liechtensteinstrasse and in spite of having taken the elevator to their floor, Haim was painfully short of breath as Harry unlocked the door. Houdini was whining impatiently. As of one mind they turned toward their bedroom.

"All I need is to lie down for a while."

"Darling, you're really frightening me. Maybe we should call off the dinner for Megan and Egga? You need rest. And quiet."

"Call off the dinner? Certainly not! I just need a little rest, that's all. Believe me."

"I want to, but I also want what's best for you."

"*Please*, Harry! Let me be the judge of that." Both men sulked silently. Harry went to the kitchen to prepare the basics, just in case they did decide to follow through on the dinner for six. If they were really going to cancel it they should do so quickly. Megan Crespi's cellphone number and email address were on her card, thank goodness. But in his heart of hearts he did wish Haim would feel well enough to go ahead with the evening's exciting plan. He would enjoy it so.

Some minutes later he was nicely surprised to hear the sounds of a cello being tuned coming from the Makart studio. He left the kitchen and walked into the great room to smile at his beloved to whom playing music was health itself. The dinner would take place as planned.

103

𝒦arl Lueger had been absolutely disgusted by the noon sit-in demonstration along the Ringstrasse with its simpering climax of "feel our love." He returned to his motorcycle and roared back via backstreets to his parent's home. Collapsing in a large roller chair at the desk in his bedroom, he turned on the radio to his favorite heavy-metal station. With this acoustic aid, he continued the boring online homework assignment he had given himself: reading Gotthold Ephraim Lessing's five-act play *Nathan the Wise*, line by line. Yesterday he had bought a volume containing the play at an old book store and he had also physically checked the Burgtheater inside and out. A statue of Lessing was on the exterior along with other supposed greats like Goethe and Schiller. But it was too high for inflicting any damage. Online information showed the play's performances at the Burgtheater were sold out every evening. There would be a huge crowd. The enormous building's auditorium, its website claimed, had well over a thousand seats plus standing room for maybe eighty-five more. Not quite as many as the Musikverein, but still impressive.

Lifting his eyes from the play to the Burgtheater's open website he saw something had just been posted. The notice said that in response to the great interest boosted by the sit-in demonstration there would be a second performance of *Nathan the Wise* tomorrow at two in the afternoon. This in addition to the scheduled evening performance.

Fabulous! He zoomed to the online box office and within seconds had bought a ticket.

So now all he had to figure out was how to carry off something sensational. Even if he had the money, he was not old enough to purchase a firearm. No, whatever he did, it would have to be totally different from what happened at the Musikverein. Something that would attract not just Austrian TV, but international attention. The sort of attention that occurred at the Burgtheater during World War II when Karl's hero, film star Werner Krauss, played a crudely exaggerated Shylock in a purposefully anti-Semitic production of Shakespeare's *The Merchant of Venice*. A fan of films from the thirties and forties, Karl had discovered the highly controversial actor when he watched with open-mouthed fascination the notorious film *Jud Süss* in which Krauss played six negative stereotypical Jewish characters ranging from being physically ugly with hook nose and whining voice, to grasping money lender to cunning, untrustworthy, materialistic, and immoral. Would Nathan the Wise be like some of them?

Karl now realized only too fully that defacing the Judenplatz monument to the German playwright had not been enough. An amateur event compared to the sensational slaying of a Jew conducting Jewish music in the Musikverein last night. That was sophisticated. By contrast he had been a mere vandal. He yearned to commit an act that would rise to, perhaps even surpass the Gerald Chaplin murder. He was hoping to find it in the lines written by Lessing.

Karl had just reached the much-touted ring parable when he heard his parents in the living room exclaiming over something on television. Their conversation was becoming louder and he wondered why. Abandoning his laptop and joining them, he saw what had sparked their comments. The screen showed the Mahler Hall inside the Opera House with a close-up of its huge profile portrait of the composer himself set against a lake scene. Apparently, the portrait had been attacked during the noon sit-in demonstration with smudges of black ink. The phrase used to describe the act was "malicious mischief." Why were his parents reacting so noisily? Oh, damn, he'd forgotten his mother liked Mahler's music. They were both evidently upset that another anti-Semitic act had occurred so soon after Chaplin's murder and the various desecrations of Mahler's grave and Freud's statue. And that not enough serious discussion of these events was taking place on television.

Well just wait, folks. And prepare to be amazed. Because your son, whom you barely speak to when he's home except to ask why he apparently has no homework and why he spends so much time on his motorcycle, your son is about to do something spectacular. As spectacular, if not more so, as the Chaplin slaying. There will be plenty of "serious" attention focused then and your own son will be at the center.

Without a word to his parents Karl returned to his bedroom desk and continued the arduous Nathan reading. The wordy play with a confusing set of characters was set in twelfth-century Jerusalem during a pause in the fighting between Muslims and Christian crusaders. Nathan, who is made out by Lessing to be a morally upright, wealthy, and wise Jew, is asked by the Muslim sultan Saladin—whose brother's son just happens to be a Christian knight—which is the true religion, Jewish, Muslim, or Christian.

Karl Lueger's patience was in short supply. Instead of answering the question directly, this Nathan character starts to recite a long story, one which drama critics refer to as the famous "ring parable." Karl looked up the word "parable" then continued his reading. His eyes began to ache, the cobweb parable was so long and large. It was all about a man who owned a precious opal ring and whoever wore it had the power to win the love of God. When the owner died he left the ring to his favorite son, and when that son died, etcetera, etcetera, etcetera until the last possessor of the ring was a man with three sons whom he loved equally. Who was he going to leave the ring to? He couldn't decide so he secretly had a jeweler make up two identical rings and before the man died he gave a ring to each son. Big deal.

Karl looked at his watch. How long was reading this long-winded parable going to take? And what was its point? Who the hell even cares about Jerusalem in the twelfth century?

Okay, reading further, it turns out that the three sons had a court battle over who had the original ring, ah, here it comes. Nathan is pointing out that they are arguing just as Christians, Mohammedans, and Jews argue about which is the original, the true faith. The judge declares that if they each received their ring directly from their father then each can believe his ring to be the genuine ring. Okay, here comes the conclusion "ringer," Karl laughed at his own joke. Their dad wanted his sons to love one another. Moral: the three religions are supposed to get along because they're all genuine. God made them all.

Dullsville. He'd learned absolutely nothing useful from laboring through Lessing's dense lines which, according to one URL takes four and a half hours to perform! Yeah, he could see that it would, with all its plot twists, stupid surprise disclosures, and sudden revelations about the uninteresting characters. And only one intermission after the ring parable of the third act. He was going to have to turn elsewhere for inspiration. Idly, he rolled his chair in ever increasing circles around the room.

And then in a flash it came. Of course! And it had been in plain sight at the Burgtheater all along!

Without a word to his parents he left the apartment, ran down to the courtyard, kicked up the stand on his motorbike, revved the engine, and roared off. He had two errands. One was to a certain hardware store in the nearby Mariahilf district. The other was out to the heavily Muslim populated Ottakring district.

104

¶It was an agitated lawyer who announced his resignation to Erich Decker as the two men sat in the chief of police's office that Wednesday afternoon. The murder case against Cristina Paloma was simply too open and shut to defend. Although a friend of the accused had hired him to defend the harpist, the evidence against her was overwhelming and his firm had instructed him to withdraw from the case. One of the two revolvers used in the shooting murder of Maestro Chaplin had been found inside Paloma's harp. Her fingerprints were the only fingerprints on the pistol. Further damaging to her case was the discovery of a sexual relationship gone bad with Chaplin when both were employed at the Berlin Philharmonic. It was common knowledge and had been verified by a number of Berlin orchestra members. They had all been witnesses to what they referred to as "Cristina's Little Revenge," when Chaplin, unable to bear her insane jealousy, had broken off their relationship. Her revenge had been to hang a pair of the conductor's semen-stained underpants from the top of her harp during a performance of an opera called *Elektra*.

"So, I am very sorry, but the Austrian state will have to provide the defense of Cristina Paloma," announced the relieved lawyer.

105

¶They purposefully arrived some fifteen minutes early for the book signing event at the very modern Leopold Museum, newest of the museums in Vienna's cultural center, the Museumsquartier. Megan had agreed to give a brief PowerPoint presentation covering several of her scholarly books on Klimt, Schiele, and Beethoven. When she, Egga, and Henri-Claude entered the auditorium they saw that copies of her books had been set out in neat stacks right and left on a table in the center of the stage. A chair facing the audience was at the middle of the table. There was no lectern. Good. A less formal setting made it so much easier to connect with the audience. And that was something Megan always wanted to do. She liked to see a comprehending gleam in the eyes of a listener, or pry out the correct answer to a question she had posed.

And that is how the book signing progressed. People had come because they were genuinely interested in Beethoven imagery or in the works of Klimt and Schiele as discussed at length in Megan's monographs. The books were devoted not only to analysis of the artists' works but also to the cultural environment—a turn-of-the-nineteenth-century history lesson of sorts with some facts that were actually unknown to a modern Viennese audience. No fault of their own; life had moved on. But Megan was like so many other scholars and appassionati who wallowed happily in the depths of fascinating past centuries. When she showed a 1908 photograph of Kaiser Franz Josef reviewing a yearly three-hour parade along the crowded Ringstrasse and asked what the crowds were waiting to see the old emperor do, the audience, clueless, was silent. No answers were offered. Megan used her laser pointer to indicate the small oriental rug that had been laid out in front of the emperor. She waited patiently. Still no one volunteered a guess. Laughingly, Megan articulated the obvious answer and the audience chuckled with her. The professor was in her element. What she pointed out was that every year people flocked to the parade not so much for the spectacle but rather to see if this year the stoic old emperor would stand on the rug laid out for him. He never did for eight more years, until his death in 1916.

After the brief lecture, a long line of enthusiastic people waited for Megan to sign the various books they had chosen while Egga waited patiently in the back of the auditorium.

The last person in line was a tall, stoop-shouldered man with a receding hairline. His excitement was palpable.

"Professor Crespi, I am Tonik Nektar of the Gustav Mahler Society here in Vienna. It is a pleasure to make your acquaintance and I so enjoyed your presentation."

"The Mahler Society? How nice. I've never had a chance to visit your headquarters but I have heard wonderful things about it and your very active members."

"Yes, active, that we are. We turned out in force for the demonstration this morning. It was so incredibly moving when the crowd took up the mayor's words 'feel our love.'"

"It was a morning never to forget," Megan discreetly looked over at her patiently waiting friend.

"I have all your books, Professor. I am here because I want to give you *my* book. I have written the most authoritative book there is on Gustav Mahler—we are both from Iglau, don't you see."

Nektar handed her a thick volume that Megan could instantly see was self-published.

"I've written a long inscription inside. You can read it later if you like." Megan looked across at Egga and pointed to her.

"Yes, I will have to because my friend has been waiting for me and we have a dinner appointment."

Nektar looked at the waiting woman and spotted Egga's white cello case.

"I see your friend plays the cello. I have always thought that Mahler should have written more music for that lovely instrument . . . "

"Excuse me, Herr Nektar, but I really do have to leave now." Megan gently pushed the well-meaning but tedious man out of her way.

A few minutes later the two friends successfully hailed a taxi to transport them plus cello to the hallowed building on the Liechtensteinstrasse where they looked forward to what should turn out to be a most interesting evening of talk and music.

106

"Yes, there still are three tickets available for tomorrow's two o'clock performance of *Nathan the Wise*. Second row front at extreme right or standing area, back row, extreme left or extreme right," the employee at the Burgtheater box office had informed Karl Lueger when he called. He wasn't about to take the chance of just a cyber reservation.

"I'll take the standing room place extreme right," Karl Lueger said, back from his errands, his heart racing. He knew that the right side of the enormous double-winged theater was nearest the Volksgarten and the gala stairwell he had in mind was also on the righthand side. Above, on the ceiling, was one of two historic paintings done for the Burgtheater by Gustav Klimt early in his career. It depicted the London Globe Theater and the final scene from Shakespeare's *Romeo and Juliet*. The neat thing about this painting was that, in addition to the double suicide depiction, Klimt had painted, on the far right, the only known self-portrait of his career—standing to watch the action and with his signature hirsute face and an attention-getting white ruffled collar.

Wouldn't it be a pity if this single self-portrait by Vienna's most famous painter were destroyed? And all because the Burgtheater insisted on presenting a play about a Jew?

107

¶It would be his last evening walk. Ottokar decided to spend it at the nearby Prater. Always a solitaire, he suddenly felt a need to be near his fellow human beings. People out enjoying themselves. Where better on a cool summer evening like this than at the great amusement park? He could clearly see the outline of the *Riesenrad* piercing the skyline from his street and he walked quickly along the Leopoldstadt side of the Danube Canal toward the historic Ferris wheel.

He remembered reading that it had been erected at enormous cost as part of celebrations being revved up to mark fifty years of Emperor Franz Josef's reign in 1897. And that within months it had become a magnet for dramatic statements.

And this was true. Wishing to draw public attention to the economic disparity between classes, a desperately poor woman, Marie Kindl, hanged herself from the window of one of the pendant cabins as the *Riesenrad* mindlessly repeated its majestic six-minute orbit before horrified onlookers below. Such poverty was the embarrassing underbelly of Franz Josef's "New Vienna," usually kept under wraps as the city concentrated on its exterior image of *Gemütlichkeit*—geniality—elegance, and well-being.

And it was, uncharacteristically, *Gemütlichkeit* that Ottokar was seeking on this last evening of his life.

108

¶It was exciting to think they were about to have dinner in the same apartment that had once belonged to Arnold Schönberg. After the Uber driver was paid, Egga walked nippily ahead of Megan to the building and buzzed the bell of the third-floor apartment, designated on the ring panel as simply H & H Docu-Films. Inside they heard the sound of human and canine footsteps racing down the stairway and a second later a beaming Bell welcomed them. He introduced them to Houdini who had taken on the responsibility of discreetly checking out the guests. They all took the modern elevator up to the third floor, turned left, and stepped into what had once been the entry threshold of the Zemlinsky apartment contiguous with Schönberg's and that was now merged with it.

What a sight greeted their eyes! Opening up before them was the entire righthand side of the building. It was decorated with free-standing Ionic capitals and furnished with oriental carpets, comfortable period chairs and armchairs, two couches, low shelves lining the four walls adorned with musical instruments of all sorts and sizes, and in the middle of the chamber stood music stands and two pianos, one a nine-foot Steinway concert grand, the other an eighty-eight-key Korg digital. Stunning! On the Steinway piano top lay, among other flutes, a gold Haynes—a treasure that did not escape Megan's attention. And all around were large green plants, vases, and small sculptures, among them life-size bronze busts of Mendelssohn and Schönberg on two free-standing half-columns. Luxurious green plants, colorful urns, and vases were everywhere. It truly was the atelier of Hans Makart brought to life.

"Here, put your cello over here," Haim said to Egga after they had all exchanged greetings. "Shall we skip drinks and have dinner right away, everyone? That way we'll have more time for music-making."

Everyone nodded in agreement and the guests were led to the other end of the studio near the kitchen which had once been in the adjacent apartment. A long mahogany table was colorfully laid out for six and Megan and Egga were directed to the end chairs. In a matter of seconds Harry and Haim served a cool cucumber soup, for "instant air conditioning," they explained. It was delicious and promised an even better entrée: hot spanakopita. The flaky phyllo dough enfolding the spinach, onion and feta cheese was perhaps the best Megan had ever tasted. On the same large plate a small chopped tomato, onion, and bell pepper salad accompanied the spinach pie. Egga's enthusiastic reception gratified the hosts and all ate as though they were ravenous. Dessert was simply a choice of three different ice creams—vanilla, chocolate, and peppermint—and Megan was relieved not to have what she worried might be something starchy like an orange-flavored portokalopita. Red Xinomavro wine from Haim's family wineries flowed and the conversation was just as fluid. Callas and Bell were the invisible waiters who kept the food and drink coming while Houdini maintained a friendly watch from a far corner of the room.

The first topic of conversation of course was the horrific murder of Gerald Chaplin. All had been present in the Musikverein and each had an opinion as to why the Jewish conductor was killed and by what sort of maniac. Or maniacs. Forensics had discovered two bullets from different directions had entered Chaplin's head. The family had seen the maestro suddenly fall to the ground from their front row seats in the second section of the auditorium floor but they, like everyone else in the audience, had not heard any explanatory pistol shots. The climaxing music was simply too all-encompassing, a thunderous heavenly din. Haim looked expressly at Egga and raised his eyebrows in an indication of his impatience to play the duets he had laid out.

But now the conversation had turned to one of his and Megan's favorite topics: whether or not it is possible to discern "Jewishness" in music, as opposed to intentional use of the Jewish klezmer style introduced by the Ashkenazi Jews of Eastern Europe.

"What do you mean by 'klezmer'?" Egga asked. Megan and Harry looked at Haim.

"Well, traditionally it's a musical genre of instrumental spectacle, or just plain show off, and dance tunes for weddings and special occasions," he explained.

"Think of Benny Goodman, the 'king of swing,' and his virtuoso clarinet," Megan added.

"I've heard great recordings by him, but didn't realize he was Jewish," said Egga.

"Do you know the song 'If I Were a Rich Man' from *Fiddler on the Roof*?" Megan demanded of her.

"Yes, yes, I love it."

"Well, that song is intentionally 'Jewish,' klezmerich sounding."

"And think of George Gershwin's opening notes of *Rhapsody in Blue*—that's clearly a klezmer clarinet sounding," Haim declared. "That great initial declaration was most probably influenced by the Yiddish he heard at home as a youngster."

"Just as Mahler, though nominally a Catholic, consciously drew from the klezmer music he heard as a child." Megan offered.

"And I would say that those more recent Jewish composers like Aaron Copland and Leonard Bernstein also drew on klezmer memories but successfully transformed them into what, upon endless repetition, sound like American folk themes, dance themes," mused Haim. "Especially Copland's lively *Appalachian Spring.*"

"I understand what you're saying," Egga was racing through her musical memory. And she had something to contribute.

"It seems to me, as a cellist who loves to play chamber music, that some non-Jewish composers have purposefully incorporated what you've explained as klezmer thematic music, or Jewish musical clichés into their own work, like, for instance Dmitri Shostakovich. I can think of his string quartet in C minor, and his piano quintet in G minor."

"Yes, I know exactly what you mean," Haim, the other cellist at the table, agreed. "And it's interesting that they are in a minor key."

"And getting back to Mahler," Megan redirected the conversation. "We heard his brief but purposeful klezmer quoting just last night. I think that musical source fits right into his effort simultaneously to embrace both the despair and the ecstasy in all his music." Haim nodded his head in vigorous affirmation and voiced his own comment.

"Yes, just as there is a parallel, at least I believe, of Mahler's manifold musical message to spoken Yiddish, when the same phrase can mean one thing to non-Jews but another to Jews, thus being simultaneously oblique and specific." Haim had voiced this dramatically, raising his hands and bringing them to rest on his chest.

"If you don't mind my intervening right at this moment," Megan said with excitement. "The gesture you just made is connected to one thousand and five hundred years of persecution. Let me explain that with two observations of body language contrasting an Italian and a Jew. The Italian says 'Come to my house,' and expansively spreads his arms outward; the Jew says 'Come to my house,' and protectively pulls his arms inward, touching his chest with his hands. And the Italian says, 'Ah! I have an idea,' putting a forefinger to his forehead and lifting it high into the air, while the Jew who says the same thing pulls his forefinger in from the air and lands it directly on his forehead."

"There she goes again, body language reading," said Egga in fake exasperation.

"That's not my observation this time; it's something Columbia University's famous art historian Meyer Schapiro once enacted for us in class."

"Isn't it time we play some music instead of talking about it?" Haim was becoming impatient. Everyone agreed and six chairs were simultaneously pushed back from the table. They walked over to the large atelier space, passing on the way the stunning Stradivari cello and Villaume bow display. Egga gasped in admiration and Haim beamed in pride. They talked shop for a few minutes in front of the rare cello, then proceeded toward the studio's Hamburg Steinway concert grand. In front of the long piano Haim had set up two music stands and two straight back chairs facing what would be the small but appreciative audience of four. He had loaded the stands with several folders of sheet music. An excellent sight reader, Egga opened up her cello case, removed the cello, its bow, and a small block of rosin, and walked to the chair on Haim's left. She rubbed her bow briefly with the rosin and began to tune her instrument. Then the two cellists quickly tuned to each other, smiling all the while, and were ready to play.

The first piece laid out on their music stands was a languorous duet scored for two cellos called "Oblivion" by Astor Piazzolla, the popular Argentinian composer who transfigured tango music by incorporating elements of classical and jazz. It was just what they all needed, considering their heavyweight dinner conversation.

Next was a Duet in G by the eighteenth-century cellist/composer Jean-Baptiste Barrière. Delighted applause greeted their rendition.

Haim told the guests that there was a version of the duet on an album with YoYo Ma playing and Bobby McFerrin singing. They could hear it on YouTube if they liked.

Then came a radical change of pace and performers. Haim invited Egga to join the audience for the next piece as the family had a musical gift for her and Megan which they had been practicing for many weeks. Egga's place at the music stand was taken by Haim and Harry's violinist daughter Callas. Harry discreetly took his place at the nine-foot long Steinway and an expectant Houdini took his place underneath the piano. This change and augmentation of players was because the next piece was "surprisingly coincidental to our discussion at dinner," Haim explained. It was the tortured Trio No.2 in E minor for piano, violin, and cello of 1944 by the "Gentile Jewish composer Dimitri Shostakovich." Haim justified this characterization by invoking the Russian composer's daring personal fight against anti-Semitism during Stalin's reign. Shostakovich, composer of fifteen polymath symphonies, himself declared he was deeply attracted to Jewish folk music because it could appear to be joyful while at the same time being deeply tragic. Just what they had talked about at dinner.

Megan, Egga, and Bell listened with fascination to the opening cello passage, all in harmonics, and followed the trio through its four gripping often dissonant movements to its climatic, Jewish-style melody invoking a dance of death theme. The piece ended almost inaudibly in an E Major chord—hope after all? So similar in ultimate message to Mahler's Second, they all agreed afterward.

"Now Megan, Egga tells me you play the flute," Harry said. "Would you care to test out some of my flutes?" Harry had opened the cases to his valuable flutes that lay on the piano top.

"Oh dear, some other evening perhaps!" Megan was exhausted and it was getting late. "I haven't played for months so I'm not in shape. But thanks for asking me. I had been admiring your wonderful collection." It really was time to leave and their hosts realized it was so. Haim called for an Uber and fifteen minutes later, with many hearty goodbyes, Megan and Egga were on their way back to their beloved Römischer Kaiser Hotel.

What a jam-packed day! Could tomorrow be any more memorable?

As she tried to fall asleep that same night, Adele Schmidt was asking herself the same question.

109

Schwarzspanierstraße 15, Ninth district, Alsergrund, of Vienna.
Earlier that evening, after his soothing Prater stroll, Ottokar Weininger had written two letters that he desired be found on his body. Just as the earlier

Otto, author of the influential *Sex and Character*, had penned two missives, one to his father, the other to his brother. Today's Ottokar, also the author of a book that, were it only published, would impact society, today's Ottokar had written not farewell letters but two *directives*. One was to the mayor of Vienna, the other was to the president of the International Gustav Mahler Society of Vienna. Both letters claimed sole ownership of the recent slaying of Gerald Chaplin and both concurrently spelled out the growing danger of tolerating Vienna's Jewish population. The two letters eloquently communicated the message for which Ottokar was about to offer his life. The historic Otto's suicide had made his book a bestseller, exerting tremendous influence on world intellectuals. The manuscript of Ottokar's unknown treatise *Personality and Gender* would be found in the briefcase strapped across his body. Publishers would fight each other for the right to publish it. As with Otto, his book would receive worldwide publicity.

If he had to take his own life for this to happen, so be it. As the world was now, what was there to live for? To think that a citywide demonstration had been called to honor the death of a Jewish conductor! To think that his dramatic spraying of the word "Jew" onto the face of the Opera's Mahler portrait was referred to as "malicious mischief"!

Ottokar had reached the historic Schwarzspanierstrasse, where some of its houses had once faced the circular Glacis—that broad, circular military strip free of buildings which for three centuries had allowed defenders to fire freely upon invaders. Now the street looked totally different, of course, and many of the old buildings were gone. Just ahead of him Ottokar saw a garishly lit restaurant. It called itself Weltcafé. Its address was Schwarzspanierstrasse 15.

What? But Beethoven had died at this address! The lightning, the thunder that was supposed to have moved the dying composer to raise his fist defiantly to heaven just before he croaked. Of course Ottokar had never bothered to visit Beethoven sites in Vienna—what the hell had he written for contrabass trombone after all?—but surely the place where he died would have been preserved? Hugging his dangling briefcase under one arm, he rushed into the café. It was packed with noisy, pushy, inebriated students. Catching the attention of a waiter he yelled to him, asking if the café's address number 15 was correct. Yes, it was correct and the café had opened there in 2005; a huge success. Oh? The Beethoven house? Yeah, that creepy old apartment building had been torn down back in 1904. Had he not seen the two historic plaques on the café façade, one in white, one with a bronze medallion portrait of the man?

No, he had *not* seen the historical markers on the outside. God damn it to hell! His grand plan was sabotaged. Where he carried it out was no longer inside a famous historic house. But *when* he did it was still his choice. He pulled the pistol with which he had shot Chaplin out of his belt, pointed it to his heart and, just as Otto had done, fired twice. But unlike Otto, who lived on some fifteen hours, Ottokar died instantly.

What better publicity for a man with such a worthy cause?

110

Emerging from the Annagasse early that morning, Megan and Egga had reached the Opera House on their right and continued west in front of it to the Operngasse. Recklessly, at Megan's impatient behest, they took their chances crossing the Ringstrasse by foot instead of using the busy Opera Underpass with its steep escalators and noisy crowds. They walked south down the short Friedrichstrasse to the Secession Museum. The simple multi-cubed white building crowned by a huge gold leaf dome was designed by Josef Maria Olbrich in 1897 to house exhibitions by a breakaway avant-garde group of artists led by Klimt. Their movement was called the Secession and contemporaries who did not like their building referred to its dome as the "cabbage" dome.

The interior now held one of Megan's favorite artworks. They hurried inside.

Once inside Megan ignored the exhibition on the ground floor and immediately steered Egga downstairs to the basement where Klimt's magnificent Beethoven frieze of 1902 was now permanently installed. Created in casein colors on stucco with gold and semiprecious stone inlay as an allegorical introduction to Max Klinger's polychromatic statue of Beethoven, it was inspired by the composer's programmatic Ninth Symphony which in turn incorporated words from Friedrich Schiller's ode *To Joy*. Megan had devoted an entire chapter to it in her lengthy book on the changing image of Beethoven.

But was it philosophy or pornography, the public of Klimt's day had wondered? And understandably so, Megan thought once again, since the very contemporary-looking females dangling before viewers' eyes in the middle section of the three-sided, seven-foot-high, 112-foot-long frieze, were undeniably "naked," and not, as in past art, heroically "nude." The frightening ensemble of Hostile Powers included Typhon in the center, the ape-like, monstrous giant and defier of the gods, his three vampiric daughters, the Gorgons, to the left, and to the right a trio of sins: debauchery, unchastity, and intemperance. It was this seething underworld that had to be conquered by humankind in order to reach the kingdom "not of this world but of pure joy," represented on the long righthand side of the frieze by a nude kissing couple in front of a floating look-alike choir of angels, "This kiss for all the world."

Megan's admiring eyes rested briefly on the two friezes—how many times had she photographed them?—but her goal this time was the long left wall. In this six-figure-introductory frieze, humanity, represented by three nudes in profile, implores a knight dressed in a suit of pale golden armor who like his fellow humans, is presented in profile. He stares ahead with noble resolve, his helmet still on the ground but his left hand firmly grasping a sword.

It was this image that Megan had wanted to show Egga. Because, even if unrecognizable to a modern audience, the viewers of 1902 knew instantly that the knight-hero who would lead humanity to "pure joy" was symbolic tribute to a contemporary musician hero—Gustav Mahler. Klimt, whose powerful allegories for the University of Vienna had been rejected, understood only too well Mahler's combat, his dual roles as both composer and conductor against uncomprehending, brutally carping critics.

Megan told Egga how the artist had been present at that fateful dinner party held by Berta Zuckerkandl in November of 1901 when Mahler, who rarely attended social events, met the young woman pianist and would-be composer Alma Schindler, known throughout Vienna for her beauty and intelligence. After an abrupt courtship, they married a few months later.

"But Mahler was not the first Gustav in Alma's life", Megan proclaimed conspiratorially. Egga fell into the trap.

"What do you mean?" she asked.

"Well, Mahler did not know about what Alma in her diary had referred to as 'the K—t affair.' You know, Klimt was a shameless womanizer and when he met nineteen-year-old Alma he immediately embarked on a charm campaign. He even followed her on a family vacation in Italy. He stole a kiss in her hotel room in Genoa."

"Oooooh! Dangerous!" Egga played along with Megan's dramatics.

"Wait, there's more. Alma had posed for a very seductive, sexy photo of herself caressing the bear's head of a rug, and Klimt persuaded her to give it to him."

"Is that it?"

"Probably. Alma's stepfather saw what was going on and broke up the 'K—t affair.' But it was clear that something had occurred between them."

Egga knew that during Megan's first tenure in Vienna she had lived in the Argentinerstrasse apartment house just across the street from the great baroque church where Gustav and Alma were married—the Karlskirche—a short walk through two green parks to the Secession building beyond. No wonder Klimt's not-so-secret portrait of Mahler meant so much to her.

Megan went on to tell Egga about the Mahler-in-person factor. A lavish private opening of the Beethoven exhibit was arranged by the Secession artists in honor of their esteemed guest from Leipzig. Through his now close connection with his young wife's father-in-law, the artist Carl Moll, Mahler was brought into the preparations. Would he kindly supply some music? Mahler chose the closing section of the quartet and chorus from the finale of the Ninth and set to work rescoring it for brass and wind instruments only. The Schiller passage he had chosen to recast was one that pointed to astral heights, so in keeping with Klinger's Olympic conception of Beethoven seated on a throne. Megan recited it from memory for her former student.

> *Ihr stürzt nieder, Millionen?*
> *Ahnest Du den Schöpfer, Welt?*
> *Such' ihn über'm Sternenzelt.*
> *Über Sternen muss er wohnen.*

> Do you fall down, ye millions?
> Do you sense the creator, O World?
> Seek him above the starry canopy.
> He must reside above the stars.

"How did that go over?" asked Egga.

"Oh, Mahler's new arrangement was enthusiastically rehearsed in the Klimt frieze room with players and singers from the Opera and, in Alma's words, 'it rang out as starkly as granite.'"

"You see," Megan summed up her impromptu lecture for Egga, "Beethoven was the artist-messiah and Mahler, through his intrepid interpretation of Beethoven, was the artist-warrior who would lead his listeners into an aesthetic kingdom secured through the agency of music."

With this in mind the retired professor, who by this time was being suspiciously watched by the frieze area guard, began using the camera zoom app on her iPhone to photograph minuscule details of the knight-Mahler. Every inch of the elaborate golden armor covered his body including the hands and feet. A two-part neck piece covered his throat and the lower part of his chin. She took the closest details possible of the profile face. Perhaps there was something she, and history, had missed? Something she could add tomorrow evening to her Vienna University lecture on the two Gustavs?

111

Spotting Stefan's car backing into a parking place on the Dorotheergasse one block away, Adele ran to meet him. For her it was a short walk to their parents' home whereas for her brother it was much farther.

"Oh, great! It's just noon. We can go in together," Stefan greeted her. They were both eager to see the grandfather they hardly remembered. They knew that, as a Palestinian living during the present Israeli-Palestinian conflict, his life had been difficult. That he had made the trip all the way from the Gaza Strip to see his son meant so much to their father. But the children took it as slightly foreboding. Their mother had privately conveyed to them her worries about the highly specialized operation Basileus needed and their inability to afford it despite the socialist country they lived in and despite the hefty annual contribution based on their income required by Austria's health system. If she had told Opa what she had told Adele and Stefan, there was need to be worried for sure.

They hurried up the stairs to the second-floor apartment. The front door was unlocked and they could hear the sounds of lively conversation.

"Ach! here you are, *Kinder!*" Sabina swerved in her seat to clasp their hands.

"You are so grown up now!" their grandfather exclaimed, standing to embrace them. In his mid-eighties, he was tall and slender, too slender perhaps, and appeared quite fragile. His abundant hair was almost completely white whereas his full beard was still almost completely black.

"How proud you must be of Adele, of Stefan," Ahmed Suleiman said fondly, looking from one to the other. "Why, Adele, last time I saw you I could lift you high up in my arms. Remember? I certainly can't do that any longer."

"But, Opa, I will *never* be able to lift you in my arms! So be happy that you once could."

"True, true. And Stefan how wonderful about your cello position. Basileus has kept me informed of your many successes."

Instead of smiling, Stefan frowned and was silent.

"Is something wrong, son?" It was Basileus's turn to frown.

"You all should know, I suppose. I had to re-audition this morning for my place in the Opera orchestra. According to our beloved maestro, moving from second to first principal chair doesn't come automatically."

Basileus and Sabina looked shocked. This was the first time they had heard about the situation. They had taken it for granted that after the sudden death of Jared Bogenstrein their son would become lead cellist.

Sensing the suddenly heavy mood, Ahmed reached for a white leather box the size of a thick book he had set out on the coffee table.

"My children," he said gravely, looking at all four of them. "You know how much I love you and how much I care about you. I have made the long trip from home because I am concerned about Basileus's health, concerned for all of you." He looked solemnly from one to the other of his four listeners, then pulled the box closer to himself, tapping the top lightly with his right forefinger.

"But with me, in this box, I have brought something that you, dear Basileus, and your children should know. It is indeed time for all of you to know." He lifted the lid of the white leather box. An old, much handled book lay inside. Looking into his son's eyes he spoke slowly and distinctly.

"Basileus. You have always known that when you were three years old, my dear, departed wife and I took you in and adopted you as our own after your entire family was killed in an explosion during the first of the Arab/Israeli Wars. We never told you of your background. Your family background. For you to be safe, we raised you as Palestinian, just as we raised our own children Palestinian. But Basileus, you are not Palestinian. Your parents were Jewish. You are Jewish."

A stunned silence fell upon the room. No one spoke. Open mouthed, Stefan looked at his father. His father was staring blankly, oblivious of the

240

questioning looks his family was giving him.

Ahmed lifted the book out of its box. It, too, was leather bound and had seen much use. He handed it to his adopted son.

"Basileus, this is your father's Torah. I give it to you now in his name."

Instinctively Basileus took it and pressed it to his lips. Tears ran down his cheeks. His wife smiled at him sadly, realizing the shock such news conveyed. But then, to recover something of one's heritage after all this time. That was something to be appreciated and welcomed.

Neither Adele nor Stefan were able to speak, so unprepared were they for such a revelation.

Basileus, however, now talked in a torrent of words.

"Oh my god! Now I know why I always felt different. It was something I could give no name to but I always sensed it. I thought it was because I was an Arab in a Christian society. That's why I changed my surname when I got to Vienna. 'Suleiman' sounded so entirely out of the European orbit that I had entered. I desperately wanted to blend in and so I chose the very common name of Schmidt."

"Yes son, we understood that. You were only eighteen after all and you were trying to blend into a completely different world. The one thing that had no nationality was your love for and study of books. And look where you are now! Director of Austria's National Library!"

"I wonder what they would think if they knew I was Jewish?" Basileus said, growing suddenly silent.

Sabina was appalled by her husband's question. As if that mattered. Yet, in a city such as Vienna where anti-Semitism had just raised its ugly head so publicly, it might. What a wild world it was now. Hatred on so many sides. Recently it had been against the Muslims because of the enormous migration problems spreading all over Europe, now it seemed to be the Jews' turn again. When would it ever stop?

Stefan abruptly stood up and looked at his father disdainfully.

"What would they think if they knew you're Jewish? Just what I would think. They would make mean remarks about you, make fun of you behind your back, resent you, *hate* you. Just as I've hated Jared Bogenstein all these years!" Stefan stopped for breath. He was livid.

"Stefan! How can you talk this way?" Sabina was shocked by her son's diatribe.

"How can I talk this way? Because what Opa has told Papa makes me *half Jewish*, that's why! All my adult life I've competed with Jews at the Opera. Detested them. And now I learn *I'm half* Jewish? God damn all of you! And you, Papa, you can go to hell!

Stefan bolted out of the house. He never looked back.

112

There was not a single seat or even *Stehplatz*—standing place— to be had at the Burgtheater's special two o'clock performance that Thursday. The audience was equally divided between older, regular theater goers and very young people, most of whom had been in the sit-in demonstration of the day before. They were all eager to see Lessing's morality play, *Nathan the Wise*, with its message of religious tolerance. One of the older audience members was Tonik Nektar, thankful to have a balcony seat on audience right and eager to witness a live performance of Lessing's famous play. He wondered whether Mahler had ever seen it. Perhaps even contemplated composing music for it? Yes, had Mahler lived longer, he might indeeed have composed an *opera* on *Nathan the Wise!*

A singular sight to which many Viennese had become used to was a tall woman dressed in a burqa standing in the back row of the *Stehplatz* area far to audience right. Her black clothing completely covered her body and face. Even her eyes were concealed behind a mesh screen. One elderly man threw her a hateful glance: no wonder there was Islamophobia in Vienna with its two-hundred thousand plus Muslim inhabitants. Why couldn't they just fit in? A curious woman in her forties eyed the Muslim woman up and down. Where was enforcement of the recent government law against persons wearing clothing that obscures the face in public? She must have slipped by because police now have the power to order that anyone doing so is subject to a fine of 150 euros and must remove the offending garment on the spot. Oh well, live and let live.

Two female students standing next to her whispered to each other, commenting with approval about how wonderful it was that a Muslim woman could come by herself, unaccompanied, to see Lessing's play pleading for tolerance among Christians, Jews, and Muslims.

A few minutes before the end of Act Three and intermission, the Muslim woman quietly disappeared. Apparently she had wanted to beat the toilet line, or perhaps she was simply shy about being stared at as people passed her and poured into the long narrow foyer that followed the oval course of the building's entrance façade into the two large foyers of the gala staircases where people would be streaming down from the four balconies.

But this time the streaming was dramatically uneven. Those descending on the Landtmann side of the Burgtheater were surprised to hear sounds coming from the ground level. And the closer they got to the ground floor, the more urgent the sounds. Men and women were all shouting the same word which now became terrifyingly distinguishable.

"*Fire!*"

People began running toward the nearest exits. Ushers pointed the way, urging them to leave. The first police began to arrive. Now the odor of smoke fumes filled the air. Other people, the curious ones, ran toward the right stairwell from where the cries were coming. As the curiosity seekers got closer to the staircase they saw a tall young man standing at the front of one of the two long side balconies projecting toward them from the staircase landing. He was dressed in black shirt and pants and gathered about his waist was a discarded black garment of some sort. On an extendable pole he was holding out at full length an ignited gas torch was bellowing forth roaring flames almost as high as the ceiling above. That ceiling section with Gustav Klimt's self-portrait. The insane man was shouting the same thing over and over again. The crowd hushed to hear him.

"*Leave this Jew play now or I will torch your precious Gustav Klimt!*"

"You wouldn't dare!" one young man yelled up at him.

"Don't encourage the idiot," a woman standing next to him screamed as others took up the shout of defiance. A sudden hush fell on the crowd as the man with the torch began to lift it high above his head, dangerously close to the Klimt image.

"*No more Jews at the Burgtheater! No more Jews in Vienna. Hear our hate! Hear our hate! Hear our . . .*"

A pistol shot sounded through the stairwell. The bullet hit its target and the man with the torch fell to the balcony floor. His slayer was Tonik Nektar.

113

"You seem a bit out of sorts today, love."

Haim was watching Harry as he played with an ever-ready Houdini, played a bit too frenetically he thought. As though he were trying to avoid something or push a thought out of his mind.

"Out of sorts? Oh, no. Just a bit frustrated, dear, that I have to skip dinner at home with you this evening. You remember, don't you, I have to meet that Benjamin Britten biographer who's going to provide us with a lot of previously unknown photos for our new documentary. But the prima donna insists we meet at that horrible new Moxy Hotel all the way out by the airport. He absolutely refuses to come into town. Says he needs to be ready for a late evening flight back to London. Frustrating!"

"Oh, I had forgotten. Well, Houdini and I will miss you but we'll try to get by." Haim laughed and called a tail-wagging Houdini over to him.

Harry was relieved his cover story for being out this evening at dinner time had been so readily accepted by his unsuspecting lover. He hated the deception, but his meeting with the Muslim mystery woman who was selling him the Rodin Mahler bust had to be kept secret. What a fabulous, unique way to celebrate their fiftieth anniversary tomorrow!

114

Erich Decker was personally interrogating Tonik Nektar. Police on the Burgtheater scene had unanimously identified him as the man who brought down the lunatic, torch-bearing teenager threatening to destroy Klimt's self-portrait. The fact that all the officers had used the words "brought down" rather than "shot" or "killed" impressed Decker. Nevertheless, he had to be thorough in his questions.

"Did you come to the play with the intention of killing this person?"

"Of course not! I have no idea who he is. Still don't. But there he was suddenly at intermission, defaming Jews and shouting out threats that he would destroy a rich part of Vienna's heritage if we did not leave what he called 'this Jew play.'"

"Do you always carry a pistol when attending cultural events in the city?"

"No, of course not. But I am Jewish, and in the wake of what's been happening in the city, I have felt the need to defend myself should I be attacked."

"But it is true, is it not, that you yourself were in no danger?"

"*Don't you understand*?" Nektar was almost hysterical. "The boy was about to sear Klimt with his torch flames unless everyone left the theater immediately. It was the only right thing to do."

"You could have left it to the police. They were at the scene, you knew that."

"No, no, I did not! I was only concentrating on the insane person standing on the balcony under the Klimt ceiling painting. I didn't look around the stairwell. I didn't look at the lobby. I only looked at him. And when he raised his torch I had to stop him. I didn't mean to kill him. But I had to stop him."

Decker believed the man. He decided the man sitting before him could be charged with third degree manslaughter; that would be the least severe of the charges against him. But the man was a hero to the crowd and in this heightened anti-Semitic atmosphere that had taken over Vienna, the man had indeed acted like a hero. Erich Decker saw no need to press charges against the earnest Jewish man quivering before him.

115

Over a late lunch at the Annagasse's convenient Burger King, Megan was sounding off to Egga on one of her favorite topics: the, what she called, " the shrinking" of education in America.

"And just think! Cursive writing is no longer taught in most grade schools. Pretty soon people won't even know how to sign their names. They'll just use Xs. And there will be a whole new epidemic of unproveable forgeries. Can't you just see someone falsifying a stolen check with just an X?"

"Yes, I worry about what my boys are *not* being taught at school in Germany now. As for handwriting, they are still taught what's called '*Lateinische Ausgangsschrift.*' But I think that pretty soon block printing will replace handwriting. It's the transformation introduced by the Internet. I can see that in the future children will be born with larger, "cellphone" thumbs."

"And, being serious now in the wake of the Mahler Bomber, has the collective memory of the Holocaust been completely wiped clean?" Megan asked. "I think it's barely mentioned in some schools' modern history classes in America now."

Egga was silent. As someone born in Germany *after* the Holocaust, she had to admit she had experienced irritation that world blame seemed to include her and her contemporaries. She voiced her thoughts to Megan who listened attentively.

"I hadn't thought about it from that point of view. To blame later generations is unfair, of course." Megan admitted.

"Racial hatred in all directions seems to be flaring up again, everywhere. In Berlin right now some recent Muslim emigrants have been committing acts of terror against our Jewish residents."

"Yes, just like Paris. The newly arrived Muslims face discrimination in employment and in their treatment by police, so they seem to take it out on Paris's Jewish population. It's so bad that thousands of Jews have left the peripheries of Paris where Muslim populations are rising. They've retrenched in neighborhoods with larger Jewish populations, say, like the seventeenth arrondissement for example."

"And it isn't only Muslim against Jew. Look at that terrible murder of eleven Jews in a Pittsburgh synagogue by a loonie who accused Jews of bringing invaders to harm America."

"Can't we talk about something else?" Egga wanted to return to the elation they had both felt while viewing the Klimt Beethoven frieze earlier in the day."

"Of course we can." Megan pulled out her iPhone, initiated several commands, then handed Egga an image that filled the screen. It was a detail of Klimt's golden knight from armored chest to up just above his head. In that picture plane on the left a square-jawed staring brunette held a green laurel wreath above the warrior while on the right, raised arms together, a hand-clasping red-haired woman looked down benignly upon the knight/Mahler figure.

"Do you see it?" Megan asked conspiratorially.

"See what?"

"Keep looking."

"I am."

"Concentrate on the knight's face."

"All right. It's in profile and he seems to be staring past the clasped fingers of the red-haired woman above him."

"Correct. Now look at that area *closely*."

A silence ensued as Egga stared at the image.

"I give up. Don't be mean. Tell me!"

"I will, dear. At tomorrow evening's lecture."

116

¶It was time.

Time to load up the Mahler bust, drive to the Prater, change into her burqa, and meet the man who was willing to pay for the Rodin bust of the composer.

Adele Schmidt had not yet digested the shattering fact revealed at her parents home. For years she had felt a deep dislike for Jews because of the blatant discrimination against her brother at the Opera by Jewish first-cellist Jared Bogenstein and Jewish conductor Gabor Alexander. Yet just a few hours ago she learned Jewish blood flowed through her own veins!

But for the present what was primary was her mission. The delivery of a Rodin bust that would bring in fifty-thousand euros and enable her family to pay for her father's operation. The meeting was set for six o'clock in front of the *Riesenrad* where one of the special closed cabins had been reserved for her and her "guest." She must concentrate completely on the mission.

Parking at the Prater was difficult but Adele knew about places reasonably near the main entrance. To go to the Prater parking lots would put her too far from the *Riesenrad*. This time she was not lucky, however, and had to search several streets with no luck. The only free spot she could find was a handicap place in front of a small bank near the Praterstern public transportation hub. Probably okay to park there at night for just a couple of hours at the most. She hid her driver's license and credit cards in the back of the glove compartment. This was not the safest part of town ever since the recent renovation, or perhaps because of it. Drugs were being sold openly on the street. While still in the car she slipped her burqa on over her blue jeans without being observed. She hated the way there were no sleeves in the almost floor-length veil and how she had to hike up the sides just to get her arms out. She got out of the car looking in all directions, then from behind the driver's seat carefully pulled out a twenty-inch-high roller tote with its precious cargo. Aware that she would have to surrender the bag as well as its contents, Adele had bought a new one that did not have the telltale label "Singer" on it. Underneath the burqa, Adele wore a large sling bag, empty and ready to receive the fifty-thousand-euro payment her client would hand over to her. She walked briskly back to the huge roundabout and the Prater's main entrance. She was ready.

By design Harry Howell had arrived at the *Riesenrad* half an hour early. He stood on the opposite side of the crowded walkway and stared at the Ferris wheel entrance with its small ticket office and low roped corridors that kept waiting passengers in orderly lines. A woman wearing a full-length black burqa would certainly stand out.

For what had to be the sixth time, Harry seriously considered alerting the police and simply standing by, letting the arrest take place as he met the woman. The thief would certainly be easy to identify in that hideous burqa. Yes, that is what he should do. Denounce her. The Mahler bust would be returned to the Opera House. And next time he and Haim attended a performance there he could let Haim know what almost took place—that they had come very close to having the bust on that pedestal between Mendelssohn and Schönberg. Wouldn't that be joy enough?

Harry made his decision. Pulling an old Blackberry cellphone out of his breast pocket, he dialed the police emergency number, 133. A female voice sounded immediately.

"*Notfall.* State location and emergency."

"Oh. Um. *Riesenrad.* Arab woman in burqa, Rodin bust of . . ."

Abruptly Harry hung up. Dread overcame him. Goose bumps rose on his forearms and the back of his neck. He simply could not go through with it. There would be too many questions, too many explanations. Terrible publicity that could affect him, Haim, and the kids. No, better to keep to the devil's bargain that he, after all, had initiated. The image of Haim's delight at seeing the Mahler bust was stronger than was his fear. He must try to stay calm and let things go forward as had been planned.

There she was! A burqa-clothed woman pulling a rolling tote bag had just walked up to the *Riesenrad* ticket office. She appeared to talk briefly to someone inside, then turned and began scanning the crowd in front of her.

Harry did not disappoint. With bulging briefcase pressed tightly under his left arm he strode toward her, his face expressionless. She was the first to speak.

"I have our reservation. We wait here until the wheel stops turning. Then we are first onboard after the cabin is cleared." They stood side by side looking at the slowly revolving giant wheel hung with cabins, without exchanging another word. The great wheel came to a stop a few minutes later and happy riders spilled out of the first cabin, now flush with the ground—their cabin. After two formally dressed waiters entered the cabin carrying dinner boxes, clearing, cleaning, and setting up—all seemingly in one minute—they were invited to enter. At Adele's gesture, Harry stepped in first and she followed, pulling her tote carefully inside behind her. As they waited for the wheel to move up one slot for the next cabin passenger exchange, Adele began drawing the blinds over the four huge windows on her side of the cabin. Following her lead, Harry closed the blinds on his side. They sat down at the long table between them and stared at each other without speaking for a few moments. At the far side a full chicken casserole with a bottle of Austrian pinot noir had been laid out for them. This was ignored, as each waited for the other to speak first.

"How do you wish this to proceed?" Harry asked finally in frustration.

"I shall place the Rodin bust on this table for your examination. It can be as thorough as you wish, with whatever non-invasive tools you have brought with you. When you are satisfied and I have counted the euros you have brought, the exchange can be made."

"Fair enough." Harry watched as the mysterious woman turned to her roller tote and with notable exertion lift the forty-pound bust of Mahler out and onto the table. She peeled away the bubble wrap that protected it. Harry gasped. He sensed he was in the presence of the two greats—Rodin and Mahler. He tried not to show his excitement. Never, in all his visits to the Vienna State Opera, had he been this close to the Mahler bust. He pulled a large magnifying glass out of his briefcase. It had an excellent LED light and three lenses; the weakest was 2.5X, the largest, 16X. Harry laid his photographs of all sides and views of the Model B Rodin Mahler bust on the table and began making his comparisons. Everything matched, including the foundry mark. Carefully he touched the bronze, running his fingers over the surface then up into the hollow interior. The nostril holes should not be accessible from the inside. They were not.

This was the original bust.

Harry looked across the table and addressed the woman who had been watching him through her concealing eye mesh.

"I see that this is indeed the bust that was in the Opera House until last Sunday. How you came by it is not my business. Nor am I interested. I am now ready to buy the bust for the sum offered in my newspaper bulletin."

"I am glad you realize this is genuine," Adele allowed.

"Here is the money." Harry opened his briefcase and counting slowly he laid out twenty piles of bundled banknotes on the table. Each pile contained 2,500 euros in denominations of one hundred euros. Adele slowly counted the bills in each pile as their cabin leisurely ascended to the top of the *Riesenrad*.

"Good, I have verified the amount. It is correct." Somewhat awkwardly, she transferred the stacks to the sling purse underneath her burqa. Then she reached over for the roller tote on the floor beside her and gingerly passed it over the table to Harry.

"You will be wanting this."

"Yes, thanks."

Harry gathered the bubble wrap, and placed it around the bust with the tenderness of a new father. Once protected, the bust was slowly lowered into the tote which Harry had placed on the floor next to him. He zipped it close. Now there was nothing to do except wait for the cabin to return to the exit point.

The two sat in silence. There was nothing more to be said. The uneaten dinner grew cold, the bottle of pinot noir remained unopened.

A sudden loud noise and noticeable jerk to their cabin had them both instantly on their feet.

The giant Ferris wheel's slow rotation had ceased.

117

Stefan was not answering his phone and his mother was worried. In fact Sabina Schmidt had been unable to reach either of her children. Where was Adele? It was definitely unusual that neither of them picked up right after the dinner hour. That was ordinarily the time for family catch-up. She did not want to alarm Basileus, who was talking with his stepfather, the two of them happily reviving early family memories. Her husband had taken the news of his Jewish heritage amazingly well, considering what a total surprise it was. Adele had made no comment about the revelation whatsoever, not even when she left, but she had seemed a bit agitated. And Stefan! How could he speak to his father that way? And what a terrible thing to do, storming out of the house that way. Was he still so furious? He had already been angry over the cello auditions at the Opera. Was he about to do something dramatic, something that might get him into trouble?

Or was Sabina just being a worry wort?

118

Megan's six o'clock lecture at the Albertina was well attended in spite of the seemingly narrow scope of the announced topic: "Of Passion and Prudery: Early Collectors of Egon Schiele." But the audience was in for an unexpected and occasionally hilarious treat as Megan introduced a variety of twentieth-century acquisatory fans of the Austrian artist in countries ranging from China and Japan to Canada and South America. Museums did not figure very much in Megan's history of the century's collecting because of the enormously high price of Schiele works. The rare oil painting that came up now and then on the auction block brought in millions of dollars and the slightly more available mature drawing with watercolor or gouache heightening averaged a million and a half dollars. It was not, however, the price paid upon which Megan's lecture was focused, it was the sometimes *bekloppten*—loony—private collectors who would sometimes resort to extreme means to own a Schiele drawing or oil. The lecture ended on a happy note as Megan recounted how she had received a gift, now in the Dallas Museum of Art, of a 1913 Schiele self-portrait titled *Recollection* to honor the completion of her dissertation on the artist. Early in her research, the generous collector family from Graz, Austria, had adopted her as the "fifth" daughter in their family and although "Mommy Dollie" and "Daddy Foga" had passed away, Megan continued to be in close contact with the four daughters—in fact, "here they are!" The audience turned to where Megan was pointing and spontaneously applauded at the touching sight of four older women modestly waving at their "sister."

"I wonder where Harry and Haim were tonight," Megan said to Egga as they left the museum after the lecture.

"Hey, you're right! They told us they were free to come to your lectures both tonight and tomorrow evening. What a pity. As collectors themselves, they would have enjoyed your tales of avarice and largesse."

"I guess they would have. Too bad."

"Perhaps they'll come to 'The Two Gustavs' at the University tomorrow then."

"Hope so."

The two friends turned into the Annagasse and at the same instant looked at each other inquiringly as they passed the Burger King.

Yes! With Klimt in the morning and Schiele in the evening a single scoop hot fudge sundae was definitely in order.

119

"Why do you think it isn't moving?" Adele looked at Harry through the mesh cloth covering her eyes.

"I don't know. Let's try to see what's going on down there." He turned to the bay of windows on his side and began pulling up the blind. Adele followed his initiative and the cabin was flooded with sunlight.

"Can't see much from here," Adele murmured crossly as she strove to make out anything unusual on the ground below.

"Nor can I. And these windows don't open. They're all just glass panels." Harry looked at the woman's back as she strove to see downward past the wheel's intricate support structure. A dark thought came to mind. What if he were to knock the veiled woman unconscious? Retrieve his money and when the cabin finally got to the ground, grab the tote and disappear into the crowd as quickly as possible?

Adele turned toward Harry at that moment and boldly sized him up. The man was in his seventies, she was in her twenties. If she weren't imprisoned in this goddamn burqa thing she'd probably be able to hit him with the unopened wine bottle and bring him down. Render him blanko. Flee with both the money *and* the bust!

A tremendous mechanical groan just then jump-started the great turning wheel and slowly the cabin made its way from the highest point of the *Riesenrad* to the ground. Neither occupant uttered another word nor looked at each other again. As soon as the cabin was anchored in place, Harry jerked open the door and, hugging the roller tote to his chest, walked swiftly toward the roaring wave of pedestrians moving up and down the wide amusement path fronting the *Riesenrad*. Within seconds he had blended in with the crowd.

Adele was not so lucky. Still garbed in the hampering burqa, under which she now had to stuff her crammed sling bag, her exit from the cabin was not as swift as her customer's. When she did step to the ground, she suddenly felt restraining hands on both her arms. A policeman was telling her to remain in place. She was under arrest!

120

¶It was the unmistakable sound of howling. Harry had heard it even before he unlocked the door to their Liechtensteinstrasse flat. When he entered, pulling the roller tote with its fabulous contents behind him, something strange happened. Houdini did not come bounding to greet him.

"Houdini? Haim?"

There was no answer. The high howling continued unabated. Harry walked to the bedroom. The door was partly ajar. He pushed it open and saw the unthinkable. Haim lay face up on the floor, his right hand behind his head, his eyes rolled upward and his mouth open. Crouching next to him and whimpering now was Houdini. He did not leave Haim's side as Harry rushed over to them. He touched his shoulder and his face. They were cold.

"*Haim! Haim!*"

The dog's immediate barking echoed the urgency.

Harry pressed his right ear to his partner's chest. He could hear no heartbeat. It can't be! He placed his index and middle fingers to the right side of Haim's windpipe directly on the carotid artery. No pulse. He pressed harder and waited.

"*Haim! Haim!*"

Harry tried frantically to remember what one does in CPR. Interlocking his hands he knelt by Haim's side and pushed down hard on his chest, then released, then pushed again. Nothing. In desperation he locked his mouth over Haim's and tried sending his breath down into the motionless man's lungs. Nothing. No movement. No response.

His despair was matched only by their faithful dog's mournful howling.

121

Stefan had spent most of the night and early morning hours at Flex, the upbeat nightclub ensconced inside one of the unused tunnels under the Danube. An indie-electro musical group from Tel Aviv was providing the frenetic dance music and for once in his cello-dominated, intensely regulated life, Stefan had let loose. No "holds barred," he laughed out loud at his insider cello joke. He drank beer and he danced; always a new brand, always a different partner. After some four frenetic hours of this he was ready to sit down and size things up. Get real. Well, the reality was he was half Jewish. The reality was that he actually felt at home with the *BustMyEars* music being played by the Tel Aviv band. It evoked some klezmer tunes he himself had played in symphonic orchestral music. Could it be that he felt at *home* in this ambience? Was this his new reality? Was being half Jewish really so bad?

Filled with these questions he lazily quit the noisy establishment at the Augartenbrücke, lurched to his dependable, welcoming car nearby, and drove home. He would call his parents and apologize to his father after he got some sleep. No, perhaps wait until after the results of the Opera cello auditions were announced. That might influence his mood and he didn't want to be in a bad mood when he talked to his father. He had already caused him enough pain by walking out of the house without saying so much as a goodbye.

When he woke up around one o'clock he realized he was in hangover status—something he had rarely experienced. He would wait a while longer before contacting the family. Meanwhile he would drop in at the Opera and see who had won first principal chair of the cello section. There were two finalists: himself and a woman who had recently joined the Opera Orchestra, Natalie Silverstein.

He found maestro Gabor Alexander in the musicians lounge and when their eyes met, Alexander beckoned to him.

"Just the person I want to see! There is no need for another audition. Fräulein Silverstein just told me that she wishes to cede first chair to you. So that is that. She will be second principle; you are now first."

Stefan was nonplussed. He found himself taking Alexander's extended hand and shaking it warmly.

"Do you know where she is now?" he asked.

"I think you can catch her if you hurry to the Operngasse exit. That's where she was headed."

"Thanks." Unencumbered by his cello, Stefan raced toward the stage door exit. There she was, her black cello case strapped to her back.

"Hey! Wait up, Natalie, wait!"

Natalie Silverstein turned toward Stefan with an inquiring look.

"I want to thank you for pulling out of the auditions."

"No problem. I hated our being musical antagonists and beside that, our maestro might not know, but *I* know you are a better cellist than I. I still have a lot to learn and you're such an inspiring example."

"My god, I'm stunned. You are too gracious, Nat."

"Just calling it like I see it."

Stefan accompanied the older woman past the Albertina Museum to the beginning of the Augustinerstrasse. They started to say goodbye.

"Where are you off to, anyhow?" Stefan asked the sturdy, smiling brunette.

"The Hard Rock Café."

"*What?*"

"Ha! I thought that might throw you for a loop. No, a bit further along than that. I'm off to the Stadttempel Synagogue. Play for them from time to time. Like right now. I'm playing a memorial service." Natalie paused.

"Wanna come?"

Before he could even think, Stefan answered.

"Yes. Why not." Why not indeed.

If he were Jewish he might as well find out what synagogues and the faith were all about.

122

⁋It was early morning. Harry could not bring himself to make any calls. How to break the news to Callas, to Bell? And whom do you call when someone dies at home? He could not think beyond the fact that Haim was gone. That he had died alone. That he hadn't been with him when his heart attack occurred. That's what it must have been. Why had he *believed* Haim when he belittled his symptoms?

He was lying beside his beloved on the floor. He had placed a long pillow under his head and lowered his out-flung right arm onto his chest. He himself had lain next to him through the night, holding him, rocking him gently. Their sweet canine companion never left them, but he was quiet now except for an occasional moan. Thus the night had passed. They had said their final farewells.

Now an image seized Harry. It was the image of Mahler's bust. The intended anniversary gift. The cursed anniversary gift! He would have been home with Haim if he hadn't been in a stupid suspended *Riesenrad* cabin swinging over the Prater crowds, buying the damn thing from an unpleasant Arab woman whose face he couldn't even see. How can I make up for my greed? I wanted us to have the Mahler bust more than I wanted to be at home for dinner with you, my dearest Haim.

Harry sat up and held his face in his hands as sobs racked his body. Houdini whimpered in consternation. At last the sobs ceased and Harry's mind cleared. There were three things to be done. First, call Callas and Bell to tell them their father had died. He would wait for them to come. Second, after the children had made their final farewells, he would call 144 for an ambulance to come and take them to MedUni. He would present Haim's willed body document to the official in charge of body donation at MedUni. Both he and Haim had filled out forms with the Center for Anatomy and Cell Biology at MedUni at the Vienna General Hospital years ago, when they first settled in Vienna. Other than their children they had no close family members. Harry would accompany Haim in the ambulance and take care of things there.

And then and only then he would carry out an equally crucial third task. Haim's voice was urging him to do so.

"Do the honorable thing, dearest, do the honorable thing!"

123

$\mathcal{T}$he eight am phone call was shattering. Sabina Schmidt had answered only to hear her daughter sobbing, her words inarticulate.

"Calm down, darling, calm down. What is it you're trying to say?" She signaled urgently to her husband to pick up the phone on the table next to him.

"It's Adele," she hissed across the room to him. "I think she's in trouble." Basileus lifted the phone to his ear and listened to the shrieking voice on the other end of the line.

"Mutti! I am in jail! I was arrested by the police. I've been locked up in a cell all night. They only just now are letting me make a phone call. You've got to get me out of here!"

"*Liebling*, speak more slowly. I'm having trouble understanding you."

"What is it you're trying to tell us," Basileus added, as mystified and worried as his wife.

"It was all for *you*, Papa, all for *you*. And in revenge for Stefan."

"*What* was all for me and Stefan? What are you talking about?"

"The money they found in my purse when they searched me. I had fifty thousand euros to pay for your operation. And they found it. Said I was under arrest."

"I don't understand. You had fifty thousand euros with you?"

"Yes, yes, and it's all because I answered an ad in the paper."

"Answered an ad? *What* ad?"

"Didn't you see it? An ad offering to pay fifty thousand euros for Rodin's bust of Mahler that was removed from the Opera House the night of the explosion."

"My god! Are you telling us you removed the bust?"

"No, no." Adele had found her tongue and there was a rush of blurted words, only half of which her parents comprehended.

"But I did find a bronze head that morning that had been dumped by somebody in our tailoring department garbage. I didn't realize it was Mahler. I just liked it. So I took it home. Then the next morning the paper came out with this ad offering lots of money for a Rodin bust of Mahler. I looked Rodin up on the Internet and found photos of Rodin's different busts of Mahler. One of them looked a lot like what I had. So I was pretty proud of having saved it from the trash and I contacted the person who'd placed the ad and we agreed to meet and I'd bring the bust thing and he'd bring the payment in cash. And we'd meet in the Prater and make the exchange in a cabin of the *Riesenrad*. And then the police were there when I got out and they arrested me and . . . "

". . . stop, *Liebchen*, stop!" Sabina screamed into the phone. "You're going too fast. We're not getting what you're saying."

"Mutti! I am in jail! You've got to get me out! I'm innocent."

"Just tell your mother where you are, Adele, and she'll come down there right away. And I'll find a lawyer to get you out."

"Okay, okay. I'm at the Police Detention Center on the Hernalser Gürtel."

"On the Hernalser Gürtel," her mother repeated.

"Okay, *okay*!" Adele was obviously yelling to someone at the detention center. "Mutti, Papa, I have to go now. They're making me hang up. I'm innocent, I'm innocent, I tell you!"

"Stay strong, *Liebling*," Basileus said even though he'd heard the line go dead.

"Thank god Opa is still sleeping in his room." Sabina suddenly remembered the old man visiting them.

"Yes, thank god. Now you drive to the jail and I'll see how soon Peter Hanslick can get there. Thank god we have a good lawyer!"

It took a few calls but Basileus got hold of the family lawyer and he promised to meet with Sabina and Adele right away.

It was still morning but Basileus decided he needed a drink—something rare for him to do. He poured himself a shot of whiskey and sat down in the kitchen, talking to himself out loud.

"Let's see. We've got a daughter who is in jail, accused of a serious crime, and we have a son who has left the house cursing me and now we don't know where he is. What would a Jew say? *Oy vey*!" Basileus snorted at this misplaced bit of humor when the situation was so serious. Another sip of whiskey and he became deadly serious.

Here was a thankless son whom he had favored over his daughter. He had even applauded his son's clever revenge attack on fellow cellist Bogenstein at the Opera when he caused him to fall on his cello during performance.

Basileus took another sip of whiskey.

How mistaken he had been, condoning that tactic in blind love for his son. The son who had just told him to go to hell. Here was a son who did not deserve what he had been keeping in his safe for him all these many years.

But he knew someone who did deserve the treasure. Someone whom he now knew in person. Basileus went in search of his wallet and pulled out a business card he had recently received.

He dialed the number on the card. It was to Henri-Claude de la Granger.

124

This was the trio's last leisurely breakfast together at the Römischer Kaiser. Egga would be returning to Berlin tomorrow at noon, Megan had a late afternoon flight back to Dallas, and Henri-Claude would be flying back to Paris and his dog Vito very early in the morning, leaving the hotel long before Megan and Egga would even be up.

But this morning the talk was about Henri-Claude and Megan's upcoming impromptu visit to the home of Basileus Schmidt. The distinguished librarian had phoned Henri-Claude in his room half an hour ago inviting him and his American professor friend to visit him. He sounded urgent. They settled on two o'clock that afternoon. That would give Megan plenty of time to prepare for her final lecture this evening at the university.

"What on earth could be on his mind, I wonder?" Megan asked after Henri-Claude told them about the call.

"He did not specify. He merely said he wanted to show us something. Something terribly, terribly important. Something I in particular should know about."

"Something you should know about?" asked Egga intrigued.

"That could only mean one thing, couldn't it? Something to do with

Mahler. But of course you know *everything* about Mahler."

"Not so, but thank you for the compliment. You would be surprised how many truly new tidbits of information on the composer are submitted to my *Médiathèque*. And occasionally letters written by the composer to someone we don't know about. I may or may not already know what Herr Schmidt wishes to tell us about, but it certainly is worth a visit. The man did not sound at all well though. And as I said, he seemed to be rather agitated. As though there were not much time to be lost."

125

Harry's children insisted on accompanying him and the ambulance to UniMed's body donation reception room. Haim's living will donation papers were in order and everything proceeded more rapidly than any of them had imagined. A payment of 990 euros was necessary. Something Harry had known was required and for which he was ready. Neither Callas nor Bell could bear to mention that today would have been their dads' golden anniversary. They were all in agreement that there would be no service of any sort. Bearing the death was already so difficult. A public ceremony would have put them through too much stress.

"Do you have time to get something to eat?" Harry asked, feeling sudden hunger pangs. It had been hours since he ate anything.

"Sure, Dad. I'll just call my museum and alert them that I'll be back later," Callas said.

"Absolutely," confirmed Bell. "I don't need to be at the Belvedere until four this afternoon for the evening shift."

"Do you think we should go to a Kosher restaurant in honor of Dad?" Callas asked.

"Oh, no, I couldn't bear it, dear heart. And you know he was not religious, not at all." Harry was surprised at his own immediate rejection of the idea, but neither of them had ever been religious.

"Let's go back to town then and eat at your favorite restaurant, Dad, *Zum Weissen Rauchfangkehrer*." Bell looked at them questioningly.

"Yes, I would find that comforting. Haim and I always loved the cozy atmosphere and the private booths. You know what? We could actually make our lunch there our own private memorial service for Haim." Harry had smiled for the first time since yesterday afternoon before he had left home for the Prater.

It was twenty to four in the afternoon when they left the restaurant. Food and wine had helped lift the family's spirits and after exchanging long hugs each went in separate directions—Callas to the Jewish Museum, Bell to the Belvedere, and Harry back home. He had a final task to accomplish. Returning the Mahler bust to the Opera. Not for one moment had he lost his resolve, but he had been glad of the delay in timing.

He knew exactly what to do. The bubble-wrapped bust was still untouched in its tote bag and this was the way Harry intended it to remain. All he needed to do now was write a short message on a card, enclose it in an envelope, seal it, and address it. Then he would call an Uber and have himself driven to the Café Mozart within very short walking distance of the Opera House. He would have the Uber wait.

All went as he envisioned and twenty-five minutes later, wearing a large pair of sunglasses, Harry was wheeling his tote toward the Kärntner Strasse side of the building.

He stopped at the stage door, tote bag at his side. The portier on duty, Rudi Wittkower, had just arrived and was in a good mood. He greeted the elderly man and asked what he could do for him.

"Would you kindly see that this bag is delivered to Maestro Alexander when he arrives this evening? As you can see, the envelope is addressed to him." There was a pause as the portier read the conductor's name on the card out loud. He seemed to hesitate.

"You do know that today is the twentieth anniversary of the maestro's tenure with the Opera, don't you?" Harry spoke up quickly.

The portier brightened.

"No, sir, I did not. And yes, sir, I will see the bag is given directly to him. He usually comes in on this side of the House."

Harry thanked the portier, turned, and rejoined the waiting Uber in front of the Café Mozart. Today was not an anniversary for the Opera conductor, but the contents of the bag would be cause for celebration. The accompanying message contained just six words:

"This belongs in our beloved Opera."

In the mid 1880s a reverent young Gustav Mahler visited Beethoven's house on the Schwarzspanierstrasse and came away with the original keyhole cover-plate of the green door to the apartment where the composer died. In the early 1900s, as conductor of the Vienna Court Opera, he gave the historic item to the Pasqualatihaus Beethoven Museum in Vienna.

126

Just as they had begun walking from their hotel to Basileus Schmidt's apartment, which was on the Augustinergasse just past the Albertina Museum, Megan's iPhone rang. She saw the call was from Erich Decker and answered immediately.

"Erich?"

"Ah, Megan, I'm glad I caught you before you leave Vienna. Wanted to bring you up to date on things. A lot has happened. Is this a good time?"

"I'm walking with Henri-Claude to an appointment right now, but do tell me what you have, *please*. May I put you on speaker so he can hear you as well?"

"Yes. All right. I'll try to be brief. We've confirmed the identities of the two shooters at the Musikverein. One was, as you well know, the harpist Cristina Paloma. Her prints were all over the pistol she used and she's in jail without bail. Raising hell, I might add."

"I bet." Megan laughed.

"The other assassin killed himself."

"What?"

"Yes. He was the contra trombonist for the Opera orchestra who left at the end of Act One—Ottokar Weininger. We encountered him in the Karlskirche, remember?"

"Boy, do I ever! I followed him inside after I saw him talking to two young kids across the street from the Musikverein. I thought they might be the two hoodlums who interrupted Egga's concert."

"Right. Well last night he committed suicide. Shot himself twice in the heart in a café that used to be Beethoven's address out on the Scwarzspanierstrasse. There were two letters, or rather I should say directives found on his body. One was addressed to Vienna's mayor and the other was addressed to the president of the International Gustav Mahler Society right here in the city. They were filled with anti-Semitic ravings. Both letters bragged about the slaying of Gerald Chaplin and also about having spray-painted the word 'Jew' on the portrait of Mahler at the Opera House."

"Good heavens! What a turn of events."

"It sure is. One of the odd things about the Weininger confession is that he claimed he was the only assassin of Chaplin. Obviously he did not know about the second shot. Seemed to be furious that the killing had been reported as having been carried out by two persons."

"Talk about vanity!"

"And we've also determined who was responsible for that spate of hate graffiti and vandalism of Jewish monuments all around the city—you know, the spray-painting of the new statue of Freud at MedUni, the desecration of Gustav and Alma Mahler's tombstones out in Grinzing, Lessing's statue here in town, and the memorial to Franz Werfel in the Schiller park. And the hate handbills found at the University. We think it was all the work of one man; I should say one boy because he was still a teenager."

"You say 'was'?"

"Yes, *was*. A first-year student at the University named Karl Lueger. And yes, before you ask, a distant relative of Mayor Karl Lueger. I presume you've heard about the shooting at the Burgtheater yesterday afternoon. And the crazed person who threatened to destroy the ceiling Klimt self-portrait unless the intermission audience immediately left what he shouted was a 'Jew play.'"

"I did see the coverage on television late last night when I got back to the hotel, yes."

"Well, the boy was shot dead by a man from the Mahler Society who happened to be in the lobby. His name is Tonik Nektar. Ever heard of him?"

"I certainly have. He was an over-enthusiastic Mahler fan who came up to me at my book-signing event. Whew! So much has happened since I talked to you last!"

"For sure. But I think we've rounded up the vandals now."

"Does that include the Mahler Bomber then?"

263

"Ha! No. I wish I could fault the Ottokar Weininger character, but he sounded so egotistical in his manifesto letters that I'm sure he would have claimed responsibility for the Opera House explosion if he were responsible for that. We have determined that he was not involved."

"So for now the Mahler Bomber is still a mystery?"

"We have one possible lead, Megan. Last night *Notfall* received an anonymous tip from a male caller clearly uttering the following words: '*Riesenrad*, Arab woman,' and 'Rodin bust of' before he hung up. We got a team there right away and initiated surveillance on the wheel from several vantage points. About thirty minutes after the *Notfall* call, a fully veiled woman emerged from one of those special cabins rented for meals during an hour's worth of full rotations of the wheel. From the way she was dressed we presumed she was Arab, as the call had indicated, but then in the holding cell she suddenly pulled off her long over-body veil, or whatever it's called, and looked like any Viennese kid in jeans and shirt.

"And that's not all. She refused to identify herself but when we searched her purse for an ID we found *fifty thousand euros*! All in denominations of a hundred."

"So *she* is the one who stole the Mahler bust, substituted the surmoulage, and then *sold* it!"

"Sure looks that way. We were hoping to arrest the buyer but he or she had already exited the cabin and disappeared into the crowd. The woman we'd arrested would not answer a single question. But you remember the mysterious ad in the paper the day after the explosion, and how it offered fifty thousand euros for the bust, no questions asked."

"I didn't see the ad but you told me about it when we met in the Café Museum after the Belvedere attack."

"Oh, that's right. Well, early this morning, we received a very interesting call from the Praterstern district police telling us they had been called by a branch of the UniCredit Bank to remove a car found parked in front of it. Their security camera showed that a woman wearing a burqa had left it overnight in the disabled parking slot."

"Ah ha!"

"There's more. After it was hauled off, we conducted a standard search of the interior and guess what they found in the glove box?"

"Well, I guess a car glove compartment is a bit too small for a Rodin bust of Mahler." Megan laughed at her own poor joke.

"We found a driver's license and credit cards all belonging to one Adele Schmidt."

"Your case is narrowing down!"

"Very possibly. We allowed the girl to make one phone call this morning. Her family lawyer is here now and I'm about to interrogate her. Wish me luck."

"I certainly do. Funny you're dealing with a Schmidt. Henri-Claude and I are on our way right now to meet a Schmidt. But this is Basileus Schmidt, the director of the National Library."

"Interesting coincidence. Ha! There must be five hundred Schmidts in Vienna."

"Will you call me if your non-Arab Schmidt girl admits anything? I'll be lecturing at seven o'clock this evening at the University, but do call me regardless, please! Even if it's during my lecture, understand? By god, you could be closing the case on the Mahler Bomber."

"I'll call you, Megan, I promise. *Tschüss!*"

They had reached Basileus Schmidt's address on the Augustinerstrasse. The National Library was conveniently just across the street.

"What an incredible location, considering his job," Megan murmured as they rode the elevator up to the top floor.

The apartment's front door was already open and a glum Sabina Schmidt introduced herself, then ushered them into the living room. Basileus Schmidt slowly rose from the couch to greet them, introducing his father who was visiting from Palestine.

"And now please come with me to my office upstairs where the item is that I wish to show you." Taking in deep breaths and obviously in great physical pain, he began to walk toward the attic stairway.

" *Liebling*, should you be climbing the stairs?" asked his wife.

Basileus waved her aside.

"I am all right."

Sabina turned imploringly to their guests, taking them into her confidence.

"My husband has ankylosing spondylitis—AS—and it has affected his breathing. He should not be exerting himself."

"Just this one time, *Liebling*. There's something very important that needs tending to and that's why I've asked Monsieur de La Granger and Frau Professor Crespi to come here." He stopped and waved to his two visitors.

"I think perhaps you should go up first. My slowness will detain you unnecessarily. Just turn to the left when you reach the top. That's my study. I will join you as quickly as I can."

Megan and Henri-Claude climbed up the narrow flight of stairs and entered the study. It contained a great mahogany desk, two straight back chairs, and a leather-covered roller stool in front of a large safe. What caught their eye, however, was not the furniture but the bronze bust on top of the safe. It was Rodin's bust of Mahler! A surmoulage at closer glance, but all the same, a bust of Mahler. Model B, they whispered to one another in confirmation.

Ignoring Sabina's continued protestations, Basileus slowly mounted the stairs and joined his two visitors. Quickly sitting down on the stool, he waved his visitors to the two chairs. His breathing was loud and labored but after five seconds or so he began to speak gaspingly, but intelligibly.

"In my safe here there is a treasure that I found in our National Library and which I brought home for preservation and study. Study because I wanted to be sure before revealing my find to the world. But the time has come." He wheeled around to the safe, entered its combination and drew out a large, heavy, and definitely ancient file. With a last effort of strength Basileus lifted the file to his desk. He turned to his worried visitors and smiled.

"You are about to see something wondrous."

Slowly he began unwinding the ancient strings that had strapped the file box closed for many decades. Now they could see that printed on the top was the name "Hugo Wolf." Megan and Henri-Claude exchanged quick glances. Slowly Basileus lifted a multi-staved score out and placed it on the desk, moving the empty box out of the way.

"What do you see?" His wheezing voice inquired. His deep brown eyes were bright with anticipation.

"What I see," said Henri-Claude with disbelief, "is Gustav Mahler's distinctive handwriting on top of the initial staves of an orchestra overture."

"And what else do you see?" Basileus asked.

Megan, eagerly leaning past Henri-Claude, supplied the answer so obvious to them both.

"The title of an opera."

"And the title?"

Henri-Claude looked puzzled. He frowned and almost unwillingly enunciated the title.

"*Der Corregidor*"

"Yes, in Mahler's own hand."

"But that's an opera composed by Hugo Wolf, not by Mahler," Henri-Claude said firmly. Megan nodded, vaguely remembering something about that.

"Of course you are both correct," Basileus answered with a wry smile. "It is well known that Wolf and Mahler were fellow students at the Vienna Conservatory in eighteen-seventy-seven and that they developed a close friendship. At one point, unable to afford separate rooms, they roomed together. But Wolf rebelled at the Conservatory's strict discipline and was expelled, as I'm sure you know."

Henri-Claude nodded affirmatively if with a tad of impatience.

"And perhaps you remember that years later, when Mahler was director at the Opera, Wolf begged him to stage *Der Corregidor* but because of the weak libretto and the composer's declining mental coherence, Mahler had to refuse."

"Yes. But Mahler did make an arrangement of the opera's prelude," said Henri-Claude. "It's eight minutes of Wagnerian color." Megan looked at the two men. She was confused.

"So is that what we're looking at here? Is this the manuscript of Mahler's arrangement of Wolf's prelude?"

"No." Both men answered at the same time. Henri-Claude began leafing gingerly through the pages of the thick manuscript. Basileus watched him intently, nodding his head in agreement each time the Frenchman voiced reactions of amusement or admiration.

Megan stared over Henri-Claude's shoulder at the score pages. The instrumentation was enormous and, following the flute and wind lines, melodious as well.

"This is quite a find, Herr Schmidt, quite a find. Mahler composed the entire last act of *Der Corregidor*." Henri-Claude placed the manuscript reverently on the desk and looked at Basileus.

"It is as if the two friends had a competition to see who could best compose music for that Spanish comedy of a love triangle. But how did you come upon it? There are no Mahler original manuscripts at the National Library."

"That's just it. This manuscript was not filed under the name of Gustav Mahler. It was in the trove we received after Wolf's death. A collection which contained sixty pages of his own unfinished opera, *Manuel Venegas*. Along with it were the score pages you see here in Mahler's hand. Wolf must have hung on to his colleague's apparently discarded manuscript all his life."

"Do you consider this composition important, Henri-Claude?" Megan asked.

"I'd say more interesting than important."

"But it certainly deserves a place in Mahler biographies, doesn't it?" asked Basileus.

"Definitely. Sheds an interesting light on Mahler's personality and on his instrumentation in the mid-nineties. What do you intend to do with this prize, Herr Schmidt?"

"I am donating it here and now to your *Médiathèque Musicale Mahler*. I know it rightfully belongs in our National Library, but as director I am making an exception since it's been unknown and out of circulation for well over a century. It might as well go 'home.'"

"Ah! But this is wonderful! There the many scholars who visit us can study and analyze a Mahler composition previously unknown. A new insight into the man and his music. We shall announce the important news in our monthly newsletter if that is all right with you. And we shall identify it as coming from a source that wishes to remain anonymous. Correct?"

"Yes. This is good. Very good. I am pleased to be able to add to Mahler research and I want as many people as possible to hear the music one day. Now let us transfer the score in this box and you may take it with you." Basileus lifted an empty file box from the floor by his desk and carefully packed the manuscript.

"And this time the name 'Mahler' will be on the file!" he added triumphantly, printing the composer's name on the box as he spoke. But the effort had been too much for him and his wheezing told his visitors that it was time to take their leave. The same procedure as before dictated that Megan and Henri-Claude go down the stairs before their host.

They found Sabina standing at the foot of the staircase. She seemed to be fighting back tears. Ignoring them and as soon as Basileus was near enough on the staircase to hear her, she hissed something to him that made him freeze in place. Sabina turned to his guests and made a commanding gesture toward them.

"I will have to see you out now. A family matter has come up." Without a further word she escorted them to the front door.

Back in the elevator Megan and Henri-Claude looked at each other in unvoiced wonderment. What on earth could have prompted that strange little domestic scene?

"I know where there's a piano in our hotel," Megan was hurrying Henri-Claude back to the Römischer Kaiser. She had had a whopper of an idea and she needed his help. She glanced at her Apple watch. It was already four. There wasn't much time. Her lecture at the University was at seven o'clock. They might have to postpone dinner.

127

"Oh, we just missed a service," Natalie Silverstein had said to Stefan Schmidt as people poured out of the synagogue. "But if you want to talk Jewish ideology and history let me introduce you to our rabbi. I see her over there."

"*Her*?"

"Yes, *her*. We're Progressive Jews here."

Before Stefan could answer, Natalie called the rabbi over to where they were standing.

Greta, may I introduce my colleague, first principal cellist of our Vienna State Opera, Stefan Schmidt. Stefan this is Rabbi Greta Berman.

"How grand to meet you," Greta Berman initiated a sincere and hearty handshake. She was of average height with short auburn hair and thoughtful, penetrating brown eyes.

"Stefan has indicated that he'd like to learn a bit more about our faith and I know you'd be the perfect person for him to talk with."

"Glad to do so. Shall we go to my office, Stefan, if I may call you that?"

"Of course you may." Stefan realized that, for someone who had never entered a synagogue, he was feeling strangely at home

"And I'm off to play a memorial service," Natalie said, taking her leave of them.

Stefan followed the rabbi to her office, noted admiringly the crowded book shelves, and sat down in the comfortable chair she indicated to him. She did not go to her desk, but instead took the chair facing Stefan, inviting him to speak with a concerned, inviting smile. He decided to be brutally frank.

"Rabbi, you are not going to like what I'm about to tell you. Up until yesterday I have been an anti-Semite. This has been based on unpleasant interactions I have had with Jewish colleagues over the years and just general impressions I've had of Jews being, how shall I say, grasping."

"I see," commented the rabbi, apparently not upset by Stefan's confession.

"But also, until yesterday morning I thought, took it for granted, that I was part Muslim, part Catholic. My mother, in fact, is Catholic. Although no one in my family has ever been the least bit religious or practiced any religion."

"I see," the rabbi said again.

"At noon yesterday, however, I learned, and *my father* learned that he is Jewish. Which makes me half Jewish. I, who don't like Jews and never have!"

"And how did you and your father learn this?" the rabbi asked calmly.

"Because my father's adoptive father from Palestine is visiting us. My father's entire family was killed in a bombing during the Arab-Israeli wars, you see, and Opa kindly adopted him. Opa is a Muslim and so was his wife. Papa had never been told anything about his real family or how they had been killed in the Gaza Strip. And yesterday Opa ceremoniously gave Papa a Talmud that belonged to Papa's real father. Although he was surprised, Papa seemed to accept that, but I could not. In fact, hatred and resentment overtook me and I left the house cursing my father." Stefan's voice quavered and he realized tears were forming in his eyes. He looked at Greta Berman beseechingly.

"Patrilineal descent has been debated for centuries. But regardless, it is not so bad to be a Jew, Stefan. It is harder on a person to be someone who hates Jews. Feeling hatred slowly putrefies the soul."

Stefan looked at the rabbi in astonishment. Yes, he had been feeling a certain interior "rotting" A dissatisfaction, a distancing of himself *from* himself as a means of escaping the obsessive Jew-despising person he had become. Yes, feeling grudges only hurts oneself. Why hadn't he understood that before?

"I think I see what you mean, Rabbi Berman."

"Oh, do call me by my first name, Stefan."

"I don't think I could, Rabbi. I feel too much respect for you."

"In that case let me give you more to think about. Clichés about Jews— like your 'grasping' adjective, or 'miserly' or 'whining'— have been in existence since before the Middle Ages, back even to the Roman Empire. One shield against such clichés by Jews was to practice what Sigmund Freud would later call self-deprecating humor. This sort of harmless self-defense was sparked by two ancient sources: Christian *theological* anti-Semitism and Christian *racist* anti-Semitism."

"Slow down, please, Rabbi." Stefan was interested in following everything the rabbi had to communicate.

"Let me put it this way. There have been three categories of anti-Semitism over the centuries. The first was religious, centering on the age-old notion that 'Jews killed Christ,' something that finally required a papal decree of repudiation."

"I didn't realize that."

"Yes, many people still think Jews killed Christ. This incites what you could call 'holy hatred.' The second category we could characterize as pseudo-racial. It preaches an opposition between non-Jewish 'Aryans' and Jewish 'Semites.' But it just so happens that, linguistically, Arab Muslims are Semites."

"I've never thought about that."

"Yes. And the third category is the bitter economic argument. That finance and capitalism are controlled by Jews. This charge certainly found credence in Europe and here in Austria in particular, didn't it?"

"Yes, I can see that."

"That's why Karl Lueger was so successful as mayor. He played to anger, didn't he?"

"So that's what changing the name on that particular part of the Ringstrasse was all about."

"Just think how long it took for that change to come about, Stefan."

"I have to admit, I did not realize its having been named after Lueger was insulting to Jews."

"Of course not. You didn't know you were Jewish then either, did you?" They looked at each other in mutual understanding.

"You are a musician and know about Gustav Mahler and his circle, yes?" Stefan nodded.

"Here is a real-life example of imbedded day to day Jew hatred. Just think, Stefan, that his future wife Alma once noted that if she were to marry his colleague Alexander Zemlinsky, it would mean she would bring 'short, degenerate Jew-children into the world.' *Think* about that. Her comment was meant to be and was understood to be *witty*!"

Stefan shook his head in bewilderment.

"So," Greta Berman continued, "to bring things up to date, think about the emergence of neo-fascist groups. They are feeding on a growing dislike of refugees. Just as Jews have been for centuries, these new refugees are the embodiment of otherness, and how easy it is to hate those who are 'different.' Also, a subject that is taboo, because one could be accused of Islamophobia, is that many of the anti-Semitic outrages in Europe are committed by Muslims."

"So, Rabbi, do you think Muslims might become the new Jews of the world?"

"Only time will tell. But I know that we have to fight against all types of prejudice and fear-mongering whoever we are, Muslim, Christian, or Jew. We are all equally loved by God. But we must fight constantly against what could again become 'holy hatred.'"

"You've given me a great deal to think about."

"Then here's something lightweight for you to put into the mix, Stefan. I'm reminded of an old Jewish joke by your characterization of Jews as 'grasping.' Are you ready?"

"Shoot."

"An elderly devout Jew goes to synagogue every day and prays the same prayer: 'Please, God, send me the money to pay off my debts.' Every day he does this. And one day a tall young Jew walks in, strides up to the glass-encased Torah on exhibition at the front, pounds on it and says loudly: 'God. I need five thousand euros by tomorrow.' Then he turns around and walks out. The Jew who has been praying is horrified and continues his plea. Well, the next day our devout Jew is there again, once again asking God for money to pay his debts. All of a sudden the obnoxious Jew from the day before appears, walks up to the Torah, raps the glass cover twice, and says in a loud voice: 'Thank you, God.' Then he leaves. The devout Jew prays: 'God! Why did you give him money and not me? I've been here every day.' A voice booms from above: 'Because you *nag, nag, nag.*'"

Stefan had to hold his sides in laughter and the rabbi joined in, old as the joke was. Finally Stefan pulled himself together, stood up, and spoke with newfound strength.

"You know, Rabbi, I think I shall like being Jewish. And I know what I must do next."

The Schmidt apartment was filled with gloom.

Sabina had told Basileus and Ahmed about the phone call that came in while her husband was upstairs with his guests. The family lawyer had phoned to say that at the *Untersuchungshaft* Adele had broken under the police interrogation. She admitted stealing the Rodin bust of Mahler and substituting her father's surmoulage loaded with an improvised explosive device and a triggering cellphone. That she had set it off with a keyed cellphone from her apartment while watching the Vienna State Opera's performance of *Fidelio* being televised live that evening. And admitted she had left a hateful note against Jews to be discovered on the scene. Adele had also confessed to selling the original bust to the mysterious man who had placed an ad offering fifty-thousand euros for it. They had met in one of the *Riesenrad* rental dinner cabins last night and exchanged the bust for money. When their cabin came to the ground again the man had rushed out ahead of her. She did not know who he was and could only give a general description. Adele maintained that she had stolen the Mahler bust to raise money for the operation her father so desperately needed. The charges against her would keep her in jail until a court hearing.

"We can only plead for mercy and understanding," the lawyer concluded.

And now the family sat in silence. There was no more to be said. A daughter in jail and a son who had cursed his father. No one moved at the sound of the front door being unlocked. They were too tired, too numb to even wonder who it was.

"*Papa! Mut*ti! *Opa!*" It was Stefan's voice. He ran into the room and threw himself down on his knees before them.

"I beg your forgiveness! I am so sorry I reacted the way I did. Papa, forgive me. I have been with a rabbi and have come to terms with our being Jewish. I *want* to be Jewish. And I beg you, all of you to forgive me."

Agonized, Stefan held out his hands toward his father. Tears were streaming down both men's cheeks. Sobs from father and son sounded in the silence. Then the father spoke.

"The prodigal is returned. Come, be embraced by me, my son."

128

"I have never seen this auditorium so full," Megan thought to herself, remembering her time as a student there so many decades ago. She, Egga, and Henri-Claude had arrived at the main University on the Ringstrasse half an hour early for the technical setup which included setting up her minuscule Spiderman thermos at the lectern. She also made sure that her Tascam would play its musical example into the mic. Now they were standing in the aula watching people enter and head toward the small lecture room on the ground floor. Megan knew it seated a hundred, but at the rate people were arriving it looked as if there might be an overflow and some would have to stand. The two Gustavs could still attract Vienna's attention it seemed!

Megan was dressed in her tried and true lecture outfit of black slacks, red shirt, black vest, and a cheerful red scarf with black music staves knotted below her neck. Certainly appropriate for the *Mahler* Gustav. Her *Klimt* Gustav homage was the glasses holder that hung from her neck. Its gold and white spiral-laden design was a detail from the painter's famous *The Kiss*.

White "Reserved" signs had been placed on three seats in the center of the front row: two for Egga and Henri-Claude, and one for Megan which would then be occupied by Dr. Gerhard Singer-Scharf after he had introduced the guest speaker to the audience. They still had ten minutes.

"I haven't seen Haim and Harry yet," Egga said, scanning the people coming in from the Ringstrasse.

"Yes, it's odd, isn't it? They had seemed so positive about coming to both lectures, and they didn't show up last night and looks as though it will be the same this evening. Something must have come up. Too bad. I was looking forward to seeing them again before we leave."

"Me too," said Egga.

"And I would really like to meet them after what you've told me about them," Henri-Claude told them.

"Oh look!" exclaimed Egga. "There's Mary Neff entering over there and here comes Hanskarl Klug. And that woman over there is Rita Rausch—we saw her on ORF television news, remember?"

"I do now. She looks very intelligent," Megan said. Hanskarl gave her a peck on the cheek as he passed by and she patted him fondly on the shoulder.

They were joined just then by Professor Singer-Scharf who was rubbing his hands in anticipation of what he knew would be a fascinating and lively lecture. He had heard Megan before at the New York Austrian Embassy and knew he had a worthy surprise for the audience. He glanced at his watch and turned to Megan and her two companions.

"It's time. Let's go get seated so I can get the introduction out of the way and our speaker on her way." The trio followed their host into the lecture hall. All the seats were taken and some ten people were standing in the two side aisles.

"Your reputation precedes you, my dear," Gerhard whispered. After everyone was seated he walked to the lectern on the far side of the room to introduce the speaker.

It was a short, robust, and to the point introduction, exactly what Megan had hoped for. She always cringed when introductions covered too many scholarly accomplishments. If such a listing tired her, think how the audience must feel. She used the interim to remind herself "there are two steps to the podium, two steps to the podium, none at the lectern, none at the lectern." Being in one's mid-eighties did have its slight drawbacks.

The introduction ended with a quip about Megan's being from Texas and not from Austria. When the applause began she rose from her seat and climbed with measured steps to the podium, then quickly to the lectern where she placed her iPhone and her Tascam within easy reach on the small shelf lining the slant-topped high desk. Her Spiderman thermos was already in place. Unlike most of her lectures, this time Megan did not use a written text. She had decided to go solo; she knew her subject matter thoroughly, including the special points she wished to make. "*Woit's es, doss I mit eich auf hochdeitsch red oder auf texanisch?*—Would you prefer that I speak with you in high German or low Texan," she asked the audience in perfectly pronounced Viennese dialect, sparking a roar of surprised laughter. The professorial barrier had been broken. Now she and the audience were one. The way she always gave her best.

She began with two Alma Mahler quotations about the two Gustavs. Concerning Klimt, the flirtatious Alma had written in a diary entry of June 1898: "He is an attractive fellow—one can have no idea what a free spirit he is." This was followed by a November entry in 1901 concerning Mahler: "I knew him well by sight; he was a small, fidgety man with a fine head."

Megan then offered a year-by-year summary of both men's careers during Vienna's Golden Age, addressing their successes and their failures. Projecting the pertinent images, she documented the rejection of Klimt's three controversial allegories of *Philosophy*, *Medicine*, and *Jurisprudence* painted for the University, asking what the University professors had asked: whether they were philosophy or pornography? In Mahler's case she showed contemporary newspaper cartoons and anti-Semitic articles, pillorying the modernist composer and savaging the severe conductor. She concluded with the year 1907, with Mahler's departure for America and a glorious career in New York, and Klimt's successful turn to sumptuous society portraiture and stunningly resonant landscapes. The screen went blank and Megan turned to the engaged audience.

"All this you are familiar with; I have only illustrated and revisited it with you." She paused. "But it is always good if a lecturer can offer something new."

"And this evening I can."

The audience leaned forward in cheerful suspense. Megan showed two images: they were large excellent photographs of Alma and Gustav Mahler and they faced each other. In actuality Alma was facing in the same direction as Mahler, but ever since her teaching days Megan had felt it was always justifiable to reverse an image if the situation required it.

"Let us remember that on the ninth of March nineteen-two, the forty-two-year-old Gustav Mahler married, after a very brief but intense courtship, the twenty-two-year-old Alma Schindler." A new image appeared. It showed Alma and Gustav again, but now a matching photo of Klimt faced them both.

"And let us recall that the thirty-nine-year-old Gustav Klimt had long since returned to Vienna from his pursuit of Alma when she was vacationing with her family in Italy the previous year." The audience murmured its agreement.

"While the Mahlers were on their wedding trip abroad, Klimt was putting the finishing touches to his Beethoven frieze which would be shown to the public the following month, April. It was an elegant event that would open in the evening with members of the Opera House chorus and orchestra performing under Mahler's baton."

The audience nodded its understanding.

"Now let's look even more closely at the knightly stand-in for the composer." A closer detail of the knight's profile head and the red-haired woman's head gazing down protectively at him from above him appeared on the screen.

"Let's jump ahead now to April and the exhibition of Klimt's sensational Beethoven Frieze at the Secession. We all know it: a suffering, kneeling humanity begs the knight in golden armor to take up the quest for happiness, but first the knight must pass through the threatening hostile powers before he enters into the kingdom of pure joy, signified by this very, nude, no, *naked* kiss." Chuckles sounded around the room. Megan acknowledged them with a complicitous smile and continued.

"Let's look at that golden knight more closely." An image of just the knight showed on the screen.

"We know he signified another knight and another, more contemporary battle—Mahler and the anti-Semitic attack against him in the press. But let's look closer." The next image showed the knight from shoulders up.

"Do you see anything unusual?" The audience stared at the detail. No answers were heard. Megan changed the image again. Now there was an amazingly close detail of the knight's head and the attentive woman's long strands of red hair. One could see the knight's horizontal eyebrow which ended at the tip of one of the woman's locks of hair.

"Now do you see anything unusual?"

Silence reigned until a man's voice sounded. "I may be wrong but there seem to be some letters in the knight's eyebrow. Could that be so?"

"Excellent! It is so. The initials are...." Megan showed the macro detail she had taken at the Secession the previous morning.

"The initials are S G M B S D G." The audience gasped. They clearly saw what Megan had read out.

"What could they mean? Would the two Gs stand for the two Gustavs? Perhaps. But what do the other initials stand for?" In addition to the detail on the screen, Megan beamed up the previous images of Klimt on the left with Alma in the center and Gustav on the right. Above them was a small map showing the upper part of Italy and Austria.

"After much combining on the computer, I have come up with the indisputable sentence these seven letters stand for. Are you ready?"

"*Yes!*" The audience shouted as with one voice.

"They stand for: *Sie Gehörte Mir Bevor Sie Dir Gehörte*—She Belonged to Me Before She Belonged to You."

Silence struck the audience. A full fifteen seconds passed as the audience strained to fit the letters to the chronology of events the speaker had provided. Then sounds of comprehension and someone began clapping loudly. Within moments the entire room was applauding. Megan smiled and bowed to her excited audience. Then she held up her hand for silence.

"Now, would you like to hear—and I literally mean *hear*—something new to the world about the other Gustav, about Mahler?"

"Tell us, tell us!" some of the student members of the audience shouted.

Large portrait photographs of Mahler and Hugo Wolf facing each other appeared on the screen. Megan narrated the sequence of events concerning *El Corregidor* that she and Henri-Claude had discovered. She paused.

"And now, in piano reduction, you will be the first persons in the world of music to hear the fandango-studded last act of Mahler's version of the complete opera." She fit her mic into its stand, lowered it, and tapped her Tascam enter button. There followed Henri-Claude's rendition of the finale. This is why they had hurried from the Schmidts to the piano in the basement of the Römischer Kaiser. The French Mahler scholar had expertly written out a piano transcription of the sprightly, vaguely Wagnerian score they had recorded on Megan's Tascam portable digital recorder just for the lecture.

When the lively music concluded, the thrilled audience stood up and it seemed they clapped endlessly. Over the noise, the amplified sound of a cellphone rang out. It was Megan's, right next to the lectern's microphone. She saw the ID of the caller and immediately picked it up and listened intently to Erich Decker's words. Then she turned to the audience, urgently tapping the mic for attention. A general hush followed. Megan held her iPhone up.

"Ladies and gentlemen. I have Vienna Chief of Police Erich Decker here on the phone. He tells me that the stolen bust by Auguste Rodin of Gustav Mahler has been anonymously *returned to our Opera House!*" Shouts of joy and triumph pierced the air and Megan, Egga, and Henri-Claude joined in.

The Mahler mayhem had ended.

READERS GUIDE

1. During the intermission of a performance of Beethoven's *Fidelio* at the Vienna State Opera, retired art history professor Megan Crespi, in the city to give lectures and a book signing, looks at Rodin's bust of Gustav Mahler and realizes there is something "terribly wrong" about it. Do we know what? Crespi voices her concern to her former student and travel companion, the cellist Egga Streicher, and they make the acquaintance of American Mary Neff. What is Neff's connection with the Opera House? Act Two of *Fidelio* begins and just as the despairing tenor sings the words "horrible silence," something totally unexpected occurs. What has happened?

2. We meet the director of the Austrian National Library, Basileus Schmidt. What was his birth name and why did he change it? And what are the professions of his adult children, Adele and Stefan, that connect them to the Opera House? Do we know what Stefan's self-imposed task is? The one that "requires total concentration and exquisite timing"?

3. Although there is no scoring for his instrument in the trombone family in the original score of Beethoven's only opera, Ottokar Weininger, contrabass trombonist at the Vienna State Opera, never misses a performance, even if the orchestration does not include his instrument. There is no exception at tonight's opera, scored for only two trombones. He sits behind the brass section during the first act, his black instrument case by his side like a large, faithful hound. Is he in the pit for Act Two? What are we to make of this?

4. Once cleared to leave the Opera House premises, Megan, Egga, and Mary adjourn to the nearby Café Mozart. They discuss Megan's speculation that the explosion was the work of a rabid anti-Semite. Their conversation is interrupted by Officer Erich Decker, an old friend of Megan's. Joining them, he relates what

his police investigation has revealed so far. What is the intriguing information?

5. We meet Homer Schlager who used to play oboe. Why has he switched instruments? What large instrument does he now play and is there anything suspicious about him or his instrument case?

6. While still at the Café Mozart, a major discovery at the Opera House is reported to Decker by his officers. It is a note with handprinted capital letters saying:

TAKE THIS AS A WARNING. NO MORE JEWS IN OUR OPERA HOUSE! NO MORE JEWS DEFILING OUR CULTURE!

Do we have an idea yet who might have left this note?

7. We return to the Schmidt family who had been watching *Fidelio* live on television. They worry about the possibility of Stefan's having been injured in the Opera House explosion. Why does Basileus have an additional worry about Stefan?

8. At the Café Mozart, Decker is informed by one of his men that a disposable cellphone has just been found. Where was it and how is this meaningful to the investigation? Megan is convinced that the original Mahler bust was spared and a surmoulage substituted. What further consequence could this have? At Decker's invitation Megan and Mary return with him to the Opera House to help with the interrogations. Why does he think they could be helpful?

9. We meet Ottokar Weininger again and learn a bit of his recent history. Three evenings earlier when he was leaving the opera he had been approached by a young man who presented him with a curious yet fascinating proposition: would he be interested in trading his ancient contrabass trombone for a brand-new German-style Kühl, with modern capacious carrying case? And for any inconvenience he would also receive 1000 euros. Why is Ottokar open to this proposition and what are the terms dictated? What does Ottokar have in common with an earlier Weininger?

10. Megan and Mary are with Erich interrogating members of the orchestra. They begin with the percussion section. The first person interviewed is asked to tilt his kettle drums. Why? He mentions an incident that happened in the

first act of *Fidelio*: the principal cellist crashed to the floor with his instrument and was thrown out by the guest conductor. Who confirms this story and what instrument does Megan notice in the orchestra pit for which there is no part in *Fidelio*?

11. Cristina Paloma, the Italian harpist, absolutely has to reach her concert harp languishing in the orchestra pit, never mind the "esplosione." Why is she so agitated? And a second French horn has been found in a nylon kit next to the principal French hornist's rectangular case. What is his explanation?

12. Pit manager Kerstin Jesse discovers the large black box she had kicked underneath the pit storage bench and calls Officer Decker over to see it.. The box is quite heavy. She tries to open it at Decker's command, flips the two side latches, but the lock latch will not lift. A set of small keys and a crowbar are sent in. The keys do not work but the crowbar does. What are the contents?

13. Rudi Wittkover, longtime garrulous portier on the Kärntner Strasse side of the Opera House stage doors, calls the police with what he thinks could be an important piece of information. About whom is this information?

14. We meet the elderly couple American Harry Howell and Greek Haim Elisaf, who have been married for almost fifty years. They make documentary films and have lived in Vienna with their two children, Bell and Callas, for many years, having managed to buy the third-floor adjoining apartments 22 and 23 at Liechtensteinstrasse 68/70. To what famous composers did these apartments once belong? What have Harry and Haim done to the two apartments? Who is Hans Makart?

15. Stefan arrives at his parent's home. His sister Adele is there and Stefan narrates what happened in the orchestra pit when the principal cellist crashed to the floor. In the kitchen Stefan tells his father what really occurred to cause the man to fall. It had indeed required "precision and exquisite timing." What happened?

16. Each of Harry and Haim's children have exciting things to tell them. Bell, a guard at the Upper Belvedere Museum, has brought a musical gift for their fiftieth anniversary on Friday. And Callas, curator of Vienna's Jewish Museum, tells them the new exhibition she opened, "Genosse.Jude—Comrade.Jew," has been such a success that it will be extended for another three months.

17. We learn much more about Adele Schmidt, head tailor of the opera's women's repertory costumes division. What convoluted actions has she taken to avenge the outrageous mistreatment her cellist brother Stefan has suffered in the Opera House orchestra?

18. At an emergency meeting called by the International Gustav Mahler Society the morning after the opera explosion, the group is trying to word a statement for the press amid great disagreement. Was the incident a crime against Austria's great cultural figure or was the incident a hate crime against a Jew? Wacky Tonik Nektar, from Mahler's home town of Iglau, insists it is both. Newspaper reporter Rita Rausch asks him for an interview. What does Nektar, to his surprise, learn from her?

19. Adele Schmidt's mother Sabina calls her at work to say that Papa is going to have to have an operation and that their health insurance will not cover the costs as the operation is "optional." Adele is surprised to learn that her father has been in such pain and that her parents have money worries. She determines to do something about it. Do we know what that is?

20. Karl Lueger, great grandnephew of Vienna's anti-Semitic mayor of the same name, is watching the morning news on television. He realizes he has a purpose now: to prevent Jews from defiling his culture. And he would begin at the University, where he is a first-year student.

21. Megan visits the Upper Belvedere Museum to study the Rodin bust of Mahler displayed there in the Gustav Klimt gallery. Is the bust Model B or A? What is the difference? A friendly guard, whose name is Bell, follows Megan into the adjoining small salon, where an exact replica of Gustav Klimt's *The Kiss* is displayed for the benefit of those who want to take selfies. He asks Megan if she would like him to photograph her in front of the iconic image. Amused, Megan accepts the offer. Just as Bell hands her iPhone back something happens that makes them both stop dead in their tracks. It is an overwhelming, nauseous stench and it is coming from the Mahler bust room.

22. In the morning newspaper Ottokar Weininger reads about the "Mahler Bomber" and finds this in the editorial: "The hatred issuing from the bomber's note is reflective of historic anti-Jew sentiments in our city from the likes of Otto Weininger and Adolf Hitler." Intrigued by a historical namesake, Ottokar researches him on his computer. It is a fascinating revelation. Otto was Jewish, like him, and Otto was anti-Semitic, also like him. What is the name of Otto

Weininger's sensational book and when was it written? What actions does Ottokar take next?

23. An interesting ad appears in the morning paper after the Mahler Bomber event. It offers a reward of 50,000 euros for the "missing" Rodin bust of Mahler. Who places the ad and what is the result?

24. Seizing the right moment in the Upper Belvedere Klimt gallery, Ottokar pulls out a squirt pen filled with black ink and a glass ampoule filled with a pungent malodorous liquid. He steps into the middle of the room. The Mahler bust is a mere three feet away. What does Ottokar do?

25. Harry Howell is seated at the back of Adolf Loos's famed American Bar waiting for the arrival of whoever the "mahlerorbust" emailer is. A woman arrives wearing a burqa and huge sunglasses and heads directly for him. After verifying each other's cyber identities, they get down to business and agree to meet at the entrance to the Prater's *Riesenrad* three evenings later at seven. The mystery woman will have reserved one of the modernized cabins for them and they can conduct business "simultaneously in private and in public."

26. After practicing with her quartet all day, Egga returns to her hotel room and finds Megan's note with a suggestion that they eat early at the Wienerwald restaurant on the Annagasse. Egga goes over the ad libs with which she will preface each of the four string quartets her group will perform that evening: Haydn, Mozart, Beethoven, and Schulhoff. Just before the modernist Schulhoff is played, Egga will tell the audience about the skull snatching of the heads of Haydn and Beethoven, grim information which always makes the audience all the more receptive to the jazzy cheerfulness of the German-Jewish composer Emil Schulhoff, who died in a Nazi concentration camp in 1941.

27. Karl Lueger designs and prints handbills and at three that afternoon walks over to the University, where he is a first-year student. He posts them in the empty lunchroom and even in the Great Reading Room. What do the handbills say?

28. Rita Rausch is among the first newspaper reporters to arrive where the life-size statue of Sigmund Freud at the MedUni has been sprayed with red paint. Who is the culprit? And what does the broadside he has left say?

29. Stefan and his sister Adele exchange their secret stories. What are they and how much bearing do they have on the plot development? In addition, Adele has arranged with a bronze casting firm in Tulln to do a rush job casting her a copy of Rodin's bust of Mahler, as she has a committed buyer for it. The new surmoulage is going to cost a fortune, but it will be ready in two days. She will be able to pay for it if her "plan" works out. Do we know what that plan is?

30. Mary has saved a front-row seat for Megan at the Brahms-Saal for Egga's quartet concert, and the first three numbers by Haydn, Mozart, and Beethoven are well received. But as the Schulhof quartet begins its presto al fuoco, loud shouting is heard in the back of the auditorium. Two young men with shaved heads are yelling "No Jewish music in Vienna!" What happens next?

31. Haim suffers what seems to be a heart attack and Harry drives him to the Allgemeines Krankenhaus where Haim is given a TTE. Everything seems normal despite slight increases in Haim's blood pressure, cholesterol and amino acid levels. They are free to go home. At home, Harry decides to tell him a little bit about what sort of anniversary surprise to expect in two days. He gives him a big hint. "I can say that you should only play music within the time frame of Mendelssohn and Schönberg...." What can that possibly mean?

32Adele plans to get to work very early tomorrow and open the large floor safe in the costume room where she had once made an amazing discovery: a box in the back of the safe containing a diamond tiara. A label on the box bore the name of the great Wagnerian soprano under Mahler's baton, Anna von Bahr-Mildenburg. The box and its contents had been left forgotten through two world wars. Sometime that tiara would come in handy, Adele had thought. The time had come.

33. Megan searches the nearby Karlskirche during a concert there of music by Vivaldi. She finds the man she had seen across the Musikvereinplatz talking to the two ruffians who had disrupted Egga's concert. Erich Decker rushes in and pulls a gun on the man. He identifies himself as Ottokar Weininger and cleverly sidesteps all of Erich's inquiries, instead imploring him to find his stolen instrument, the contrabass trombone. It is a draw.

34. Adele has taken the Anna von Barr-Mildenburg tiara home unobserved. She changes clothes and drives out to the famous pawnshop in the crowded, Muslim-populated Favoriten district, the Dorotheum. She herself is dressed

in a full-length black burqa. The store manager examines the tiara and confirms that it contains the rarest of diamonds, the red. He offers a loan of twenty thousand euros for thirty days at fifteen percent interest. Adele agrees, although she knows the tiara is worth much more. There is only one other thing, says Herr Schau: "your proof of ownership." Do we know yet how Adele will circumvent this demand?

35. On their drive to her lecture site, Neulengbach, Megan asks Egga to read aloud to her Mahler's vast instrumentation for the work they will be attending this evening: the Second Symphony. It will be led by the famous, self-taught American Jewish conductor Gerald Chaplin. What are some of the instruments called for in this "Resurrection" Symphony?

36. The renowned French expert on Mahler, Henri-Claude de La Granger, checks into the Römischer Kaiser. He has been given a front row ticket by his friend Gerald Chaplin to the Mahler performance that evening. Henri-Claude visits the Christian Nebehay Antiquariat next door and learns his dear friend Megan Crespi is in town giving lectures.

37. Ottokar visits his widowed mother who is now almost completely overtaken by Alzheimer's. He finally locates his father's service pistol, a Glock 19 and leaves. What is his other acquisition?

38. In the Judenplatz people are gathering around the Lessing statue staring at the malicious poster taped to the pedestal. Callas, who had been visiting the branch of her museum, ponders why there is so much anti-Semitism and why is it "necessary" to know that a composer or a personal friend is Jewish? She cannot find any plausible answers to her questions.

39. University students have formed a ring around the Musikverein and are uttering a continuous chant: "We say yes to Jewish music in Vienna, we say yes to Jewish conductors in Vienna!" It is customary for players and singers at the Musikverein to arrive early, and this evening's conductor had asked them to be on stage at exactly six forty-five at the latest. Ottokar Weininger is among the instrumentalists who enter the Musikverein early. He is carrying a contrabass trombone case and he knows exactly what his musical cue will be. Do we know what is in the trombone case?

40. There is a four-minute late start to the seven o'clock performance of Mahler's Second Symphony. A death threat has been found in Chaplin's dressing room.

The maestro himself comes out and says he believes Mahler is "indestructible" and if the audience wishes, the symphony will be performed. A standing ovation takes place and the symphony begins. We are taken through all five glorious movements but in the fifth, when the chorus and soloists sing a certain line something unthinkable happens. What are the cue words and what happens?

41. Karl Luegar has just heard the news of a sensational happening at the Musikverein. He is inspired by an unknown comrade's bold anti-Semitic act. It is a challenge. He will have to think of a similar audacious deed. In fact he will strive to outdo his predecessor. Perhaps, like his great-uncle of the same name, his name will be in the history books.

42. Early the next morning Rita Rausch walks the Ringstrasse, determined to find the best site from which her TV crew can film, and she can report on the sit-in called for by the media to honor the conductor Gerald Chaplin. What historic Ring buildings does she consider? And what is her choice? Why is it an ideal spot?

43. Ottokar takes the D tram as far as it can get through the gathering crowd on the Ringstrasse and walks to the Opera House. He goes up to the foyer floor and looks down on the Ring where hundreds of people are already gathering for the sit-in. He turns and walks into the recently named "Mahler Hall." What, to him, "maudlin" large item does he study there? What is his plan and at what point during the noisy demonstration will he execute it?

44. Vienna's inner-city traffic has come to a standstill. The city sit-in planned for noon has taken over the Ring and the side streets. Megan and Egga walk, almost run, to the nearest site of the rally, the Sigmund-Freud-Park. The voice of Vienna's mayor blares a message over the loudspeakers. What are his moving words? Where have Megan and Egga been that puts them on this far side of the Ring from the Opera House?

45. As people begin dispersing at the Sigmund-Freud-Park, Bell recognizes Megan from their encounter at the Upper Belvedere and introduces his family to her. They get along famously and Megan and Egga agree to come to the Liechtensteinstrasse flat for dinner that very evening. When Haim learns Egga is also a cellist he urges her to bring her cello along. What professional event does Megan have to attend before that dinner?

46. Rita Rausch is the first television reporter to arrive with her crew at the Opera House in response to the shocking incident that has just taken place there. She confers with the director of Opera properties, Harriet Hausmann. Before other reporters arrive Rita and Hausmann decide to underplay what has happened because publicity is exactly what the Mahler Bomber or his copy cats covet. When other press members arrive, they are urged by Rita to underreport the event as "malicious mischief" so as not to gratify the perpetrator. What has actually happened?

47. During the afternoon at her parent's home, Adele makes an unobserved substitution for the surmoulage bust of Mahler she had borrowed without her father's knowledge. Her mother arrives with exciting news. What is it and why does she want Adele and Stefan to appear for lunch tomorrow at noon? And why is Stefan so glum when his sister phones with the news?

48. Back in his apartment, Ottokar learns from television coverage that something that had occurred in the Mahler Hall at the Opera House was "malicious mischief." He is incensed. After having risked his life during the Chaplin-Mahler performance at the Musikverein, the city had answered with a sit-in demonstration in honor of Viennese Jews! And now to dismiss what he had done at the Opera House? Depression takes hold of him. He remembers that his namesake Otto Weininger experienced much the same lack of grateful understanding and that he therefore committed a supreme act of publicity. All Europe had then read his masterpiece, *Sex and Character*. Now Ottokar knows what he must do to get his own vitally important manuscript published and read. What does he plan to do and at what specific location?

49. Even though taking the elevator to their apartment, Haim feels so weak he must lie down. Harry pleads with him to take it easy and goes to the kitchen to prepare the basics in case their planned dinner with Megan and Egga takes place. Suddenly he hears sounds of a cello being tuned in the studio. He enters, smiling at the man to whom music was health. The dinner will take place as planned.

50. Karl Lueger, disgusted with the successful demonstration sit-in, is in his bedroom reading Lessing's boring *Nathan the Wise* play with its Jew hero, hoping to find a clue as to how he can perform an anti-Semitic act even greater than what happened at the Musikverein. He has already physically checked out the Burgtheater, where the play is being performed, but he is not inspired.

He reads the plot of the famous "ring parable"—every religion is the true one. Dullsville. Turning to the Burgtheater's website, he learns an extra performance of Nathan the Wise will be given at two o'clock tomorrow afternoon. Suddenly Karl sees what's to be done. And it was there in the Burgtheater all the time! He goes on two errands What are they? Do we know what he plans to do?

51.Megan and Egga have a delicious Greek dinner with Harry and Haim and their children Callas and Bell. They marvel at their hosts' Makart-like home with its many exotic furnishings. A stimulating dinner conversation takes place about whether or not there can be "Jewishness" in music, Mahler's for example and in that of Shostakovich, who although not a Jew himself, treasured his Jewish friends. Egga unpacks her cello and joins Haim in performing two pieces. Then she trades places with violinist Callas, Harry goes to the piano, and they play Shostakovich's shattering Trio No. 2 in E Minor. They all hear the same message of hope in the trio's E Major ending, as is sounded in Mahler's "Resurrection" Symphony. Who are some of the other composers the group discusses or plays?

52. Megan takes Egga to the Secession to admire Klimt's great *Beethoven Frieze*, which is on permanent display in the basement. She photographs many details, more magnified than she has ever taken before. Do we know why? And what is the program of the frieze? Whom does the Golden Knight really represent?

53. Basileus's adoptive father, Ahmed Suleiman, has arrived from Palestine and greets his grandchildren fondly. Stefan is glum because of having to re-audition for the position of first chair at the Opera House. Ahmed presents Basileus with a treasured book his birth father owned. Basileus is stunned. Then he talks about how he had always felt different in a Christian Europe. Stefan has said nothing but suddenly stands up, curses his father and rushes out. Do we know what has triggered this? What religion was the birth father of Basileus?

54. As the balcony audience starts to pour down the two grand stairwells during intermission at the Burgtheater's afternoon performance of *Nathan the Wise*, the shout of FIRE is heard. A tall man, dressed in black and holding a lit torch on a pole, is shouting from the projecting balcony at the crowd to leave this play by a Jew or he will set fire to the ceiling image above. Who is this man and why does he have an abandoned black garment looped around his waist? What is the image he threatens to set aflame? What happens next?

55. Harry reminds Haim that he can't be home for dinner this evening because he is meeting the man who is supplying lots of photos for their next documentary. Haim buys the story and Harry is relieved. He hates the deception but the meeting this evening with the mystery Muslim woman, who is selling him the Rodin Mahler bust must remain a secret. At what famous Vienna location is the meeting taking place? And for what jubilant occasion the next day is Harry acquiring the Mahler bust?

56. During a late lunch at their Burger King, Megan and Egga are talking about the spate of anti-Jewish attacks by Muslims. They bemoan subjects from poor education to hate attacks and then change the subject to something cheerful: the Klimt *Beethoven Frieze* they had seen that morning at the Secession. Megan wants Egga to study a photo she had taken there: a detail of the Golden Knight/ Mahler's face. Egga cannot see what Megan wants her to see, and Megan will not tell her what it is until tomorrow night's lecture at the university. Mean! Do we know what Megan has photographed in detail? And why?

57. Keeping watch over the *Riesenrad* a half hour before he is to meet the woman in a burqa with the stolen Mahler bust, Harry succumbs to the urgent temptation to call the police and report a crime about to be committed. He dials 311 but hangs up in mid-sentence. He will go through with the exchange. Minutes later he and Adele—clad in her burqa—are inside the *Riesenrad* cabin she has reserved and the exchange is made: Mahler's bust for 50,000 euros. What is the mid-sentence Harry blurts out to the Notfall operator? Will this be helpful to the police?

58. Harry can hear the dog's howling before he even unlocks the door to their flat. He searches for Haim, calling his name. Opening the bedroom door he sees the inconceivable. What has happened and what does Harry do?

59. After spending most of the night and early morning at Flex dancehall, where an Israeli band was playing, Stefan pulls himself together. What is his new reality? Why does he go to a large edifice just beyond the Hard Rock Café? What is the building and in whose company is he?

60. After sobbing his heart out, Harry decides upon three things. He will call the children, he will have an ambulance take him and Haim to the Vienna General Hospital, and finally, with Haim's voice prompting him in his ear, he will return the Mahler bust to its rightful home. What are the painful circumstances prompting Harry's three decisions?

61. An agonized, incoherent Adele phones her parents—she is in jail! She fabricates a tale of why she has 50,000 euros on her when arrested the night before. Basileus contacts his lawyer and Sabina drives to the holding center. Now Basileus is really angry: he has a thieving daughter and a thankless son who has told him to go to hell. What does he decide to do?

62. Megan receives a call on her iPhone as she and Henri-Claude are walking to Basileus Schmidt's address on the Augustinierstrasse. It is Erich Decker, eager to update them on events concerning the Mahler Bomber. When Megan asks whether the Mahler Bomber case has now been solved, Decker has to say no. But the police have an encouraging lead. What is it?

63. And what extraordinary thing happens when Megan and Henri-Claude meet with Basileus Schmidt? With what are they entrusted? After they leave, another extraordinary event takes place within the Schmidt family. What is it?

64. The closing episode takes place at Vienna University where Megan has arrived early for her lecture on "The Two Gustavs." The technical setup includes her personal lectern equipment: her small Spiderman thermos, her iPhone, and her Tascam portable digital recorder. Megan is dressed in her tried and true lecture outfit. Of what does that consist and how does it pay homage to both Gustavs?

65. After engaging with the audience by asking an initial question in Viennese dialect, Megan offers a year-by-year summary of the careers of the two men in Vienna's Golden Age, addressing both their successes and their failures. She then announces that she has some new information concerning both men. Would the audience like to hear it? As with one voice the answer is an adamant yes. Suspense grows as Megan leads her listeners through the close monthly chronology of Alma Schindler's flirtation with Klimt in Italy and then her marriage after just a few months of courtship to Mahler. Klimt's *Beethoven Frieze* appears on the screen and Megan's listeners are reminded that the Golden Knight symbolizes Mahler. Then she shows a close detail of the knight's head. His profile faces the floating female figure at his side. His eyebrow is at the level of a lock of her long red hair. Megan asks if the audience can spot something unusual. No answer. Closer details are shown. Finally a member of the audience identifies what is suddenly obvious to all. Exclamations of astonishment fill the air. What have they seen?

66. Megan has a similar amazing find concerning Mahler. For this she utilizes her Tascam, placing it right in front of the lectern mic. What happens next and why is the audience so amazed? Just as Megan's lecture ends her iPhone rings. Who is it and what is the extraordinary news conveyed by the caller that signifies the Mahler mayhem is ended?